Praise for *New Yor*
RaeA

"RaeAnne Thayne is quickly becoming one of my favorite authors.... Once you start reading, you aren't going to be able to stop."

—*Fresh Fiction*

"RaeAnne has a knack for capturing those emotions that come from the heart."

—*RT Book Reviews*

"[Thayne] engages the reader's heart and emotions, inspiring hope and the belief that miracles are possible."

—#1 *New York Times* bestselling author
Debbie Macomber

Praise for *USA TODAY* **bestselling author**
Patricia Davids

"Patricia Davids pens a captivating tale... *The Color of Courage* is well researched, with a heartwarming conclusion."

—*RT Book Reviews*

"With its even pacing, *A Matter of the Heart* is a touching and wonderful story that's not to be missed."

—*RT Book Reviews*

RaeAnne Thayne finds inspiration in the beautiful northern Utah mountains, where the *New York Times* and *USA TODAY* bestselling author lives with her husband and three children. Her books have won numerous honors, including RITA® Award nominations from Romance Writers of America and a Career Achievement Award from *RT Book Reviews*. RaeAnne loves to hear from readers and can be contacted through her website, raeannethayne.com.

After thirty-five years as a nurse, *USA TODAY* bestselling author **Patricia Davids** hung up her stethoscope to become a full-time writer. She enjoys spending her free time visiting her grandchildren, doing some long-overdue yard work and traveling to research her story locations. She resides in Wichita, Kansas. Pat always enjoys hearing from her readers. You can visit her online at patriciadavids.com.

New York Times **Bestselling Author**

RaeAnne THAYNE

NEVER TOO LATE

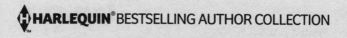
HARLEQUIN® BESTSELLING AUTHOR COLLECTION

If you purchased this book without a cover you should be aware that this book is stolen property. It was reported as "unsold and destroyed" to the publisher, and neither the author nor the publisher has received any payment for this "stripped book."

ISBN-13: 978-1-335-01630-0

Never Too Late

Copyright © 2018 by Harlequin Books S.A.

The publisher acknowledges the copyright holders of the individual works as follows:

Never Too Late
Copyright © 2005 by RaeAnne Thayne

His Bundle of Love
Copyright © 2006 by Patricia Macdonald

Recycling programs for this product may not exist in your area.

All rights reserved. Except for use in any review, the reproduction or utilization of this work in whole or in part in any form by any electronic, mechanical or other means, now known or hereafter invented, including xerography, photocopying and recording, or in any information storage or retrieval system, is forbidden without the written permission of the publisher, Harlequin Enterprises Limited, 22 Adelaide St. West, 40th Floor, Toronto, Ontario M5H 4E3, Canada.

This is a work of fiction. Names, characters, places and incidents are either the product of the author's imagination or are used fictitiously, and any resemblance to actual persons, living or dead, business establishments, events or locales is entirely coincidental.

This edition published by arrangement with Harlequin Books S.A.

For questions and comments about the quality of this book, please contact us at CustomerService@Harlequin.com.

® and TM are trademarks of Harlequin Enterprises Limited or its corporate affiliates. Trademarks indicated with ® are registered in the United States Patent and Trademark Office, the Canadian Intellectual Property Office and in other countries.

HARLEQUIN®
™ www.Harlequin.com

Printed in U.S.A.

CONTENTS

NEVER TOO LATE   7
RaeAnne Thayne

HIS BUNDLE OF LOVE   273
Patricia Davids

Also by RaeAnne Thayne

HQN Books

Haven Point

Snow Angel Cove
Redemption Bay
Evergreen Springs
Riverbend Road
Snowfall on Haven Point
Serenity Harbor
Sugar Pine Trail

Harlequin Special Edition

The Cowboys of Cold Creek

The Rancher's Christmas Song
The Holiday Gift
A Cold Creek Christmas Story
The Christmas Ranch
A Cold Creek Christmas Surprise
A Cold Creek Noel
A Cold Creek Reunion
Christmas in Cold Creek
A Cold Creek Baby
A Cold Creek Secret
A Cold Creek Holiday
A Cold Creek Homecoming
The Cowboy's Christmas Miracle
Dalton's Undoing
Dancing in the Moonlight
Light the Stars

**Don't miss *The Cottages on Silver Beach*,
coming July 2018 from HQN Books.**

For a complete list of books by RaeAnne Thayne,
please visit www.raeannethayne.com.

NEVER TOO LATE

RaeAnne Thayne

For Kjersten Thayne,
the best daughter in the world!

I couldn't have written this one without you.

Chapter 1

What was wrong with her? Kate Spencer wondered as she watched her brother twirl her best friend—his new wife—around the room. The small train of Taylor's elegantly simple ivory gown brushed the floor and her face glowed with joy at being in the arms of the man she loved.

They looked perfect together, the lanky cowboy author and his lovely, serene bride. But instead of sighing over the romance of the moment, Kate only felt restless, edgy, uncomfortable inside her skin.

She sipped at her champagne as an odd combination of emotions floated through her veins along with the bubbles.

She was thrilled for Wyatt and Taylor. How could anyone look at the two of them together and not be thrilled for them? She loved Taylor and wanted her friend to be happy and though she couldn't say she'd really had the chance to get to know her brother in the nearly six weeks since he had found her, her gut told her Wyatt was a good man who would rather cut off his arm than hurt his new bride.

And there was the cause of her restlessness—that she didn't really know Wyatt at all. She shifted and set the flute on the table. Wyatt was her flesh and blood yet she barely knew him. Or her other brother, Gage, or their parents, Lynn and Sam.

She was suddenly overflowing with family. A mother, a father, two strong, handsome brothers. And now two sisters-in-law and even two step-nieces from Gage's marriage to Allie DeBarillas.

For a woman who had grown up believing she was nothing—less than nothing, just the throwaway kid of a homeless junkie—this sudden surplus of relations was daunting.

Intellectually she knew she belonged here with them. DNA tests proved without a doubt that she was the child of Sam and Lynn McKinnon, sister to Gage and Wyatt. But emotionally, they were still all strangers to her, all but Taylor.

If circumstances had been different, she would have known that her father wasn't very graceful on the dance floor and that Gage and Wyatt both looked strong and masculine and gorgeous in their tuxedos.

She would have known her mother didn't drink anything stronger than white wine and that Gage had broken both his legs earlier in the summer and that Sam had the incredible skills to carve the delicate wood angel that graced the soaring twenty-foot-high Christmas tree.

She was only now just learning all of those things because her entire life with these people had been stolen from her one hot summer afternoon twenty-three years ago.

She needed to move, to channel some of this restless energy into something constructive.

As Taylor's maid of honor, shouldn't she be doing something? Mingling or labeling gifts or helping out in the kitchen? She jumped up, intent on finding something to occupy her mind beyond her own problems. Before she could escape, though, Lynn whirled past her in the arms of her oldest son, Gage.

Blond and petite, Lynn looked radiant and far too young to have two sons in their thirties, one a decorated FBI agent and one a bestselling true-crime author.

And a daughter, Kate had to remind herself, a daughter who barely knew her.

Bitterness welled up inside her and threatened to spill out but she staunchly suppressed it just as Lynn disengaged from her son's arms and wrapped Kate in a sweet-scented embrace. Her mother was a toucher, she was discovering. Lynn rarely let a conversation go by without holding her arm or squeezing her hand or patting her knee.

Kate had wondered more than once if perhaps Lynn needed somehow to make up for the twenty-three years they'd been apart, for all the hugs and kisses they had missed. Or maybe she was afraid if she didn't touch her to make sure she was real, Kate would once more disappear.

"Hasn't this been the most wonderful day?" Lynn beamed. "I'm so happy I just want to dance all night."

Kate managed a smile and hugged her back. "It's

lovely. Everything is perfect. I don't know how you and Taylor threw this together on such short notice."

Lynn laughed. "We didn't have any choice. Wyatt refused to wait once he found his Taylor. Gage was the same way."

Gage smiled at both of them and Kate thought again how ruggedly handsome the FBI agent was. "We Mc-Kinnon men are impatient creatures," he said. "Once we find what we want, we move fast."

She watched his gaze scan the room until it rested on his wife, Allie, who was laughing as she tried to show her daughter Gabriella the steps of a waltz. Allie didn't seem to mind Gaby's shiny black Mary Janes planted on top of her own evening shoes as she moved through the dance.

Gage smiled at them both and the love in his eyes blazed brighter than all the stacks of candles gleaming around the room.

Kate knew Gage and Allie had been married for three months but they still acted as if they couldn't bear to be out of each other's sight. She hadn't been there, of course. She hadn't even known she had a pair of brothers three months earlier.

"I'm sorry I missed your wedding," she said on impulse, then regretted it when Lynn hugged her again, her eyes sorrowful.

"Oh, my, darling. We're just so glad you're here now. It seems like a dream, the most wonderful of miracles, that we've found you again after all these years. And just in time for the holidays!"

Kate blew out a breath. She had barely given Christmas a thought between helping Taylor with her wedding, finishing up her E.R. rotation in her second year of residency and dealing with this wild tangle of emotions at learning her true identity.

Finding out she had been kidnapped at the age of three from the arms of a loving family and thrust into the hell she'd lived as a child tended to make everything else on her to-do list fade into the background. How was she supposed to adjust to the fact that the person she thought she was all her life didn't exist?

She supposed she needed somehow to summon the energy and get busy about the holidays. It was unlike her to procrastinate so long—her friends always teased that she usually had her shopping done by Halloween.

Though she typically only bought a few gifts—something for Taylor and a few other friends, and for Tom and Maryanne Spencer, her foster parents in St. Petersburg—she was stunned by the sudden realization that her list had now grown by leaps and bounds.

She already had something for Taylor, a stained-glass wall hanging she had purchased at the arts festival in Park City last August, but now she would have to find something for Lynn and Sam, for Wyatt, for Gage, and for Allie and her children.

Before she could give in to the panic spurting through her at the idea, Lynn squeezed her hands. "I know I've mentioned this at least a dozen times before," her mother went on, "but I wanted to remind you again that I'm having dinner Christmas Eve at my home in Liberty. We'll all be together. Even Sam is staying until after the holidays."

A blush stole across Lynn's still-lovely skin like autumn's touch on a delicate leaf and Kate wondered at it. She looked for her father and found him on the dance floor with Allie's youngest daughter, Anna.

Sam McKinnon was still a handsome man, she thought, even though he was probably nearing sixty. He was exactly the kind of man she would have selected for a father if she'd been given a chance—quiet and strong, with powerful shoulders, a deep desert tan from years of living in Las Vegas, and the nicked and callused hands of a carpenter.

Her parents had divorced decades ago, a year after she'd been kidnapped. Could Lynn still have feelings for Sam after all this time? And if she did, why had she never acted on them?

Did their divorce stem from the trauma of losing a child? Though she knew it was irrational, she couldn't help a pang of guilt, as if somehow she had been responsible.

"We'll be eating around seven," Lynn said. "A little early because of the girls."

"I'm looking forward to it," she lied smoothly.

The fact that her words were a lie only made her more angry. These were wonderful people—loving and kind and painfully eager for her to take her place in their family. Why couldn't she? Why was she so damn conflicted every time she saw the love in their eyes?

Why couldn't she become the daughter they had lost?

Sam suddenly swung Anna around in their direction through the crowd to join them. The moment they were close enough, Anna jumped from his arms and threw her arms around Gage's waist.

"Gage-Gage-Gage," she chattered. "Grandpa Sam and me were dancing. He says I dance just like Clara in *The Nutcracker*. Wanta see?"

She didn't give him a chance to answer as she pulled

him out to the area of the room that had been cleared of furniture for dancing.

"Looks like I've lost my partner," Sam said with that warm smile of his. "How about if I take my beautiful little girl for a spin around the dance floor instead?"

She gazed at that smile. How many other dances had she missed with her father over the years? What would her life have been like if she'd had Sam, with his broad hands and his warm smile, to help her over all the rough patches along the way?

She thought of the times when her home had been the back seat of a broken-down car, when her stomach had churned with hunger more often than not, when her only friend had been a tattered doll Brenda had picked up at the Salvation Army during one of her good moods.

Suddenly she couldn't bear this. She cared about these people and she wanted to love them. But how could she, when she couldn't see past her own bitterness over all that had been taken from her?

She blew out a breath, loath to disappoint this kind man more than she feared she already had been a great disappointment to all of them. "Um, I'm a bit warm. I think I need to sneak out for a little air. Do you mind?"

"Not at all, honey." He winked at her and slipped an arm across Lynn's shoulders. "I've been waiting all night for my chance to sweep the mother of the groom off her feet."

Lynn blushed again but went willingly into his arms. Neither of them noticed as Kate slipped through the huge gathering room of the Bradshaws' ski lodge in Little Cottonwood Canyon with its heavy log beams and soaring cathedral ceiling.

The large home was the perfect place for a December wedding. Besides the huge tree in front of the floor-to-ceiling windows, with its twinkling gold lights and plump burgundy ribbons, more lights winked from fresh garlands hanging on the stairway and around the doorways. Gold and burgundy candles speared out of more greenery on the mantel of the huge rock fireplace, where a fire burned merrily.

It was a magical scene, one she would have delighted in for Taylor if circumstances had been different. She barely noticed, though, as she hurried through the house and slipped out the door leading to the wide deck that circled the rear of the house.

The twinkling lights extended out here and gave her just enough light to pick her way carefully across the deck. The December cold was a welcome relief from the warm house and from the heat of her own emotions as she leaned against the railing and lifted her face to the gentle snowfall.

After a moment, she could feel the tension in her shoulders begin to seep away as tiny flakes caught on the mossy-green velvet of her dress, in her hair, on her eyelashes. She relaxed enough that she even stuck her tongue out to catch a few stray snowflakes.

Growing up in Florida, she'd never seen snow as a child. It wasn't until she came to Utah for college that she had experienced her first snowfall and she still remembered how entranced she'd been by the sheer beauty of it.

Eight years later, she'd seen enough snow for it to lose much of its magic—it was mostly just a pain to drive in and a hassle to scrape off her car on her way to class or to the hospital.

Until moments like this.

Inside, the string quartet played something low and lovely and the mountains gleamed white in the moonlight. Tiny, gentle snowflakes kissed her cheeks.

She wasn't sure how long she stood there, but she did know this was the nearest thing to peace she had known since Wyatt had revealed to her the results of the DNA testing he had secretly ordered after they'd met through Taylor.

"You stay out here much longer, you're going to catch pneumonia."

The voice from the darkness startled her and she whirled so quickly she nearly lost her footing on the snow-slick wood of the deck. A large, dark shape stepped out of the shadows at the edge of the deck and into the light spilling from the lodge windows.

She recognized Hunter Bradshaw, Taylor's older brother, and pressed a hand to her suddenly racing heart. To her chagrin, she suddenly wasn't sure if her increased pulse stemmed from being caught unawares or from suddenly finding herself in such close proximity to Hunter.

In a dark suit and white shirt, he was gorgeous, with dark hair the color of hot cocoa, lean, elegant features and dark blue eyes that gleamed in the night. And, she had to admit, he had been making her pulse race since they'd met five years earlier.

"Sorry," he said. "Didn't mean to scare you."

"I didn't realize anyone else was here." Her voice sounded breathless and she cleared her throat to conceal her reaction to him. "How long have you been standing there?"

"Oh, about fifteen minutes before you showed up."

He had watched her the whole time? While she lifted her face to the sky and caught snowflakes on her tongue like a kid on the playground at recess? Heat rushed to her cheeks, surely enough to melt any flakes left there.

"I'm sorry I interrupted your solitude."

"Don't worry about it," he finally said after an odd pause.

"I'll leave. You obviously wanted to be alone."

He shrugged. "Not really. I just can't seem to spend enough time outside."

He didn't add any other explanation, but he didn't need to. She knew exactly why he craved fresh air, even cold and snowy fresh air. It all must seem heavenly to a man who had only been out of prison for a little over a month.

Hunter had spent more than two years on death row for a hideous crime he didn't commit. He had only gained his freedom after Taylor and Wyatt had uncovered the truth behind the slayings of Hunter's pregnant girlfriend, her mother and her unborn child.

Relieved to be able to focus on someone else's problems for a change, she studied him in the moon's glow and the twinkling lights. He looked tired, she thought, and the doctor in her wondered how he'd been sleeping since his release.

"How are you doing? I mean, really doing?"

He was quiet for a moment, as if not very many people had asked him that. "When I was first released," he finally said, "I wanted to do everything I'd been dreaming about inside that miserable cell for thirty months. I wanted to climb the Tetons again and feel the water rushing around my waders as I stood in a stream with a fly rod and now for some strange reason I can't seem to generate enough energy to do anything but sit out here and breathe the mountain air."

She knew exactly what he meant—his discontent and malaise mirrored her own.

"You've been through a terrible ordeal. It's going to take a while to adjust to normalcy again. Give yourself a little time."

Hunter had to smile at that crisp, professional note in her voice. "Thank you, Dr. Spencer. I don't believe I realized psychiatric medicine was your specialty."

He watched as color climbed her high cheekbones and wondered if Kate had any clue how very much she resembled Lynn McKinnon.

"You know it's not," she said. "But in family medicine you need to do a little of everything. Sorry for the uninvited advice. Hazard of the profession. I'm afraid I always think I know what's best for everyone."

"No, I appreciate it. Intellectually I know you're right—I just need more time to adjust. But I've never been a particularly patient man and I'm having a hard time trying to figure myself out right now."

He paused, uncomfortable talking about this with anyone, but especially with Kate Spencer, and decided to change the subject. "Taylor tells me you're doing well with your residency."

"Right. I just finished an E.R. rotation and on Christmas Day I start one in the neonatal intensive care unit at Primary Children's Medical Center."

He hadn't been a cop for a while now but even his rusty detective skills could hear the definite lack of enthusiasm in her voice and he wondered at it. As long as he had known her, Kate had been focused on only one thing—becoming a doctor. It had been the strongest tie binding her to his sister, the common ground that had led them to becoming friends.

"You don't sound very thrilled about it."

"I am. I've been looking forward to working in the NICU. I know I'll gain valuable skills there."

"But?"

She sighed and turned back to the ghostly mountains. "But just like you, I can't seem to work up much enthusiasm for anything right now."

"You've had a wild few months, I guess."

"We both have."

They drifted into a comfortable silence. After a moment, she stirred next to him and he caught the scent of her, that mouthwatering smell of vanilla sugar, and suddenly became *very* uncomfortable.

With her blond hair piled up on her head and that slender green dress, she looked elegant and graceful and delicious. He wondered what Dr. Spencer would do if he gave in to his sudden urge to yank the pins out of those luscious curls, bury his fingers in them, and pull her toward him.

He hadn't had much to do with women since his release and his body was loudly reminding him of the fact.

That had certainly been on his to-do list, one of those things he'd dreamed about in prison—sex with a different woman every single day for a month.

But the reality was, he didn't enjoy meaningless sex. He'd had plenty of offers since his release from prison but all from the kind of women who didn't appeal to him at all, the kind who found his dark history a turn-on and wanted to make it with an ex-con, even an innocent one.

He cleared his throat and tried to figure out how he could escape without being rude.

"Do you think you'll take your old job back?" she asked, unaware of his torment.

If any question could deflate his fledgling lust, it was that one. He stared out into the night. "That's still one of those things in the undecided column. I don't know."

"You were a good cop, Hunter."

"Yeah, I was." He didn't say it out of ego. "I loved it. But I have to admit I don't have much faith left in the system."

How could he, when that system he'd worked so hard to uphold had failed him so miserably? Despite an unblemished—even stellar—career with the Salt Lake City Police Department, he had first been arrested and then convicted of taking three lives, one of them an unborn child, one a dying cancer patient and one the woman he thought he loved.

He would still be in that cell on death row if not for his sister's unwavering faith in him. God knows, his former buddies on the force had all turned on him. The system of justice he had built his life around had failed him with disastrous consequences, and he didn't know if he could ever believe in it again.

And if he didn't believe in it, he sure as hell couldn't pick up his detective shield again and take up where he had left off before his arrest nearly three years earlier.

"So what will you do?" Kate asked.

He shrugged. "For now, I guess I'll just stay out here and watch the mountains."

She laughed a little, then shivered as a cold gust of wind blew across the porch. "We're both going to turn into blocks of ice if we stay out here much longer."

"I suppose we'd better go inside."

He was surprised to see her expression become guarded, reluctant.

"Why the hesitation? That's your family in there."

"I don't know. I must be crazy, right?"

He gave a harsh laugh. "Believe me, I know crazy. You can't spend thirty months behind bars and not get real good at telling the nuts from the wackos. You're neither—in fact, you're one of the most sane women I know."

"Not the last six weeks. I'm a mess, Hunter."

She faced him then and he was stunned to see tears gathering in her vivid blue eyes. He didn't know what to do for a wild moment, then he placed a hand over hers, struck by her icy fingers.

He squeezed her hand and she gave him a tremulous smile. They stood there for a moment, then she slipped her hand away and returned to the deck railing.

"I should be happy. I *know* I should. I'm suddenly surrounded by this wonderful family, people who love me and want me to be part of their lives. I want that, too, but I'm just so damn angry."

"At what?"

"Whoever did this to us! I'm filled with rage toward the person who kidnapped me, who took me away from a sane, normal, happy family and dragged me into..."

Her expression closed up and he wondered about her childhood after she was taken from her family, about what she might have been through to put that bleak look in her eyes. "Into a world far removed from the safe, happy life I likely would have known as Charlotte McKinnon."

Someone had kidnapped her more than two decades before. He hadn't been so self-absorbed that he didn't know all about that. Who was it? he suddenly wondered. And had they paid for the crime that had devastated the lives of so many people?

For the first time since his release—hell, since the shock of his arrest three years ago—he found himself concerned about someone else's problems, found himself actually interested enough to want to solve the mystery.

He wasn't sure he wanted to care, but he had been a cop too long to turn it off completely.

"Any idea who kidnapped you?"

"Until six weeks ago I thought my mother was a woman named Brenda Golightly. She's all I can remember until I was taken away from her and put into foster care when I was seven."

"And you think she was the one?"

"She must have been. My earliest memories are of her—driving beside her along a lonely stretch of highway. Sleeping in some dingy motel somewhere. Eating peanut-butter sandwiches and washing them down with warm soda. She's the one listed on all my records as my mother. I have a birth certificate and everything. I don't know how she did it but my name was Katie Golightly until I changed it at eighteen to Kate Spencer."

At least she had a name. He could work with a name. "Any idea where she is?"

"We don't exactly exchange Christmas cards. Brenda was a prostitute and a junkie, stoned more often than she was sober. After I was taken from her, she used to write or phone me once in a while but by the time I was in high school, she seemed to have lost interest—the letters and calls had trickled down to maybe once every couple of years. I was glad she didn't seem to want much to do with me. It was easier that way."

She paused, and again he wondered what dark images she was seeing in her memory.

"Anyway," Kate went on, "I haven't heard from her in eight years, since I left for college, but last I knew she was living in Miami somewhere."

He could drive to Florida in two days if he pushed it. The thought sneaked into his mind and Hunter drew in a sharp breath. Now who was the crazy one, contemplating a drive across the country on what was probably a fool's errand?

On the other hand, he didn't have anything else to do right now. He was restless and edgy and a road trip might be just the thing to help him figure out what to do with himself.

"Either she kidnapped me herself," Kate went on, "or she had to know who did it. I only want to know why. Why me?"

He studied her there in the moonlight, this small, beautiful woman with shadows in her eyes. He could help her. Like she said, he'd been a damn good detective once. Maybe he could be again. He had considered going into private-investigator work, the logical second career for a burned-out cop. This could be a way to test if he had the temperament for it.

One of them at least ought to be able to put some ghosts aside and move on. With a sneaking suspicion that he was going to have some serious regrets later about ever opening his mouth, he took the plunge.

"You want to know why you were taken," he finally said. "Why don't I find this Brenda Golightly and ask her?"

Chapter 2

Kate stared at him. He looked perfectly rational, his eyes dark and intense as he stood there in the cold night air with the soft snow sifting down around him like powdered sugar. But looks could be deceiving, she thought.

"Didn't you hear what I said? She's probably in Florida! The last address I had was Dade County."

"Sunshine sounds nice right about now."

No wonder, she thought. Since his release, sunny days had been few and far between in Utah. The state had seen a wet, cold fall—a boon for the ski resorts but probably not so enjoyable for someone who had been incarcerated for more than two years.

She had to admit, though she had grown to love the Utah mountains, the first place she would head if she had just been released from prison would be somewhere with an ocean view. Somewhere she could bask in the sun and lick salt from the air and dig her toes into warm sand.

But how could she ask him to travel across the country for her on little more than a whim?

"I haven't heard from Brenda in nearly a decade," she said. "She might not even be in Florida anymore. Heavens, for all I know, the woman could be dead."

"Then I'll find out where she's gone. Or at least where she's buried."

He said the words with complete confidence. She would have thought it an idle boast if he hadn't been such an outstanding detective. But if Hunter Bradshaw put his mind and energy into finding someone, he would. He had been dogged about his job, completely focused on it.

She had so many unanswered questions. Since finding out she had been kidnapped, her mind seemed to be racing on an endless loop of them.

Why had she been taken? Not for ransom, certainly, since the McKinnons said no one ever contacted them. And why *her*? What about Kate had made her a target of the kidnapping?

If Brenda had taken her, why had she then just surrendered Kate to the foster-care system, keeping only enough contact to ensure that no one could adopt her?

Finding the answers to those pressing questions was tantalizing. But the idea of Hunter Bradshaw offering to help her baffled her.

She was nothing to him, only the roommate of his younger sister. She couldn't even say she was a friend. Before his arrest and imprisonment, he had always been distantly polite to her but never more than that.

She had even wondered if he disliked her because he seemed to go out of his way to avoid situations where they might be alone.

Yet here he was offering to chase after her past.

"Why would you do this for me?" she asked.

"Why not?" Hunter asked. In the dim light, his eyes wore an inscrutable expression. "You deserve to know the truth. I know how frustrating unanswered questions can be, just as I know what it's like to be punished for someone else's sins. I'd like to help you find out why."

She wasn't sure why—perhaps something in those shadows in his eyes—but she sensed another reason, something deeper. "What else?"

Hunter turned away from her to lean his forearms on the deck railing and gaze out at the shadowy mountains.

"Because I can." His voice was low and without inflection but suddenly his offer of assistance made perfect sense. It had nothing to do with her at all, she realized, but with him and his new freedom.

He had spent nearly three years of his life behind bars, where his choices had been severely limited. Others told him what he could eat, where he could go, even how he could dress. What a heady sense of control he must find in the idea that he could pick up and drive across the country on a whim!

"I see," she murmured.

He slanted a look at her. "Do you?"

"You know, you could take a trip wherever you want without having the burden of tracking down a drug addict and a prostitute who could be anywhere."

"I've been at loose ends since my release. I could use a distraction. This is a good one."

"It might take weeks, Hunter. I can't ask you to give up so much of your time."

His shrug rippled the fabric of his well-cut suit. He had always been a good dresser, she remembered. Back when he was a detective, he always took care with his clothing.

Before his arrest, he would sometimes stop by Taylor's house after work for some reason or other. Even with his tie loose, a hint of dark shadow stubbling his jaw and his white shirt perhaps not as crisp and starched as it had likely been in the morning, he had been enough to make her mouth water. She had always thought Hunter Bradshaw was strong and masculine and gorgeous.

She wasn't sure which she preferred, that slightly rumpled end-of-day Hunter or this elegant man in evening wear.

"You didn't ask, I offered," he said in answer to her earlier comment. "Anyway, my time is my own now."

"So take a cruise around the world if you want to go somewhere!"

Kate knew that like his sister, Hunter didn't need to work. He could spend the rest of his life traveling the world if he wanted to. Both of them had fathoms-deep trust funds that would support them forever if they wanted to live lives of luxury and ease.

Their parents had come from old money, although like Taylor, Hunter had always shunned the accoutrements of wealth. He had become an underpaid Utah public servant and lived quietly here in the family ski cabin.

"Let me do this, Kate. You're looking for answers and I'm looking for something to fill all this free time

I've suddenly got. Seems to me this is a good way for both of us to get something we want."

She looked inside the house and caught a glimpse of her family. Wyatt danced with their mother now, Lynn small and delicate next to his lean rangy height. Gage stood in one corner talking to Sam, with a tired-looking Anna in his arms.

A gust of wind blew across the deck, sending the fairy lights dancing, and Kate shivered.

She should be inside with her family. They would be looking for her soon. But despite the cold out here and the snow that was swirling around a little harder, she dreaded returning to that happy, bright group inside. The joy that lit their eyes whenever they caught sight of her scraped along her spine like a chipped fingernail.

She couldn't be the daughter and sister the Mc-Kinnons wanted and her own failure to be open and relaxed around them sat heavy and thick in her chest.

Brenda Golightly had stolen twenty-three years of her life. She had taken so much from Kate—didn't the woman who had caused such horrible pain in so many lives deserve to pay for what she had done?

Perhaps if Kate could find answers to some of the questions that had haunted her for six weeks since learning her true identity, she might at last be free to accept the love and nurturing this family seemed painfully eager to shower on her.

Didn't she owe it to the McKinnons and to herself to try to reclaim some of what had been taken from her?

She blew out a resigned breath. "It won't be easy to find her," she warned. "She could be anywhere. Brenda was always good at slipping under the radar."

Hunter gazed at her for a moment, his expression

unreadable, then he nodded, recognizing she had decided to let him help her.

"If you have a previous address for her, I can work with that. I can leave tomorrow and start digging. I should be able to call you with information by the end of next week."

She looked at him standing in shadow, then shifted her gaze to that bright, gleaming window again. Laughter and music spilled out into the night. Would it always be this way? Would she always be on the outside looking in, separated from her family by the walls a stranger had erected between them by snatching her away so long ago? Would she always be unable to let herself partake of the love the McKinnons so wanted to give her because of her anger and bitterness?

That restlessness prowled through her again, edgy and fretful, and she blew out a breath and turned to face Hunter again in the shadows.

"You won't need to call me to report your progress."

He frowned. "Why not? Don't you think you'll want to know how things are going."

"Absolutely. That's why I'm going with you."

His mind already busy mapping a route and making plans, Hunter barely heard her. When her words pushed their way through his crowded thoughts, shock just about sent him toppling over the deck railing. She wanted to go along? Yeah, right!

He would never have suggested helping her if he thought for one second it might involve spending time alone with Kate Spencer.

"Really, that's not necessary."

Not necessary and not at all appealing.

"It is to me. This woman stole my life. My identity, my family, everything. If you can find her, I believe I have the right to confront her to find out why."

Okay, he would give her that. If he had been in Kate's shoes, he would have moved heaven and earth to locate this woman who had wreaked such havoc in her life.

He understood her need for answers and her desire to be involved in finding those answers but he didn't think she quite comprehended the implications.

"If I were flying out there for a quick trip," he explained, "I would have no problem with you going along. But I won't be taking a plane. If I go, I'm driving."

For one thing, he couldn't leave Belle, especially with Tay and Wyatt leaving for their Cozumel honeymoon in the morning. Since his release, his Irish setter clung to his side like a mother hen watching her chick. Though normally calm and well-mannered, she turned into a nervous wreck if he left her alone for even a few hours.

He wouldn't put her through the stress of a lonely kennel for a week or two, nor was he willing to subject her to the trauma of putting her on an airplane. The one time he had taken her on a plane before his arrest, she'd been a quivering mess for a week afterward.

He had to admit, Belle was part of the reason behind his sudden desire to drive, but she was by no means the only reason. The thought of taking off across the wide expanse of the United States with the road in front of him and Utah in his rearview mirror seemed just the thing to shake this malaise he'd suffered from since his release.

Those months he had spent on death row sure his

life would end there in that miserable prison, he used to dream about hopping on his Ducati and zooming off across the country. When he would lie awake at night in that thin, lumpy cot staring up at cement walls, he had grieved for the trips he had never found time to take, for the scenery he would never have the chance to savor.

The Ducati would have to wait since December wasn't the greatest time for a motorcycle trip—not to mention the minor little detail that he hadn't yet taught Belle how to hang on behind him. But he could enjoy a cross-country trip from inside the brand-new Jeep Grand Cherokee he'd bought just days before.

What better way to celebrate his newfound freedom than loading up his dog and trekking across the country—eating in greasy diners, blasting his favorite songs on the radio at top volume, outrunning his past with every white line passing under his tires.

He would have thought his announcement would be enough to dissuade her, but Kate didn't seem at all fazed by his declaration. "Driving is fine. I don't mind a road trip," she answered.

Damn. So much for his peaceful jaunt across the country.

"Don't you have to work?" he asked, not willing to give it up just yet. "I thought residents worked sixty hours a week without a day off."

The Christmas lights sparkled in her glossy hair as she shook her head. "I'm free until I start my new rotation on Christmas Day. That gives me two weeks of freedom. This is a perfect time for me to go. I should have thought of it myself."

Now what the hell was he supposed to do? He

couldn't just come out and tell her she couldn't go. For one thing, he was oddly loath to hurt her feelings. For another, from his admittedly limited experience with Kate, he knew she was enough like Taylor that she would push and poke at him until she pried out the reason he didn't want her along.

He was well and truly stuck. He should have kept his big mouth shut about the whole thing.

It would take them a bare minimum of two days to drive to Miami. Two days alone in a car with Kate Spencer. For a man who hadn't been sexually intimate in nearly three years, that prospect was guaranteed to be a recipe for disaster.

He couldn't do it. He couldn't sleep with his sister's best friend just to slake his hunger. If he did, he would be exactly the kind of beast he'd been trying to prove to the world—and himself—that he wasn't.

"Look, Kate—" he started to say, but his words were lost when the door opened and Lynn McKinnon walked out onto the deck, her lovely features concerned.

"There you are, Charlotte!" She winced and reached for Kate's arm. "I'm so sorry, Kate. I keep forgetting. It's just that I've thought of you as Charlotte for so long. But I'll get it, I promise."

"It's fine," Kate murmured. The animation of the last ten minutes was gone from her features as she gazed at the small, energetic woman who looked so much like her.

"You're going to catch your death out here! Is everything all right?"

"We were just enjoying the snowstorm."

"Your father is still waiting for his dance."

"Of course." Even in the pale light, Hunter thought

her smile looked strained. "I just need a few more minutes of air, okay? And then I'll be in."

Lynn's mouth softened as she gazed at her daughter, and Hunter thought she would have reached up and
grabbed the moon for Kate if she asked for it. "Take
as much time as you need, darling. Sam will be there
whenever you're ready."

Kate managed another smile before her mother
slipped back inside, though Hunter was surprised to
see a bleakness in her eyes.

He muttered a string of curses in his mind. He
couldn't leave her here twiddling her thumbs while he
went off dragon hunting. This was her *life*.

Of all the people at this wedding gig, he could certainly understand her need to take back some kind
of control over the circumstances that had buffeted
her for the last six weeks. If finding and confronting
her kidnapper would help her achieve some measure
of peace—would help her move past her pain and be
ready to accept the McKinnons' love—how could he
deny her that?

Surely he was tough enough to control himself
around her for a week.

"What time are we leaving?" she asked after Lynn
closed the door behind herself and returned to the fes-
tivities, leaving them once more in the still, quiet night.

"Early. I'll pick you up at eight. Does that work?"

"Perfectly."

Was it just his imagination or did the pinched look
around her mouth ease just a little?

"I can't tell you how grateful I am for this," she said.
"Going after Brenda is a brilliant idea."

"Let's see how brilliant you think it is after a week
on the road."

* * *

This had to be the craziest idea she had ever come up with.

Worse, even, than the time when they were second-year med students and she and Taylor had tried to break into the anatomy lab for a little extra study time working on their cadavers.

In the cold, pale light of a December morning, what had seemed so logical the night before seemed short-sighted and foolish when faced with the cold, hard reality of spending at least a week in intimate quarters with Hunter Bradshaw.

Kate stood at the front window of the small second-floor apartment she had moved into the month before, watching for him to pull into the driveway below.

A quick glance at the clock on the microwave told her that even if he was obsessively punctual, he wouldn't arrive for at least ten minutes, but she couldn't seem to pry herself away from the window where she stood tracing the filigreed frost collecting on the other side.

She hadn't slept well, with her nerves on edge and her mind racing. She had finally tired of her tossing and turning a few hours before dawn and had climbed out of bed to start preparing for the trip.

The few things she planned to take had been packed and waiting by the door for hours and she spent the rest of the morning wrapping her few Christmas presents and scrubbing her apartment. Since she barely spent any time at all here, she could find little to clean, but at least she wouldn't be coming home to a mess.

With all her preparations done, she had little else to do now but stand here at the window watching for him and panicking about the sheer insanity of this situation her impulsiveness had thrust her into.

Whatever had compelled her to insist on traipsing along with Hunter Bradshaw? In what feeble-minded moment would that ever seem like a good idea?

How could she ever have been stupid enough to think she could travel blithely across the country with him when simply finding herself in the same room with the man left her flustered and giddy?

He had always made her insides tremble and her heart rate accelerate. She had been friends with Taylor since their first semester of medical school, more than five years ago. She could still remember the first time she met her friend's older brother. She and Taylor had been cramming for finals their second semester and had decided to grab a midnight snack at their favorite all-night diner, a humble little place downtown that served divine mashed potatoes with thick, creamy gravy.

They had walked in and Kate had only a few seconds to register a gorgeous man sitting in a booth in the front window with a couple of uniformed cops when Taylor had let out a delighted laugh and dragged her over to meet the brother she often talked about.

She could still remember her first impression—that the two of them shared an obviously close, affectionate relationship completely foreign to someone who had never had siblings of her own, except in a few foster families where she had been barely tolerated.

Her second impression of Hunter Bradshaw had been far more elemental and astonishing—an intense physical awareness of him unlike anything she'd ever experienced. As she gazed into dark blue eyes while

Taylor introduced them, her stomach did a long, slow roll and she felt as if something had just squeezed out every molecule of air in her lungs.

The off-duty uniform cops had been flirtatious and charming to a couple of weary young med students and had insisted she and Taylor join them. To her growing dismay, Kate found herself squeezed next to Hunter in the red vinyl booth.

Throughout the next hour she had been painfully aware of every movement he made—the way he leaned an elbow back on the seat cushion, how his mouth quirked up a little higher on one side than the other when he smiled, the way his dark hair curled just a little on the ends.

Her sudden absorption with him had been as unexpected as it was mortifying.

She had always considered herself rather cold when it came to the opposite sex. Men had never been a high priority in her life. Sometimes they hardly seemed worth the energy it took to cater to their egos and their self-absorption.

She thought perhaps she'd been passed over on the whole libido thing because most of the kisses she had experienced in her twenty-six years on the earth to that point had been pleasant, certainly, but nothing to write home about.

In that tired old diner looking out at neon gleaming in the wet street, with her pulse jumping every time Hunter's long legs would brush against hers under the table or his shoulder would bump her, Kate finally started to get an inkling what all the fuss was about.

Taylor often gave her a hard time because she rarely dated the same man more than a few times. She never told her friend this but she was always looking for that same crazy, exciting, terrifying breathlessness she experienced whenever Hunter was around.

Not that she ever did anything about it. How could she? When she first met Hunter, he had just started dating Dru Ferrin, the ambitious, talented crime reporter at a local television station.

A few months later, Dru had announced she was pregnant and Hunter had become totally absorbed in trying to convince Dru to marry him, in the prospect of becoming a father.

Or so he thought, anyway. After Dru and her terminally ill mother were murdered, DNA tests proved Hunter had not fathered the eight-month-old fetus that had also died from his mother's gunshot wound.

She had grieved right along with him, first at the child's death, then when he found out Dru had lied to him throughout her pregnancy. And then had come the horror of his arrest and the subsequent trial and wrongful conviction.

She had had a major crush on him. The knowledge mortified her. She was a doctor, for heaven's sake. Twenty-six years old, well on her way to being established in her chosen career path, and she had a crush on a sexy, dangerous, unreachable male as if she were thirteen years old fantasizing about a pop star.

How on earth would she keep her silly feelings to herself for a week or longer when it would be just the two of them alone on the road?

She would just have to do her best to treat him like she did male colleagues and her other male friends—casual and cheerfully friendly.

Could she pull it off? She was still trying to figure that out when she saw an SUV turn into the small parking area behind her battered six-year-old Honda.

As usual, her stomach performed a long, slow tremble at the sight of that muscular body climbing out of a gleaming Jeep Grand Cherokee the color of a mountain forest.

He wore jeans and a suede jacket that did nothing to hide his powerful build. His years in prison had turned what had already been a sexy, muscled build into something potent and dangerous.

Kate huffed out a breath, heat crawling across her cheeks. Not the kind of thing she should be noticing. She would never survive riding in such close quarters with him if she couldn't shove those kinds of thoughts completely out of her head.

She was a doctor who had seen more than her share of men's bodies, both muscled and otherwise. It might require a great deal of effort on her part but she needed to treat Hunter Bradshaw with the same courteous, impersonal distance she treated her patients.

The man was doing her a huge favor by helping her trace her past. The last thing he probably wanted was for her to go all gooey over him.

The doorbell chimed through her apartment and Kate pressed a hand to her stomach, where a whole brigade of butterflies were doing their thing.

After a few deep, cleansing breaths, she pasted on a polite smile and opened the door.

"Good morning," she said.

He returned her attempt at a smile with one of those shuttered looks he excelled at and she could feel more heat crawl across her cheeks.

"I'm all ready." She gestured to the few bags by the

door—one suitcase, her laptop case and the emergency medical kit she always carried with her.

He blinked a few times at her meager luggage. "This is all you're taking? We might be gone a while."

"I don't need much. A few pairs of jeans and a toothbrush and I'm set."

He looked even more surprised by that piece of information. She wondered why, until she remembered his most recent experience with females, not counting his sister, had been Dru Ferrin—a girlie-girl if Kate had ever met one.

Dru probably wouldn't even have driven to the all-night grocery store at 3:00 a.m. unless she'd worn full battle armor. Kate doubted if Dru Ferrin could have gone anywhere without a footlocker full of makeup.

As soon as the thought flitted across her mind, she felt small and catty. She hadn't much liked Dru Ferrin, but the woman had died a horrible death. She deserved better than to be the object of malicious spite, simply because Kate was jealous that Hunter had loved her.

She made a face at herself and her own small-mindedness but Hunter must have misinterpreted the reason behind it.

"Are you sure you want to do this?" he asked quickly. "I can go by myself. It's not too late if you want to back out."

For just one moment she was tempted—horribly tempted—to do just that, especially when a hint of his aftershave wafted to her. He smelled divine, something leathery and outdoorsy and male, and for a moment she wanted to stand right here in her tiny living room just sniffing him.

She could handle this. Yes, she was attracted to the

man but that was nothing new. She'd been dealing with that for five years now and had never done anything about it. A few more days wouldn't make much difference in the scheme of things, especially if she could keep the purpose for the whole trip uppermost in her mind.

"I need to do this, Hunter. I realized during the night that I have to try to make some kind of peace with my past. I can't spend the rest of my life being eaten alive by my anger."

"You think finding the woman you thought was your mother will help you find that peace?"

"I can only hope. I won't know for sure until I find her, will I?"

He studied her for a moment, then shrugged. "Let's go, then."

He reached down and picked up her luggage effortlessly, then headed back down the stairs.

With an odd, tingly feeling in her toes like she teetered on the brink of something precarious and shaky, Kate made one last check of her apartment to ensure she had turned everything off, grabbed her coat, then locked the door behind her and followed him down the stairs.

Chapter 3

Hunter was stowing her suitcase in the cargo area of his new SUV next to Belle's travel crate when Kate walked down the steps of the old Victorian that had been split into three or four apartments.

"All set," she said. "Everything's turned off and locked tight."

He wondered if she realized her chipper tone seemed as forced as her smile—and about as enthusiastic as he felt about this whole thing.

Was she as apprehensive as he was about this whole road trip? He ought just to back out right now, let her fly down to Florida by herself on this quest of hers.

He couldn't do that, though. If he hadn't opened his big mouth and suggested it, she wouldn't even have grabbed onto the idea.

No, he had started this and he would see it through.

He had offered to help her, had made a commitment, and he was a man who honored his promises, no matter how difficult.

How tough could it be, anyway? All he had to remember was that those columbine-blue eyes and that honey-blond hair and those lush delectable lips were off-limits. No worries.

To his surprise, Kate immediately opened the back door of the Jeep to greet Belle.

His setter barked in greeting and jumped from the vehicle, writhing around Kate with her tail wagging like crazy. Hunter was about to apologize and order Belle to settle down but before he could, Kate knelt down and wrapped her arms around the dog's neck.

"Oh, I've missed you, sweetie. How've you been?"

She didn't seem to mind Belle's slobbery greeting or the dog's enthusiastic licking of her face, or the hair she was undoubtedly depositing on Kate's gray sweater.

He supposed he shouldn't have been surprised by their happy reunion. While he had been locked up, Belle had lived with his sister and her roommate and best friend. Kate.

In truth, Belle had probably spent more time with Kate than she had with him. She was really more theirs than his. Belle had only been a few years old at the time he had been arrested.

His dog certainly hadn't suffered at all under their care. By the looks of things, the Irish setter adored Kate as much as him.

He let Belle work out a little of her energy by dancing around Kate a few times, then opened the door of her crate.

"Belle. Kennel."

With one last enthusiastic lick of Kate's hand, the dog leaped into her travel crate and settled in.

"It's safer for her to ride back here," he explained. "For her sake and for the driver's. Belle's a good traveler but she can be a distraction."

"I know. Once she tried to attack the rear windshield wiper in Taylor's Subaru—from the inside of the vehicle, of course. She spent about ten minutes trying to figure out why she couldn't wrap her teeth around the thing."

Her smile looked more natural, a little less forced, and he had forced himself to look away, focusing instead on the clouds hanging heavy and dark in the December sky.

"We'd better get going," he said brusquely.

"Right," she said after an awkward moment, then headed for the passenger door of the SUV.

He beat her to it and held it open for her, earning himself an odd look, as if she weren't quite sure how to react to that small courtesy.

As he walked around the Jeep, he couldn't help thinking about the somewhat old-fashioned lessons his father had constantly drilled into his head about how to treat a woman. With respect and civility and basic human courtesy.

He and his father had certainly had their differences but he could never fault the Judge in that regard. His father's example had been lesson enough. Even when his mother had been at her most difficult—days when she had been barely coherent and had raged at everything in sight—Hunter never saw his father treat her with anything but dignity.

He doubted the Judge would find anything courteous about the thoughts he was entertaining about this particular woman. Like how the ivory December morning light gave her skin the soft delectability of a bowl of fresh apricots and how that full mouth begged to be devoured.

He paused outside the driver's side for one more last-minute lecture to himself. He had to send those kinds of thoughts right out of his head.

Okay, so he'd been a long time without a woman. He could have remedied that anytime these last six weeks if he'd chosen, but he hadn't and now it was too late. It was his own damn fault if he found himself in a near-constant state of arousal for the next few days.

With a heavy sigh, he opened the driver's side door and immediately wished he hadn't. He felt invaded. Overwhelmed. Instead of the comfortably male scent of leather and new car he expected, he smelled *Kate*—that subtle, alluring scent of shampoo and woman and the vanilla sugar that always clung to her. The smell seemed to slide over him like silk and he wanted to close his eyes and sink into it.

He gritted his teeth and climbed into the SUV.

They drove in silence for a block or so before he dared unclench his teeth to speak. "Your apartment seems comfortable."

She looked a little nonplussed by his comment coming out of nowhere. Okay, so he was a little rusty at making small talk. His companions for the past two years had been the other inmates on death row, who weren't exactly big on social chitchat. He was going to have to work on it, though, or this trip with Kate would be excruciating.

"Thanks," she said after a moment. "I had to find

something in a hurry and this was one of the first places I looked at. I thought it was a graceful old house and I liked the fact that it was an established neighborhood. That was one of the things I enjoyed most about sharing Taylor's house in the Avenues, having neighbors who actually knew your name."

Guilt pinched at him and he felt like he had shoved her out onto the street. "You had to find somewhere else in a hurry because of me, right? I'm sorry about that."

"I'm not. You were coming home and that was the important thing. Anyway, the house in Little Cottonwood Canyon was yours. Taylor and I were only staying there temporarily after her cottage burned."

"After it was torched, you mean."

Her mouth tightened at the reminder. "Right. I was always planning on finding somewhere else. You and Taylor deserved some time alone without me hanging around."

"You could have stayed. There was plenty of room."

She laughed a little. "Right. The roommate who would never leave. That's me. Don't worry about me, Hunter. I like my new place, even if I don't expect to be there long. I only signed a six-month lease— I imagine when my residency is over and I start my own family-medicine practice somewhere, I'll buy a house somewhere."

Her words reminded him of his own aimlessness since his release. He needed to give some serious thought to what he was going to do with the rest of his life, now that it had been handed back to him. Maybe with the open road stretching out ahead of him, he might find inspiration.

"I do like my apartment," Kate went on, "but this is

the first time I've ever lived alone and I have to admit I'm finding it a little odd."

"You've always had roommates?" There. That sounded just right. Casual and interested but not too inquisitive. They were almost having a normal conversation.

She nodded. "I've been a struggling med student, remember? I found it hard enough to make ends meet. Sharing the rent helped ease the financial strain a little."

She lifted one shoulder. "Maybe by my second or third year I would have decided I'd had enough of roommates and moved out on my own but then Taylor bought her house and asked me if I wanted to share it. I couldn't say no."

Hunter had to admit, that decision of his sister's to take on a roommate had come as a surprise to him. Taylor had bought her little cottage in the Avenues outright with her inheritance from their father. She certainly hadn't needed a roommate to share expenses but she had taken one, anyway, for the company.

Taylor wasn't like him in that respect, he reminded himself. He had never been much of a pack animal, but his sister loved having people around her. He knew she had been lonely those first few months after she'd bought her house and she'd been eager for Kate to move in.

Kate seemed to be waiting for him to respond, so he fished around in his mind until he found an appropriate question. "So do you miss having a roommate?"

She gazed out the windshield, at the minimal Sunday-morning traffic, then finally looked back at him. "I miss Taylor," she admitted. "That sounds silly, I know, but she was more than just a roommate. She was my best friend. The closest thing I had to a sister."

"You'll still be close."

"It's not going to be the same. I understand that. Don't get me wrong, I'm thrilled for her and Wyatt. They're perfect for each other, I could see that right away."

"Your brother is a good man."

"I know. Wyatt is strong and smart and funny. Just the kind of man Taylor needs."

What kind of man do you need? he almost asked but stopped himself just in time. None of his business. That kind of question would lead their fledgling conversation in a direction he absolutely didn't want it to go.

"He makes her happy," she said. "When it comes down to it, that's all that matters."

"Right," he murmured. He had to admit, he enjoyed seeing Taylor find some happiness. She deserved it. Both she and Wyatt did.

If not for the efforts of his sister and of Wyatt McKinnon, he would still be in that prison, feeling his soul shrivel more each day. Taylor had worked tirelessly to free him. She had put her dream of becoming a doctor like Kate on hold, switching instead to law school so she could fight for his appeal. Taylor had finally enlisted the help of Wyatt, who had been writing a book about Hunter's case.

In the process of trying to free him, she had been threatened, her house set ablaze, and finally had faced down death for his cause. He hadn't wanted her to sacrifice her dreams for him—or, heaven forbid, her life—and Hunter knew he could never repay his sister for all that she had done.

He supposed that was another of the reasons he was

driving through the sparse Sunday-morning traffic heading south on I-15. He owed Taylor and Wyatt everything for all they had risked. Maybe by turning around and helping Kate—someone both of them cared about—he could start to check off a little of that debt.

"You're not taking I-80?" Kate asked as he passed the interchange—the Spaghetti Bowl, as the locals called it, for the various lanes twisting off in every direction like pasta in a dish.

He shook his head. "The weather report said that light snow we had last night gathered strength as it headed east and was due to hit Wyoming with a vengeance today. I figured if we head south now, down through Albuquerque and Amarillo, we'll escape the worst of it."

"Good thinking."

They encountered no delays traveling south across the Salt Lake Valley and, all too soon, they reached Bluffdale where the Point of the Mountain state prison sprawled out to the west of the highway, its buildings squat and depressing.

This was the first time he'd been this way since his release, Hunter realized. Perhaps he had made a point of staying north of the area without even realizing it.

If he had come this way before, he might have been prepared for the rush of anger and hatred rising like bile in his throat.

His hands tightened on the steering wheel. Sunday mornings were relatively quiet at the prison. Many prisoners chose to sleep the day away, while others attended the various religious services offered.

Hunter had quite deliberately chosen to stay in his cell reading. By the time he'd found himself on death row, he had lost whatever faith might have lingered in his soul.

He had been less than nothing in prison. Inhuman, like a dog locked up in a cage at the pound. He had been out for six weeks and he wondered if that feeling would ever go away.

"It's hard for you to see the prison, isn't it?"

It seemed a sign of weakness to admit the truth. It was just a cluster of buildings, after all. A part of his life that was over forever.

He opened his mouth to deny he was at all affected by the sight but somehow the lie caught in his throat.

"I lost two and a half years of my life to that bastard Martin James. Three lives were lost while he tried to protect his web of lies and deceit. Who knows how many more he would have taken? It's a little hard to get past that."

Her blue eyes softened with understanding and she reached a hand across the width of the SUV and touched his arm with gentle fingers. "I'm so sorry, Hunter."

Despite his grim thoughts, heat scorched him where she touched his arm and he was suddenly aware of a wild, terrible hunger to drown in that heat and softness, to lose some of this rage always seething just under the surface.

He jerked his arm away, just firmly enough to be obvious. "I'm sorry enough for myself. I don't need your pity, too."

She paled as if he had slapped her—which he guessed he had done, verbally at least—and quickly pulled her hand away.

"Right. Of course you don't."

He opened his mouth to apologize for his rudeness, then closed it again. Maybe it was better this way. They weren't buddies. It was going to be tough enough for him to stay away from her on this journey without having to endure shared confidences and these casual touches that would destroy him.

He had been without any kind of physical affection since his arrest and he hungered for gentleness and softness as much as for sex.

It was a grim realization, one that certainly didn't make their situation any easier.

She had two choices here, Kate thought as his blatant rejection burned through her like hydrochloric acid. She could let herself be hurt and pout for the rest of the day. That was the course that appealed to her most, but what would that accomplish?

Yes, her feelings had been hurt. All she had been trying to do was offer comfort and he had slapped her down like she was one of those inflatable punching bags she used to beat the heck out of when she was in foster care, angry at the world and unsure of her place in it.

But she decided not to let herself be offended. Hunter was a proud man who had seen his entire world crash down around him. He had lost friends, his job, his standing in the community.

It must have been agony for him to know the whole world believed him capable of murdering a pregnant woman and her dying mother.

He had a right to be prickly about it, to deal with his wrongful conviction and everything else that had happened in his own way. If that way included being surly and hostile when an unsuspecting soul tried to offer comfort, she couldn't blame him.

His bitterness and anger must be eating him up from the inside and she could certainly understand all about that.

She would take the higher road, she decided. Instead of snapping back or sulking all day, she would swallow her hurt feelings and pretend nothing had happened.

She decided a change of subject was in order. "I brought music if you're interested," she said, then risked a joke. "I figured your CD collection might be a few years out of date."

He sent her one of those dark, inscrutable looks she could only imagine must have been torture for any crime suspect he was questioning. He said nothing, but she thought she registered a vague surprise in those dark blue eyes at her mild reaction to his rudeness, and she was immensely grateful she hadn't gone with her first instincts and thrown a hissy fit.

"What are you in the mood for?" she asked. "Jazz? Rock? Country? Christmas music? I've got a little of everything."

"I don't care. Anything."

"Okay. I'll pick first and then you can find something."

She chose Norah Jones and felt her own stress level immediately lower as soon as the music started.

They drove without speaking for several moments, Belle's snoring in the back and the peaceful music the only sound in the vehicle, then Kate reached into her bag again and pulled out Wyatt's latest bestseller that had come out a few months earlier.

"You don't mind if I read, do you?"

"Go ahead. We've got a long drive ahead of us. I imagine we're going to run out of small talk by the time we hit Spanish Fork."

She laughed. "*You* might. I never seem to run out of things to say. But I'll take pity on you and pace myself."

To her delight, that earned her a tiny, reluctant smile, but it was more than she'd seen since his release. It was a start, she thought. Maybe by the time this journey was through, he would be smiling and laughing like the man she had met five years ago with Taylor in that all-night diner.

She picked up her book, one of only a few of Wyatt's she hadn't had time to read yet. She had actually discovered his books long before she ever knew he was her brother, and had read each one with fascination.

He wrote true-crime books—usually not one of her favorite genres—but Wyatt had a way of crawling inside the heads of both the victims and the killers he wrote about, and she found his work absorbing and compelling.

This one was no different, and she was surprised by the warm contentment stealing over her as she rode along with Hunter's sexy male scent drifting around her senses and the tires spinning on the highway while the windshield wipers beat back a light snow spitting from the sky.

Combined with the peaceful music, Kate felt herself begin to relax and slip further into that warm, cozy place where she didn't have to worry about the family waiting patiently for her love—or the man beside her who wouldn't want it, if he ever guessed it might be his for the taking.

* * *

She must have drifted off to sleep. One moment she was reading the introduction to Wyatt's book, the next she woke facing Hunter, with her left cheek squished into the leather seat.

She blinked, disoriented for a moment, then whispered a fervent prayer that she hadn't done something humiliating in front of the man, like snore or drool or—heaven forbid—talk in her sleep.

They had stopped moving, she realized. The cessation of movement must have been what awakened her. The SUV was parked at the gas pump of a dusty, dilapidated filling station, far from the traffic and houses of the Wasatch Front.

"Where are we?" she asked, her voice gruff with sleep.

"A ways past Price. Sorry to wake you but Belle needed to get out."

"No. It's fine. I can't believe I fell asleep."

"Don't worry about it. You looked comfortable so I figured you needed it. I know what kind of hours you M.D.s keep." He started to say something more but Belle's sharp, impatient bark cut him off.

Kate winced. "That sounds urgent bordering on desperate. Why don't I go to that park across the street and play with her for a few moments while you fill up?" she offered.

"Thanks. I brought along a ball and a Frisbee. She likes either one." He looked a little embarrassed. "But I guess you know what she prefers, don't you? Probably better than I do."

That bitterness tinged his voice again and again she had to fight her instinctive urge to offer comfort.

He opened his car door and she caught sight of the gas pump again, which reminded her of something she meant to bring up earlier in the trip. She reached for the huge, slouchy purse she'd bought in Guatemala when she was there on a medical mission a few months earlier, and dug through it until she found her wallet.

She pulled out a credit card and handed it to him. "Use this for the gas."

With one hand on the frame of the SUV and the other on the door, he gazed at her, another of those unreadable expressions on his face. His mouth quirked a little as if he wanted to say something but he just shook his head.

"No," he said, and shut the door in her face.

Undeterred, she climbed out after him before he could come around and open her door. A cold wind nipped at her and lifted the ends of her hair. The air felt heavy, she thought. Moist and expectant, as if just waiting for the right moment to let loose. Maybe they wouldn't be able to skirt around the snowstorm, after all.

She shoved away inane thoughts of the weather and focused on what was important. With her Visa tight in her hand, she marched to the rear door of the Grand Cherokee, where he stood hooking on Belle's leash so he could let her out of the crate.

"I mean it, Hunter. The only reason you're even here at some armpit of a gas station in the middle of nowhere is because of me. I intend to take care of expenses on this trip."

"I'm here because I want to be here," he corrected her. "It was my idea to go after the woman you're looking for."

"Right. The woman *I'm* looking for. That's my point. For all intents and purposes, you're my private investigator. You're working for me, so I should be footing the bill along the way."

He paused at that, his hands on Belle's crate as he closed the door. "Let's get one thing straight. I'm not working for you. I'm doing this because I want to do it, because I was looking for something to occupy my time, and because I need to be doing something useful."

"And I appreciate all those reasons. Believe me, I do. But you're still here because of me."

He sighed at her obstinate tone. "Look, I can afford it, okay?"

She lifted her chin. "So can I." So she had a pitiful resident's salary with medical-school debts that would probably take her the rest of her natural life to repay.

"Anyway, that's not the point," she went on, thrusting the card out to him again. "You're already going to have to give up a couple weeks out of your life on this quest. Please let me pay for expenses."

Belle chose that moment to break in, a slightly frantic note to her bark this time. Hunter let her jump from the vehicle, where she danced around them, eager to be off.

"You'd better take her," Hunter said, holding out the leash.

"Okay, as long as you take this."

She didn't wait for an answer—as she reached to accept the leash, she handed the Visa to him in return. With a victorious laugh, she hurried away after Belle, certain she was leaving him glaring after her.

Chapter 4

By the time he finished pumping gas into his Jeep, that cold, damp wind seemed to have picked up and a few stray snowflakes drifted down.

Hunter looked up at the heavy gray sky. The weather forecasters said the storm wasn't supposed to hit this part of the state, but it sure looked to him like those black-edged clouds were boiling around up there, ready to blow.

Maybe they could still outrun it before the center of the storm passed over. If the storm was heading east, as most low-pressure systems moved here in the Intermountain West, it might clip past them.

He might still have to drive through a little snow, but by the time they hit southern Utah in a few hours, it would probably be mostly rain.

Anyway, he didn't mind snow. He had spent his

youth driving the canyons of the Wasatch Front, skis strapped to the roof, looking for fresh powder.

When he was a kid, skiing had been his passion. He'd even been on the junior U.S. ski team for a while.

For the adult in him, skiing had been therapy. When he was stressed over a case and couldn't quite find the answer to whatever puzzle he was working on, he would take a few hours of personal leave and head for the slopes. More often than not, while his body focused on turns and terrain, his mind was able to come up with an answer.

He was chagrined to realize that even though most of the ski resorts had been open since mid-November, he hadn't been able to summon the energy to go yet.

The nozzle clicked off, signaling the tank was full. With a sigh, Hunter tightened the gas cap, then went inside to pay.

On the way, he pulled Taylor's credit card out of the pocket of his jacket and shoved it in his wallet before pulling out one of his own, new since his release and still shiny enough that the gilding on the numbers hadn't worn off.

He had absolutely no intention of letting Kate foot the bill for this trip. He meant what he'd said to her—this whole thing was his idea. He would pay his own way.

He decided he wouldn't make a big deal about it, though. He would just keep her card in his wallet until the trip was over, then give it back to her. He wasn't prepared for another confrontation with her, not when it made her eyes look bright and vibrant and gave her skin that appealing flush, raising all kinds of questions in his vivid imagination, like if she would look like that in his arms.

Inside the convenience store, he grabbed some liquid caffeine from the soda dispenser. He probably should have asked Kate if she wanted something, but he hadn't thought of it and he didn't have the first idea about her beverage preferences.

Being forced to consider someone else's likes and dislikes was a novel experience. Or at least not something he had considered much since his arrest three years earlier.

That was one of the unfortunate side effects of prison—behind bars, the world condensed to one of survival, to thinking of self before anything else.

At least for him it had. He knew men with families on the outside could spend their time thinking about them. He hadn't had anyone but Taylor. Though he worried about her, in his heart he had known she could take care of herself, as she had proved so adroitly a few months earlier.

It would take him a while to get into the rhythm of having someone else to consider.

He paid for the gas and his drink, then carried it outside. He moved the Jeep so someone else could use the pump, and a few moments later he walked across the street to the park, where he could see Belle still gleefully chasing after a ball.

Without direct sunlight, colors were saturated in the overcast sky. The russet, sleek dog and Kate with her bright blond hair and gray sweater looked vibrant and alive playing in the light snow covering the ground.

Even from a hundred yards away, he could see Kate's smile light up her face as she watched Belle scramble through the snow after that ball as if it were made of raw hamburger.

She was breathtaking in that pale light, like something out of an impressionist painting.

He had always been attracted to Kate, he acknowledged now. He had never done anything about it, in fact he had gone out of his way to avoid situations like this one where they would be alone.

He *couldn't* do anything about it. For one thing, she was Taylor's closest friend. His sister hadn't had all that many close friends and he wasn't about to screw this up for her by messing around with Kate.

He had a poor history with women. Until Dru, most of his relationships had ended after only a few months, usually because the women he dated tired quickly of his complete dedication to his job. Dru hadn't minded; in fact she had encouraged him to talk about work. In retrospect, he wondered how much of that was genuine interest and how much was her reporter instincts, nosing around for a good story.

He had a feeling their relationship would have gone the way of all those others if she hadn't told him after only a few months of dating that she was pregnant.

Since her murder, he'd had plenty of time to think about things between them. He knew now that he had tried to convince himself he loved her because he'd thought she was pregnant with his child and he'd wanted fiercely to make things work between them.

His son deserved a father and Hunter intended to be part of his life. The best way to accomplish that— the right thing to do—was to marry his child's mother.

Dru had refused, though. Oh, she hadn't minded him taking her to doctor appointments and fussing over her, but she wasn't ready to marry him, she said.

Now he knew the reason why. She had likely known—or at least suspected—that he wasn't her baby's father.

Kate's laughter rippled across the cold air suddenly, distracting him from the grim direction of his thoughts.

He could never act on this attraction simmering through him, he thought as he approached them. He didn't have room in his life right now for a woman and, even if he did, it wouldn't be this particular one.

"Hey." She greeted him with a smile. "I've almost worn her out. A few more throws and I think she'll be good for a while."

He held a hand out for the ball. When she gave it to him, he hurled it to the other side of the park.

"All right, show off." Kate laughed as Belle let out an ecstatic bark and set off after it. "Let me guess. You were a baseball player in another life."

He shrugged. "All-state in high school. When I wasn't skiing, I was throwing a ball through a tire hung up in the backyard. I played one year of college ball and had dreams of the majors, then I messed up my shoulder." Not that the Judge had ever encouraged those dreams for a second.

"So you decided to become a cop instead."

"Right." He didn't add that he had dreamed of being a cop as a boy but had entered the police academy mostly in an effort to piss off his father, who would see nothing else for his son except that Hunter should follow in his footsteps and study law.

To Hunter's surprise, he had thrived at the academy. By the time he'd graduated first in his class, he knew he had discovered his calling.

Or he thought he had, anyway. As much as he had loved being a cop, first on the beat then as a detective, he had been betrayed by the brotherhood. He couldn't work upholding a system he no longer respected.

"Do you miss it?"

He wasn't sure what to say, since the answer to that question was anything but an easy one. Did he miss it? Yeah. He'd been a good cop, a dedicated one. But he certainly didn't miss it enough to jump right back into the fray.

He was spared from having to answer by the return of Belle, who came panting back with the ball tightly clenched in her teeth. She rushed to Hunter and dropped the drooly thing like an offering at his feet.

"Good girl." He rewarded her with one of the treats he'd brought from the Jeep. She gulped it down, then barked with joy when Hunter threw the ball hard for her again.

What was it about dogs? he wondered. They never seemed to get tired of the same activity. Give Belle a ball and a little attention and she was content for hours.

"Do you?" Kate asked again. He sighed. He hoped she would let the matter drop, but he supposed he wasn't really surprised when she didn't. The woman was nothing if not tenacious.

"Sometimes," he admitted. "I loved being a detective, helping people find justice. Giving them answers. The badge meant something to me." He gazed across the park at a pair of forlorn swings, chains rattling in the cold wind. "But I had already come to hate the politics of the job before I was arrested."

She nodded her understanding. "I suppose it's the same as medicine. I love treating patients but I can't stand dealing with insurance companies and HMOs. I guess it's true that sometimes you have to take the bad with the good."

"And sometimes it's easier to walk away from both."

She opened her mouth to argue but before she could say anything, Belle came bounding back with the ball. She came running at them just a little too fast, though, and bumped into Kate's legs in her rush to get to Hunter.

Kate wobbled a little and tried to keep her balance but the light layer of snow made gaining traction difficult. She gave a small cry as her legs started to slip out from under.

He didn't take time to think—if he had, he would have known reaching for her was a bad idea. Still, he couldn't let her fall.

He grabbed her to keep her upright, blocking her from falling with his own body. Her hands came out to grab something solid to hang onto—his shirt, as it turned out—and his arms came around her.

Though she was small, only five-four, maybe, she was sturdy. Still, she felt tiny and fragile in his arms.

"Are you all right?" he asked, his voice gruff.

"Yes. Yes, I think so."

Hunter wasn't. He felt frozen, cast in bronze like that statue in the corner of the park of a couple of soldiers crouched over what looked like a piece of World War II heavy artillery.

How long had it been since his arms had held a warm female? Forever. So long, he'd forgotten how absolutely perfect it could be to feel all those intriguing curves and angles, to be surrounded by the mouthwatering vanilla-sugar scent of her, to know he only had to bend his head down a little to capture that perfect, lush mouth for his own.

He had to let her go. The thought flickered through his mind, then flew away like a killdeer on the side of the road.

Her eyes, wide and lovely in that delicate face, gazed up at him, full of confusion and embarrassment and what he thought might be sexual awareness—though it had been a hell of a long time since he had seen it, so maybe he was wrong about that last bit.

She made no effort to pull away. Instead her hands seemed to curl in his sweater and her dewy lips parted a little as she hitched in a ragged little breath.

They stood there, eyes locked and bodies entwined, as the moment seemed to drag on forever. He was vaguely aware of the cold seeping through his boots, of those swings creaking in the wind, of a pickup truck driving past. But nothing else mattered but this moment.

This woman.

He had to think he would have gotten around to letting her go eventually, but Belle took matters out of his hands. She whimpered as if she knew she'd messed up and nudged the back of his leg.

The contact seemed to jerk him back to his senses. What was he doing? In another second, he would have thrown caution to that cold wind and done exactly what his body was loudly urging him to do. He would have kissed Kate Spencer right here in a public park in Nowheresville, Utah.

And what a disaster that would have been!

Kate took a step backward quickly, and he was instantly cold, far colder than he should have been even with the chill wind.

"We should probably be on our way again," Kate murmured. Her voice sounded a little thready, a little breathless, as if she had just hiked the steep trail behind his family's ski cabin in Little Cottonwood Canyon.

"Yeah. You're right." He scrambled for something to say. Should he apologize? No, he hadn't done anything. Not really, only held her a moment—or two or three—longer than strictly necessary.

"I, uh, need to give Belle some water now. That will take me a few moments, if you need to make a trip inside the gas station."

She looked blank for a moment, as if she couldn't quite figure out why she might need to make a trip inside the gas station, then he saw understanding dawn in her eyes.

Despite his best intentions, he couldn't help being amused, charmed, by the color that spread across her elegant cheekbones.

She was a doctor who had undoubtedly seen things that would make his hair curl, but she could still blush at a suggestion that she might need to use the ladies' room.

"Right. Yes. I'll only be a moment."

They walked across the street together, then their paths diverged as he headed for the SUV and she went inside the gas station. He paused and watched until she went inside, reliving the heat and *rightness* of holding her in his arms for those few seconds.

If he responded so forcefully just to a platonic embrace, how the hell was he going to keep his hands off her this entire trip?

* * *

In the surprisingly clean restroom of the gas station, Kate stood at the sink for several moments, her cold hands covering the heat still soaking her cheeks.

She was such an idiot. She wanted to die, to sink through the floor—or at least to hide in this bathroom for the rest of her natural life.

What must he think of her? He had only been trying to keep her on her feet after that lovely show of grace and poise she had demonstrated. Just extending a courteous hand—like his habit of opening the door for her, keeping her upright had been only another polite gesture.

But the moment she found herself in such close contact, surrounded by those hard muscles and that rugged, masculine scent of him, she dug her hands into his sweater and held on for dear life.

And then she had made things worse by standing there, staring into his eyes, willing with all her heart for him to kiss her.

She fought the urge to bang her head against the mirror a few dozen times. She was an *idiot*! One who should certainly know better than to make mooneyes at a man who had no interest in her whatsoever.

Still, there had been a moment there when she thought she saw something in those dark blue eyes. Something intense and glittering and just out of reach. And he hadn't exactly pushed her away either, even after she regained her balance.

Why not? she wondered.

She certainly wasn't going to find any answers staring into the mirror of some convenience-store bathroom. If she didn't hurry, they would be on the road forever.

She blew out a breath, did her best without a comb to straighten the wind-tangles from her hair, then walked out into the convenience store.

By the time she bought a couple bottles of water, some power bars and deli sandwiches that looked surprisingly fresh for later, she had nearly regained her equilibrium. At least she felt a little more centered, almost in control.

At the Jeep, Kate found Belle in her crate and Hunter leaning against the vehicle gazing up at the dark clouds, his arms folded across his chest. He straightened at her approach.

"Sorry I took so long," she said, hating that breathless note in her voice. "I bought some provisions so we don't have to stop for lunch."

"Good idea." He moved around the vehicle to open the passenger door for her, which reminded her of something else she meant to bring up.

"Would you like me to drive for a while?" she asked.

He shook his head. "Maybe later. We've barely started."

She wanted to remind him not to overdo it, to pace himself, but she was afraid that would sound entirely too much like a nagging wife, so she held her tongue. Besides, she knew if she had just spent the last thirty months in prison, she wouldn't want to give up one iota of control to another person, in driving or anything else.

With her small bundle of provisions, she climbed into the passenger seat. He closed the door, then walked around to the driver's side and a few moments later they were back on the road.

After they left the gas station, she tried a few times to make conversation, but gave up when his answers were short and choppy.

Fine, she thought. If the man wanted to ride three thousand miles as quiet as a post, she could entertain herself. She popped in a CD—a group she'd fallen in love with at the Snowbird Bluegrass Festival the summer before—kicked off her shoes, and pulled her book out again.

It was difficult to focus with Hunter sitting next to her but she called on the same powers of concentration that had helped her survive medical school and was soon lost in Wyatt's prose.

She wasn't sure how long she read, but she finally wrenched her attention away when her stomach growled again. If she wasn't mistaken, that was at least the second time through the CD. She knew one corner of her brain had registered hearing that song already.

She reached to stop the CD player. "Sorry. I'm afraid Wyatt sucked me right in."

He shifted his gaze briefly to her before returning his attention to the road stretching out ahead of them. "Yeah, your brother spins a good story, doesn't he? I read a few of his books in prison."

"Is that why you agreed to let him interview you?" Kate knew Wyatt was writing a book about the Ferrin murders. That was how he had met Taylor, the impetus behind the sequence of events that had led to Hunter's sentence being voided by the state supreme court.

"I knew someone would write about the case. It was sensational enough that I knew it was only a matter of time. I was impressed by McKinnon's writing and the way he treated the victims, with a dignity and respect that's missing in a lot of other books of that genre. That's why I agreed to cooperate with him instead of any of the other authors who contacted me."

What must it have been like for him, she wondered, knowing he was innocent but being bombarded by members of the media who all thought him guilty as sin?

"You know, it was odd," she said. "I don't normally pick up true-crime books for my leisure reading—when I have time for leisure reading, which isn't very often. But Wyatt's books really appealed to me, right from the first. I read nearly his entire backlist before I ever knew…"

She tightened her lips as her voice trailed off. Why could she never seem to squeeze those words out? They tangled in her throat, lodged there like she'd swallowed a rock.

To her relief, Hunter finished the sentence for her. "Before you knew he was your brother?"

"Right," she murmured.

She didn't know much about siblings but Wyatt and Gage certainly didn't feel like brothers. They were simply two very nice men who happened to share the same blood as her.

She admired them and enjoyed being in their company, but when she dug around in her heart for something deeper, she came up completely empty. Would that ever change? she wondered.

"What's this book about?"

She passed him a sandwich from her provisions and the bottled water, and outlined the case *Blood Feud* focused on and a few of the key players in it. While they ate lunch on the go, they spent several moments discussing other Wyatt McKinnon books they had each read. To her surprise, they actually were able to carry on an intelligent discussion. As a former homicide detective, Hunter had interesting insight about police procedure.

Fledgling hope stirred inside her. Perhaps this trip didn't have to be days of long, awkward silences, after all.

"You certainly know enough about that world. Both sides of it, actually—the inside and the outside of the criminal justice system. Maybe *you* ought to write a book."

He stared at her for a moment, then he actually laughed. Kate almost couldn't believe it! It was short and abrupt, but was definitely genuine.

"I can't imagine anything more torturous. I'm no writer. It was all I could do to pass freshman English in college. Filling out my case paperwork was a nightmare."

"Well, you could always collaborate with Wyatt."

"Been there, done that. No thanks. After he finishes the book about Dru and Mickie's murders, I think my collaboration days are over forever."

"You don't want to go back to being a cop and you don't think you're cut out to be a writer. What will you do?"

He sent her a sidelong look over his sandwich. "I've been thinking. Maybe I'll just spend the rest of my life driving around the country helping damsels in distress."

Was that a joke? She stared at him, unable to believe her ears. Hunter Bradshaw actually made a joke!

"Interesting career choice," she murmured. "But I'm sure you can make a go of it. If you put out an ad, I'm sure you'll have distressed damsels crawling out of the woodwork."

Especially if you include a picture, one that shows your dark and dangerous side, she wanted to add, but didn't quite have the nerve.

"I'll be sure to include advertising in my business plan, then."

She smiled. "And if you need a reference, let me know."

"Better wait to see if we actually accomplish anything on this quest before you make an offer like that."

"We will. I have great faith in you."

"Good thing one of us does," he muttered, his features austere once more, with no trace of that fleeting lightheartedness.

Unsettled at his rapid transition, Kate turned to look out the window. They rode in silence for a few moments, but she thought it was a little more comfortable between them now.

Not *easy*, exactly, but getting there.

"I love this part of the state," she said after a few more miles. "The hoodoos and the mesas and the slickrock. It's like we're on another planet from the high mountain valleys of northern Utah."

"I haven't been this far south for probably five or six years. I'd forgotten how raw and primitively beautiful the desert can be in the winter."

"Taylor and I drove down to Moab to mountain bike a few times during med school."

"Really?"

"Why do you sound so surprised?"

"Every time I saw the two of you, you had your noses stuck in medical school textbooks. I wouldn't have thought you would make time for a vacation to shred up the slickrock."

"We weren't completely obsessed," she said with a laugh. "We took time away from studying when it was for something really important, like mountain biking."

"You've been a good friend to Taylor," he said after a moment.

"She's been good to me," Kate said simply. "I'm glad she's going back to finish her last year of med school. It's been so wonderful these last few weeks to have the old Taylor back."

"What do you mean, *have her back*?"

She regretted her words as soon as she uttered them but it was too late to backpedal. She picked her next words more carefully. "You know how she's been since your arrest. She was driven before as a medical student—both of us were, that was the big link between us. But when she switched to law school to help with your appeal, Taylor went beyond driven."

"She was obsessed with the case. You don't have to sugarcoat it."

"*Obsessed* is a strong word and I'm not sure it's the right one, but she didn't allow much room in her life for anything else."

"For anything but trying to bail out her jailbird brother."

The bitterness in his eyes pierced her like a lancet. "No," she said firmly, earnestly. "Trying to right a terrible wrong. Trying to save the life of an innocent man."

He didn't say anything for a few more miles. She was just about to ask if he wanted to listen to another CD when he finally spoke.

"What about you?" He made his voice quiet, deceptively casual. "Did you think, like everyone else, that I was guilty as hell, that Taylor was wasting her time?"

"Never. Not for one single moment."

The vehemence in her voice stunned him enough that he shifted his gaze from the road to look at her. He saw no dissemination in her columbine-blue eyes, no hint of doubt. Only pure trust, absolute certainty.

He jerked his gaze back to the road, his mind barely registering the passing yellow lines under his tires. "How could you be so sure? You barely knew me. My closest brothers on the force thought I was guilty."

Men he had worked beside, would have taken a bullet for. Of all the crushing betrayals of the last thirty months, that had been the worst, that more police officers hadn't been willing to stand with him.

"They all thought I did it," he went on. "How could you be so sure I didn't?"

She paused so long he finally looked at her again. What had he said to put that light blush across her cheekbones? he wondered.

"I saw you with Dru," she murmured. "Even though you were angry that she refused to marry you after she found out she was pregnant, you still treated her like fragile, priceless glass."

"The prosecution would have said that was all the more reason for me to be furious when I found out she was cheating on me, when I found out the baby wasn't mine. All the more reason for me to kill her in a jealous rage—because I had been a blind, besotted fool."

"Whatever Dru did—no matter how she treated you—you never would have hurt her. And you absolutely would never have done anything to harm that baby. Never."

That solid, unwavering faith shook him to his core, somehow managed to sneak under all those hard, crusty protective layers he had worked so hard to build these last thirty months. The cold, hard knot that had been tangled around his heart, his lungs, eased just a little and he almost thought he could breathe just a little easier.

Except for Taylor, he had felt completely alone in prison. Even Taylor's unwavering support had been small comfort, he was ashamed to admit. As his sister, she was supposed to believe in him. He had both needed and expected her faith in him.

Kate definitely wasn't his sister but she had believed in him, too. He shouldn't have found the knowledge so achingly sweet.

But he did.

Hunter was quiet for a long time after she uttered her fervent declaration, so long Kate wondered if she had embarrassed him by it.

Maybe she shouldn't have been quite so ardently enthusiastic in her support of him. She couldn't help it, though. She was so *angry* at what had been done to him, first by that bitch Dru Ferrin and then by the system of justice he had risked his life day after day to uphold.

The miles ticked by and for a long time she stared out the window watching dark clouds scud by above the desert, moving even faster than they were. Finally, she turned back to her book but she found it much harder to concentrate than she had earlier. She was relieved when Hunter stopped the SUV on the outskirts of Moab to fill up again and let Belle out.

Their first pit stop earlier in the day set the pattern for this one. Once more they worked as a team— Hunter pumped gas while she found an open space to exercise Belle for a few moments.

This time, though, when they finished she offered to drive again. To her surprise, he agreed.

The SUV handled even better than her little Honda, she was pleased to discover. Kate took off heading south while Hunter, big and rangy in the seat next to her, leafed through her CD collection for several moments.

She waited, curious as to what he might pick. Music was one of her passions and her collection was eclectic and extensive. Most men she dated tended to favor her blues or classic-rock CDs but she had to admit to some surprise at Hunter's ultimate choice—Dianne Reeves, one of her favorite jazz vocalists.

"I saw her in concert once at Red Butte," he explained at her raised eyebrow.

They listened in silence for a few moments while she adjusted her driving instincts to the SUV's bigger frame and longer braking time. By the third song, she glanced over and was further surprised to find Hunter's eyes closed.

At first she wondered if he might be feigning sleep to avoid making conversation, but after a few moments of the steady rise and fall of his chest, she was certain he was genuinely asleep.

This was nice, she thought. Driving along through harshly beautiful scenery with a gorgeous man sleeping in the seat beside her, while soft jazz kept her company.

Not a bad way to spend a Sunday afternoon at all.

Chapter 5

He was in heaven.

A paradise of sensations—heat and hunger and the sweet tug of anticipation.

He was lying on a beach, palm fronds rustling and clicking overhead. Sunlight seeped into his bare skin, his toes dug into warm sand and his arms were filled with naked womanly curves.

Heaven.

Kate.

She was everything he hadn't let himself imagine. Her skin was creamy and smooth and when he pressed his mouth to the curve of one shoulder, she tasted like sun-warmed vanilla candy. He wanted to lick every inch of it, to work his way from her pink-polished toes to that sweetly bowed mouth then back again.

"Mmmm, that's good," she murmured, arching her

back as she stretched beneath him so that the tight buds of her nipples brushed against the hard muscles of his chest.

He groaned and kissed her neck, that intriguing hollow just above her collarbone, then shifted his body just enough that he could cup one of those warm, tantalizing breasts in his fingers.

She made a soft, erotic sound and arched again, long, smooth legs sliding against his. She wrapped her arms around him, pulling him close.

He couldn't seem to breath as a torrent of sensations crashed over him like those sea waves buffeting the shore. So long. It had been so terribly long since he had tasted and touched and explored the mysteries of a woman's body.

She called his name and her low voice rippled down his spine like a slow, warm trickle of suntan lotion on his skin. He reached for her again, craving her touch with every cell, every synapse. She came to him with an eagerness that stunned and aroused him, with that secretive, seductive smile that hinted of female delights he had nearly forgotten.

"I want you," he murmured.

Her sleepy-lidded eyes beckoned him. "I know."

One hand slipped from behind his back between their bodies. He waited, stomach muscles contracted, not a single particle of air in his lungs, as she reached for him.

Her hand moved with agonizing slowness, down, down and it was all he could do not to whimper.

He had never been so aroused, never wanted so ferociously. He couldn't wait, he wanted to consume her.

To take her until neither of them could move. Fast, slow, and every way in between.

"Hunter?"

The voice came again, more insistently this time. Instead of a warm, sensuous whisper, this time it blew across his skin like the Arctic Ocean had suddenly come crashing over him.

In an instant, everything disappeared, yanked away with such cruel abruptness he wanted to bellow with rage. The warm sand, the sunshine, the naked and beautiful Kate in his arms. It was all gone.

He blinked quickly back to awareness, to the inside of his Jeep, to Belle snuffling around in her crate. Instead of warm tropical breezes, snow whirled around outside the SUV, blowing hard across the highway.

A dream. He was having a dream about Kate Spencer, about making love to her on some tropical beach, while she sat oblivious two feet away.

Holy hell.

He drew in a ragged breath, more grateful than he had ever been in his life that sometime while he'd slept she must have covered him with that fleece blanket he'd put behind the front seat in case of emergency.

This definitely qualified as an emergency. He was so aroused, it was a wonder he hadn't popped a few buttons on his Levi's.

He was sick thinking about what might have happened if she hadn't awakened him—and if the blanket wasn't hiding his obvious arousal. In another few moments, he would probably have embarrassed them both, something that hadn't happened to him since he'd hit puberty.

He would have had to move away, to another country, possibly another continent. Though he would have hated it, he would have had to break off all contact with his own sister to avoid ever having to see Kate again.

He had been far too long without intimacy. While on one level it was good to know he was still capable of all the normal hunger he thought had shriveled away during his incarceration, he would really rather not have discovered this salient fact on a long road trip with the one woman he couldn't have.

He could only hope and pray he hadn't said anything incriminating while he'd slept, that he had only done all that moaning and groaning in the feverish recesses of his mind.

Hunter blew out a breath and tried to focus on anything but the need still centered in his groin.

Even though the electronic clock on the dashboard read only five-thirty, the sky had darkened while he'd slept. They were approaching the shortest day of the year, he remembered. Outside the window, he saw nothing but snow swirling in their headlights. No house lights, no headlight beams from other traffic.

It was otherworldly, that total absence of life, as if they were completely alone in their own intimate little universe. His shoulder blades itched and he almost— not quite—forgot about that horrifying dream.

"Where are we?"

"On the Navajo Reservation. The last road sign said five miles to Shiprock, so we should be seeing some signs of life soon."

"How long has it been snowing?"

"Right before I hit Blanding."

That must have been a hundred miles ago! He couldn't believe he'd slept that long or that deeply. He couldn't remember the last time he'd slept three hours at a stretch.

Of course, he couldn't remember the last erotic dream he'd had either.

His lingering embarrassment turned him surly. "I told you to wake me up if the weather turned bad. Why the hell didn't you do what I said?"

"There was no reason to wake you. I was doing fine. I'm still doing fine. You looked like you needed the rest and I didn't see any need to disturb you. I wouldn't have awakened you now except I thought since it's your vehicle here I'd better check to see if you want to stop in Shiprock and wait out the storm or keep driving onto Farmington or points south. I've been listening to weather reports on the one station I've been able to get and they're saying it's snowing hard between Farmington and Albuquerque and the Weather Service has issued a travel advisory."

Damn. So much for his plans to reach Albuquerque that night—or his hopes of outmaneuvering the storm by heading south. He had to hope this wasn't a grim precursor of what was to come on this trip.

"I guess we'd better stop in Shiprock for the night. Pull over and I'll drive from here."

She slanted him a quick, amused look before turning her attention back to the road. "Why? I'm perfectly comfortable driving in snow."

But *he* wasn't comfortable with her driving in snow. It was irrational, he knew, as from what he could see she was handling his SUV just fine.

She wasn't exactly driving at a snail's pace but her speed didn't seem at all excessive for conditions. She had engaged the on-demand four-wheel drive, he noted, and she seemed very competent behind the wheel.

She was a doctor. No doubt her hands were probably capable of all kinds of things.

The thought reminded him of that damn vivid dream, of those hands caressing him, reaching for him...

Hunter pushed the memory aside quickly.

"We should keep an eye out for a hotel, since it looks like we're starting to hit civilization."

They discovered as they drove slowly through town that Shiprock had very little in the way of overnight lodging. At last, almost at the outskirts, they stumbled past a small two-story hotel with a neon Vacancy sign out front. Underneath it was an even more encouraging message—Pets Welcome.

Kate pulled a U-turn in the deserted street. The Jeep slid a little as she made the turn but she expertly maneuvered out of the skid and pulled up in front of the modest brown brick building.

The parking lot was crowded with vehicles. His heart sank until he remembered that Vacancy sign out front.

"Wait here. I'll see what they have," Hunter said.

Kate nodded and he climbed out, relieved that any lingering effects from that dream had expired.

The lobby was pleasant but impersonal. The only bright spots were a striking woven Navajo rug hanging behind the front desk, a homely Christmas tree that looked like some kind of juniper gleaming cheerfully in one corner, and a sign that read Happy Holidays and what he assumed was the same sentiment in another language, undoubtedly Navajo.

The clerk was about forty with a round, cheerful face and smooth black hair that reached past her hips. She looked frazzled but still managed a smile as he approached the desk.

"You're in luck," she said in response to his request. "You'll be taking my last two rooms. Usually this time of year we're pretty empty but I guess you're not the only ones looking to get out of the snow today. Don't blame you a bit. Looks like a bad one out there."

He let out the breath he hadn't realized he'd been holding. At least they wouldn't have to share a room. He wasn't sure if his taut nerves could handle that. After nine hours in the car with her, he desperately craved a little distance to regain his much-needed control.

He handed over his credit card. As he waited for her to process it, his gaze shifted out the window. While he had been speaking to the clerk, another vehicle had pulled up behind his SUV and, out of habit, Hunter automatically catalogued the make and the model and the occupants—a woman and what looked like two small children, in a late-model extended-cab pickup truck with a sleeper shell, Utah plates.

The woman lumbered out and rocked her torso back and forth on her hips for a moment, her hands pressed to the small of her back. As soon as she turned, he realized why the need to stretch. She looked at least eight months pregnant and even from here he could see the fatigue and discomfort in her features.

She walked inside the hotel lobby shaking off the snow that had collected on her parka just in the short distance between her vehicle and the building.

The woman mustered a tired smile that didn't come close to reaching her eyes, the color of creamy hot cocoa. "*Ya'at eeh*. Your sign out front says Vacancy. I need a room for one adult and two children."

Any minute now, it looked like that tally would rise to three children, Hunter thought.

The clerk's hair rippled in a sleek black waterfall as she shook her head regretfully. "Haven't had time to turn off the sign yet. Sorry, but I just gave our last two rooms to this fellow here. You might try the Sleep-Easy, down at the other end of town."

Everything about the pregnant woman seemed to sag in defeat. "I just came from there. They were full, too. Guess we'll try to push on through to Farmington."

She looked as if she barely had the energy to walk back to her truck, forget about driving through a blizzard to the next town.

Hunter muttered an oath. He couldn't turn a pregnant woman and her children out into the teeth of a blizzard—even if his spontaneous act of generosity would mean he had to spend the night trapped in a room with Kate Spencer.

"Stop." The word burst out of him just as the woman reached the door. Damn, he was going to regret this. But he knew he would regret it even more if he let her walk out. "Look, we can get by with one room. You take the other one."

The woman turned, wary and hopeful at the same time, as if fate had handed her so many disappointments she was afraid to believe this chance wouldn't be snatched out of her hands.

"Are you…are you sure?"

"Yeah," he growled, though his mind was already filling with all kinds of forbidden images. Kate walking out of the shower, her hair damp and that beautiful face scrubbed clean. Kate curled up in the next bed. Kate waking up in the morning, all soft and warm and welcoming...

"Both rooms have two double beds," the clerk offered helpfully.

That was something, at least. If he had to share a room with Kate, he knew he would be up all night. But at least with two beds he could pretend to sleep on a bed instead of pretending to sleep on the floor.

He grabbed the two key envelopes the clerk had prepared and handed one to the woman. "Here you go."

"I can pay for it," she said, somewhat stiffly.

"The charge has already gone through on my card. It would be a hassle to void it, so don't worry about it."

"But..."

Something in his expression must have stopped her argument. Tears swelled in her eyes but to his relief they didn't spill out. She was gazing at him like he had handed her the keys to Fort Knox. "Thank you. Thank you so much for your kindness."

"You're welcome," he said gruffly, then turned to the desk clerk. "Is there somebody who can help with her bags?"

The clerk nodded and paged someone named Vernon to come to the front desk.

When he was certain the woman was taken care of, he walked back to the SUV. Now he only had to explain the situation to Kate.

And wonder how he would survive twelve hours of driving the next day on no sleep—except for one brief nap, tormented by dreams he had no business entertaining.

* * *

"I'm sorry again about this."

Kate, perched on the edge of one of the two double beds, gave Hunter an exasperated look. So they had to share a room. It wasn't the end of the world. He didn't have to glower like it was the worst thing that had ever happened to him. The man had spent more than two years in prison—as punishments went, sharing a hotel room with her shouldn't even rank in the same stratosphere.

"It's no big deal," she said again, trying not to be hurt by his obvious unease. "What else could you have done? That woman needed it worse than we did. I wouldn't have been able to sleep knowing we sent her on her way into that storm. You did exactly the right thing."

He didn't answer, just continued standing at the window gazing out at the snow still falling heavily.

Kate swallowed her sigh. What were they supposed to do for the rest of the evening? It was far too early for bed and the idea of sitting in this hotel room with Hunter edgy and restless all evening was about as appealing as cleaning out an impacted bowel.

She stretched a little to take the driving kinks out of her back and was debating whether she should turn on the television set to watch the news when he turned from the window abruptly. "I'm going to take Belle for a walk."

"In the snow?"

"She needs the exercise. Anyway, I have a parka in the Jeep. I'll be fine. Do you want me to bring back something for dinner? On the way here, I saw a diner a block or so away that looked open."

"Sure. If they have some kind of soup and maybe a dinner salad, that would be great."

"What kind of soup do you like?"

"Any kind except broccoli."

"You're a physician. Don't you know broccoli is good for you?"

"Unfortunately, it's usually the things that aren't very good for me that I find the most desirable."

He made a sound that could have been a laugh. "You and me both, Doc."

"Can you carry a take-out bag and hold Belle's leash at the same time?" she asked.

"I'm a man of many talents," he said drily. "I'm sure I'll be fine."

Kate had to admit she was relieved when he slipped on Belle's leash and walked out of the hotel room. Her muscles seemed to relax and for the first time all day she felt as if she could take a deep breath into her lungs.

This was all so much harder than she thought it would be, spending every moment in close proximity. With each passing minute, she found something else attractive about him. By the time this trip was over, she was going to be a quivering mass of hormones.

Unless she did something about it. The thought whispered into her head, seductive and beguiling.

Maybe he wasn't completely immune to her. After he had awakened while she was driving, she thought she caught a glimpse of *something* in those midnight eyes, something dark and hot and hungry. He had quickly veiled it before she could be sure but there had been an instant there when she thought maybe that hunger had been directed at *her*.

The thought made her stomach muscles quiver. If

she tried hard enough, perhaps she could seduce him. What better way to spend a snowy night trapped together in a hotel room than in each other's arms?

She rolled her eyes at herself. Right. As if she could entice a man like Hunter Bradshaw. She was just a master of seduction, wasn't she? That's why she was the only twenty-six-year-old virgin left in the civilized world.

To distract herself from such unproductive thoughts, she flipped on the television just in time to catch the end of the six-o'clock news. She watched the Albuquerque station for a few moments, long enough to learn the whole area was socked in by snow. When the news was over, she flipped through the twenty or so channels with little success.

Though she didn't necessarily feel like going out into the teeth of that storm, she could use some exercise to work out a little of this dangerous restlessness. The hotel didn't have a pool or an exercise room. About the only course open to her was walking the halls.

At least she could get some ice while she was up and moving, she decided. She found her room key and grabbed the ice bucket, then walked out into the hall just as the door to the room next door opened.

The woman in the doorway was lovely, with thick dark hair that brushed her shoulders and delicate light bronze features. She was also hugely pregnant, near the end of the third trimester, Kate thought.

This must be the woman Hunter had given their second room to. His career in the damsel-rescuing business was certainly off to a promising start.

She turned her sudden grin into a friendly smile and gestured to the ice bucket the woman held. Inside the room, she could see two dark-headed children propped on their stomachs on the bed watching cartoons.

"Hello. Looks like we're heading in the same direction. Can I fill that for you? That way you don't have to leave your children."

"That would be great." The woman mustered a strained smile that didn't conceal her sudden wince or the hand she placed on the small of her back.

Kate took the ice bucket from her and quickly filled them both, then returned to the room. The woman was still standing in her doorway, her expression pinched.

"Here you go," Kate said.

"Thank you."

"You're welcome. I'm Kate Spencer, by the way."

"Mariah Begay. You're with the nice man who gave us the room, aren't you?"

Nice? She didn't hear that word used in connection with Hunter Bradshaw very often. It should be, she thought. He *was* nice, even if he would probably jump down her throat if she ever called him that. What else would you call a man who had sacrificed at least a week of his life to help his sister's best friend?

She nodded. "Right."

"Thank you again for giving up your room. I hope it hasn't been too much of an inconvenience."

"Of course not." She smiled. "Your children are beautiful. I'm guessing they're about five and two, right?"

The woman's small smile revealed a narrow gap between her two front teeth. "Yes," she answered proudly. "Claudia will be six in February and Joey will be three next June."

"You're going to have your hands full with the little one."

"I know. But they're worth it." She winced again and pressed her hand to her back again. It was almost rhythmic, Kate thought, watching her carefully.

"I noticed you had Utah plates."

"Yes. My husband flies F-16s in the air force. He's stationed out of Hill Field but he's been in the Gulf for the last six months."

"Hunter and I are both from Salt Lake City."

Mariah's eyes widened. "I thought I recognized him! That's Hunter Bradshaw you're traveling with!"

Kate could feel her friendly smile cool and she braced herself to defend him. Hunter's case had been widely publicized in Utah. Dru Ferrin had been a popular television personality and her death had been front-page news for months, both in the aftermath of the murders and during the trial.

She doubted there was a resident of Utah who didn't know Hunter's name.

Even though his vindication and subsequent release had also been widely publicized, Kate knew there were many who still believed he got away with murder.

How he must hate his notoriety, she thought, aching for him.

"Yes," she said tersely.

"I followed the trial a little. I was bedridden during my pregnancy with Joey so I had a lot of time to watch the news. I thought it was terrible what happened to him! A horrible injustice. Mike and I never thought he was guilty, even during the trial."

She pressed a hand to her back again and Kate wondered if she was even aware of it.

"You know it's not really safe for a woman past

her eighth month to do a lot of traveling, especially not alone."

"I know." Grief spasmed across her face. "I wouldn't be here but my father died two days ago. Cancer. We knew it was coming."

"That doesn't make it any easier. I'm sorry."

"I had to come back to the Rez for the funeral. My mother doesn't have anyone else."

Kate watched her for a moment, wondering if she ought to mind her own business. But when Mariah pressed her hand to her back again, she couldn't contain her suspicions any longer.

"How long have you been having contractions?" she asked.

Mariah stared at her, her eyes as wide and dark as the desert at midnight. "I'm not!"

"You're having pain, though, aren't you?"

"Some. My back has been bothering me. But that's only because I've been driving for the last six hours."

"You would know, I suppose. Can I just point out that we've been standing here talking for ten minutes. I've counted the times you tense up and I'm up to four now. That's less than three minutes apart."

Mariah stared at her, her features slack. "You're... you're wrong. I can't be in labor! I'm only thirty-six weeks along!"

"Well, babies sometimes have their own timetables. One more week and your baby would be considered full-term."

"No," Mariah wailed. "I can't have my baby on the reservation! I can't! I swore when I left for college that any children I might have wouldn't be born here."

She seemed horrified at the very idea and Kate instinctively tried to calm her. "I'm sure there's fine medical care here. Shiprock is a good-sized town. They should have a clinic, at least."

"They do," Mariah said automatically. "They built a new one a few years ago. Farmington has a hospital, too. That's where my father was treated during his illness. Maybe I should just try to make it there."

Before Kate could answer, Mariah moaned with pain and held both hands over her abdomen, as if Kate had made the contractions more real just by mentioning them.

"How far away is the Shiprock clinic?"

"I don't know. The other side of town. Three, maybe four miles."

"With these conditions, it will take at least ten or fifteen minutes to drive that." Kate frowned. "I'm not sure it's safe to try to make that, not as fast as these pains seem to be coming and not in this blizzard. Is there an ambulance service?"

Mariah looked taken aback by that and for the first time, she started to look scared.

"I…I think so. Do you really think that's necessary?"

"From what I've seen, your contractions are coming fast and regular. Without an internal exam I can't be certain, but I'm willing to bet you've been in labor all day without realizing it. You're probably close to fully dilated, which means that baby's going to be here soon, ready or not."

"Are you a nurse?"

Kate tried to look professional, something tough for somebody who wasn't even five feet four inches tall. "Doctor, actually. I'm in my second year of residency at the University of Utah."

Some of the fear seemed to ease in Mariah's eyes. "Oh, thank heavens! Have you delivered any babies?"

"Three or four dozen."

Mariah grasped her hand. "Driving into that hotel parking lot was the best thing that's happened to me since Michael was sent to the Gulf."

"I believe I can deliver your baby if it comes to that but I'd really prefer to do it under better conditions than this, at least somewhere with a fetal monitor. I think we need to call an ambulance."

"Okay. Okay, whatever you think is best."

She bent over with another pain and Kate decided the time for discussion was over. She hurried to the phone.

"Don't leave me!"

"I'm not leaving. I'm just going to call the ambulance. Hang on, honey. Find a comfortable position and I'll be right back."

Mariah nodded and sank into the small armchair in the room, her eyes full of fear and pain and no small amount of trust.

Kate could only hope she would be worthy of it.

Chapter 6

The storm continued to howl and blow as Hunter made his slow, tedious way back to the hotel, the bag of take-out in one hand and Belle's leash in the other.

He had taken her as far and as long as he dared. At least she'd had plenty of exercise for the night. Walking into that ferocious wind made every step twice as much work.

By the time he'd circled the block twice and stopped at the diner down the street, his muscles burned as if he'd run a marathon.

The cook and solitary waitress had looked at him like he was crazy to venture out into the storm to the empty diner. He wasn't so sure they were wrong. Still, his stomach had rumbled pleasantly at the aromas of baking bread and fried onions.

Food was another thing that had held little interest

to him since his release and he took heart at the idea that maybe that particular appetite was returning, too.

He ordered soup for Kate—a double order of chicken noodle with noodles that looked homemade—and beef Stroganoff for himself, and he had the waitress throw in two orders of boysenberry pie.

By the time the waitress packaged it up for him and sent him on his way with a warning to be careful, his earlier footprints had all but disappeared under the new onslaught of snow.

He made new ones as he trudged on, wishing his past could disappear as easily as those footprints in the snow. That he could be clean and new again.

At the hotel, warmth washed over him as he opened the door. With no free hands, he couldn't brush off the snow that coated his parka. He could only wish he could shake it all off like Belle did. Instead, it fell off in little clumps as he and Belle walked through the lobby and climbed the stairs to their second-floor room.

He let himself into the room, expecting to find Kate either asleep or curled up on one of those beds watching television. When he found the room empty, he frowned, concerned. Where could she be?

The hotel wasn't exactly overflowing with leisure diversions. No pool, no exercise room, not even an on-site restaurant. What else could have drawn her from the room?

He would have seen her on his way up if she'd gone down to the lobby for a little company. Where else could she be?

He took off his wet parka and hung it over the shower-curtain rod where it could drip into the tub, then put out food and water for Belle. While she chowed down, he ate a few bites of the beef Stroganoff while he tried to figure out where Kate might have disappeared to—and tried not to focus on the worry gnawing at his gut.

Was that her voice? He wondered at a low murmur from next door. It sounded like her along with the sound of children crying behind the door. Before he could analyze it further, he distinctly heard the sound of a woman crying out in pain.

Without taking a moment to think about it, he pulled his Glock out of his suitcase and rushed out into the hall, then banged on the door. "Kate? Kate, are you in there? Open up!"

He waited, his heart beating a loud cadence in his ears. When she opened the door, he darted his glance inside to assess the situation.

The two dark-haired children he had seen earlier were curled up together on one of the beds while the woman he'd given the room to was stretched out on the other one, her face drenched in sweat and her features contorted with pain.

He jerked his gaze back to Kate, who was looking at him with a naked relief that stunned him.

"Oh, Hunter. I've never been so glad to see anybody in my life!"

Before he could respond, she dragged him into the room behind her. "Can you take Claudia and Joey over to our room and see if there's a movie on they might like? They're a little frightened right now."

"What's going on?" he asked in a harsh undertone, engaging the safety on his Glock and shoving it into the waistband of his jeans, at the small of his back, out of sight.

"We're having a baby. Well, Mariah's having a baby," she corrected. "I'm just helping."

"Now? Here?" His voice rose on the last word. The children, who had stopped crying momentarily, started up again and Kate's look of relief at seeing him shifted to one that bordered on dismay.

"We called an ambulance at least twenty minutes ago but Shiprock only has two crews and they're both out on traffic-accident calls right now. The dispatcher couldn't give us any idea how long it would take to get paramedics here."

Well, at least he wouldn't have to worry about spending the evening staring at the walls of the hotel room to keep from jumping Kate. Thank the Lord for small favors.

"What do you need me to do?"

The woman on the bed moaned again. "I'm coming, Mariah," Kate said in a calm, reassuring voice at odds with the slight panic in her eyes. "I'll be right there. Hang on."

She quickly turned back to Hunter but he could tell her attention was on her patient. "If you can keep the children entertained in our room, that would be a huge help. Maybe they'd like to play with Belle."

What did he know about a couple of kids? He shifted his gaze to the two rug rats watching him with tearstained dark eyes. He hated to admit it but he'd rather be helping deliver the baby than be in charge of a couple of bawling kids. And he wanted to deliver a baby about as badly as he wanted to strip naked and run through the streets of Shiprock in the middle of that blizzard.

But Kate was looking at him with such faith and

entreaty in her expression he knew he didn't have a choice. He tried not to let her see how daunted he was by his assignment. "Okay. Sure. No problem."

Famous last words. It took every ounce of guile he possessed to convince the children to come through the connecting door. They didn't want to let their mother out of their sight, so he agreed to leave the door open and at last they came with cautious curiosity once he let Belle out of her kennel.

To his great relief, the dog worked her usual magic. The children were nervous at first around her but as soon as they realized Belle was a big softy, they relaxed. In a few moments, the three of them were happily wrestling on the floor.

There. That wasn't so tough. With a thoroughly ridiculous sense of accomplishment, Hunter helped the girl find Belle's favorite rubber bone from her pile of supplies and showed her how to toss it to the other side of the room.

Each time Belle padded after it with a weary, puzzled obedience, the two children giggled as if she were wearing clown shoes and a big rubber nose.

As they seemed to be sufficiently distracted, Hunter returned to the connecting doors between the rooms so he could watch the drama unfolding next door.

Kate Spencer in action was an incredible sight, one he couldn't manage to wrench his eyes from.

She never seemed to stop moving—she wiped the forehead and held the hand of the distressed mother; she called the hotel desk clerk for extra linens; she measured and timed contractions; she took heartbeats and blood pressures and temperatures; all the while she kept watch out the window through the whirling snow for the paramedics with an expression on her face that seemed to grow more worried by the moment.

A cell phone buzzed suddenly on the bedside table and the woman—Mariah, Kate had called her— grabbed for it.

"Oh, Michael," Mariah said, then began to weep. The baby's father? Hunter assumed so, by her reaction.

He wasn't trying to eavesdrop but he couldn't help hearing snippets of her side of the conversation. "I should never have tried to come by myself. I know. I'm so sorry. I wish you could be here. I miss you so much."

Kate wandered over to him during the phone call to give Mariah a little more privacy. "Her husband is a pilot out of Hill Air Force Base," she told him. "He's stationed in the Persian Gulf. Her father died of cancer a few days ago and she's come home to the reservation to help her mother with arrangements."

"That's tough." He was suddenly vastly relieved he had gone with his instincts and surrendered this room to the woman.

"How's it going in there?" she asked.

He glanced back at the children, who had finally tired of catch and were snuggling on the floor with Belle while they watched the animated movie he'd found on cable. The girl looked like she was going to nod off any minute while the younger boy seemed hypnotized by the movie.

"Fine. What about you?"

She aimed a careful look toward Mariah Begay. When she saw the woman was still wrapped up in her phone conversation with her husband, Kate turned back to him with a frown. "Not as well as I'd hoped. The baby is a frank breech. If we were in a hospital I would recommend a C-section to get him out quickly but I don't think we're going to make it in time. He's already moved down into the birth canal."

"What can you do?"

"Try to help Mariah hang on until the paramedics get here. With any luck, that will be soon."

"She's in better hands with you than with some frazzled paramedics." The gruff words sounded awkward and stilted but he meant every word.

Her eyes widened at the compliment and she gazed at him with such touched gratitude that he had to grip his hands into fists to keep from reaching for her right there, despite the circumstances.

Before he could do something so foolish, Mariah moaned a little and Kate hurried back to her patient's side.

Twenty minutes later, Kate's nerves were as tightly wound as a bowstring and she was as sweat-soaked as Mariah.

She had never felt so inept, all fumbling hands and indecision. During her ob-gyn rotation, she had participated in dozens of deliveries but only a handful of *those* had presented in labor as breech. All but two of those had resulted in C-sections.

Her total sum of experience was in the controlled environment of a sterile, well-equipped hospital with all the latest diagnostic equipment, not in a small, slightly shabby motel in Shiprock, New Mexico, where she had little but a stethoscope.

Every decision she made here seemed life or death. Never had she felt the pressure of her oath more keenly.

If only those blasted paramedics would get here!

She turned back to her patient. "Okay, I need you to hold on, Mariah. Breathe, sweetheart. Try not to push."

"I have to push," the woman wailed. "I can't stop!"

Kate drew in a ragged breath. She was afraid they were past the point of no return here. The baby was coming, ready or not.

She would just have to make sure they *were* ready. A quick check told her the baby's rump was already presenting.

Every moment she continued to try to delay delivery increased the chance of cord prolapse, where the blood and oxygen supplies were cut off from the baby with each uterine contraction.

Fear was a heavy weight in her stomach, but she recognized she had no choice.

While she was considering the best course of action, she caught sight of Hunter. He had angled his chair in the connecting doorway so he had a view into both rooms. Kate couldn't see Claudia, but Hunter held little Joey on his lap and the boy was sound asleep.

The sight of Hunter looking so solid and big, his eyes a deep, concerned blue, gave her an odd sense of comfort. She felt a little less alone.

She turned back to Mariah. "Okay, let's do this."

The hotel staff had supplied them with every clean towel in the place. They had already stripped the bed of all its linens and covered it with a plastic sheet, also supplied by the nervous desk clerk. Now Kate spread several layers of towels under Mariah and had her scoot to the edge of the bed.

"I want you to lie on your side. It's going to be a little awkward to deliver that way but that position will increase blood flow to the baby. That's important right now since we don't have any real way of checking for fetal distress."

"I don't care how hard it is. Just keep my son safe!"

Kate settled her into position just as another contraction hit her. Mariah cried out. "I have to push."

"Okay. Go for it."

With Kate offering encouragement and positioning help, it only took two pushes for the baby's legs and torso to slide free.

"You'll be happy to know your OB was right. It's still a boy. One more push and you'll be able to hold him. Come on, now."

This was the trickiest part. A dozen possible complications rattled through her mind as she supported the baby's torso in the crook of one arm and inserted the fingers of her other hand inside the uterus to keep the cervix from contracting around the baby's neck and strangling him.

On one high, thin cry, Mariah pushed again and pushed out the baby's head in a gush of blood and fluid.

"Lots of hair on this one," Kate said, trying to hide her fear at the baby's blue color. "He's a tiny one."

Mariah started to weep and shake in reaction. "Why isn't he crying? What's wrong? Is he okay?"

Out of the corner of her eye, she saw Hunter rise to his feet, the boy still sleeping in his arms, but she had no more than half a second to register that. "I'm working on him. Let me clean him up."

With the bulb syringe from her medical kit, she suctioned out the tiny boy's nasal passages, then rubbed him vigorously with a clean towel, both to clean off the birth fluids and to wake up his nervous system.

The baby wasn't breathing on his own, though his

little heart was still beating. She had to hope he was getting some oxygen from the placenta that Mariah had yet to deliver but without a monitor, it was impossible to know for sure.

She needed to get him breathing fast. Off the table she'd set up as an improvised instrument tray for the few inadequate supplies she had with her, Kate grabbed her pocket mask and covered the infant's nose and mouth.

She gave two gentle puffs of air and saw the infant's lungs expand. *Come on, kiddo*, she thought. *Take over now.*

Her own heart raced as she waited. Just when she was afraid she would have to start compressions, the infant gurgled a little then started to cry, weak at first then building in intensity.

Kate grinned as a vast relief washed over her. "There you go. You get good and mad at me. That's the way," she crooned, wiping off the rest of the fluids, then wrapping the tiny figure in another towel before handing him to Mariah.

"Will he be all right?"

"He's pinking up great now. He's tiny, probably no more than five pounds, but I think he'll be just fine."

For a few moments, Kate admired the elementally beautiful sight of a mother holding the tiny life she had brought into the world, then she got down to business cutting the cord and delivering the placenta.

Just as she was wrapping things up, voices and a flurry of activity in the hallway signaled the arrival of the paramedics—a good hour after they'd been called.

"I guess this is our patient?" A burly Navajo with

a solid chest and two thick braids led the way with a stretcher.

"Yeah, but now you get two for the price of one," Kate answered.

"Bonus." He grinned at her and then at the new mother and her baby. His eyes widened when he saw the woman. "Mariah Begay? That you?"

"Charlie Yazzi! Last I heard you were in Phoenix." Mariah's eyes lit up despite her obvious exhaustion.

"No. I married a woman of the Bitter Water Clan, born for the Salt Clan. My wife, her folks live here. She wanted to be close to them so we been back in Shiprock for a few years now." His features sobered. "Heard about your pop. I guess you came back to the Rez for his funeral, yeah?"

Mariah nodded and held her baby just a little tighter.

"Mike with you?" the paramedic asked.

She shook her head, her chin wobbling a little, but didn't speak as the other paramedic started checking vitals.

"He's stationed in Iraq and is trying to swing leave right now," Kate said quietly.

"You're by yourself? Didn't I hear you already had two little kids?"

Mariah gestured to the other room, then sudden panic flickered across her tired features. "Joey and Claudia! I can't leave them here. What will I do with them while I'm at the hospital until my mom can come up from Naschitti?"

Kate started to offer to watch them but Charlie Yazzi cut her off. "They can stay at our place tonight. Marilyn and the kids will love the company. My house is just a block away and she can be here in five minutes to get them. Don't even think about arguing. It's the least we can do. Now let's get you two to the hospital, where you belong."

Forty-five minutes later, Kate shut the door after Charlie Yazzi's wife had bundled up Claudia and Joey and taken them out into the night.

The room seemed unnaturally quiet after all the chaos of the evening. She turned back to find Hunter standing in the connecting doorway, his midnight eyes glittering.

"Wow. You sure know how to show a guy a good time."

She laughed even as exhaustion seeped through her, so overwhelming she suddenly felt as if her bones had dissolved.

He moved toward her. "Seriously, you were incredible, Kate. Watching you in there was the most amazing thing I've ever seen in my life. That baby would have died if you hadn't been here, wouldn't it?"

She shrugged. "I don't know if I'd go that far."

"I would. I saw how blue he was and how worried you were. Then you were working on him and suddenly he was this crying little creature, flailing his arms around and looking normal."

"No matter how many babies I deliver, it still hits me hard every time. Knowing I'm the very first one to welcome this new little person to the world is an indescribable feeling."

"Wasn't it Carl Sandburg who said a baby is God's opinion that the world should go on?"

Her insides quivered at hearing such a tender sentiment from a man who had been forced to walk a hard, ugly road. She thought of the child he had thought was his, the tiny boy who had been murdered with Dru Ferrin, and grieved for him.

She gave him a watery smile. "I'll have to remember that one."

"You never ate your soup," he said. "I could probably find a microwave somewhere in the hotel and heat it for you."

She tried to assess her appetite and decided exhaustion trumped her hunger. "Thanks, anyway, but I just want to sleep."

She looked at the room where she had delivered the baby. The desk clerk had sent housekeeping in as soon as the paramedics had left for the hospital and there was no trace now of the miraculous event.

"I guess since Mariah and her kids won't be using this room, we don't need to double up, after all. I'll just use this one."

Some unfathomable expression flickered in his eyes, something she feared might be relief, but he quickly veiled his expression. "Right."

"I'll just grab my things then and move them over here."

"I'll get it. Sit down for a moment."

She ignored his order. If she sat down, she would probably fall instantly asleep.

Fatigue was a heavy weight around her shoulders. Little wonder at it, she thought. They had survived a tumultuous day, emotionally as well as physically. Nine hours on the road, a blizzard, and a frank-breech delivery. She had to hope the rest of their trip would proceed a little more smoothly or they might never make it to Florida.

He returned a moment later with her suitcase. "Here you go." He set it on the folding chrome luggage rack in the small closet, then turned to go back to the adjoining room. She roused herself enough to stop him with a hand on his arm.

"Thank you, Hunter. Not just for the suitcase. For everything. I was scared tonight." She could admit it now. "I've never had to deliver a baby under these kind of conditions and it was a complicated delivery. I was doubting every decision I made. But then I looked at you and you were watching me with complete faith. I can't tell you how much that meant to me."

His eyes darkened suddenly, the black of his pupil nearly consuming the blue as he met her gaze. "You're welcome," he said gruffly.

The atmosphere between them seemed to pop and sizzle and she couldn't look away from the intensity of those glittering eyes. Against her will, her gaze shifted downward slightly and she found herself staring at his hard, unsmiling mouth.

She was still holding his arm, she realized. His skin was hot beneath her fingers and the muscle of his biceps was tight, hard as granite.

She swallowed, trying to summon the will to release his arm. Just as she started to move her fingers, her gaze met his again and she froze at the raw heat in his eyes.

She thought she made some kind of sound but it was swallowed when his mouth captured hers.

In an instant her exhaustion trickled away, leaving only a stunned and fiery heat. So long. She had wanted him to kiss her for so very long. To find herself in his arms seemed an impossible dream, something she had hardly dared hope for.

She had an odd, random memory of being six years old, moving from town to town with Brenda, never knowing where their next meal would come from. On the TV of some dingy motel room or other she had seen a commercial for a Cabbage Patch Kids doll and she had wanted one with every fiber of her little six-year-old heart.

Of course, she had known better than even to ask Brenda, but that hadn't stopped her from hoping and praying.

That year at Christmastime Brenda had found herself between men—and jobs—so they had wound up living in a Miami homeless shelter. Some do-good organization had brought toys for all the children. Kate could still remember her instant of heart-stopping, stunned glee when she had opened her present to find exactly the kind of doll she'd dreamed of, the kind she'd never thought she would have.

Kissing Hunter Bradshaw was a million times better than getting the toy of her dreams.

He was big and solid and wonderful and she kissed him back with all the eager enthusiasm she had never been able to give another man.

Every single nerve cell in her body hummed with need and she wanted to wrap her arms around those hard muscles and hang on for the rest of her life.

His hunger was a slumbering beast that suddenly roared awake, wild and barbaric and urgently ravenous.

Mindless, heedless, he devoured Kate's mouth with his tongue and his teeth, tasting and biting and sucking.

She tasted like vanilla sugar, like everything sweet he had ever craved. She was small and curvy and he wanted to wrap himself around her, inside her.

He gripped her soft hair with one hand to angle her mouth for his kiss and slid his other to the seat of her jeans, drawing her closer to his instant, fierce arousal.

Heaven.

This was better than any half-baked fantasy of making love on some sandy beach. This was real. *She* was real.

He wasn't sure how long they stood in that connecting doorway, mouths and bodies tangled together. He lost track of time, of everything, until she made a soft sound low in her throat and he realized she was trembling.

What the hell was he doing?

A tiny, insidious voice of reason slithered through his ravenous hunger. He wrenched his mouth away, his heartbeat thundering in his ears.

Another few seconds and he would have ripped off her clothes and impaled her against the wall.

She was exhausted, so tired she could barely stand up, and he was taking advantage of that to ease his own lust. His hands fell away and he forced himself to step back a pace even as his body howled at the loss of physical contact he hadn't even realized he had been so desperately craving.

Kate looked tousled and windblown, as if she'd just come from the blizzard outside. His fingers had played havoc with her hair, her cheeks were flushed, and her mouth was swollen from his kiss.

Finally he met her gaze and found her staring at him with an odd, unreadable expression in her blue eyes. He was afraid to look too closely, not sure he could bear seeing the same disgust there that he suddenly felt for himself.

Before his arrest, he had always considered himself immune to the world's opinion of him. He had become a cop when his father and the rest of those in the Judge's social circle had tried to discourage him, when some had openly disdained him for his career choice.

His father had pushed him and Taylor both hard to go into law. Hunter might have considered it if not for the constant pressure—which, predictably, made him contrary enough to run in the opposite direction.

When he had applied and been accepted to the police academy, the Judge had been furious at his stubbornness. Friends had called him crazy but Hunter hadn't cared.

He had always prided himself in going his own way, impervious to what others thought of him.

After his arrest, it had been a bitter lesson to discover he *did* care what the world thought of him. He cared deeply. He had hated knowing people deemed him the kind of monster capable of killing two women, of taking the life of an unborn baby.

He suddenly discovered that this woman's opinion of him mattered far more than the rest of the world.

He didn't want her to think he was some kind of monster, some kind of rampaging beast. But he had certainly behaved like one.

She continued staring at him, her eyes huge and solemn, and he knew he had to say something.

"Kate, I—" *I'm sorry* would have been a lie he couldn't quite bring himself to utter and any other words seemed to lodge in his throat.

After a long moment, she let out a breath. "We have

a long day tomorrow." Her fingers curled around the doorknob between their rooms. "We'd both better get some rest."

He could think of a million things to say but he couldn't seem to work any of them past the lump of self-disgust in his throat.

"Right. You're right," he finally said. "Good night, then."

She all but pushed him through the door and closed it with a decisive click behind him.

He closed his own connecting door, then stood on the other side for a long time, hungry and aching and ashamed of the beast he had let prison turn him into.

Chapter 7

"**H**e's beautiful, Mariah. Absolutely gorgeous."

Kate smiled down at the little blanket-wrapped bundle in her arms. Big dark eyes studied her solemnly from underneath a tiny blue knit cap. The boy had dusky, delicate features and a little cupid bow of a mouth. He smelled wonderful, of baby lotion and milk and brand-new life, an irresistible smell that made her want to sink her face into his softness and just inhale for a few hours.

He yawned suddenly and flailed one curled fist out of the bunting toward his mouth like a little kitten ready to lick a paw and Kate tumbled completely into love, as she had with every single infant she'd ever helped deliver.

She had toyed with obstetrics as her specialty because she loved moments like this so much, knowing she had a small but important part in helping these little ones arrive safely.

In the end she decided she liked the idea of family medicine more, the variety of treating a grandmother's arthritis one moment and a five-year-old with tonsillitis the next, of being the first line of defense in the fight to keep her patients healthy.

Holding this little one was definitely enough to make her reconsider, though.

Propped in the hospital bed and looking radiantly maternal, Mariah smiled. "He has Michael's eyes and my nose. Not a bad combination."

"Have you heard from your husband today?"

"Yes!" Mariah beamed. "He's coming home! He called me this morning, right after he was granted leave for two weeks. He probably won't make it for my father's funeral tomorrow but he'll be here by the end of the week. He's hoping he can swing being transferred back to the States in the next month or so."

"I'm so happy for you." Kate smiled, stroking the soft skin of the baby's cheek. She laughed when he rooted toward her finger. "What name did you decide on?"

"Franklin James Begay, after my father. We'll call him Jamie. It seemed right."

"It's a good strong name for a healthy little baby."

"He wouldn't be here if not for you. I don't know how to thank you for what you did."

Mariah's gaze landed on Hunter standing silently in the doorway and her smile widened to include him. "Both of you. I hate even thinking about what I would have done if I had been alone. If you hadn't given up one of your rooms for us, I could have gone into labor on the road somewhere in the middle of the blizzard with only the children to help me. Jamie wouldn't be here if it weren't for you."

"I'm glad things worked out the way they did," Hunter said quietly.

Kate risked a look under her lashes at him. Instead of looking at Mariah, he was watching her hold the baby, his expression unreadable again.

She would give anything to know what thoughts were spinning around in that head of his. Probably reconsidering this whole damsel-in-distress rescue thing. Wishing he were back in his mountain hideaway, away from emergency deliveries and fretting infants and twenty-six-year-old virgins with mortifying crushes.

To keep from blushing and embarrassing herself further, she held the baby out to him. "Here. You were part of this whole thing, Hunter. You should hold him."

Alarm flickered in the stormy dark blue of his eyes. "No, really. That's okay."

"Come on."

She didn't give him much of a choice, just transferred the tiny bundle into his arms. For a moment Hunter held the tiny baby with awkward reluctance, like a ball player about to bobble a catch.

After just a moment, he tightened his hold. His hands looked huge around that tiny bundle, square-tipped and strong, and the sight plucked funny little strings inside her.

He relaxed by degrees, until finally the nervousness gave way to a baffled kind of wonder.

Franklin James Begay tolerated the manhandling for a few precious moments and Kate cherished up the image of big, tough ex-cop and ex-con Hunter Bradshaw staring into tiny, solemn eyes. Soon hunger won out, though, and the baby let out a couple of squawks and started flailing those little fists around.

One side of Hunter's mouth lifted and he handed him back to his mother with alacrity. "He's got good lungs, anyway."

Mariah smiled. "I have a feeling things won't be quiet at our house, with three kids demanding my attention every moment."

"You, ah, had better feed him," Hunter said. "Kate, we should probably go soon. We've got a long drive."

"Right." Kate rose obediently, though she didn't want this visit to end—not necessarily because she loved holding new life, though she did, but more because she dreaded climbing into that SUV again and enduring hours of tension.

All morning, the ghost of the kiss they shared the night before seemed to seethe and stir around them as they checked out of their hotel and shared a quick breakfast at the café down the street, the same place where Hunter had picked up her uneaten dinner.

She saw his muscles flex as he loaded her suitcase into the Jeep and remembered the hard strength of those arms around her. She watched him take a bite of his ham and cheese omelette and remembered how those teeth had nipped at her lip.

She tried to be surreptitious about it but she couldn't seem to help noticing little details like that about him while Hunter would barely even *look* at her all morning. When he did, his eyes were always remote, veiled, and she felt as if she were talking to the mast-shaped mountain that gave Shiprock its name.

She wasn't sure she could endure two or three more days of this before they reached Miami.

What was the big deal, anyway? They were two adults, both unattached. If they wanted to share a passionate, toe-curling kiss at the end of a crazy, stressful day, it certainly wasn't the end of the world.

He seemed to think it was, though. Though the kiss followed them around like a ghost, neither of them mentioned it until they left Shiprock heading across the eastern border of the reservation toward Farmington and the hospital.

"It won't happen again," Hunter suddenly said out of the blue after they had been on the road for ten minutes or so.

Though she knew exactly what he was talking about, she pretended ignorance. "What won't?"

His face looked carved from granite, harsh and austere. "I don't make a habit of accosting women in hotel rooms. I don't want you to be on your guard all the time around me, afraid I'm going to suddenly grab you."

Maybe I want *you to grab me*, she thought, but couldn't quite find the courage to say the words.

Hunter had stared out the windshield, his jaw tight and his mouth firm. "It was a momentary lapse in judgment, one I swear to you won't happen again. That said, I understand if you're uncomfortable now. I can arrange a flight home for you when we reach Albuquerque."

She didn't want to admit how tempting she found his suggestion. Now that she had something concrete to focus on instead of just vague awareness—like how fragile and feminine she had felt in his arms and how he kissed her like his life depended on it—this trip was bound to be hell.

Still, she couldn't give up. She wouldn't, if only to prove to herself that she was made of stronger stuff.

"Don't be ridiculous," she had snapped. "I'm going with you to find Brenda. Did you really think a little thing like a kiss between friends would send me running home?"

His only answer had been to draw those lips even tighter and turn his attention back to the road.

Oh, she couldn't *wait* to get back into that SUV for more of the same. Kate pushed away the depression settling on her shoulders and smiled at Mariah now. "Hunter is right. We should be on our way. But we have to keep in touch."

From her purse, she pulled out a business card. On the back she had added all her contact information—her home phone, cell, snail mail and email addresses.

She handed the card to Mariah. "I'm going to want pictures of little Franklin James. He was my first—and hopefully only—hotel birth and I want to keep tabs on him."

"I'll contact you after I get back to Utah," Mariah promised.

"Good."

Kate hugged her, baby and all, and received more effusive thanks and even a few tears. To her secret delight, when Kate stood up, Mariah held her arms out to embrace Hunter, too. Hunter complied a little stiffly but Mariah didn't seem to notice.

They said their goodbyes and a few moments later they walked out of the hospital into the thin December sunshine.

The storm's fury had blown itself out in the early morning hours and Kate had awakened in the strange hotel room to the sound of snow plows and life returning to normal. Already, the sunshine had started to melt the thin layer remaining on the road and the storm seemed as much a memory as that kiss.

He held the door open for her, as she had come to realize was an ingrained habit. She slid inside, trying hard to ignore the tremble of her insides at the scent of soap and expensive aftershave that clung to him.

Belle barked a quick greeting then settled back in her crate as Hunter climbed in then drove out of the parking lot and headed southeast, toward Albuquerque and the interstate.

"You looked good holding little Franklin," she said once they left Farmington behind and headed across the raw, stark beauty of the snow-covered high desert. "A bit more practice and you'll be a natural, just in time for any little ones Wyatt and Taylor might have. Or one of your own, I guess."

If she hadn't been watching, she might have missed the tiny flex of a muscle in his jaw. Was that grief in his eyes?

Suddenly she again remembered the child that had died along with Dru Ferrin, the child Hunter had believed was his.

"I'm sorry, Hunter." She wished she could slide right into the upholstery and disappear. "I wasn't thinking at all. I made you hold that baby, completely forgetting that it was probably painful for you after the child you lost."

His fingers stiffened around the steering wheel. "Most people would say I didn't really lose anything. The baby wasn't born yet and he wasn't even mine."

"I would never say that. I know what you lost."

He looked surprised by her words. "This is horrible to say but I think I grieved more for that baby than I did for Dru, even after I found out I wasn't his father. DNA tests weren't important to me. He was my son, in every way that mattered."

"Of course he was." Kate curled her hands in her lap from reaching out to him in comfort at his blunt confession. Given the tension between them, she didn't think he would welcome her touch right now.

She wondered if he was remembering, as she was, those months before the murders. To his sister's surprise, Hunter had been ecstatic about the baby. He had read baby books and gone with Dru to Lamaze class and showed off ultrasound pictures to anyone within reach. She could still remember trying to smile woodenly and look excited for him.

She knew he had begged Dru to marry him when she told him she was pregnant and that she had continued to refuse, right up to her murder.

Kate had watched Hunter become more thrilled about the birth of the child—and increasingly frustrated with Dru's refusal to marry him—and she had wanted to grab the woman and shake her until her teeth rattled out for the careless, callous way she treated him.

"You would have been a wonderful father," she murmured.

"Maybe then. Not anymore." As soon as he said the words, he looked as if he regretted them.

"Why not?"

He gazed out at the desert. "I'm a different man than I was then. Harder. Less forgiving. Doing time on death row has a way of taking away all the good and leaving a man with nothing. I'm not a good bet for a father anymore. Or anything else."

His last words were pitched so low she had to strain

to hear them over the humming of the tires on asphalt. Was that some kind of warning? she wondered.

If so, she was afraid it was coming far too late to do her any good.

Without the weather to slow them down, they made good time once they passed through Albuquerque. Traffic was relatively light and they didn't hit any delays.

All night as he had stared at the textured ceiling of the motel room berating himself for losing his head and giving into the heat, Hunter worried things between them would be tense and uncomfortable for the rest of this journey.

It wasn't as bad as he'd feared. Though he couldn't stop remembering their kiss and the hot and urgent hunger that still gnawed at him, with every mile he drove more of the thick tension seemed to seep away.

He wasn't sure he would ever feel completely comfortable around her, not with this constant attraction simmering beneath his skin. But he could at least try to be polite.

Prison might have distilled his psyche down to the bare elements of raw survival but he wasn't a wild animal in a cage anymore. It was time he started acting like a civilized human being again.

Between Albuquerque and Amarillo, she seemed content to listen to the radio—country music stations, mostly—and read her brother's book. They made only one stop to gas up and exercise Belle.

She offered to drive again when they finished their pit stop but he was wary about relinquishing the wheel. The last time she drove, he had spent the time in the middle of a hot, erotic dream that had most likely contributed to his boorish behavior later in the evening.

When they were back on the highway, Kate picked up her book again but she seemed restless. He was aware of every move and knew when her attention wandered. Though the book was still open on her lap, she spent more time looking out the window, her expression pensive.

What forces had shaped her into the woman she had become? he wondered. Strong and gutsy, brave enough to delivery a baby under relatively primitive conditions yet nervous about confronting her painful past.

He wanted to know about her, he realized. The information would be helpful for finding the woman she had always believed to be her mother. It might also help him understand the woman Kate had become.

"How old were you when this Brenda Golightly turned you over to the system?"

She looked as startled by his question as if he'd suddenly pulled over and started eating road kill. "Where did that come from?"

"Just wondering. Trying to figure everything out. I like to have all the pieces of the puzzle in front of me so I can see how they fit. I guess it's the detective in me."

He thought for a moment she wasn't going to answer him. She took a deep, steadying breath, the fingers of her left hand clenched on the armrest. He couldn't see her eyes behind her sunglasses but he thought he could guess at the emotions in them. Remembering her past obviously wasn't a gleeful skip down memory lane.

"Seven. I was seven years old."

"You spent four years with her then, after you were kidnapped from the McKinnons' front yard."

"Right." Her voice was terse.

"Why then, do you think? Why keep you only four years?"

"It wasn't like she made some kind of conscious choice in the matter. She went on a three-day bender and left me alone in a motel room with no food or running water. After two days when I couldn't bear the hunger pains anymore, I finally ventured out looking for something to eat. A cop found me rooting through a garbage can outside a doughnut shop."

Hunter's own stomach twisted at the cool, almost clinical way she described what must have been a terrifying childhood, full of hunger and fear and uncertainty.

"It was a stupid mistake," she went on in that same eerily calm voice. "I knew better than to go anywhere near a cop hangout. Brenda taught me early to avoid cops and social workers and anybody else who might ask too many questions. When I grew old enough to figure out that wasn't normal behavior, I just thought it was just because of our transient lifestyle. But knowing what I do now, I can't help thinking there was likely a more sinister explanation. She was probably afraid of someone finding out about Charlotte McKinnon being kidnapped and somehow link the two of us together."

She spoke about her true identity as if Charlotte McKinnon was a completely different person. He supposed in a way, she was.

"What happened after you were removed from her custody?"

She shrugged and adjusted her sunglasses higher on her nose. "Foster care. I moved around a lot at first. Nine placements in five years."

His own childhood hadn't exactly been easy, but he couldn't imagine what it would have been like never knowing stability. Even when his mother was at her worst shortly before her death, he always knew he had a home. The same four walls, the same bedroom furniture, the same grandfather clock ticking away in the hallway.

The Judge had been a harsh, autocratic father in many ways, but Hunter had never doubted his father loved him, even if that love had been more controlling than kind most of the time.

He couldn't imagine being seven years old, living with strangers, shuffled from place to place.

"Why so many?"

"My fault, mostly. I was confused, angry. Unmanageable. I guess you could say I didn't play well with others."

"Why not?"

"What did I know about other kids? Brenda always kept me away from anybody close to my own age. I didn't have any friends and of course I never went to school."

"At all?"

She shook her head. "Teachers and principals tend to ask nosy questions. We were never in one place long enough for school officials to come after us and drag me to class. So there I was a seven-year-old kindergartner. Luckily I'd taught myself to read—cereal boxes, mostly. The Kellogg Corporation was responsible for most of my nutrition during those years. Thank the Lord for fortified cereal."

"You must have caught up, education-wise. You're only, what, twenty-six, and you've already finished med school."

"I skipped a couple grades later and finished my undergrad work in three years. Those first few years after I was removed from Brenda's custody were tough, though. I had no idea how to interact socially with others. I lied, I stole from my foster parents, I beat up other kids at school and at home. And that was on my good days."

He couldn't quite swallow the idea of delicate, lovely Kate Spencer battling it out on the schoolground.

"Hey, don't laugh," she said at the amused look he sent her. "I was a tough little scrapper. I made up for what I didn't have in size in sheer evil ingenuity. One time I was mad at a foster mom for making me pitch in and help with laundry so I gleefully emptied a whole gallon of bleach on four baskets of clean clothes. That little tantrum of mine ruined just about every stitch of clothing in the house. Not a pretty sight. I was out of there by dinnertime."

"You were in pain and children in pain lash out."

"Oh, I lashed out with a vengeance." Her features softened. "Finally when I was twelve I got lucky. I was placed with Tom and Maryanne Spencer. They were an older couple who never had any children of their own. I was the third foster child they had taken in. The other two were both in college when they accepted me."

"They were good to you?"

Her smile was soft, tender, and gave her such an air of fragile beauty that Hunter had to remind himself to keep his eyes on the road. What he really wanted to do was bask in the glow of that smile, even if it wasn't directed at him.

"Wonderful. Maryanne is the most gentle, patient woman I've ever known. No matter how hard I scratched and clawed and fought to keep them away, she always returned my anger with love. And Tom's a doctor. Family medicine."

"That where you got the bug?"

"Yeah. I guess so. Whenever I had a day off from school, he would take me to his practice with him to file paperwork or stock supplies. The summer before my senior year in high school he took me on a three-week medical mission to central America. It was an incredible experience to watch this humble, unassuming man change people's lives. I watched the rapport he had with his patients, both in Central America and in his regular practice, and knew I wanted to be just like him someday."

"Looks like you're on your way."

She shook her head. "I have a long journey ahead of me if I want to follow in the footsteps of Tom Spencer."

"They must be proud of you. Taylor told me you went on your own medical trip to Guatemala last month."

"Whatever I've become, I owe to them. I don't know where I would have ended up if not for them. Probably just like Brenda—an addict on the streets. They saved me."

She didn't give herself nearly enough credit, he thought. All the best intentions in the world mean nothing if they don't find receptive ground to take root.

Despite the insecurity and trauma of those years with Brenda Golightly and her first few years in foster care, Kate had become a remarkable woman. He wanted to say so but the words clogged in his throat.

"You still keep in touch with the Spencers?" he asked instead.

"Oh, yes. We email all the time and I go back to St. Petersburg as often as possible. I spent Thanksgiving with them a year ago but I haven't been able to schedule another visit in a while."

"Maybe if we have time, we could stop on the way back through."

She lowered her sunglasses for just a moment but the delight in her eyes sent warmth trickling through him.

"That would be great!"

He was in trouble, Hunter thought as they once more lapsed into silence. Deep, deep trouble. Every moment he spent with her not only added fuel to the fire of his growing desire for her but made him think all kinds of tender thoughts he had no business entertaining.

She had been through enough in her life. She didn't need the added complication of a bitter ex-con who had no idea where he fit into the world anymore.

To her relief, her few answers about her history seemed to satisfy Hunter's sudden curiosity. He turned his attention back to the road and the easy, rolling hills of West Texas. After a while she pulled out her brother's book again.

She was having a harder time focusing today. Despite Wyatt's intricately crafted story, the words seemed to blur on the page and she couldn't seem to concentrate. Images from the past seemed to crowd everything else out and she once more felt like that skinny, frightened seven-year-old with an empty stomach and a two-day-old bear claw in her hand, facing down that bald, fatherly looking cop.

What she had told him was ugly enough but she

wondered what Hunter would say if he knew she had whitewashed some of it.

She hated thinking about that time in her life before she went to live with the Spencers.

Kate was sure all the well-meaning social workers thought they were rescuing her from a horrible fate when they took her from Brenda Golightly. She had no doubt they were, but some of the situations she had been thrust into during those first five years in foster care had only been slightly less terrible.

Ugly things could happen to a young girl with few social defenses, things that made her feel sick inside to remember.

In her first foster home, a fourteen-year-old sexual-predator-in-training had seen a frightened little girl as a convenient victim.

The first few times he touched her, she had been too stunned and sickened and too afraid to do anything to defend herself. The next time he came to her room, she had been ready for him with a kitchen knife she had carefully hidden in the folds of her nightgown when she went into the kitchen for one last glass of water before bed.

When the little bastard tried his funny stuff again, she had pulled the knife out from beneath her pillow and stabbed him in the leg. She hadn't been strong enough to shove the blade in very deep but he had screamed and cried and bled all over her room until his parents came running to the rescue.

Nobody believed her version of events, of course. Why should they? She was just the white-trash troublemaking kid of a junkie who attacked an innocent boy without provocation.

After that, she was labeled a Problem Child. And she had done her best to live up to that reputation. She became suspicious, wild, angry, rejecting anybody who tried to reach out to her.

The Spencers had been her final chance, the last-ditch whistlestop before she was shipped to juvenile detention. She fought their efforts to help her as hard as she had everyone else but they never gave up.

For a long time, she thought she deserved everything that had happened to her. The abuse, the beatings, the vicious cruelties that children—and sometimes adults—show to anyone weaker than they are.

As far as she knew, she was Katie Golightly, the bastard kid of a junkie and a whore who had basically thrown her away.

After she finally came to trust the Spencers, counseling had helped her shake off that victim mentality. She had worked hard to put those dark, ugly years behind her, to see herself as more than the sum of where she had come from because that was the way the Spencers saw her.

She wasn't sure even the best counseling in the world would help her now.

Her anger was like sulfuric acid eating away at the edges of everything she had worked so hard to become. She had lived through hell not because she'd been born to it but because someone had stolen her away from something else and thrust her into it.

If not for Brenda, she would never have been scavenging through Dumpsters or fighting off fourteen-year-old perverts with a kitchen knife. She would have been safe, happy, loved, living a far different life with the McKinnons.

She couldn't seem to get that image out of her head of a loving father and mother and two older brothers she knew would have fought to the death to protect her.

Brenda had taken all of that from her. Family vacations and Christmas mornings and Fourth of July picnics. She had taken an innocent little girl from her happy life and shoved her into a nightmare, and, dammit, Kate wanted to know why. She *had* to know why.

Maybe then she could finally put that past behind her and move forward.

Chapter 8

Rain found them in Oklahoma and followed them across Arkansas where they had stopped for the night, and now to northern Mississippi.

Kate didn't mind. She found the steady, hypnotic rhythm of the windshield wipers and the rain sluicing under their tires soothing, relaxing. It was almost cozy driving along through the rain, safe and warm in their car with B. B. King and Buddy Guy wailing out the blues on the stereo.

"Good choice," Hunter had said when she'd dug through her CD collection for her favorite bluesmen that morning when they'd passed the Arkansas state line an hour or so earlier.

"We have to listen to the blues in Mississippi. I think it's the law."

"If it's not, it should be," he had answered. She could

swear he had almost let loose with a smile that time, but he'd poker-faced it before she could be sure.

He smelled wonderful, as usual—soap and expensive aftershave and just-washed male. In the close confines of the SUV, she couldn't take a breath without inhaling the scent of him. She found it erotic and disturbing at the same time.

What would he do if she closed her eyes for the next few hours, just listening to the rain and the music and filling her senses with his smell?

Oh, Kate. What a fine mess you've gotten yourself into.

The ultimate goal of this trip was certainly something she wanted, to make her peace with what had happened to her, or at least to gain understanding. As she had feared, though, she was discovering an unfortunate side effect.

Hunter.

More precisely, her feelings for him.

For all of the five years she had known him, Hunter had been making her pulse skip and her insides quiver. Though she knew it was hopeless—and embarrassing, when it came right down to it—she had long ago accepted the fact that she had a powerful crush on the man.

Now, after more than two days of being with him constantly, she had finally faced the grim, inevitable truth. Her feelings for Hunter Bradshaw ran much deeper than a simple crush.

If she wasn't careful, she would find herself headlong, foolishly in love with the man.

That would be disastrous, she knew. All she would get from him would be a shattered heart. Though there might be some physical attraction stirring between them—and she still wasn't sure whether that had only been one-sided—that was as far as things went.

If anything, her revelations the day before about her life in foster care seemed to have given him a definite disgust of her. After they had talked about her history, he'd said little throughout the afternoon and evening, and had barely made eye contact with her when they'd stopped at a motel off the freeway in Little Rock close to midnight.

She was only glad she hadn't told him the whole of it.

Kate tried not to let his reaction hurt, but she wasn't succeeding very well. With every centimeter he withdrew further into himself, tiny sharp barbs lodged under her skin.

A big baby, that's what you are, she chided herself. *The man is doing you a huge favor. He doesn't need you making a fool of yourself over him.*

Still, as they drove southeast across northern Mississippi with rain clicking against the windshield, she listened to B.B.'s mournful guitar and you-treat-me-bad songs and thought she could write a few pretty decent blues songs of her own right about now.

"Belle is probably ready for a run to work off her breakfast," Hunter said after only a few hours on the road. "Thought I'd stop in Tupelo for gas."

"Great. I need to stretch my legs, too. At least the rain looks like it's letting up."

By the time they took the exit east of town, the rain had slowed to a drizzle, then stopped altogether.

Hunter pulled up to the pump at a busy truck stop. Really busy, Kate thought. The convenience store inside was full of people, about twenty or so. She wondered at it until she saw a Greyhound bus pulled up to one of the diesel pumps on the other side of the building.

By now, she knew the drill. He started to fill up the tank while she opened the cargo door, hooked the leash on the dog and let her out of her crate.

Hunter scanned the bustle of activity inside. "There might be a wait if you need to use the restroom."

"I'm good. I'll just take Belle for a little walk around the block. We'll be back in a minute."

"Be careful. It looks like a safe enough neighborhood, but you never know."

She mustered a smile. "I'll keep my guard up, Detective."

She was warmed by his concern, even though she knew he was the kind of man who would show that same solicitude to anyone. Tempting as it was, she couldn't let herself read anything more into it.

She walked away from the truck stop and took off down a small cluster of businesses. The air was cool and misty, but she didn't mind. Compared to the bone-numbing cold of the Utah December they had left, she found this milder weather refreshing.

Belle kept up a fast clip as they walked through the largely industrial area. Kate didn't mind that either—her cramped muscles welcomed the activity. Maybe a little vigorous exercise would take her mind off the futility of her feelings for Hunter.

A few more days, she thought. They would probably reach Miami late that night or the next morning. If all went well, they would find Brenda quickly, shake some answers out of her and then be back in Utah by the end of the week.

She would be ready for her next rotation, Hunter would figure out what he wanted to do with the rest of his life, and their paths would probably rarely intersect, only through their connections to Taylor and Wyatt.

Her hand tightened on the leash and she forced herself to keep walking, even though she suddenly wanted to stop and have a good cry.

When they were about half a block from the truck stop, Belle suddenly spied a convenient tree at the mouth of an alley. As Kate slowed to wait for the dog to mark territory she would likely never see again, she heard voices and saw a trio of people standing a dozen yards away.

An older black man was deep in conversation with a couple of white boys who looked to be about fifteen.

She raised a hand in greeting and was about to say a polite good morning when Hunter's words echoed in her mind. *Be careful*. Something didn't sit right about the scene. She couldn't quite put a finger on what—maybe just a subtle vibrating tension in the air.

The three hadn't noticed her yet. She was going to keep on walking when Belle suddenly growled low in her throat, something so rare for the dog that for a moment Kate could only stare.

She shifted her gaze back to the group down the alley at the same moment the sun found a thin spot in the heavy layer of dank gray clouds. A shaft of light caught on the man and flashed off something silvery in one of the boy's hands.

A knife! One of the boys was holding it close to the man's side!

Kate caught her breath; her fingers tangled in Belle's leash. Every instinct urged her just to keep walking. This was not her business and the last thing she needed right now was to jump into the middle of somebody else's trouble. She had plenty of her own to deal with.

Even as she thought it, she knew she couldn't walk away. Two young, muscled, shaved-head little punks against one frail old man just wasn't fair, and the tough little scrapper she'd been at seven urged her to help even up the odds.

The smaller teen must have heard Belle's growl. He turned, a triple row of earrings swaying in his ear. He looked tough and wiry, with a pierced lip and a jagged scar above one eyebrow.

He nudged the other boy—the one with the knife— who shifted his gaze from the old man to her, his eyes small and mean.

Unlike his companion, this one had no earrings or scars, but a tattoo of a hissing snake slithered up his neck, the forked tongue licking his jawbone.

They both looked rough and scary, though she saw they were heartbreakingly young, maybe only fourteen or fifteen.

For just a moment, Kate stood in the alley, her nerves buzzing and her mind working frantically to come up with a plan. She had to do something and fast, so she went with the first thing that came to her.

"There you are!" She stepped into the alley, dragging a bristling Belle along with her. "Where have you been?"

As she continued moving toward them, all three males looked at her as if fireworks had just started shooting out of the top of her head.

"We've been looking everywhere for you!"

She reached for the elderly man's elbow as if he were her best friend. He was bony and slight and she wanted to punch both of these little punks for terrorizing an old man.

"Come on, let's get some lunch," she said to the stranger. "You know how your blood sugar dips if you don't eat on a regular schedule."

The man frowned in her direction though his eyes didn't make contact with hers. As soon as he stepped away from the building with a baffled kind of look, she realized why. In the heat of the moment, she had missed the white-tipped cane resting at his feet.

He was blind!

All the more reason to intervene. What kind of evil spawn preyed on a blind man? She reached for the cane, shaking with the urge to whack these two young delinquents over the head with it.

One of the teens—Snake Boy—slid a combat boot over the cane so she couldn't pick it up. "Stay out of this, lady. This ain't none of your business."

"What isn't? I'm just here to take my friend back to the car."

"Don't try to play us, bitch. He ain't your friend. He walked off the Greyhound, same as we did. You weren't nowhere on there." His cold eyes scoured her from head to toe, a suddenly dangerous light in them. "Believe me, I'd a noticed a li'l hot thing like you."

Now what? Even as adrenaline pumped through her, her mind felt slow and dull. "Um, we were meeting up here to take him with us the rest of the way. Come on, Grandpa."

The two punks seemed to think that was the funniest thing they'd ever heard. "Hear that, old man?" Snake Boy said. "This little white girl says you're her grandpa."

"Hi, honey." The blind man smiled in her direction. "I was wondering when you'd get here."

Charmed by him and grateful he was willing to play along, Kate smiled even though she knew he couldn't see it. She tucked his arm firmly in hers. "I'm right here. Now let's go on and get some lunch. I know how you love that chicken-fried steak they serve at our special place."

She started to drag him toward the street, hoping sheer cojones would get them out of the alley, but the boys weren't having any of it.

The twitchy little one stepped forward and grabbed the man's other arm. He produced a knife of his own and Kate's heart sank.

She had an awful feeling that two tough punks with knives against a woman, a dog and a blind man wasn't a scenario that was likely going to end happily.

"You ain't going anywhere, Grandpa, until you hand over that roll we saw you flashin' around back there."

"Okay. Okay. I'll give you what you want. Just don't hurt the young lady here."

"You ain't calling the shots here, Grandpa. We're the ones with the pig stickers." As if to emphasize his point, Snake Boy started to grab for Kate.

Kate wasn't exactly sure what happened next. Belle barked, protective of her, as Kate tried to wrench her arm out of the punk's grasp. In the confusion, the elderly gentleman stumbled a little—right into the nervous boy holding the knife.

He grunted with pain then staggered and fell to the

ground. Kate took a lurching step forward, a strangled cry in her throat and her hold on the leash going slack.

Belle took advantage of her newfound freedom and escaped the thick tension between humans, running out of the alley with her leash trailing behind her like the tail of a comet.

Panic spurted through Kate as she rushed to the fallen man but she did her best to push it away. She had to keep a level head. One of the first lessons in med school was how to stay calm in a crisis.

The kid holding the bloody knife looked like he was about to cry. "Damn! I didn't mean to stick the old dude! He fell right into my knife."

"His own frigging fault." Snake Boy scratched his tattoo, his eyes cold. "If he'd just handed over his stash, everything would have been cool."

She would have expected them to take off but they loitered there in the alley as if not quite sure what direction to run, while she assessed the man's injuries.

Kate pulled the elderly man's crisp blue dress shirt from his slacks and lifted it free of the wound, a two-inch puncture just below his rib cage. She had just finished her rotation in the emergency room of a level-one trauma center. Stab wounds had been an everyday occurrence and this one looked cleaner than most.

The old man grimaced as she probed the wound. To her relief, it looked as if the knife had glanced off the rib.

She didn't think he would have any internal injuries, but the wound was bleeding copiously.

"Kid made a mess of my best suit," the man said in a disgusted voice. "I'm probably bleeding all over it, aren't I?"

"We want to help you keep as much of your blood as possible inside, for your sake and for your suit's. I'll do my best to keep the damage to a minimum," she promised.

"One of you will have to go for help," she told the teens. "We need an ambulance to take Mr...." She stopped, realizing she didn't know the man's name. "To take my grandpa here to the hospital."

Snake Boy raised an eyebrow. "You can forget that, lady. We're out of here."

"You might want to reconsider that."

The deep voice from the alley's mouth was the most welcome sound in the world. She looked up from applying a makeshift pressure bandage from her sweater to find Hunter standing there, Belle right behind him. *Good girl*, she thought. *Way to go for reinforcements.*

As the cavalry, Hunter was perfect. He had never seemed so big, so mean, so dangerous.

"Screw this." Snake Boy didn't look intimidated. "Come on, Juice."

Hunter moved farther into the alley and, for the first time, Kate noticed he carried a gun.

"Like I said—" his voice was as dark and as deadly as the gun that had suddenly appeared in his hand "—you might want to reconsider."

The smaller boy again looked like he was just an earring away from bawling, but the older one just looked resigned.

"You a cop?"

"Used to be."

Snake closed his eyes and gritted out a raw epithet that would have singed Kate's eyebrows if she hadn't spent plenty of time in an E.R., hearing much worse than this gangsta wannabe could ever hope to dish out.

"Watch your mouth," her patient said from the ground. "There's a lady present."

With the gun pointed at the two juvenile delinquents, Hunter fished out his cell phone and dialed 911 to report the armed robbery and assault.

"An ambulance is on the way," he told them, after he'd summed up the situation and given their location in a brisk, efficient way, which said better than anything else that he still had plenty of cop left in him.

"What a bother. I don't need an ambulance." The older man's voice was smooth, well-modulated, with only a slight Southern accent. "He barely nicked me. I've done worse than this shaving."

Hunter looked to Kate for confirmation, but she shook her head.

"I'm sorry, Mr...."

She knew he must be in pain but he still mustered a smile. "Mr. Henry Monroe, miss."

Charmed again by his polite manners, she smiled back. "I'm Kate Spencer and this is Hunter Bradshaw. Mr. Monroe, I'm sorry but you've got a deep puncture wound that's going to need several layers of stitches. I don't think they'll have to operate but you need to be treated at a hospital."

He appeared to digest this information for a moment but it didn't sway him. "Well, now, I appreciate your help, miss, but if I don't get back to that gas station in a real hurry, I'm afraid I'll miss the Greyhound. My granddaughter is dancing in *The Nutcracker* tonight in Memphis and I decided to ride up and surprise her."

"We'll find you another bus," Kate promised. "Don't worry, we'll make sure you get to Memphis, won't we Hunter?"

As sirens wailed in the distance, Hunter shifted his gaze from the two punks at the business end of his gun to her.

He gave her a long, inscrutable look out of eyes, the color of a stormy sky, then he shook his head and she could swear she saw one corner of his mouth turn up and amusement flicker in those dark eyes. "Sure we will, Mr. Monroe. Don't worry about a thing."

A squad car pulled up with a couple of Tupelo's finest before she could say anything else and Kate turned her attention back to her patient.

Hunter leaned back in the uncomfortable chair in the E.R. waiting room of the Tupelo hospital and surveyed Kate as she sat down in the chair across from him.

She had bloodstains on her shirt, her hair had slipped free of the casual ponytail she'd pulled it into that morning and her makeup had washed away in the drizzle that had descended on them while they were trying to get Mr. Monroe into the ambulance.

She looked bedraggled and tired and worried, and he had to just about sit on his hands to keep from reaching for her.

How was it that she seemed to grow more beautiful with every moment they spent together? Physically, yes, he had always thought her attractive. Even without makeup her features were elegant, soft and lovely like a woman in an old-world painting.

But more than that, *she* was beautiful, deep inside where the rest of the world couldn't see. She had faced down two little dumb-ass punks to protect an elderly blind man with nothing more than her own courage—and now she refused to leave the hospital until they made sure she found the man's treatment acceptable.

"It took three layers of stitches but everything's closed up tight now. They're just bandaging him up but I thought I'd better come find you to give you a status report," she said.

"I appreciate that. You know, I didn't realize part of our trip itinerary was a tour of hospitals across the country," he couldn't resist adding.

She made a face. "I'm sorry. I had to come along. I don't suppose it makes sense to you but in a way Mr. Monroe feels like a patient of mine. I couldn't just leave him alone in a strange city."

As someone who used to have the same level of caring about his own job, he had to admire her dedication to her chosen profession; at the same time, part of him seethed with envy. How long had it been since he'd cared about anything that passionately? He couldn't remember—and he wasn't sure he ever would again.

"Are they keeping him overnight, then?"

"The attending physician is pushing hard for it. He seems like a bit of a jerk. But Mr. Monroe is a stubborn one—he insists he's got to leave. *The Nutcracker* is waiting."

Hunter studied her. "You want to take him to Memphis, don't you?"

A hint of color dusted her cheekbones and she gave him a sheepish look. "The thought had occurred to me," she admitted. "I just don't feel good about sending him off alone on a Greyhound with his injury. If I really were his doctor, I would order him to bed for a few days but I don't think he would take that advice."

"You do realize Memphis is more than two hundred miles out of our way round trip, right?"

She fretted with a loose thread on her sweater. "Yes. And you've already done so much for me, I know I can't ask this of you, too. I don't know, maybe I could call the daughter and have her come get him."

"Would she have time to drive down here and still make it back in time for the granddaughter's performance?"

"Probably not." She fell quiet. "I'm willing to entertain other suggestions if you have any."

He wondered if Kate was even aware of her habit of collecting strays. Mariah, Henry. Himself. She tried her best to heal the whole world, whether they wanted healing or were content to stay mired in the muck of their own angst.

Was it because she'd been a stray herself? Because she knew what it was like to be lost and alone and hurting and she couldn't stand to see anyone else in that condition?

Two hundred more miles meant at least three more hours with her. A hundred-eighty more minutes for her to wrap her fingers around his heart and keep tugging it out of the cold, dark corner he'd shoved it into after Dru's murder and his arrest.

He sighed. "What's two hundred miles when we've already come this far?"

Chapter 9

"So there I was, blind as a bat, stubborn as a one-eyed mule and stuck out in that fishing boat with no idea which way to row toward shore." Henry Monroe, seated in the back where he could theoretically stretch out, guffawed a little.

Despite the blood covering his shirt and the heavily bandaged abdomen Hunter knew was underneath that shirt, Henry sat up straight as an ironing board and never lost his smile the entire drive from Tupelo. It seemed as permanent on his features as that punk kid's hissing viper tattoo.

"Let me tell you," he went on, "I did some mighty serious praying that day. Turns out God *does* listen to stubborn old fools who ought to know better. Next thing I knew that fishing boat was touching bottom and I was touching dry land. That was the last time I tried that, you can be sure. I still go fishing but I now force myself to have the patience to wait until my good friend Lamont Beauvais can go along. He doesn't hear too well and I don't see too well so between the two of us we make a pretty fine team."

Kate's laughter bubbled through the vehicle like a spring deep in the mountains—sweet and clear and refreshing.

Hunter loved listening to that sound. It seemed to seep through all the bloody cracks in his soul like healing balm.

He hadn't heard her laugh in a long time—not a real one, anyway, the kind of deep laugh that started low in the pit of the stomach and burst out like water from an uncapped irrigation pipe.

Amazing how one elderly man with a vision impairment and a cheerful smile could lighten the mood in the SUV so dramatically.

He wasn't sure he had fully recognized how strained things were between him and Kate, the finely tuned tension always humming under their polite conversation, until Henry Monroe climbed in the back seat at that hospital parking lot and set about shaking things up.

He only wished they could take Henry along the rest of the way to Florida with them, but they were only about twenty minutes from Memphis and his daughter's house.

Henry and Kate had gotten along like a house on fire. During the hundred-mile journey from Tupelo to Memphis, Hunter had listened while Henry told her about his life as a Baptist preacher and how his macular degeneration didn't stop him from tending to his flock.

Kate, in turn, had told him the reason for their journey, about the stunning discovery six weeks earlier about her kidnapping, that everything she thought she knew about herself and her life had been a lie and how they were on a quest for answers.

Hunter had mostly been an observer to their conversation. Nothing new in that, he thought, suddenly realizing how detached he had been from life in the last three years.

Maybe it had been a form of self-preservation, the only way he had of protecting anything good and decent left inside him, but he had somehow distanced himself from the events that had turned his life upside down.

From the moment of his arrest for the murders of Dru and Mickie, he had retreated to a safe, private place inside his psyche. He was only coming to realize on this journey that a part of him was still inside that place peeking around the corner, afraid to venture out even though he knew the coast was clear.

"That fishing trip was in the early days after my vision started going south, when I was still fighting and bucking against fate. I've become a lot smarter since I hit seventy."

Kate smiled but her eyes were serious. "It must have been difficult for you at first."

"Oh, it was. I was angry for a long time. I fought against it as long as I could, held onto my driver's license long after I could safely drive. That was the worst, giving that up. I still miss taking off in my old Mercury and driving for hours down country roads."

In the rearview mirror, Hunter saw him shake his head. "I spent many a night on my knees crying out to God, asking why I was being punished so. First he took my wife, Eleanor, then he took my vision so I couldn't even see the faces of the children and grandchildren my Ellie left behind. It seemed a mighty cruel trick to play on a man who had tried to spend his whole life in service to him."

Hunter thought of the long nights in prison when he had cried out to anyone who might be listening. He too had felt forsaken, forgotten. Prison is hell for an innocent man and day by day his faith had dwindled. He wasn't sure now that he could ever find it again.

"What changed?" he asked suddenly, earning a surprised look from Kate. "You seem to have accepted your condition now. How did that happen?"

In the mirror, he could see Henry's soft smile. "I realized I had two choices. I could sit there in my house until I died, scared and angry and bitter. Or I could go on living. I decided to go on."

That's what Hunter hadn't done, he realized. He had been out of Point of the Mountain for six weeks but his bitterness against Martin James for what he had done was keeping him in another kind of prison, one with bars just as strong.

He would stay there, hiding inside his anger and betrayal, until he made the choice to go on living.

He wasn't sure he could. After three years of believing he would be executed, he was finding the transition to contemplating a future a little difficult to maneuver.

He was still lost in thought as they drove the rest of the way to the comfortable suburban neighborhood where Henry directed them.

"It's a mighty kind thing you folks have done here, driving me all this way," Henry said as they neared his daughter's home.

He wasn't kind at all, Hunter thought. He just couldn't say no to Kate Spencer.

"We're happy to do it, aren't we, Hunter?" she said.

Just hearing her say his name shouldn't send heat trickling down his spine like the rain dripping down the windshield, but there it was.

"Right," he murmured.

"I can't thank you enough. I'd have been in a real fix if you all hadn't come along when you did."

Kate smiled. "I'm just glad we were there to help."

"Is this the right place?" Hunter asked as he pulled up in front of the address Henry had given. "It's a white house with green shutters and a tire swing in a big maple."

"That's the one."

Hunter pulled into the driveway. He turned off the Jeep then climbed out and opened the passenger door to help Henry from the back seat.

He wasn't at all surprised when Kate climbed out too and came around to offer her other arm.

"Oh, now, you don't have to mollycoddle me. I'm just fine."

"I want to talk to your daughter about caring for your injury," she said firmly.

They made quite a trio, Hunter thought as they made their way with slow care through the light drizzle to the front porch hung with garlands of fragrant pine.

Henry rang the doorbell and a few moments later a young woman with long bead-tipped braids and a harried expression opened the door, sending out a rush of warm air that smelled of gingerbread and cinnamon and sugar cookies.

A coltish little girl about eight with Henry's warm eyes peeked around her.

Hunter decided the whole detour was worth it to see the stunned glee in the little girl's eyes.

"Grandpa! You came! You came!"

She rushed to throw her arms around Henry, something that would undoubtedly have been painful with his injuries, but Kate stepped in front of him first.

"Grandpa, you're bleeding!" the little girl said, her voice suddenly fearful. "What happened?"

The daughter's eyes were wide with shock. "Dad? What are you doing here? Who are these people? What's going on?"

"I came to see *The Nutcracker.* I couldn't miss my little Antonia. On the way I was in a little accident but I'm fine. Just fine. Don't you worry, Raquel. My friends Hunter and Katie here helped me out and offered to give me a ride from Tupelo."

"What kind of accident?"

"Now that's a long story. The important thing is I'm fine and I made it here. I may need to borrow one of Marcus's shirts, though. I'm afraid this one is beyond saving."

He bent to his granddaughter. "I see pink. Are you wearing your costume? You're going to have to tell me all about it."

Antonia dragged him over to the couch and started describing her frothy tulle costume. Hunter didn't miss the way Kate made sure he was settled before turning back to the daughter.

In her calm, clinical way, she described the attempted mugging and Henry's subsequent injury, assuring Raquel quickly that his injury wasn't serious.

She then gave the woman Henry's hospital discharge papers and explained the care his wound would need.

The daughter was effusive in her gratitude for what they had done. She insisted on sending them on their way with two huge bags of home-baked goodies—several kinds of holiday cookies, a tin of fudge and thick gingerbread.

Finally, they said their goodbyes, again with Kate leaving her contact information and insisting Henry email her and let her know how his wound was healing.

At the rate she was acquiring her strays, she would have email penpals across the country.

Though they urged him to rest, Henry insisted on walking them to the door. He shook Hunter's hand solemnly, then hugged Kate.

"I hope you find the answers you need," he said, those blind eyes filled with more wisdom and serenity than Hunter could ever hope to gain. "Both of you."

With that advice, they walked out into the cold drizzle.

Kate didn't know what kind of magic wand Henry Monroe had waved inside at Hunter before they dropped him in Memphis, but whatever Baptist-minister voodoo he'd whipped up packed a heck of a punch.

Hunter seemed like a completely different man than the one she had traveled with for three days. He seemed younger, somehow. Lighter.

He had smiled more on the stretch of road between Memphis and Atlanta than he had the entire trip and she could swear she'd even heard him laugh once, though it had been so fleeting she couldn't be a hundred percent sure.

How long had it been since she had seen him like this? she wondered. Probably since before his arrest. No, before he became tangled up with Dru Ferrin and her lies.

She wasn't sure what had caused the big change and she couldn't take the time to figure it out—not when it was taking every iota of her strength to protect her heart from this version of Hunter Bradshaw.

She had a tough enough time trying to resist him at his most terse and moody. This relaxed, teasing man was positively dangerous.

Maybe the magic taking away that haunted look in his eyes had something to do with Raquel Monroe-Payton's fudge. Hunter certainly seemed to be enjoying it.

He grabbed for another piece out of the tin, then made a face. "Sorry. I'm being a pig, aren't I?"

"Eat it all. I'm not a big fan."

"I am. Always have been. In fact, I dreamed of fudge in prison. That sounds really stupid, doesn't it?"

She laughed a little but shook her head.

"Yeah, it does," he said. "After my mother died, we had this housekeeper who made this absolutely incredible fudge. Real butter, walnuts, the works. I think she sold her recipe to one of the big Salt Lake candy companies. Made a fortune. Anyway, she used to make it for Taylor and me whenever we were upset about something. A punishment from the Judge, a bad grade on a test. A particularly bad day when we were missing having a mother. Whatever. Helen McKay's fudge is exactly what I think of when I hear the words *comfort food.*"

If ever there was a time he had needed solace, it

was during his prison time, she thought. "You should have told Taylor about your craving," she said. "I'm sure she would have moved heaven and earth to keep you permanently supplied."

"It was hard to admit I needed anything," he said, his voice low.

In that moment, with the soft rain falling on the roof and the smell of leather seats and fudge and Hunter surrounding her, Kate faced the truth.

She had worried earlier that morning about trying to protect her heart from him, but the damage was already done. This was no silly schoolgirl crush.

She was in love with him. She suddenly realized that she had been for a long time, probably as long as she'd known him. She loved his honor, she loved his strength, she loved the small kindnesses he always seemed a little abashed to show.

"Kate? Everything okay?"

She fought the urge to press a hand to her reckless, destined-for-disaster heart. "Um, fine," she lied. "Great. Why do you ask?"

"You just looked a little funny there for a minute. Are you a little carsick? Need me to stop?"

"No. I'm fine."

Though he still looked concerned, Hunter let the subject rest. Kate gazed out the windshield, her thoughts whirling. What was she supposed to do with this information now? Her first instinct was to tell him to drop her off at the next airport so she could catch a flight home. Even as the thought whispered in her mind, she discarded it. She couldn't do that. She had to stick this out, no matter how difficult the road.

Maybe she shouldn't be looking at this time together

as torture, she thought, but as an opportunity to store up as many memories as possible. After this trip, they would go their separate ways, but for the next several days at least, he was hers.

Her cell phone bleeped just as she drifted off to sleep in a hotel room that seemed to whirl around a little like she was still riding shotgun in Hunter's Jeep.

Kate thought about ignoring the blasted thing. In the chaos of their quick trip, she had forgotten all about it in the bottom of her purse until she went digging through for a business card to leave for Henry. Now she wished she'd left it off.

It bleeped again, vibrating on the bedside table like a tiny angry cat. The temptation just to let it ring was overwhelming, but then she thought of the dozen messages she had yet to check and sighed.

She had ignored real life for three days, cocooned in Hunter's SUV, loath for some strange reason to let the world intrude on their quest. What if she'd missed something important?

With another sigh she grabbed it and hit the talk button just before the call would have gone to voice mail.

"Hello?"

"You're there! Oh, thank heavens!"

Kate heard Lynn McKinnon's soft, cultured voice on the other end and let out a long breath, wishing she had followed her instincts and ignored the call.

"Yes, I'm here."

"Oh, Charlotte." Lynn paused slightly and Kate could picture her mother's fair skin turning rosy with embarrassment. "I'm sorry—Kate. Drat. I keep trying to think of you as Kate but it's hard after so many years of you being our Charley. I'm sorry."

"It's all right. I know who you mean."

"Thank you, darling. Anyway, I'm so glad I finally caught you. I've been worried sick! I've been trying to reach you for days!"

Kate lay back on the bed and closed her eyes, unused to the guilt that pinched at her with sharp aggravating fingers.

"I'm sorry," she said. "My cell phone has been off for a few days and I only realized it this afternoon. I haven't had time to check messages. Is everything okay?"

"Yes. Everything's fine. Now I feel silly for worrying about you. It's just that I was in the city Monday for a little last-minute Christmas shopping and stopped by your apartment to see if you might like to have lunch since you weren't working."

"Oh?"

"Your car was in the parking lot but your next-door neighbor said she hadn't seen you around for a few days."

Lynn fell silent, obviously waiting for some kind of explanation for the anomaly. She should have told her family what she was doing, Kate realized. She was embarrassed and a little ashamed that the idea of vetting her travel plans past them had never even occurred to her.

"I'm not trying to crowd you or anything," Lynn said after an awkward pause. "You don't have to report your every move to me. I suppose I'm a little paranoid. We've only just found you and I can't bear the thought of losing you again."

Thick emotion rose in her throat as Kate heard the concern in Lynn's voice. She wanted so much to be able to accept the love this woman and the rest of her family stood ready to embrace her with. But she felt as if her hate and bitterness formed a heavy magnetic shield around her like something out of a science-fiction movie, repelling any of the McKinnons' attempts to reach out to her.

"I'm sorry. I should have told you where I was going. I'm in Florida."

"Florida!" Lynn's voice sounded as shocked as if Kate had announced she was trapped deep in the Congo. "My goodness! You didn't say anything about a trip Saturday night at the wedding. Or did I just miss it somehow?"

"You didn't miss anything. This was a spur-of-the-moment thing." She hesitated to tell Lynn the reason for the trip, then decided there was no reason to pre-varicate. "I'm looking for answers to my past. I'm hoping to find Brenda Golightly, the woman I thought was my mother until six weeks ago when Wyatt and Gage found me."

There was dead silence on the other end, stretching out so long Kate wondered if she'd lost the connection. She was afraid she had hurt the other woman by her announcement, but when Lynn spoke, all Kate could hear in her voice was concern and a love so clear and pure, her eyes started to burn.

"Oh, sweetheart. Are you sure this is something you want to do?"

Kate blinked away the tears that threatened but her eyes still stung. "I don't want to. Not really. Until a month ago, I would have been happy never seeing her again."

Lynn made a distressed kind of sound. Kate hadn't told the McKinnons much about her life with Brenda, only that she had been taken away from her and put into foster care when she was seven.

She thought the grim reality would be too painful for them to hear. Most parents want their children to have lovely, shiny-bright childhoods, free of darkness or despair. Hers was tarnished and grim and she hadn't wanted to burden the McKinnons with any of the details.

She had the unsettling thought as she lay on that hotel bed with the cell phone to her ear that maybe that was one of the ways she kept them at arm's length. If they didn't know what she'd lived through, they didn't really know *her*.

"I have so much anger inside me," she confessed to Lynn, with an odd feeling that she had just stretched out a bridge of sorts. "I need to know why me. And right now Brenda is the only person who might have the answer to that."

Lynn was quiet for a long moment. "I wish you had told me you were going. Maybe I could have come with you. Or Sam or one of your brothers. You have endured so much alone. I hate the idea of you going through this by yourself, too."

"I'm not alone," she assured her. She rose and wandered to the window, restless suddenly. "Hunter came with me."

"Taylor's brother? That Hunter?"

"Yes."

There was another awkward silence then a long, drawn out "Ohhhh."

Kate flushed at the speculation she heard in Lynn's voice but didn't correct her.

"Have you spoken to her yet? To this Brenda person?"

Kate gazed out at the courtyard below. Her room faced the swimming pool and the pool lights glowed green in the night.

"No. We're only in Jacksonville. The last I heard of Brenda, she was in Miami so that's where we've decided to start. We should be there tomorrow. I believe she had a sister there we're going to try to contact but for all I know, this is a wild goose chase. She's probably halfway across the country."

Wouldn't she feel horrible if, after all this effort and energy, they couldn't find Brenda at all? She would be mortified if she'd dragged Hunter all this way for nothing.

"Did you talk to Gage about what you're doing?" Lynn asked.

Kate thought of her oldest brother, the FBI agent. Of all the members of her newly discovered family, she found Gage hardest to read. Sam, her father, seemed quiet and steady. He worked with his hands but he still had a bright mind and a deep calmness about him.

Lynn was open and sincere, eager for Kate to love her.

She knew it wouldn't be hard to care for Wyatt—he was her best friend's husband now and she would have loved him for that alone, but he had earned a special place in her heart for helping to free Hunter.

Gage, though, was still a mystery to her. He was abrupt to the point of reticence but he obviously adored his new wife and daughters, and Kate had seen moments of great sweetness between the four of them.

Kate knew Gage and Wyatt had never given up finding her and she had learned enough about the FBI agent in the past month to guess that her disappearance probably contributed at least in part to his career choice.

"No," she said now to Lynn. "I didn't talk to anyone but Hunter."

"Your case is still technically open. Gage may have some information on this woman's whereabouts."

Of all the members of her family, he had been the one most interested in details about her childhood as Katie Golightly and the woman she had believed to be her mother.

"Do you think he's still working the case?"

Her mother sighed. "If I know my oldest son, I have no doubt whatsoever. Even though we've found you again, Gage won't be able to rest until he finds out why you were taken and by whom."

Maybe she was more like her brother than she thought. "I need that, too. That's why we're here."

"I'll talk to Gage. He may have some information that could be helpful to you."

"Thank you."

Kate didn't know what to say after that. She hated this distance, this awkwardness she always felt when talking to Lynn, and wondered if it would ever ease.

"I'm so glad I finally reached you," Lynn said after moment. "I know it's silly but I'll sleep easier tonight. Will you forgive me for panicking?"

"Of course."

They said their goodbyes, with Lynn's repeated promise to talk to Gage, then Kate hung up her phone.

She set it carefully on the dresser, then opened the sliding doors to the small terrace of her room, suddenly desperate for air.

The night was lovely, clear and comfortable. Kate wandered to the railing, gazing out at the garden around the pool. Though still just off the freeway, this was a better scale of hotel than they'd stayed in yet on this journey, with an extravagant pool and lush landscaping, complete with twinkling little Christmas lights in the palm trees.

She and Brenda never would have stayed in a place like this. Their accommodations were usually the kind of scary, hole-in-the-wall motel that had shifty-eyed clerks, cardboard-thin walls and bedsprings that creaked.

Kate would usually make a bed for herself on the bathroom floor and curl up while Brenda entertained a gentleman friend in the other room or would pass out on the bed.

Most of the time, she doubted whether Brenda knew—or cared—that Kate was even there.

Kate thought of Lynn McKinnon's loving concern, and the stark contrast between what should have been and what was brought those tears she had been fighting to the surface again. This time she couldn't stop them and they burst free.

She stood there for a long time with the moist breeze eddying around her and tears trickling down her cheeks.

She didn't realize she was no longer alone until Hunter spoke from the balcony next to hers.

"In prison, nights were the worst. During the day you could wear a facade of indifference. But at night we were all locked into our cells, alone with only the guilt to taunt and torment us. Those of us who didn't have guilt had nothing left but our fear."

"I'm sorry." She sniffled, embarrassed at herself for letting her emotions out.

"Don't be. Nothing wrong with crying."

"It's either cry or scream right now. And I'm afraid if I start screaming, I won't stop. I don't know what to do with this anger. I can lock it away for long stretches of time but sometimes no matter how hard I try to keep it contained my hate and bitterness bursts free and I can't think about anything else."

"Are you angry? Or are you just hurting?"

She gave a ragged-sounding laugh. "Both."

Only about two feet separated their terraces. Before Kate realized what he intended, Hunter grabbed his railing and swung his body over to her terrace with an agility that left her blinking.

It was a crazy thing to do, he thought, but he couldn't bear her crying over there by herself. He leaned with her on the railing, gazing out at the twinkling palm trees and the bougainvillea and the deep green of the pool lights.

The cool breeze lifted his hair and Hunter thought how odd it was that three days earlier they had stood together on the deck of his canyon home while he'd watched her catch snowflakes on her tongue.

"What let it out this time?" he asked quietly. "Your hurt or anger or whatever it is?"

In the moonlight, he saw her chin quiver a little but she quickly straightened it out again.

"Lynn McKinnon just called me. My mother." Her laugh was short and bitter. "My *mother*. I can't even say the word. The woman has loved me for twenty-six years—never gave up hope of finding me again—and I can't even do her the courtesy of calling her by her rightful title. She's a stranger to me. A stranger I seem to be doing my damnedest to keep at arm's length."

"Give yourself time. You can't expect to love the McKinnons as if you spent your whole life with them. They understand that. From what I've seen of them, they're decent people. I'm sure they'll give you whatever space you need until you're comfortable with them."

"What if that day never comes?"

He couldn't bear the murky pain in her eyes, the heartache threading through her voice. Though he knew it wasn't the wisest of ideas, he reached for her.

She was stiff with surprise for just a moment before she sighed and settled against him, small and fragile.

"It will," he murmured. "And if you can never love the McKinnons as the daughter and sister they lost, you can at least learn to care about them as good, kind people with your best interests at heart."

She said nothing, only settled closer against him. Hunter's arms tightened and he was stunned by the tenderness welling up inside him.

He cleared his throat and continued. "You didn't have them for a big part of your life and that really stinks. But you have them now. That has to count for something, doesn't it? It's more than you had two months ago, more than a lot of people will ever have."

She rested her cheek against his chest, where he was certain she could hear his heart pounding away. "You're right. Intellectually I know you're right. I feel horribly guilty that I can't just lighten up and accept that my life has suddenly taken a bizarre turn. Just be grateful for what I have. But my time with Brenda and…and what came after was awful. Something no child should have to live through. Talking with Lynn just made me contrast what those early years should have been like with the ugly reality."

"I'm sorry, Kate. I wish I could change it for you."

"Contrary to what you must think right now after I just blubbered all over you, this trip is helping. Even if we never find Brenda, being away from the situation has given me a little perspective."

She lifted her face, tearstained but heartbreakingly beautiful in the moonlight. "I think you've got a brilliant future in the damsel-rescuing business."

He mustered a smile, even though it took every ounce of strength he possessed not to kiss her.

Though he was definitely rusty at it, he tried a joke. "Thanks. We're a full-service operation. Finder of lost souls, chauffeur of stranded crime victims, and shoulder to cry on. It's all part of the package."

She smiled and hugged him tighter and Hunter had to clamp his teeth together to hold in his moan of sheer wonder at how good it felt to hold this warm, soft woman.

"Thank you, on all counts," she murmured. "You're very good at what you do."

The pay might be lousy but the benefits sure as hell rocked, he thought.

After a moment, he tried to carefully extricate himself from her arms before he embarrassed both of them by enjoying her touch a little *too* much, but it was like trying to slip out of a warm feather bed on a cold January morning.

He managed to pull one arm away but the other one,

curved around her shoulders, refused to budge. While he was trying to remind it who was boss, Kate lifted her face to his again.

In the moonlight, her eyes looked fathomless, deep pools of emotions he couldn't even begin to guess at. She studied him for several heartbeats, then drew in a deep breath, which unfortunately had the side effect of lifting her breasts in even closer contact to his chest. He was trying to keep control and remove the other arm when she spoke, her voice low, throaty.

"Would you kiss me again?"

Every synapse snapped to attention and blood gushed to his groin. "I, uh, don't think that's a very good idea right now."

She gazed at him. "Why not?"

He decided he had no option left but stark honesty. "I haven't been with a woman in three years, Kate. If I kiss you right now, I'm afraid I'll eat you alive."

She appeared to digest his words for a long moment, then she smiled. "And you see this as a problem because...?"

Chapter 10

For the space of about two heartbeats, Hunter managed to resist that look in her eyes, the invitation in her voice, then with a groan he surrendered and dragged her against him, his mouth descending with raw, unbridled hunger.

He wasn't gentle. He swept his tongue inside her mouth and pressed her hard against his erection, his body aching with need.

She made a low sound he took for arousal and wrapped her arms around him, her mouth warm and welcoming.

They stood on the balcony locked together for a long time, mouths and bodies tangled together.

All his pent-up need seemed to explode as he kissed her, roaring through him like a wildfire in high winds.

Finally he dragged his mouth away. "We're going to put on a hell of a show if we don't go inside."

She blinked several times, color stealing over her cheekbones. "Right. You're right."

With hands that fumbled, she slid open the terrace door and led the way into her hotel room. He was afraid to say anything, afraid she might change her mind, but she kept her hand tucked in his while she slid the door shut and straightened the curtains.

When she was done, she turned back to him, her mouth swollen but her eyes bright with desire and something else he couldn't identify.

He made a low, raw sound and pulled her against him, his mouth finding hers again.

He had never been so aroused, so ravenous for a woman's touch. When she slid her hands inside his shirt to spread those small, elegant fingers across the muscles of his back, he shivered.

He ached to touch her, to fill his hands with feminine flesh, but he felt strangely paralyzed, afraid when he did he would lose whatever thin hold he had on his tenuous control.

He brought his hand to her rib cage, just under the cotton of her shirt, but couldn't seem to move it farther. Her skin was incredible, soft and warm and sweetly scented, and he could feel her small, delicate ribs move with each breath.

"Touch me," she commanded softly against his mouth.

His stomach twirling with anticipation, he slid his thumbs up, up until they brushed the undersides of her breasts through the fabric of her bra.

This time she was the one who shivered, a delicate, erotic tremor. He closed his eyes, overwhelmed by the sensations pouring over him. He felt like a randy teenager again, all raging hormones and fumbling hands and stunned disbelief that she was actually letting him go so far.

"Funny thing about three years of celibacy," he said hoarsely. "I feel like this is the first time I've ever done this."

"I know just what you mean," she murmured, a small smile curving her lips.

He puzzled over that remark but didn't have the brain power to figure it out as she arched against his hands. He had to touch her. Really touch her.

To his vast relief, she wore a front-clasp bra and it only took him a moment to work the tricky thing. At least he hadn't forgotten that particular skill. An instant later his fingers were brushing against warm, soft flesh.

Her breath came in short little gasps as he spent what seemed like hours relearning the feel of a woman's body.

Later he had no conscious memory of slipping off her shirt. One moment it was there, the next she stood before him wearing only her unhooked bra hanging free.

She had small, high breasts, her nipples dark against her creamy skin and he devoured the sight as long as he could stand without touching her again.

With nothing in the way now, he lowered his mouth to the slope of first one breast and then the other, then he drew one taut nipple into his mouth. She smelled of hotel soap and vanilla sugar and woman and he couldn't get enough.

She let out a low, ragged sound and buried her hands

in his hair while he savored the incredible wonder of exploring a woman's body again.

Not just any woman, he thought. He had had a dozen chances or more since his release for meaningless sex, but he had wanted none of those women. Only Kate, with her big eyes and her soft heart, made him almost frantic with need.

He was going to explode, right now, he thought. His arousal jutted against the fabric of his Levi's and all he could think about was coming inside her.

Driven by sudden urgency, he yanked his own shirt over his head, then went to work on the metal buttons of her jeans. To his embarrassment, though, his hands were trembling too hard to work them free, and finally her hands stopped his increasingly frustrated efforts.

"Here. Let me."

Seconds later she slid out of her jeans and her panties, until she lay before him on the bed, an exquisite, naked offering.

He couldn't breathe, could only stare, his blood racing and a wild surge of emotion in his chest.

"I'd forgotten how beautiful a woman's body could be," he said hoarsely. "The hollows and curves and dark places. Do you mind if I just stand here for a moment?"

She blinked, her eyes wide. "I... No. Of course not."

Kate tried not to feel self-conscious as he devoured her with hot and hungry eyes. He had warned her he would eat her alive. She just hadn't expected him to do it with his eyes.

He was the beautiful one, she thought, all muscles and sculpted strength. He had always had a powerful body but his years in prison had turned him into something hard and dangerous.

Finally he slipped out of his jeans, then pulled something out of his wallet and tossed it onto the bedside table.

At the sight of the square metallic packets, Kate's insides twitched with a combination of nerves and anticipation.

"You're prepared."

She thought his short laugh had a layer of self-mockery to it. "I bought a jumbo pack when I got out but they've been gathering dust for the last month."

"Why? I'm sure you've had women banging down your door for the chance to, um, bang down your door."

At last he joined her on the bed and she almost forgot the question when he kissed her again.

"I don't know why," he admitted. "I wanted to but I couldn't manage to work up the enthusiasm—or anything else—for anybody. Until you walked out onto that deck three nights ago."

His words slid through her like an intimate caress and her whole body seemed to catch fire.

He kissed her, a slow, deep mating of tongue and mouth. She wrapped her arms around him, her love for him a heavy weight in her chest.

She was doomed to heartbreak with this man. She knew it as surely as she knew the names of every muscle and tendon his mouth and hands explored, but she wouldn't waste this moment worrying about the future.

Right now she would savor this moment and add it to her precious store of memories.

He kissed her deeply, intensely, as if to memorize each centimeter of her mouth, until she was weak and trembling. After years of second and third dates—and nothing more—she had become a bit of a connoisseur of kissing. She had never experienced this wild desperation, the edginess of his mouth on hers, as if he were afraid this was his last kiss and he wanted to make it matter.

While he kissed her, his hands began to wander over those curves and hollows and dark places he had talked about, until she was breathless and near frantic with need.

Finally, when they had touched and tasted and explored until she lost any coherent thought, he found the tight, aching bud between her thighs and she nearly rocketed off the bed.

He made a low, raw sound and, still kissing her, began to dance his fingers across her. Heat and desire and love wrapped her tightly in a cocoon of need, tighter and tighter until she couldn't breathe; her heart raced and her vision blurred. Finally he thrust a finger deep inside her and she cried out his name as the cocoon burst free and she soared.

When she fluttered back to earth, she found him watching her with those hot, hungry eyes. She pulled him to her for another kiss, one hand fisted in his hair, the other clutching him to her.

"I have to be inside," he groaned.

"Oh, yes," she said fervently, then added a polite "please."

He laughed hoarsely. "I'm afraid I won't last very long," he said as he reached for one of the foil packets from the bedside table. "It's been so long for me."

She was breathless—nervous and still painfully aroused at once. "That's all right. We can take it slow the next time."

His eyes darkened at her inference that once

wouldn't be enough, then he entered her with one powerful motion.

Though she tried to brace herself for it, Kate stiffened and swallowed her instinctive cry as she felt the resistance of her hymen break free with a deep, burning ache.

Hunter froze, his features stunned. "You're a frigging virgin!"

She had the completely insane urge to giggle at the oxymoron as the first pain began to ease. In the face of his fury, she decided it probably wouldn't be a good idea.

"Well, technically, not anymore."

He held himself rigid, unmoving for a few seconds, long enough for her to marvel at the novel, wonderful sensation. A man was inside her! Not just any man but Hunter Bradshaw. The man she had loved forever, long before she even could admit it to herself.

The ache all but forgotten, Kate wrapped her arms around him and arched to angle him in deeper. Hunter's breathing was ragged, tortured, his neck corded with veins.

After a moment of holding himself absolutely still, he groaned. "I can't stop. I'm sorry."

"I don't want you to stop." She kissed him, her arms tight around him, as he surged deep inside her.

He drove into her no more than four or five times then with a hoarse cry he found release.

Kate held him close as long as he would let her, until his frenzied heartbeat slowed and his ragged breathing returned almost to normal.

After a moment, he slipped out of her arms and rose without a word, crossing to the bathroom to take care of the condom. She heard running water and then he returned to the bed with a warm washcloth for her to wash the streaky blood off her thighs.

"Why didn't you tell me?"

The quiet anger in his voice, so at odds with his considerate gesture, sliced at her composure but she took a deep breath and forced herself to meet his baffled, angry gaze. "Why? What difference does it make?"

"One hell of a lot! You know it does! I never would have let things go so far if I had known you had never been with a man before."

"Then I'm glad I didn't tell you. I wanted to make love to you, Hunter. I'm a grown woman and can make my own choices. Tonight, this was what I wanted."

"Why?"

He looked genuinely baffled at her behavior. She wanted to tell him she loved him, but she knew he wouldn't welcome the information.

Finally she shrugged, heat crawling up her cheekbones. "The moment seemed right," she said. She didn't want him to know the depth of her emotions—the last thing she wanted right now in addition to his anger was his pity—so she tried for a light, casual tone.

"You were here—a strong, warm, attractive man who appeared more than willing. Maybe I decided I was tired of wondering what all the fuss is about."

She regretted her glibness when a feral expression crossed his features. "I don't like being used, Kate. If you wanted a stud, you're looking in the wrong pasture."

Tears burned at his coldness but she knew she deserved it. "If that's all I wanted, why would I still be a virgin at twenty-six years old?"

He yanked on his jeans. "That's a question I would certainly like to know the answer to."

Kate drew the sheet around her, compelled to be honest about this, at least. "I've always thought I was too picky. Sex just never seemed a priority to me. I had my goals and I preferred to focus on them, not on anything that might be distracting. I never dated anyone who seemed worth the energy for all of this."

He continued watching her out of hooded eyes and she yearned for even a hint of softness in him.

"During one of her psych classes, Taylor told me I never date the same man more than a few times as a self-protective mechanism. She believed I use my experiences in childhood as a shield and a crutch. I don't let people too close because I look at everyone through the suspicious, wary eyes of a child who has been hurt one too many times.

"I don't know if either of those theories is true, mine or Taylor's," she went on. "I only know this was my choice, Hunter. One I'm glad I made, even if it will likely make things a little awkward between us for a while."

He made a disbelieving sound, as if to imply they had moved beyond awkward into excruciatingly uncomfortable.

"You should have told me," he said again. "At the least, I could have made things easier for you and not attacked you like some rutting beast."

"I'm sorry." The words seemed inadequate but she had nothing else to offer.

He studied her for a moment then he picked up his shirt. "I think it's best if I leave now," he said, his voice low, reserved. "Tomorrow will be a long day of driving to Miami."

She absorbed his rejection without even flinching. Determined to hide her hurt, she lifted her chin.

"I don't regret what happened between us, Hunter. Most of it was wonderful, until the last part there and even that was starting to feel good. I don't want you to regret it either."

He opened his mouth to say something, then closed it again and walked toward the door.

"Good night," he said brusquely, then he walked out into the hall. A moment later she heard the click of the door to the room next to hers, then all was silent.

Kate let out a long, pained breath. She meant what she'd said to him. She didn't regret making love to him, even with the empty bed and the empty space in her heart he had left behind.

She had a feeling years from now she would remember this wild-hair trip to Florida as one of those pivotal, life-changing events. Making love to Hunter would certainly qualify as pivotal in any woman's life, especially one who had loved him for years.

He might leave her heart bruised and her body aching. But every single moment had been worth the price of admission for the chance to be in his arms.

Kate had a feeling she was in for a long, uncomfortable day.

For one thing, a few restless hours of sleep did not put her at her best for traveling. She also had a whole range of sore muscles she hadn't expected from their extracurricular activities the night before.

To top it all off, her traveling companion could

hardly force himself to look at her in the early morning sunlight.

"Ready?" Hunter asked, his voice terse and his eyes shielded behind Ray-Bans the color of espresso.

As I'll ever be, she thought, but gave him only a polite smile in response. What else could she do? Tell him that although she had been as close to him as two people could possibly be the night before, in the light of morning the idea of sitting next to him in a moving vehicle for eight hours seemed about as daunting as taking her boards with her eyes closed.

She decided not to risk saying anything, so she just climbed into the passenger seat of the SUV.

"I grabbed coffee and a bagel for you while I was walking Belle earlier," he said tersely once he had climbed into the driver's seat.

"Thanks," she murmured.

His only response was to shrug and reach for the radio. Soon the low voices of NPR's Morning Edition filled the vehicle, effectively squashing any conversation, had she been at all inclined to attempt any.

They rode for fifteen miles in a tense, awkward silence. She wondered if they would spend the whole day with this morning-after discomfort between them. Just when she was about to say something, her phone bleeped from her bag.

For the first time she could remember, she reached for it eagerly, grateful for any interruption in the tension between her and Hunter.

"Hello?" she said after the second ring.

"Kate, this is Gage. Gage McKinnon."

Despite her grim mood, she couldn't contain a little smile at her brother's formal greeting—as if she knew any other strong, commanding men named Gage besides her oldest brother that he felt he had to qualify with his last name.

"Hello, Gage. How are Allie and the girls?"

"Good. Great. Well, Anna picked up a bit of cold at the wedding so she's been home from preschool since Monday. Poor thing is miserable. Runny nose, sore throat, sniffles. The only thing that makes her feel better is me reading *Yertle the Turtle* to her. I've read it at least a hundred times in the last few days. Good thing her mother's a nurse because I don't know the first thing about comforting sick kids."

Her smile was a little broader by the time he wound down. She found it funny—and terribly sweet—that her taciturn brother could wax positively eloquent when it came to his stepdaughters. "Have you taken her to her pediatrician yet?"

"Yeah. Allie's got her all fixed up. Cough syrups, pain relievers, the works."

"Good. Give her a kiss for me."

"I'll do that." He cleared his throat. "That's not why I called, actually. Mom phoned me this morning and told me what you've been up to down there. I really wish you had talked to me first. I could have saved you three days of driving."

Her hands tightened on the phone as she absorbed his meaning. "You know where Brenda Golightly is?"

Gage didn't answer for a moment. When he did, she heard the regret in his voice. "Yeah. I know."

"Is the FBI investigating?"

"Twenty-three-year-old kidnapping cases are a fairly low priority to the bureau so Wyatt and I did a little digging on our own. We hired a P.I. and he tracked her down a few weeks ago. She's living in the Keys."

Her brothers had known where Brenda was all along. She stared out the windshield, her mind whirling. She didn't know much about the whole sibling dynamic but she was fairly certain keeping secrets like this one shouldn't be allowed.

"You and Wyatt both knew this and yet you never bothered to tell me?"

"We talked about it but we didn't think you wanted to know," Gage said warily. "If you'll remember, when I questioned you about the woman right after we received the DNA tests back confirming you were Charlotte, you said you didn't know where she was and you didn't care. You said you lost contact with her years ago and you didn't seem all that eager to find her again. I believe your exact words were *She can rot in hell as far as I care.*"

Kate winced, remembering her words. She had meant them at the time but that was before she had come to see that she would never be free of Brenda until she faced her one more time.

They knew where Brenda was. The implications of her brother's words started to seep in. She hadn't needed to drag Hunter into this at all. If she had only talked to Wyatt or Gage, she could have flown out and confronted Brenda on her own.

She had made a royal mess of this whole thing.

"Did you talk to her? Ask her how she ended up with me?"

Gage was quiet. "I didn't. Not personally," he finally said. "I wanted to but I had some pending cases here I couldn't break away from for a trip right now. I had a friend of mine out of the Miami field office pay her a visit."

Kate waited for him to go on. When he said nothing, she fought the urge to grind her teeth. "And? What did she have to say?"

"Not much, Kate. I'm sorry. She wasn't in any condition to say much of anything."

"Let me guess. She was stoned."

"Not exactly." His voice gentled. "Brenda Golightly is in a Key West nursing home after a heroine overdose four years ago that left her with limited mental function. She wasn't sure of her own name, forget about remembering details of something that happened more than two decades ago."

The fist in her lap moved to her stomach as she tried to absorb one more blow. "Limited mental function. Does that mean she won't be prosecuted for what she did to me? To all of us?"

"I doubt it. After the report I got from my colleague, I don't see how Brenda Golightly could ever be found competent enough to stand trial, even if the Nevada statute of limitations on kidnappings hadn't run out years ago."

The woman had destroyed so many lives, had wrecked a good marriage, had taken an innocent child and thrust her into hell. Yet she would never pay for what she had done. The injustice of it was staggering.

"I'm sorry I didn't tell you," Gage said. "I see now I should have, no matter what you said about not wanting to ever see her again. But I never imagined for a moment you would suddenly decide to take off in the middle of the night to go after her."

"It was a last-minute thing," she said, still reeling.

"I had some time off and it seemed like a good idea at the time."

"Well, you could always go to Disney World or something while you're down there. Or visit that foster couple who took such good care of you, the couple whose name you took."

Kate had a sudden powerful yearning to walk into the warm, cheerful kitchen of Tom and Maryanne Spencer, to smell Maryanne's African violets and see Tom's familiar, sturdy frame. She pushed it away and tried to focus on her brother.

"Good suggestions. Thanks. I'll have to see what Hunter thinks."

"Which brings us to the second reason for my call. What the hell were you thinking to head off across the country with a man like Bradshaw without telling anyone?"

Her hackles rose as she readied to defend the man who sat in the driver's seat, listening to every word as they drove past strip malls and warehouses. "I don't need a lecture from you, Gage."

"No, what you need is a hard kick in the seat. You scared Mom half to death when she couldn't reach you these last few days."

"I've already I told her I'm sorry for that. I'm not used to having anyone besides Taylor worrying about me and she and Wyatt are on their honeymoon. I didn't even think about calling anyone else about my plans."

"And the rest of it. Taking off with Bradshaw? Why is he involved?" Suspicion colored his voice. "Do the two of you have something going?"

An image from the night before danced across her

mind, of mouths and bodies tangled together, and heat crept across her cheeks. "None of your business, Gage."

She knew she sounded rude but she had just about had it with big, handsome, overbearing men who thought they knew everything.

"Be careful, Kate," he said after a pause. "That's all I'm going to say. Be careful, for your sake and for mine."

"For yours?"

"Yeah. Prison can make any man—especially an innocent one—mean as a snake in a badger hole. I don't particularly want to have to try to whip Hunter Bradshaw's ass if he ends up hurting my baby sister."

To her surprise—and no doubt to Gage's—she laughed. "Thanks for your concern, but I can take care of myself."

"I know you can," he said gruffly. "You've done a good job of it so far. I just wanted to remind you that you've got a couple brothers on your side now. I might still be hobbling around with these bum legs but that doesn't mean I can't get the job done. And Wyatt is a whole lot tougher than he looks. Between the two of us, we ought to be able to take care of Bradshaw if he steps out of line."

"I'll keep that in mind. Thanks."

Chapter 11

A few moments later, Kate said goodbye to Gage, then returned the phone to her bag. She leaned back against the leather of the seat, lost in thought.

Hunter waited as long as he could. "You planning to leave me in suspense all the way to Miami? What did he say?"

She opened one eye and peered at him. "He says he doesn't want to beat you up if you hurt his baby sister but he will. And Wyatt will help. That's what big brothers are for, apparently—a side benefit I hadn't fully appreciated when the McKinnons found me."

"Good to know. Did he have anything else to say?"

"Oh, not really."

She dropped the light tone and opened both eyes. In them he saw a mix of emotions—regret and apology and no small amount of embarrassment. "Only that I've dragged you and Belle three thousand miles on a wild goose chase."

"Oh?"

"I should have called him first. I'm so stupid. It never even occurred to me to start with Gage. I'm so used to doing everything on my own that I have to keep reminding myself I even have brothers, one of whom works for the FBI. Apparently he and Wyatt have known for a few weeks now that Brenda Golightly is in a nursing home in Key West. An OD a few years ago left her brain-damaged."

She said the last in a flat tone at odds to the tumult in her eyes.

Brain-damaged. Hunter didn't miss the implications. No punishment, no vengeance, no answers.

"I'm sorry, Kate."

She gazed out the windshield, her color high. "You must think I'm such a fool. I can't believe we've come this far for nothing."

"I don't think you're a fool. I think you're a victim of a terrible crime who wanted to find answers. Who *deserved* to find answers. What could possibly be foolish about that?"

"Well, it looks like I'll never find them now. The whys and the hows are probably locked away somewhere in Brenda Golightly's drug-ravaged mind."

He hated seeing her features haunted by pain.

"I suppose we should just turn around and start heading back to Salt Lake City," she went on. "There's no reason to drag this out any further."

A few hours earlier when he had been sitting awake in that damn hotel room after a sleepless night castigating himself and her, he might have agreed with her that they should just cut their losses and go home.

Faced with her pain, he had a difficult time remembering the anger that had prowled through him like a caged animal since making love with her the night before.

He hadn't been mad at her. Not really, though he supposed she no doubt believed otherwise after the abrupt, rude way he left her.

Wham, bam, thank you, ma'am.

While he still believed she should have told him she had never been with a man, most of his anger was self-directed. He had given into his overwhelming need without giving any thought to the consequences. For three long days he had fought his attraction for her and then in an instant all his hard work, every bit of control and self-denial, had been for nothing.

None of that seemed important suddenly. Not with Kate in the seat next to him, looking like she had just been kicked in the teeth. The need to comfort her, to ease that pain in her eyes, was stronger than any lingering anger.

"We're not turning around."

She blinked. "We're not?"

"No. We can't just give up. We're this close, Kate. We can make it to Key West in time to watch the sunset."

"To what end? There's no point in dragging this out. Don't you get it? Brenda can't tell us anything. Gage sent one of his FBI colleagues to talk to her and from the sound of it she was barely coherent."

"She might not have said much to an FBI agent but that doesn't necessarily follow that she won't have anything to say to you. I've seen brain injuries before and

I know how capricious they can be. You should know that, Dr. Spencer. Who knows, you could have better luck getting through than a stranger."

They traveled a full mile before she spoke again. "She might not even know who I am. What if she doesn't say anything more to me than she did to Gage's colleague?"

"Then she doesn't. You may never find the answers you want. I guess you'll have to be ready for that eventuality. But at least it won't be for lack of trying on our part."

She still looked unconvinced, her hands fisted together on her lap.

"Besides, I've never been to Key West," Hunter went on, undeterred by her silence. "Maybe I can take Taylor home a conch shell for Christmas."

"Why?"

"Well, I'd like to take her a palm tree but I don't think it will fit in the cargo area."

She frowned. "No, why do you insist on dragging this out? After last night, I would think you should be more than ready to turn back."

His jaw hardened at her reference to the evening before. "The job's not done. I offered to help you and I'll see it through."

"Don't you think you're carrying this damsel-in-distress thing a little far?"

Maybe. If he were smart, he would be doing all he could to spend as little time as possible with a woman who left him aching and confused. He would have seen the wisdom of cutting their trip as short as possible, returning to Salt Lake City and going their separate ways.

A sane man—or at least a smart one—certainly

wouldn't be coming up with transparent excuses to spend as much time as possible with a woman he knew he couldn't have.

"We've come this far, Kate. Let's see it through."

She looked undecided for a moment, then nodded tightly.

She wasn't sure how he did it, but Hunter was able miraculously to find deluxe lodging in Key West that welcomed pets, after only a few phone calls. The two tiny matching cottages were set in a lush tropical garden overlooking the Gulf of Mexico. Both painted a pale, cheerful pink, they looked like the perfect spot for a breezy, relaxing beach vacation.

Too bad she wasn't here to relax.

Under other circumstances she would have found it restful swinging in the hammock on the small wood porch while palm fronds rustled and swayed overhead and the ocean licked the sand twenty yards away.

If not for the low, steady thrum of anger—the deep, restlessness that seemed to have increased the closer they drove to this isolated paradise—she would have loved this.

She had come to the Keys once with Tom and Maryanne. They had stayed not far from here, she remembered.

The trip had been a panacea of sorts—a consolation prize—to offset their deep disappointment after Brenda once more had refused to relinquish her parental rights so Kate could be officially adopted by the Spencers.

Her entire adolescence had been one long tug-of-war with Brenda. With the Spencers, Kate had finally found a place where she could be content, could belong. Yet

Brenda had refused time and again to let them make their foster arrangement permanent.

Kate had been fourteen that long-ago trip to the Keys, trying desperately to figure out why Brenda didn't want her but didn't seem to want anyone else to have her either.

She and Tom and Maryanne had gone through the motions of enjoying themselves on that trip, she remembered now. They had walked and shopped along Duval Street and the rest of Old Town, had snorkeled, had even gone out deep-sea fishing where Tom had caught a swordfish that still hung in his office in St. Petersburg.

But through it all, a dark, greasy cloud had hung over them, a shadow they couldn't shake. Brenda, with her lies and her manipulations and her dogged determination that Kate remain legally hers.

It wasn't as if Brenda had wanted to play a huge part in her life in those eleven years after Kate had been removed from her custody until she'd reached eighteen and could legally change her name.

Brenda had come only occasionally for the court-approved visit, just often enough that Kate couldn't be considered abandoned and therefore become eligible for adoption.

She had come to dread those brief, uncomfortable encounters that always left her angry and depressed for weeks.

The real hell of it was that she hadn't hated Brenda. Not at first, anyway. That had come later, as she had moved further into her teens.

No, for most of her childhood before she had landed with the Spencers, Kate had loved the woman she thought was her mother—loved her with single-mindedly, childlike affection and desperately wanted her approval, waiting for the day when Brenda would claim her and they could be together again.

For all Brenda's selfishness, her addictions, her men, she had been the only constant in Kate's life as she was shuttled from home to home, the one thing she had to hold onto for as far back as she could remember.

The troubled child she had been was frightened of Brenda—of the chaos and tumult of their life—but she had loved her.

Sitting on the porch of this cheerful little cottage by the sea, Kate felt an echo of that love and couldn't stop her heavy sigh. How could she have loved a woman who treated her with such callous indifference? Why hadn't she *known* somehow that their whole relationship was a fraud?

Since finding out about her past, she had scoured the deep recesses of her memory bank trying for even one instance when she might have suspected Brenda wasn't really her mother. She could come up with nothing. She had only a vague, very early memory—not even a memory, really, more just a hazy impression—of a time when her life had been happy, safe.

Charlotte McKinnon might have been happy in her safe, comfortable world but poor little Katie Golightly had never enjoyed that luxury.

She sighed again, hating this self-pity, just as Hunter walked up the steps to the porch with the suitcase he had insisted on carrying up from the Jeep for her.

He set it down inside the cottage, then rejoined her on the porch, leaning against a pillar.

"Want to grab a bite to eat before we head over to the nursing home?" he asked.

She turned to face him, for the first time noting how the hard lines around his mouth seemed to have eased a little. In the slanted sunlight filtering through the lush growth in bright patches, his features seemed less harsh than they had four days earlier.

He was gorgeous, so beautifully male that her stomach did a long, slow roll.

"I'm not very hungry."

"No problem. We can get something a little later, after we talk to Brenda."

The dread that had ridden with her all afternoon seemed to wash over her again, drenching her like a sudden tropical rain.

She exhaled slowly. "I... Hunter, would you mind if we waited until the morning to go to the nursing home?"

He raised an eyebrow. "Why? We're here now. You've come three thousand miles for answers."

"Answers we both know I'm not likely to ever find now."

"You certainly won't find them if you refuse to even go talk to the woman."

"I will talk to her," she insisted. "But not yet. I know you probably think I'm crazy or the world's biggest coward but I...I just can't yet. I need to work up to it. Can we wait until morning?"

He studied her. "You're not crazy."

"Well, I seem to be doing a pretty good imitation of it then. I feel crazy. Restless and angry. Itchy inside my own skin. I want to scream and shout and throw chairs around one minute and curl up into a ball and cry my eyes out the next."

"Sounds pretty normal to me."

She laughed a little at his dry tone. "I guess that proves we're both a little wacky."

"That's certainly a possibility."

Kate had a sudden vivid memory of the wild heat they'd generated between them the night before and had to take a deep breath to calm her suddenly racing heart.

"Crazy or not," she said when she could think again, "I can't face Brenda yet. I just can't, Hunter. I need a little more time."

Hunter studied her in the dappled tropical light. She looked fragile and tired, her eyes huge in her pale face. With each mile they drove closer to Key West he had seen the finely wrought tension on her features, her body posture. By the time he'd found these cottages, she was so tightly strung it was a wonder she didn't vibrate.

He couldn't blame her for being nervous about meeting the woman who had caused her such pain. He still hadn't been able to bring himself to see Martin James since his release. His former defense attorney was in the county jail awaiting sentencing after pleading guilty to a host of charges, including the capital-murder charges he had ostensibly been defending Hunter on, though Martin had done everything possible to make sure his client would pay for his own crimes.

Martin was expected to receive the same sentence he had done his best behind the scenes to make sure Hunter had received—death by lethal injection.

Hunter doubted he would ever have the strength of

will to face Martin as Kate was facing her demons. A least not without wanting to be the one shoving in that needle—not just because Martin had framed him but for Dru and her dying mother and her unborn baby. And because Martin had been willing to kill Taylor to keep his deadly secrets.

He wouldn't even go see Martin, so how could he blame Kate for needing a little time to prepare herself before confronting her pain?

"Okay. This is your show," he said. "There's no reason we can't go in the morning."

Her smile flashed like a heron taking flight. "Thank you."

That smile entranced him and he wanted nothing more in that moment than to stand in the warm sunlight and soak it in.

Well, okay, he did want something more. He wanted to capture that smile with his mouth, to absorb her sighs and her pain into him.

Hunger gnawed at him, making a mockery of any hope he might have been foolish enough to entertain that the night before might have worked her out of his system.

He couldn't kiss her and he couldn't afford a repeat of the night before. The very fact of her inexperience had driven that home forcefully through the long night and their drive south across Florida.

Kate was a relationship kind of woman with a capital *R*. She obviously wasn't interested in casual sex or she wouldn't have still been a virgin, and he wasn't capable of anything else right now.

He was empty inside. No, not completely empty. There seemed to be room for his hate and anger—

and even some irrational shame—over what had happened to him. But anything good and decent had died during those grim days and miserable nights of his incarceration.

He would hurt her. He didn't want to but he knew himself well enough to know it was inevitable. He couldn't do it to her—she was coping with enough pain right now.

He shoved his hands in his pockets to keep from reaching for her, good intentions be damned. "I think I'll take Belle for a run on the beach. We can both use it after four days on the road."

She looked as if she would like to go along but right now he needed distance from her to rebuild his self-control, so he refrained from issuing an invitation.

"I'll be done in an hour or so. If you're hungry by then, we can wander out and see what we can find to eat."

He'd heard the nightlife on Key West was wild and woolly. He wasn't much of a drinker but maybe if he got good and smashed he might be able to forget the night before and the healing peace he had known so briefly in her arms.

He was still feeling vaguely unsettled after he'd changed into a T-shirt and the one pair of jogging shorts he'd brought along.

Belle was beside herself with joy, anticipating exactly what was coming. She panted with glee and raced circles around him as they headed out toward the water.

They had made good time from Jacksonville that day. Hunter had predicted they would be in Key West by sunset and, sure enough, the sun was just beginning its slow slide into the sea as he set a hard pace for himself through the hard-packed sand close to the waves.

Lord, he loved this. Euphoria churned through his veins with every step, every thud of his jogging shoes in the sand.

Of all the things he had missed during his three years of incarceration, the freedom to take off and run whenever the mood hit him had been up there close to the top of his list. Exercise had certainly been encouraged for inmates. Corrections officers figured it worked off aggression better expended in sweat and exertion than on each other. But Hunter found little satisfaction running around a prison-yard track like a rat in a cage.

He did it, anyway, along with weight lifting to keep his body in shape. But every time he would run inside those razor wire–tipped walls, he would dream of a moment like this, of stretching his legs as far as they would go and heading off into the sunset.

The ocean was a new twist. Usually his prison fantasies involved taking off into the mountains surrounding his home in Little Cottonwood Canyon, the sharp tang of sage surrounding him and the clear, high air burning his lungs while Belle chased after ground squirrels and pikas.

This was a heaven he wouldn't even have let himself dream about two months ago—water lapping at the sand, the warm sea breeze kissing his skin, the sun slipping toward the Gulf of Mexico in a fiery show of orange and purple.

Hunter enjoyed the sunset on the go, unwilling to stop even for something so spectacular, not with the endorphin high pumping through his system.

With Belle chasing the waves excitedly and shore-birds crying overhead, it was a moment of pure, stunning joy. The euphoria almost made up for his four days on the road, of trying—and obviously failing spectacularly—to keep his hands off Kate.

He ran for a long time, until his lungs ached and the sun dipped into the water. As he headed back up the beach toward their rented cottages, his mind traveled of its own will to the woman who waited there.

Small and lovely and vulnerable, she made a dangerous package, one he found entirely too appealing. He just had to do his best to resist her, no matter what it took.

His resolve was tested unexpectedly about a quarter mile from their lodging. The sun was now only a rim above the waves but he still had enough light to see a solitary figure on the beach staring out to sea, arms wrapped around her knees.

He knew instantly it was Kate.

Even if he hadn't recognized the sunlit warmth of her hair or that slender, elegant stretch of neck, he would have known it was her by Belle's joyful reaction. The dog raced to her side and leaped and writhed to see her as if they had been separated for months and hadn't just spent the last four days in almost constant company.

Kate hugged Belle to her and even from a dozen yards away he could hear her low laughter. It slid around and through him like a thin, silvery ribbon.

He stopped there in the sand, his muscles twitching and his heart still pounding from the run.

Still sitting in the sand, she swiveled a little to face him, a small smile of welcome on her face.

Coming home. That's what he felt like when he saw her, like some part of him that had been adrift for too long at last had a place to rest.

He stared at her as a stunning realization hit him with the jolt of a thousand watts of electricity.

He was in love with her.

These last few days on this trip—hell, for the whole five years he had known her—he had done his best to convince himself this *thing* between them was only physical attraction. Pheromone to pheromone, yin to yang.

Standing here with the tropical breeze cooling the sweat on his body and the sea a soft wash of colors behind him, he forced himself finally to face the truth he had been running from.

They shared an attraction, certainly. A constant, insidious heat that made him aware of her every sigh, her every breath.

But he could no longer deny the truth. This was far more than a mere physical attraction. He was in love with Kate Spencer, of the healer's spirit and the troubled past and the haunted eyes.

He loved her laughter and he loved her courage and he loved the way she gathered stray chicks around her like a lonely mother hen.

The realization horrified him. For a long moment, he could do nothing but stand there in the sand trying to catch his breath with his solar plexus tight and quivering as if he'd just taken a hard hit with one of those vicious billy clubs a couple of the guards at the Point of the Mountain took great delight in wielding against someone who had once been one of their own.

"How was your run?" she asked.

He cleared his throat, hoping she would attribute his sudden breathlessness to the exercise.

"Good. It's a beautiful place for a workout."

She lifted her face to the warm air. "I'd forgotten how much I love the sea," she said with a soft smile. "Since I moved to Utah I've come to love the wildness—the primitive strength—of the Rockies. But the ocean feeds my soul."

He should leave, he thought with an edge of desperation. Right now, run as fast as he could away from her. Instead, he found himself moving closer. He knew it was foolish but still he found himself sitting beside her in the sand, though he maintained what he hoped was a safe distance between them.

"Why did you leave Florida? I'm sure you could have gone somewhere closer to med school. What took you to the University of Utah?"

Her brow furrowed as she considered his question. "I don't know that I have a firm answer to that. Not one that makes any sense, anyway. I was accepted to three different medical schools—Vanderbilt, Tulane and the University of Utah. I was really close to going to Vanderbilt but somehow the mountains called to me. Somewhere deep in my soul were memories of aspens and pines and blue sky. I used to think it was some lingering remnant of a previous life."

Her small laugh contained little humor. "I guess it was. That first time I went back to Liberty with Gage and Wyatt, they drove me to Lynn's house, on my grandfather's ranch where we all lived for the first three years of my life. I can remember looking up at the green-and-gray mountains surrounding the ranch and feeling this deep connection, this missing piece of my life clicking back into place."

She was quiet as the first stars started peeking out of the twilight sky. "I didn't know why until this last month or so but I suppose I left Florida looking for that missing piece of myself. For my family."

"And you found them."

"Right, even though technically, they found me. Anyway, Utah is home now and was before the Mc-Kinnons ever found me but a part of my soul will always hunger for the ocean. I suppose this is one of those painful times I have to give up one thing I love in order to get something else I love."

"The ocean will always be here waiting whenever you come back."

She gave a little laugh. "You're right. I really don't have to choose, do I?"

"Not right now, anyway. Right now you can just enjoy it."

They sat for several moments in silence, Belle flopped onto the sand beside them, while the waves lapped at the shore and the stars continued to pop out like silver sequins.

"I'm sorry I disturbed your run," she said after a moment.

"We were heading back, anyway. I haven't quite got my running legs back."

Her gaze shifted to his legs and he was unnerved to see color rise on her cheeks. The brief moment of peace suddenly seemed charged with tension, awareness.

Hunter cleared his throat. He had to get out of here before he did something stupid.

He rose, shaking sand off. "I, uh, need to shower

and then we can find somewhere to eat if you're up for it." Somewhere crowded and noisy and raucous where he wouldn't have to be alone with her.

She nodded, her color still high. "Okay."

"You want to stay here a little longer?"

"No. I think I'm ready to go back."

He helped her to her feet but quickly released her hand as they walked up the deep white sand toward their cottages. He couldn't risk prolonged physical contact right now, not with this thick emotion swirling through him.

He needed space and distance from her. Too bad he couldn't swim out to some isolated offshore cay and stay there for a week or two, until she returned to Utah and her residency.

Chapter 12

How did a woman with very little experience seduce the man she loved?

Kate blew out a breath, for once wishing she'd taken more time away from medical textbooks in the last few years to gain a little practical knowledge.

She knew how to discourage a man, to slip away from wandering hands and to gently divert a man's attention until he didn't even realize he had been brushed off.

That she could do in her sleep. The opposite—letting a man know she wanted more—was a little harder to figure out. How did she do it without coming across as easy or desperate or both?

The trouble was, she only had about fifteen minutes to figure it out before Hunter finished showering and changing from his jogging clothes. Fifteen minutes to turn herself from bland to bombshell.

It was a daunting prospect.

Kate stood in her cheerful rented cottage, a ceiling fan spinning lazily overhead as she studied the pitiful offerings from her suitcase spread out across her tropical bedspread.

She might have had a fighting chance if she had brought along something slinky and sultry, an outfit sure to turn her petite, almost boyish figure into something that cried out *ba-da-bing*.

Okay, that would take more than a sexy outfit to accomplish. Still, it would be nice to have something to work with here.

When she had packed in those early morning hours after the wedding—what seemed a lifetime ago—she had opted for travel casual, clothes picked more for comfort than for their sex appeal.

The only thing she'd brought along that was even remotely interesting was the simple, no-frills black dress she'd picked up before her Guatemala trip, mostly because it was guaranteed not to wrinkle.

With a snap of her wrists she shook it, relieved when she found the short-sleeved tunic dress lived up to its hype and was ready for a night on the town. At least she had the foresight to include a pair of flat black sandals to go with it—wouldn't she have looked lovely with her little black dress and high-tops?—but she was afraid she still looked like some kind of granola lover.

The only thing she had for accessories was a handmade Mayan jade *mariposa* necklace-and-earring set she'd bought at a village market in Guatemala. No problem. At least it would match the butterflies in her stomach.

Kate blew out a breath, slipped into the dress and

went to work on her hair and makeup, something she rarely fussed with. Anticipation curled through her as she piled her hair onto her head, wishing she had time for something a little more elegant, then quickly applied eye shadow, mascara and the sexiest shade of lipstick she owned. Her color was high enough she decided she didn't need blush.

Sultry. That's what she was going for here. Maybe Hunter would be swept away by the hot, uninhibited tropical nights. She could always dream, couldn't she?

One would hope that after four days in his constant company, she could read the man a little better but he was still a mystery, a study in contrasts. There had been that odd, jittery moment on the beach earlier when he had gazed at her with an intense light in his midnight eyes that left her shaky and breathless.

But then he barely touched her. She hadn't missed how quickly he had released her hand after helping her from the sand. That hadn't been the only example. All day, he'd gone out of his way to avoid even the most accidental of touches.

Maybe the reason for his distance was something other than revulsion. She thought of the expression in those eyes and pressed a hand to her stomach through the black cotton at the nerves jumping there.

She had to believe Hunter wasn't completely unaffected by her. He had certainly been interested enough the night before, even when she had been teary and emotional.

She was just finishing up when a knock sounded at the door. Blotting her lipstick, Kate took time for one quick look in the mirror. Not bad for travel chic.

Ready or not, Hunter Bradshaw.

"Just a minute," she called, then slipped into the sandals and hurried to the door.

When she opened the door, the butterflies in her stomach turned into stampeding rhinos. He stood on the other side wearing khakis and a navy-blue golf shirt, his wet hair gleaming silvery black in the porch light. He smelled divine, that sexy, cedary male aftershave that transported her instantly to the night before, trailing kisses up his neck.

For just a moment, she thought his eyes turned hot and hungry as he looked at her in her little black travel dress, but he blinked and the moment was gone.

She tried to smile a greeting but was fairly certain her facial muscles had suddenly gone Botox-numb on her, along with everything else.

"Where's Belle?" It was the only thought her brain could grab hold of.

"Enjoying a minute to herself, I think. She was sound asleep in her crate when I left."

She continued to stand there like an idiot and only realized it when he cleared his throat. "Are you ready?" he asked.

Oh, yes, she wanted to say but she swallowed the fervent declaration. "I think so," she said instead. "Oh, wait. I forgot."

Kate grabbed the jade butterfly necklace and earrings off the dresser. To her dismay, her hands that could suture a gaping wound with tiny, delicate stitches fumbled with something as simple as inserting the earrings in her ears, but she finally managed it.

She picked up the necklace and reached her arms behind her neck to fasten it, then she happened to glance at Hunter. She found him staring at her, his eyes slightly unfocused and his respiration rate most definitely accelerated.

Hmmm. Maybe this whole seduction business wasn't as tough as she feared. She took a deep breath and decided to try the only thing she could come up with at short notice.

"I can't quite work the clasp," she murmured after a moment. "Would you mind helping me?"

He froze, a trapped look in his eyes, then she saw his throat work. "I'm not very good with jewelry thingies. You look fine without the necklace."

"I'd really like to wear it, though."

After a few heartbeats, the trapped look gave way to resignation. He took the necklace from her and moved behind her. She obliged by tipping her head forward, pulling the stray tendrils of hair that always managed to slip from her updo out of the way.

Just who was seducing whom here? Kate wondered as Hunter went to work on the necklace. She was painfully aware of him, of his just-showered scent and his crisp, clean clothes and his fingers warm and strong against her skin.

A shiver slid down her spine at his touch and she closed her eyes and leaned her head back until it rested against his shoulder.

His fingers at her nape stilled and she could feel the quick rise and fall of his chest. "What are you doing, Kate?" he asked, his voice low.

Hot color soaked her cheeks. She couldn't come up with anything but the truth, so she straightened and turned to face him. "I was hoping to seduce you, but I'm obviously not very good at it."

His short laugh was raw, unamused. "I wouldn't say that."

That sounded promising. "No?"

"If you leaned any closer, you would find out exactly how you affect me."

Her gaze locked with his. "Is that an invitation?"

A muscle flexed in his jaw. "Dammit, Kate. This isn't a good idea."

"Why not?"

He groaned. "A hundred reasons. If I were a smart man I would have turned around the moment I walked in the door and found you in that dress. I have no self-control where you're concerned."

"Good," she murmured, then stepped forward again, her arms entwined around his neck as she kissed him.

He stayed unmoving for perhaps ten seconds, then he groaned and dragged her against him.

He must have shaved again after his shower. That sexy dark shadow she had seen him grow by evening over the last few days was gone and his skin smelled of that delicious aftershave.

His kiss was edged by the same wild desperation of the night before. This time it didn't unnerve her, it only fueled her own desire.

"Make love to me again, Hunter. Please."

He closed his eyes as if praying for strength. When he opened them, they were dark, aroused. "All day I've tried to convince myself what a mistake that would be, no matter how much I might want it."

She pressed her mouth to his carotid artery, to the pulse she could see pumping just below the skin. "Did it work?"

"What do you think? I'm not very persuasive, I

guess. Right now making love to you seems like the best idea in the world."

"I'm glad we see eye to eye," she murmured and kissed him again.

"I don't want to hurt you, Kate."

He wasn't talking about the kind of fleeting physical pain she had experienced the night before. She sensed it, could almost feel a phantom spasm from the impending heartache.

"You won't," she lied, lifting her chin. "I can take care of myself."

He didn't look convinced so she kissed him again, pouring all the emotions she couldn't say into her kiss, her touch.

The dress she had selected with such care quickly ended up piled on the floor. Busy helping him out of his clothes, Kate left it there, grateful for the wonders of wrinkle-free cloth.

As inevitable as the tide, they came together, unspoken emotions simmering below the surface. This time there was no anger, no fear, only this wild, edgy heat.

"Are you still sore?" Hunter asked just before he entered her.

Kate thought about denying it but honesty compelled her to nod. "Maybe a little. Don't worry about it, though."

She should have known he would. The kind of man who rode his silver SUV to the rescue of any damsel in distress who needed him would die before he hurt his woman.

Not his woman, she reminded herself. His lover. For now, that would have to be enough.

After a moment's consideration, Hunter rolled

onto his back, pulling her atop him. Kate gasped as he guided her onto his arousal.

"You have a little better control this way." His voice was raspy, deep. "If anything hurts, you can stop."

Nice theory, but she knew she couldn't have stopped even if a hurricane suddenly blew across the Key.

Kate twisted her fingers around his, setting an erotically slow pace. With each deep thrust inside her, she had to clamp down on the words of love fluttering in her throat like trapped birds.

Heat and love and desire braided through her, tighter and tighter, binding her to this strong, beautiful man with the shadows in his eyes.

At last, just when she was sure she couldn't endure another moment, he reached a finger to the junction of their bodies and touched her. With a wild cry, she soared free. He watched her, his eyes hot and dark, then he gripped her fingers again and with one more powerful surge, joined her.

Much later, when every muscle burned with a pleasant exhaustion, she lay nestled in the crook of his shoulder, her arm spread across the hard muscles of chest.

"We didn't get dinner."

She laughed at the woeful note in his voice and raised up a little so she could see his face better.

"If not for the last hour or so I would have said some smart remark about food being the only thing you think about."

To her shock, he grinned. Hunter Bradshaw actually grinned, a slow, sexy smile that made her just about forget her name. As she looked at him sprawled there in the bed of her rented cottage, she felt as if she'd just been handed the world.

"I think about plenty of things. Food. Sex. Food. Sex. I'm a man of many interests."

Oh, she wanted to hold on tight and never let this lighthearted man go. If she had helped him, even a little, to allow some goodness back into his life she thought it would almost be worth the heartache she knew waited for her back in Utah.

"How about pizza?" she suggested. "I'm sure Ruben and Violet could suggest a decent place that delivers."

He agreed and called the small resort's owners at the front office. They recommended a place not far from their lodging that delivered delicious pizza. After some debate, they decided to be adventurous and ordered something billed as a Caribbean pie, with grilled chicken, pineapples and peppers on a plum sauce instead of the traditional tomato.

"We have half an hour before they deliver," Hunter said after he hung up.

She curled a hand across that hard chest, loving the way his pulse skipped a little at her touch. "Time management is a very important skill for medical residents. You'd be surprised what I can accomplish in half an hour."

He lifted her fist to his mouth and pressed a kiss to her knuckles. "Somehow I don't think anything you do could surprise me, Dr. Spencer."

"There's always a first time," she said with a sly smile, then proceeded to demonstrate.

He couldn't get enough of her.

After the pizza arrived and was quickly consumed, they took a shower together and made love again, this time slow and easy, with a tenderness that terrified him as much as it seduced him.

He would have been happy to stay there all night— hell, if he died in Kate's bed, he wasn't sure he would mind—but Belle had been stuck in her crate all evening.

Kate insisted on going with him and said she was eager to see Key West again, so while he retrieved Belle from his own room, Kate once more put on that sexy short black dress.

She was waiting for him on the porch of her cottage when he brought the dog out on her leash.

Even at 11:00 p.m. on a Wednesday night, the Key West nightlife was jumping. Live music blared from a half-dozen bars as they made their slow way down Duval Street, and the area was thronged with tourists.

It reminded him of a law-enforcement conference he'd attended in New Orleans just after he'd earned his gold shield. A couple of veteran detectives had dragged him down to the French Quarter with them and the rowdy party mood there had been the same.

This kind of crowd made the short hairs on the back of a cop's neck stand up. It could turn unpredictable in an instant.

He found himself scanning the crowd for any law-breakers. When he realized it, he ordered himself to cut it out. He wasn't a cop anymore. He wasn't *anything*, just an ex-con in love with a woman who deserved far better than him.

The familiar restless dark mood crept up to the edge of his psyche. Hunter knew it was there, just waiting to take over, but he pushed it away. Tonight he wasn't going to give in. Tonight he had a beautiful woman on his arm, they were in a tropical paradise, and he was a free man. He intended to do his best to enjoy every minute of it.

"I'm in the mood for some key lime pie," he said suddenly. "What do you think?"

She smiled. "Sounds great."

They found a sidewalk café where Belle could rest at their feet and they could enjoy the sights and sounds of the warm night.

After they placed their order for pie, he told Kate of that convention in New Orleans when he'd been a rookie detective and how pathetically eager he had been to return to the clear, sweet mountain air of Utah when it was over.

She told him of her culture shock after moving to Utah from St. Petersburg but how she had learned to embrace some of the state idiosyncrasies.

Throughout their conversation, he was aware of her, of the way she tucked a stray tendril of honey-blond hair behind her ears, how she fingered that jade butterfly in the hollow of her neck, the absent way she sometimes reached down to pet Belle.

He was crazy about her. Everything she did.

He wanted this moment to stretch on forever.

He was so busy watching Kate, he almost missed a couple of drunks across the street when they staggered out of a bar, drinks in hand. He only noticed them when one started hassling a couple of women walking by.

"Come on, baby. Lemme buy you a drink," one said, loud enough to draw more than just Hunter's attention.

They looked like college boys who hadn't yet learned their limits, he thought. It was months too early for spring break but maybe they decided spending the holidays drunk in Key West would be a hell of a lot more fun than stringing popcorn back home with Mom and Dad.

The women quickly walked past but the frat boys were just warming up. Hunter watched as they accosted two or three more groups of women. He was just about to get up and tactfully urge them along when he saw a middle-aged man walking with what looked like his wife and teenage daughter.

The college boys said something to the daughter that had the man bristling. He could see by the alarming red of the father's face that whatever the drunks said had been offensive.

With a growing sense of inevitability, he watched the confrontation escalate and a moment later, the older man poked one of the boys in the chest with his finger.

Hunter half rose, then forced himself to sit down again. Not his problem. He wasn't a cop anymore and he wasn't responsible for policing the whole damn world.

The frat boy apparently didn't like being dressed down by this stranger anymore than he probably did from his own father. When the man continued to get into his face, he coldcocked him with a hard right.

The women screamed as the older man went down, clutching his nose, now spurting red.

In an instant, Hunter swore, handed Belle's leash to Kate and ordered her to stay put.

He managed to reach the trio before the outraged father came up swinging. As much as he understood and applauded the man's need to defend his women, these two cocky little bastards would beat the crap out of a pasty-white tourist like him.

"Bring it on, dude. Let's see what you got." The

slightly bleary-eyed college kid stood over the tourist, baiting him to defend himself.

Hunter moved in between the two before the tourist could stagger to his feet.

"That's enough," he said in his best prison-yard tough voice. "Let's all just cool off now."

Frat Boy Number One blinked at him as if Hunter had just beamed in from the planet Zorcon. "Who'r'you?" he slurred.

Hunter ignored the question and turned to the tourist, whose wife and daughter fluttered around him like a couple of quail protecting their nest.

"Sir, are you all right?"

"Little bugger broke my nose."

Hunter was remarkably unsurprised when Kate disobeyed his order to stay out of harm's way and pushed her way through the crowd that had begun to gather. She handed Belle's leash to a bystander and knelt at the man's side. "Let me take a look at it. I'm a doctor."

Drunk far past the point of reason or discretion, Frat Boy Number Two leered at Kate kneeling there in her sexy little black dress and grabbed at his crotch. "Hey, Doc, I got something right here that hurts. Want to kiss it better?"

Hunter let out a disgruntled sigh, wondering why trouble seemed to follow them around like a greasy dark cloud, then he stepped forward, grabbed the punk by his shirtfront and shoved him into the other boy. Both of them went sprawling against the wall, amid widespread applause from the crowd.

The first kid came up swinging and managed to sneak an uppercut into Hunter's gut but the punch was so wimpy he barely felt it. He dodged the next one and returned it with a hard blow that knocked the college boy to the ground. He groaned but didn't get back up.

The other kid—the one with the dirty mouth—started to scurry away but his retreat was stopped by a couple of uniform cops on bicycles who had been drawn by the commotion.

"Why are we always in the wrong place at the wrong time?" Hunter muttered twenty minutes later when they finally returned to the café and their uneaten pie after giving their statements to the bike cops. The cops had hassled him a little about shoving the frat boys, but after they heard from various witnesses that Dumb and Dumber had started the altercation and had repeatedly accosted various women, they backed off.

The two college boys were on their way to face drunk-and-disorderly charges and the tourist's injuries had been treated at the scene.

"I think we're always in the right place at exactly the right time," Kate said.

She hadn't stopped looking at him with that soft light in her eyes, as if he were some kind of hero or something. He wanted to tell her to cut it out, that they were just a couple of drunk kids and he hadn't done anything, but he would rather just see the whole thing dropped.

She picked up his hand where his fist had been scraped a little on the kid's tooth in the altercation. "We'd better get this cleaned up. We should have had the paramedics look at it when they were helping Mr. Coletti. We can go back to the resort for my bag or I can see if the restaurant has a first-aid kit."

"It's fine, Doc. Just a couple of scraped knuckles."

"Humor me, okay? Human bite wounds can be nasty."

She grabbed their waiter on his next go-round. A few moments later he brought a first-aid kit. Hunter stoically endured her fussing over him, washing off his knuckles and bandaging the worst scrape.

Not for all the world would he admit he secretly enjoyed her nurturing. It had been so long since he'd had this kind of softness and caring in his life, and he found himself soaking it up.

"There you go," she said, rubbing a finger over one of his uninjured knuckles. "Good as new."

Now if she could only do the same to his heart, but he was afraid it would never be the same.

They finished their remaining few bites of pie, then left a hefty tip for the waiter who had held their table for them during the street scene.

"Have you given any more thought to what you're going to do when we return to Utah?" Kate asked as they walked up the beach toward their lodging.

Besides try to live in a dull, colorless world without her? He hadn't managed to move beyond that. He shook his head. "Some. I haven't figured anything out yet."

"I think you should go back to being a cop."

"Don't you think I've been punished enough?"

She made a face at him. "It's not a punishment. It was a joy for you. I know it was."

He gazed at the moonlight shimmering on the water. "Maybe three years ago. That was a different lifetime ago. I was a different person."

"I saw you tonight as you handled those drunks. You were perfect—not vicious, just firm. Exactly what a good cop does."

"A good cop doesn't punch a couple of drunk kids just for talking trash."

"You didn't. You shoved them a little but you didn't throw the first punch. They did when they hit Mr. Coletti. You didn't start it, you just ended it, which was exactly what needed to be done. Exactly what a good cop would do."

Hunter was silent as Belle sniffed at a sand crab scuttling for something to eat. "A cop needs to know his brothers and sisters on the force have his back," he said quietly. "Mine didn't when I needed them most. I can't go back to the Salt Lake Police Department."

"So go somewhere else. The county sheriff's department can always use deputies or one of the smaller incorporated areas in the valley would probably love to have someone with your experience. Or you can even go farther afield. If you were willing to move out of Salt Lake County, I'm sure there are a hundred small communities in the state who would be eager to add a seasoned veteran to their departments. Who knows, you might even find you prefer small-town crime fighting."

Hunter was stunned by the idea. He had been so consumed with anger at his department for not standing by him that he'd never even thought about moving to a different division.

"You also have an interesting perspective that most cops never get," Kate went on when he said nothing. "You know what it's like on the inside. I believe what happened to you—your wrongful conviction and imprisonment—would only make you a stronger detective, even more dedicated to finding justice. True justice, not just easy justice."

Hunter stared out to sea as her suggestion seemed

to settle inside himself. Definitely something to think about.

He had thought his days as a cop were over. He had grieved over it but hadn't seen a way past his bitterness. He was angry at the system for failing him, but the bulk of his anger was against the officers and detectives he had worked with who had done a sloppy job investigating Dru's murder. They had focused on the most obvious suspect—him—and ignored any leads that pointed in other directions.

For the first time since his release, he felt a tiny flicker of hope that maybe he could move on, do something worthwhile with the rest of his life.

"What about you?" he asked Kate. "Where do you see yourself settling when your residency is done? Will you come back to Florida?"

The breeze off the Gulf lifted her hair, caressed her skin as he would like to be doing right about now. "I'm not sure what I'll do. I thought about returning to Central America for a while. There is so much work that needs to be done there. I don't know. With Utah's birthrate, there's always a need for family doctors in the state, especially in those smaller towns I was talking about."

"Cops and doctors can always find something to keep them busy, I suppose," he said.

"Unfortunately, sick people and crime seem to be universal."

"Well, wherever you decide to practice, your patients will be lucky to have you," he said gruffly.

She stopped walking and he could see her eyes soften in the moonlight. "Sometimes you say the sweetest things," she said. "Thank you."

Before he could tell her he meant every word, she leaned on tiptoe and kissed him.

They stood there in the sand with only their mouths connected and Hunter felt something deep and elemental shift inside him.

"Anyway, I don't want to think about the future or the past," Kate murmured. "For tonight, can we just focus on right now?"

He pulled her into his arms. *Right now* was just about the best moment of his life so he wasn't about to argue.

Chapter 13

Two days later, Kate woke sometime in the reverent hush before dawn. Outside the bedroom window, the sky was just beginning to lighten to a pale, silvery pink and the world seemed peaceful and still.

Hunter had pulled her to him sometime during the night and he slept on his side facing her, one arm casually flung across her rib cage.

With each breath, she could feel the soft brush of hair on his arms against her skin.

She could watch him sleep all day. At rest, he lost the hardness, the edginess, he wore as a shield against the world.

Really, when she thought about it, during this entire trip he had been lowering that protective shield inch by inch and letting the real Hunter out a little more.

These few days they had spent together in Key West

had been so wonderful. It was as if all the dark shadows that had hovered around her since finding out about Charlotte McKinnon couldn't pierce the bright sunshine of the Key.

For two days, they laughed and talked and kissed and she had watched with delight as Hunter truly began to relax, as if he were slowly waking from a long, terrible nightmare.

She wanted to stay here forever, wrapped in this quiet, elusive peace—tangled together with him while the world outside this tropical paradise ceased to exist.

If only things were that simple. She could feel the pressure of all she had left behind begin to crowd in on her again. She shifted her gaze to the ceiling fan overhead, its plump leaf-shaped blades spinning slowly.

She had to face her past today. She had put it off too long but time was running out. Both of them needed to return to Utah. She had to start the next rotation of her residency bright and early Christmas morning, and Hunter needed to begin the process of picking up the pieces of his life.

She sighed, her heart already constricting at the pain she knew waited for her there.

She wasn't foolish enough to think they could remain in this idyllic bubble of passion and tenderness when they returned to the mountains and real life.

Hunter had given her no words of tenderness, had offered her nothing but the momentary comfort of his arms.

He was attracted to her, she had no doubt about that, and on some level he cared for her. She knew he did. But even when he made love to her, he kept a part of himself separate.

He didn't love her. She couldn't fool herself into thinking otherwise. No matter how she might wish it, she couldn't turn what they shared here into some kind of sweet happily-ever-after.

Lost in her thoughts, she was startled when she suddenly felt a wet nose nudging at her. Belle stood on the other side of the bed, her eyes deep and mournful.

"You need to go out, honey?" she whispered. "Just a minute."

Though she hated leaving this warm, soft bed, she slipped out of Hunter's arms, holding her breath for fear she would wake him. A frown twisted those hard, lean features for a moment, then he rolled over.

Kate slipped on shorts and a T-shirt, found the pair of bright-purple flip-flops she had bought at a souvenir shop the day before and grabbed Belle's leash.

The hard-partying nights on Key West tended to make early mornings quiet. She didn't mind the lack of company at all as she and Belle walked down to the deserted beach. Kate enjoyed the pale beginnings of sunrise while Belle marked her temporary territory then raced around for a while chasing the surf.

They walked until Belle's tongue lolled out from running and she started looking thirsty.

Back at the cottage, Kate made as little noise as possible while she filled the dog's water dish then carried it out to the porch.

She sat on the rocker, able to catch just a small glimpse of the surf through the lush growth.

"Next time, wake me up to take care of Belle."

Startled by the sudden deep voice, she turned to find Hunter standing in the doorway. He wore only a pair of jeans, the top button undone, and his hair was tousled from sleep, but she had never seen a more gorgeous sight.

She swallowed and tried to rearrange her suddenly scattered thoughts. "I didn't mind. I was up, anyway. We took a little walk on the beach and watched the sunrise."

"I was worried when I woke and found you gone, until I saw the empty crate and figured out Belle must have been bossing you around again."

"She's pretty good at getting her message across, isn't she?"

He returned her smile briefly, then turned serious. "I only reserved two nights here, Kate, which means we're supposed to check out today. I need to let the management know if we're staying longer."

She knew what he was asking. Though the sun was already climbing the sky, she was sure the morning suddenly seemed darker.

"It's time," she finally said. "Past time."

"Are you sure?"

She wasn't sure of anything except the inevitability of her heartbreak, but she forced herself to nod.

A strange light sparked in his eyes, one she couldn't read. He stood in the doorway looking strong and masculine and gorgeous.

"You won't be alone. I'll be right there with you."

She tried to smile. "I know."

He moved out onto the porch and pulled her to her feet and against that hard, wonderful chest. "We don't have to go yet," he murmured. "We still have a few hours."

She lifted her mouth for his kiss. The shadows could wait while they stayed in paradise a little longer.

* * *

For all her bravado earlier in the morning, Hunter could see Kate's nerves were stretched as thin as a strand of hair. She sat beside him with her hands folded tightly in her lap and her shoulders stiff as he drove the short distance from their bungalow to the Key West Terrace long-term care facility.

The building overlooked the Atlantic and was white brick with terra-cotta roof tiles and a blooming tropical garden out front that gave it the look of a Mediterranean villa.

Though it was broad daylight, he could see holiday lights strung across the small gated yard. Inside, poinsettias in bright gold pots were arranged in a cone shape approximating a Christmas tree.

The tanned, perky young receptionist behind the glass information booth registered surprise when Kate asked for Brenda Golightly's room, as if not very many people asked that particular question.

"Are you friends or family?" she asked in a syrupy Southern accent.

Kate seemed frozen by the question. She didn't answer, only gave him an anguished look that sliced at him worse than any prison shiv.

He stepped forward, his best charming-cop smile in place. "Something like that," he said.

The receptionist preened a little, like a turtledove. "Well, Ms. Golightly will be absolutely *thrilled* at the company, I'm sure. She's in the north wing, room 134. Just take the hallway to the left of the elevators. Follow that hall as far as it goes and Ms. Golightly's room is on the right. You can't miss it."

The halls had more holiday decorations, garlands

of looped green and red paper, a smiling plastic Santa Claus pulling a sleigh and eight reindeer, and even a life-size poster of the Grinch.

Kate didn't appear to notice anything about their surroundings. The closer they walked to room 134, the more her color faded, until he was afraid she would disappear against the whitewashed walls.

He stopped outside a plain wood door devoid of ornamentation. "You don't have to put yourself through this, Kate. I can go in and interview her alone."

She seemed to steel her shoulders like a soldier heading into a firefight. "No. I appreciate the offer but I have to be there. I have to face her. After all these years, I *have* to."

Watching her battle her own fears was humbling and made him grieve for a blond little girl stolen from all she knew and thrust into a world where she knew no peace.

"Have I told you I think you're one of the strongest women I've ever met?" he asked, his voice low.

Her mouth parted a little in surprise but then he saw gratitude blossom in her eyes.

His words seemed to steady her, calm her. She drew in a deep breath and pushed open the door.

In contrast to the holiday gaiety in the hallway outside, room 134 was spartan, cheerless. His grandmother Bradshaw had spent the last year of her life in a nursing home. She'd died when he was in his early teens, but he remembered her room as an extension of the prissy, orderly house she had lived in before, with frilly doilies on the bedside table, lacy curtains and her favorite oil painting of a mountain sunset.

This room was like dozens of other hospital rooms

he had seen in his life. Sterile, bland, and wholly lacking in personality.

A single bed with nobby blue institutional bedding dominated the room. A TV mounted high on the wall was playing a soap opera and the room smelled of antiseptic and the faint ammonia of urine.

The bed was empty. He wondered if they had come to the wrong room until he saw Kate's attention was focused on the window, where he now realized a woman sat in a wheelchair staring out.

She had dirty-blond hair with glaring bald patches. It wasn't unkempt, just long and unstyled. An oxygen line tethered her from a nasal cannula to the wall and she wore a sweat suit the color of kiwi fruit.

As he looked closer, he saw a face worn down by the grim ravages of time and a harsh life. She had a two-inch scar on her cheek, a quarter-sized pockmark on the other and she was missing a tooth.

There was a blankness to her features, an emptiness, and Hunter's heart sank.

Kate's brother was right, this was likely a wasted trip. How could this pitiful creature tell them anything?

Kate's eyes, blue and stormy, gave away some of her tumult as she stared at the faded shell of the woman she had both loved and hated. He saw she had reached the same grim conclusion he had—that their mission was doomed to failure—but still she drew a deep breath and walked into the room.

If he hadn't already loved her, he would have tumbled at that moment, hard and fast.

"Hello." Kate walked in and sat in one of the vinyl armchairs near the wheelchair.

Brenda Golightly narrowed her eyes then blinked

rapidly several times as if coming awake from a long sleep. "Do I know you? I don't think I know you. Are you a new nurse? I don't like new nurses. Jane is my favorite nurse. She brings me extra pudding. Do you like pudding? I like pudding."

For all its singsong pitch, her voice was rough and raspy—from the oxygen or from her life choices, Hunter couldn't tell. Her speech was slightly slurred, rounded a little at the vowels.

At least she was verbal, he thought wryly, as she went on for several moments longer about her favorite kind of pudding.

He was certainly no developmental expert but she seemed more like a child of seven or eight than a woman in her fifties. He found it rather disconcerting to hear inane, innocent chatter from someone who looked so world-weary and hardened.

After a moment, Kate put a hand on Brenda's knee to distract her from her soliloquy. "I'm not a new nurse. I... It's me. Kate. Katie."

At first, Hunter didn't see any visible reaction on Brenda's features and he wondered if she had even heard the words, then Brenda gave Kate a furtive, wary look out of the corner of her gaze.

After a moment, she gave a sharp, raspy laugh. "You're not *my* Katie! My Katie is little! You're all grown up."

Kate knotted her fingers together, obviously disconcerted.

"No." She cleared her throat, her eyes so distressed Hunter wanted to bundle her up and carry her out of here. "It's me, M-Mama. Katie."

Brenda smiled at something Hunter couldn't see. "I

have a little girl named Katie. She's so pretty. Her hair is blond like yours, but she's just a little girl. She likes pudding, too. She has a doll named Barbara. Her doll has brown hair and freckles. I wish I had a doll named Barbara. Do you have any dolls?"

"Um, not anymore." Kate's attempt at a smile just about broke his heart. He couldn't stand the defeated devastation he saw in her eyes as she listened to Brenda and absorbed the true extent of her brain injury.

He saw all her hope for answers slip away like her childhood and he knew he couldn't sit by and watch it go.

He pasted on a smile he was far from feeling and stepped toward the two women, pulling a second armchair over to them.

"Hi, Brenda. I'm Hunter."

She studied him solemnly but said nothing. As he tried to formulate a strategy for questioning her, he noticed a couple of crayon drawings taped near the bed. Simple pictures of flowers and houses and trees, but he saw one that looked like a little girl with blond curly hair.

"Do you have any pictures of your little girl?"

He thought for a moment she wasn't going to answer him, then Brenda nodded. "I drew some."

He pointed toward the pictures by the bed. "Is that one?"

Her reserve melted like an ice-cream cone under the hot tropical sun and she nodded more vigorously.

"It's nice," he said.

"I have more. Do you want to see?"

"Sure."

She pointed him toward a drawer in the bedside

table. He opened it and stared at the contents. Stacks and stacks of drawings showed the same little girl in a pink dress with yellow-crayon hair and huge blue eyes.

He took a few out and showed them to Kate, who looked stunned and baffled.

"These are very good."

"Told you she was pretty."

"You were right. Brenda, where is Katie?"

"Right there, in the pictures."

"No, where's the real Katie?" he asked gently.

Brenda blinked at him again then her eyes suddenly filled up with tears. "Gone. She's gone."

"Where?"

"They took her. It's not fair. They took her."

"Who took her?"

"The bad people. They said I wasn't a good mama but I was. I was!" The tears vanished as quickly as they had come. "I took care of her. I brushed her hair. I gave her animal crackers and dressed her in pretty pink clothes. I was a good mama but they took her and hid her from me."

Her eyes darted to his with a sly, sidelong look. "But I showed them. They hid her from me but I was smart and I found her. I found her and I stole her back."

Ah. Here it was. What they had traveled three thousand miles to learn. His heart pounding, he leaned forward. "Stole her back? How did you do that?"

She ignored his question, her eyes focused on Kate with such a fierce look of concentration Hunter wondered if somehow they were finally beginning to unwind the gauzy layers of memory. Maybe this damaged woman with her vague eyes and her worn-out body was beginning to reconcile the child to the woman.

Brenda stared at Kate for a long time, her dark eyes intense, then a radiant smile burst out, broken tooth and all. "Chocolate pudding is my favorite. What's yours?"

Kate's gaze shifted to his and the anguish in her eyes cut his heart to shreds. She swallowed hard a few times then mustered a grim facsimile of a smile. "Um, I like rice pudding. And tapioca."

Brenda rocked with sudden sharp laughter, one pale hand clapped over her mouth to contain her glee. "Ew. Tapioca tastes like fish eggs. I only like chocolate and banana."

Hunter broke in before she wandered off again about pudding. "You said you found Kate again," he said, trying to draw her back. "Where did you find her?"

Brenda didn't seem to mind his efforts to shepherd her through the conversation. She smoothed a finger over the construction-paper portrait, that hard, used-up face gentling a little. "They hid her from me but I always looked for her. You can't take a baby from her mama. It's wrong. Don't you think it's wrong?"

Hunter couldn't think how to answer that so he just nodded.

"Me, too. I looked and looked for her and one day I was driving my car and there she was. My little girl. My Katie." Her voice took on a defiant edge. "She was mine and they shouldn't have taken her so I took her back and we ran away where the bad people couldn't find us."

"But they did, didn't they?" Kate spoke up, her voice rough, strained. "She was taken away from you again, wasn't she? And this time you didn't want her back."

The sly defiance on Brenda's features just as quickly turned to anger. Her face suddenly turned an alarming puce and her thin, nearly concave chest started heaving violently. "Go away. I don't want you here. Go away! Where's my pudding? Where's Jane? I want my pudding!"

By the end she was nearly shouting, flailing her arms around violently, and Kate rose and laid a gentle hand on Brenda's arms.

"Okay. Okay," she murmured in a slow, nonthreatening voice she undoubtedly used with children in her medical practice. "We'll get you some pudding."

She had reached for Brenda's bony hand and it took Hunter a few moments to realize Kate was taking the woman's pulse.

"I think it's best if you rest now while we buzz for Jane, all right?"

Somehow Kate seemed to stow away her own distress at dredging up this painful past. Her voice was brisk, professional, but still calming. "Let's get you back into your bed now."

Hunter had never been very comfortable with strong emotion. The Judge certainly hadn't encouraged it in his only son. Bradshaw men were strong, stoic, invincible. They certainly weren't supposed to throw temper tantrums or—God forbid—shed tears about anything.

Hunter had made a conscious decision to follow his father's somewhat bloodless example rather than the wild pendulum of his mother's mood swings. Angela Bradshaw had enough strong emotions for all of them, with bitter, angry episodes or bone-deep depression followed with jarring, dizzying speed by frenetic gaiety.

Her bipolar disease had made his childhood unpredictable and precarious and he had never been sure when he came home from school whether she would smother him with kisses when he walked through the door or screech and yell at him for some infraction or other.

His father's way was safer. He had learned that even before the bitter humiliation of his arrest. In jail, he had done everything he could to shut off whatever stray emotions might flicker through him at odd moments. He couldn't afford to feel in prison, to show any sign of weakness, of fear or anger or bitterness. So he had shown nothing. Had become nothing.

But as he watched Kate carefully tuck in this woman who had brought her nothing but pain—who had stolen her from a happy, healthy home life and thrust her into a dark and terrifying world he could only imagine—all those emotions he had suppressed for so long rose up in his throat and threatened to choke him.

He was appalled at the burn of tears behind his eyes at her gentleness. He blinked them away, grateful Kate was too busy tending to Brenda to see the telltale sheen of moisture.

How could she do it? he wondered. Show compassion and kindness to the catalyst of her pain?

A nurse responded quickly to Kate's page. The infamous Jane of the extra pudding, she noted by her name tag. She was blond and round, in hospital scrubs printed with grinning cats.

"What's this now?" the nurse asked as she helped her transfer Brenda from the chair to the bed.

Though she wanted nothing more than to run out, away from this sterile room and this wild, tangled rush of emotions, Kate forced herself to focus on Brenda's physical symptoms.

"I'm afraid our visit has agitated her. I was concerned about her color and her pulse rate is nearly one-fifty."

"Oh, dear. We can't have that now, can we?"

Kate watched the nurse tuck in the blankets, then pick up the crayon drawing Brenda had been showing them from the floor where she had dropped it in her frenzy.

She slipped it through Brenda's curled fingers and Kate was startled to see the silly, childlike crayon drawing seemed to have some kind of calming effect on Brenda.

Not sure how to identify the odd emotion tugging at her insides, Kate watched her clutch it like a talisman.

The nurse's voice was calm, soothing. "Take a nap now and when you wake up, you'll feel better, just in time for lunch."

Brenda nodded, obediently closing her eyes like a child expecting a birthday surprise when she opened them.

Kate didn't expect her to sleep but their visit must have sapped her energy reserves, obviously low. A moment later her breathing slowed and her thin chest began to rise and fall slowly.

The nurse waited until she slept, then picked up Brenda's chart off the end of the bed and made a few notations.

"How often does she have these episodes?" Kate asked.

The nurse's gentle demeanor with her patient turned cool as she surveyed them. "I'm afraid federal privacy regulations prevent me from talking to you about her condition."

"I know all about HPAA. I'm a doctor."

"Not *her* doctor."

Kate drew a breath into lungs that felt tight and achy. "No," she agreed. "But I also know you can speak with immediate family. I'm her…"

She faltered, not quite knowing how to complete the sentence. "My name is Kate Spencer," she finally said. "But I legally changed it to that when I was eighteen. Before that, my name was Katie Golightly."

The nurse's eyes widened with shock, her arms going slack. "Oh, my word! You're Katie! She talks about you all the time. I thought you were dead!"

Emotions crowded Kate, too many for her to handle at once. She pushed them all away for now. "No. I'm very much alive."

"And a doctor! She never said a word."

"Can you tell me about her condition? I know she had a TBI a few years ago but that doesn't account for all her symptoms."

Jane fidgeted with the chart but not before Kate saw evasiveness war with compassion. "Perhaps you should talk to her doctor. I'm sure Dr. Singh would have no problem with you studying her charts. He should be in this afternoon."

"I won't be here that long. We're just passing through."

That information apparently didn't sit well with the nurse. Her amazed expression gave way to disapproval. "I see."

She didn't. She couldn't possibly. How could this stranger understand the layers and layers of emotions here when Kate herself couldn't comprehend them?

She decided to try a different tack. "One of the first things Brenda talked about when we arrived is how you're her favorite nurse. She said you give her extra pudding."

Jane's sudden coldness eased enough for her to smile a little. "It's just a little thing but it makes her happy. She does like her pudding."

"Please. You seem like a kind woman. All I'm asking is for a little information."

The nurse studied the drawing clutched in Brenda's hands then looked at Kate again. "She has cancer. Non-Hodgkins lymphoma."

She digested this and its implications. "AIDS?"

Jane's slow nod confirmed what Kate had already begun to suspect. Non-Hodgkins lymphoma, though it can appear in the regular population, had a greatly increased frequency in people infected with the AIDS virus.

She supposed she wasn't really surprised by the grim diagnosis. Brenda's lifestyle as a drug user and sometime prostitute made her a prime candidate to acquire the virus.

"Full blown," the nurse said, her brisk voice a contrast to the sadness in her eyes. "She's already had pneumococcal pneumonia twice this year. The cancer seems to be in remission for now but as I'm sure you know, it's very hard to control in AIDS patients. She could relapse anytime. I'm very sorry to have to tell you this way."

Kate studied the wasted frame sleeping on the bed, suddenly awash with sorrow and regret for this woman who had lived such a hard life. What had led her down this road? she wondered, slightly ashamed of herself for never bothering to find out.

She knew very little about Brenda's history. Those

weren't the kinds of questions a child asks a mother, especially one as unstable as Brenda, and as a teenager, she had been too angry and bitter at her for not letting the Spencers adopt her that it never would have occurred to her to dig into her past.

"Look, I'm going to give you my cell number and my pager number in Utah. Will you put it in her chart and have someone contact me when…when her condition changes?"

Jane looked at her for a moment, then to Kate's surprise she reached out and squeezed her fingers. "I will."

She bustled out of the room, leaving Kate and Hunter alone.

"Do you want to wait until Brenda wakes up and talk to her again?" Hunter asked after she left.

Kate touched the frail hand holding a crayon drawing, then lifted her gaze. "No. I don't want to upset her again. There's nothing for me here."

No answers to find and no one to blame.

Chapter 14

She was shutting him out, building walls around herself more effectively than all the concertina wire in the world.

Hunter's hands gripped the steering wheel as his Grand Cherokee rattled over yet another of Henry Flagler's bridges. Water surrounded them on both sides, stretching out as far as the eye could see. There might as well have been an ocean between him and Kate, too, he thought.

She sat beside him, her face as composed and serene as a burial mask, but he knew damn well it was all an act. He had seen her eyes when they walked out of that nursing home, had seen the raw emotions in those lovely blue depths.

But somehow through the past hour she found a way to hide it all away while they picked Belle up from their cottage, checked out and headed through the merry holiday traffic away from Key West toward Miami.

Until they were on the road, she had kept up a steady stream of cheerful, light conversation. Every time he tried to draw the conversation back to Brenda and their interview with her, Kate either answered him with a monosyllable or ignored his question altogether, deliberately changing the subject.

She was shutting him out and he couldn't do a damn thing about it. Worse, he didn't have the first clue how to handle the hurt pulsing through him that she wouldn't let him reach her, even after all they had shared these last few days.

"You know, you can't keep doing this forever," he said suddenly.

He couldn't read her eyes behind her sunglasses but he saw one thin eyebrow arch above the curve of tortoiseshell plastic. "Keep doing what?"

"This game of duck and run. You'll have to talk about it sometime."

She leaned her head against the seat. "I know. But not yet. Please, Hunter."

How could he ignore that entreaty in her voice? He had certainly had plenty of experience burying his emotions down deep. If she wasn't ready to talk about what had happened with Brenda Golightly earlier, he wouldn't badger her.

"I don't remember when I've ever been so tired," Kate said as the tires spun along the raised highway. "Would it bother you if I try to sleep for a while?"

"Of course not," he said, uncomfortable with the guilt pinching at him. Neither of them had slept much the last two nights. He couldn't seem to get enough of her—all she had to do was smile and he wanted her, with a fierce hunger that didn't ease even in the warm, peaceful aftermath of their lovemaking.

They would steal small slices of sleep but most of their nights—and days—had been spent in each other's arms.

Now Kate would barely look him in the eye, at least not without the buffer of her sunglasses. He tried not to feel hurt when she curled up on the seat, her back to him, but it sure as hell felt like a rejection.

Ignoring the sting and the deeper sense of loss at the apparent end to the closeness they had shared, he fiddled with the radio until he found something classical and relaxing.

"That's nice," she murmured with a soft smile over her shoulder. "Thank you. I don't need long. Wake me in an hour or so, would you?"

He didn't expect her to sleep. More likely she would feign sleep to prevent him from badgering her more about Brenda.

After a few miles with the gentle music and the low hum of the tires as her lullaby, soon Kate's breathing slowed and those slender knotted shoulders relaxed.

Good, he thought. She needed the rest. No matter what kind of bright, cheerful face she tried to put on it, he knew the visit to the nursing home had been draining for her.

He exhaled slowly. It hadn't exactly been a piece of cake for him either. Even the reading of the verdict in his trial hadn't seemed as stressful as the morning they had just endured, maybe because by the time the jury had rendered its verdict, Hunter had already resigned himself that conviction would be inevitable.

The case against him had been a strong one and public sentiment had run high that he was guilty.

What had they learned from Brenda Golightly? Kate would probably say nothing they didn't already know but in the past few hours Hunter's subconscious—the part of his brain that used to always be working a case even when he wasn't aware of it—had been busy formulating a theory.

From what little she said, he would bet his new SUV that she had given birth to a child named Katie Golightly around the same time Charlotte McKinnon had been born to Sam and Lynn McKinnon. Perhaps in Nevada, perhaps somewhere else. Kate had a birth certificate that showed her as being born to Brenda and an unnamed father so presumably a Katie Golightly once existed somewhere.

Judging by what Brenda had said, he surmised that the child had been taken away from her.

She was mine and they shouldn't have taken her so I took her back and we ran away where the bad people couldn't find us. That's what she had said.

He would talk to Gage McKinnon about following the paper trail to see if a child was removed from her custody in Nevada in the months prior to Charlotte McKinnon's kidnapping.

All this was speculation, but judging by the woman's history of substance abuse and borderline mental illness, he could guess she was probably high that fateful summer day when she happened to drive through the McKinnons' Las Vegas neighborhood.

She must have seen Charlotte playing in her yard. In a drug-induced psychosis, it would have been easy for her to convince herself the child was Katie Golightly, that she was only taking back what was hers.

Would this information give Kate any solace? He doubted it. But at least she might be able to reach some kind of understanding, a peace of sorts. Despite her problems, Brenda had obviously loved her daughter and grieved for her loss enough to try to take her back.

He shifted his gaze from the road for a moment to Kate's curved back. He had wanted so much to help her, to ease her tumult, and his failure gnawed at him.

Maybe if he could have helped her, some of his own sense of inadequacy would have dissipated a little. He had spent his time behind bars living each moment with the sobering knowledge that for all his skills as a detective, he had been powerless against the fates that conspired to put him on death row. This morning had been a grim reminder that for all his freedom now there were sometimes circumstances in life he couldn't control.

He couldn't control his feelings for Kate. Despite his better judgment—and his best effort—he had fallen in love with her, for all the good it did him. He planned to keep that little nugget of information to himself.

The last thing she needed right now was another snarl in an already tangled life.

She was having a tough enough time coming to terms with her past. He wouldn't complicate things even more for her. With all she had on her plate, she didn't need a bitter ex-con with a hazy future stepping up to clutter her life, too.

As he drove north, he couldn't help feeling like he was leaving behind warmth and sunshine and heading back into the cold.

* * *

She dreamed she was three years old again, her chubby legs planted on a wide grassy field, with the sun bright in her eyes and the world brimming with joy.

She couldn't decide what to do first, somersault across the field or twirl around, arms out and her frilly pink skirt flying high, until she was so dizzy she fell over in a heap.

She started to clap her hands with glee, then she realized instead of arms and hands she had thick braided ropes at the end of her shoulders that she could only wave helplessly.

Suddenly she found herself surrounded by all the players in the drama of her life. The McKinnons—Sam, Lynn and much younger versions of Gage and Wyatt—stood on one side while on the other were Maryanne and Tom Spencer, along with her two best friends from junior high school and Mr. Moffat, her high school science teacher, of all people.

A whistle blew somewhere and an instant later Kate felt a tug on her rope-arms and found herself in the middle of a deadly serious battle of tug-of-war. Her shoulders were nearly dislocated as both teams did their best to pull her to their side.

She cried out for them to stop but no one seemed to be paying the slightest bit of attention to her. Neither side seemed to be gaining an advantage but their efforts were fierce.

At last, when she wasn't sure she could stand another moment, a woman with dirty blond hair and a missing front tooth wheeled out onto the grassy field.

Right there in the middle of the game she picked up Kate, rope arms and all, piled her onto her lap and rolled off the field away from all the players, with Kate screaming and crying out for her to stop...

"Kate? Everything okay?"

The deep voice intruded into her nightmare and Kate woke with a start, the coppery taste of blood in her mouth. It took her a few seconds to realize she must have bitten her lip in her sleep.

She was disoriented for a moment, trapped there in that odd, surreal place between sleep and consciousness.

"You were dreaming. Must have been a doozy. You were crying out."

She found Hunter watching her, his eyes solemn and concerned, and his lean, familiar features calmed her.

Right. They were in his SUV again, heading northwest, back to Utah and the McKinnons, where she belonged.

"I'm all right now," she said, dabbing her lip with a tissue from the console.

"What were you dreaming?"

"Nothing. I don't remember." She ignored her qualm over the lie. "Where are we?"

"A ways past Fort Myers," Hunter replied. "We should be in St. Petersburg by dinnertime."

She straightened. "St. Petersburg?"

"I told you we could stop in and visit the Spencers while we're in Florida. Give you a chance to drop off those presents you bought them in Key West. We can even stay for a day or two if you'd like."

To her horror, hot tears burned her eyes. How could such a hard, unrelenting man have these astonishing bouts of kindness? She blinked back her tears, knowing they would only embarrass them both. "Thank you, Hunter."

He shrugged off her gratitude, as he had been doing all week whenever she tried to tell him how much his help meant to her.

"I'd like to meet them, anyway," he said, his voice gruff. "They sound like remarkable people."

Suddenly she was aware of a deep hunger to see her foster parents, to wrap her arms around Tom's comfortable bulk and find center again in Maryanne's calm, eternally serene expression. It suddenly seemed like exactly the place she needed to be.

"They are wonderful. You'll like them and I know they'll like you."

"Prison record and all?"

She narrowed her gaze at him. "You don't have a record. It was expunged."

"Right." He gave that self-mocking smile she hated, the one she realized she hadn't seen for a while. "Too bad I can't expunge the last three years so easily."

She hadn't heard that grim note to his voice for several days either. Its return left her inexpressibly sad. She had hoped he was moving past his anger at what had happened to him.

"If we've made it past this far, I must have been sleeping for hours," she murmured. "Through Miami and Ft. Lauderdale and Alligator Alley. You should have woke me."

"You needed the rest."

She hadn't been getting much sleep the last few nights. The reason why sat next to her in the driver's seat, just a hint of afternoon shadow stubbling his jaw. He looked big and powerful and incredibly sexy, even with the hardness in his eyes.

She hadn't *wanted* to sleep much the last few nights,

not when she was exactly where she needed to be, wrapped in his arms.

She had a fierce sudden desire to be there again, to feel him around her and inside her again, and wondered with a pang if she would ever have the chance.

A muscle flexed in his jaw suddenly and she wondered if he could somehow guess the direction of her thoughts. Color soaked her cheeks and she pretended extreme interest in the passing scenery.

"Do you feel better?" Hunter asked at her silence.

She thought of that terrible dream, the horrible sensation that she was being torn apart.

"I don't know," she admitted. "Physically, yes."

She didn't add that emotionally her psyche felt as battered and bloody as the gang members she treated after a nasty street fight.

Maybe she didn't need to share that information with him. The way he looked at her, his eyes fathomless and dark, she thought maybe he already knew.

After nearly a week on the road, Hunter likely knew her better than anyone else in the world. She found it an alarming realization, especially as she wasn't even sure she knew herself anymore.

"I should probably stop for gas soon," he said.

"I imagine Belle could use a good run."

"Yeah, probably." He took the next exit where a cluster of gas stations squatted in the sun.

"Do me a favor, will you?"

She looked at him quizzically.

"Try not to get into trouble while we're here. No more adventures. No pregnant women ready to pop, no blind men who need a lift to Memphis, no drunk college boys looking for a little action. Let's just make this a simple pit stop, okay?"

She laughed a little, as she realized he had intended. "I'll do my best. Although I'll remind you I had nothing to do with the college boys. That was all you, Detective."

As if their time together in Key West had altered their established pattern, this time Kate insisted on pumping the gas so that Hunter could exercise Belle.

"You've been driving the whole time I slept so you deserve a little rest," she told him firmly.

After a small argument, Hunter finally ceded defeat and grabbed Belle's leash and a ball then headed toward a grassy field next to the filling station.

Kate finished filling the tank, then wandered over to watch them. This was another of those moments she would store in her memory bank. The pure joy of a gleeful dog and her master at play.

How many more moments like this would she have? In a few days they would be home and would go their separate ways. She would still see him, she had no doubt of that. His sister was her best friend so it was inevitable that the paths of their respective lives would intersect again but nothing would be the same.

She wouldn't think about it, she decided as sadness slipped over her like clouds over the sun. It would be foolish to waste their few remaining days together worrying about the inevitable pain of their parting.

What if they didn't have to part? The thought, insidious and seductive, slithered across her mind. What if she walked right over to him, took his face in her hands and told him she was hopelessly in love with him?

No. She couldn't do that to him. He didn't share her feelings and she wouldn't burden him with them.

He deserved a woman who was whole and healthy, not someone fractured and damaged, someone desperately afraid the broken pieces of herself would never come together again.

The moment Hunter drove down the quiet street in a comfortably middle-class St. Petersburg neighborhood and parked in front of the dearly familiar rose brick house, Kate felt some of those stray pieces of herself start jostling back into place.

She loved this place. From the hanging begonias on the front porch to the carefully tended lawn to the colorful Christmas lights Tom insisted on stringing across all available surfaces every year.

She jumped from the car, ready to race up and fling open the door like a child racing home from school, but she forced herself to wait with hard-won patience for Hunter to let Belle out of her crate and leash her before she hurried up the walkway with him.

Though it felt odd to ring the doorbell of the house she had spent so much of her life in, she didn't feel right about bursting in when they weren't expecting her.

Long moments passed while they waited for someone to answer, until she began to have the horrible fear that perhaps they weren't home.

Maybe they were traveling. She had spoken with Maryanne a few days before Wyatt and Taylor's wedding the week before and she hadn't said a word about going anywhere, but Tom was in the habit of coming home from work with itchy feet and dragging Maryanne on one of their impromptu jaunts across the South.

It seemed desperately important that they be home. She held her breath and only let it out when she heard yipping behind the door. Their little shitzu Lily was a fierce guard dog, even if she only weighed about fifteen pounds.

A moment later she heard a deep voice ordering her to be quiet, for the love of Pete, and a moment later the door swung open.

Her foster father stared out at her for just an instant. Then his broad, handsome face lit up with joy.

"Pumpkin? What on earth?"

He opened his arms and she walked into them, closing her eyes to savor the distinctive scents of wintergreen LifeSavers and Old Spice.

He held her close, rocking a little in the doorway, while Lily and Belle sniffed each other.

"How's my favorite doctor?"

She smiled against his broad, sturdy chest. "Great. How's mine?"

"Couldn't be better, especially since my best girl's come home." He pulled away long enough to call down the hallway.

"Maryanne, you better come on out and see who's come a-knocking."

A moment later, Maryanne walked in wiping her hands on her favorite apron, one Kate had sewed for her years ago in home economics.

When she caught sight of Kate in the doorway, amazement leaped into those calm brown eyes and she gasped with delight. "Katie? Oh, darling, what a wonderful surprise!"

She pulled her from Tom's arms and wrapped her in her arms tightly. Kate hugged her back, barely able to breathe through the love coursing through her for these people who had taken her in and given her a chance.

Though they had talked several times since she learned the results of that DNA test confirming she was Charlotte McKinnon, she hadn't seen them since. Now, wrapped in the arms of their love, she finally realized how afraid she had been about this moment. Deep in her heart, she had been dreadfully afraid things had been forever changed between them.

She needn't have worried.

"Oh, I can't tell you how marvelous it is to see you!" Maryanne pressed her warm cheek to Kate's. "But what are you doing here? I thought you said last week you weren't going to be able to come for Christmas."

"I can't stay that long. I'm starting my newborn ICU rotation Christmas morning."

Disappointment flickered in those brown eyes but Maryanne squeezed her hands. "Well, you're here now and that's the important thing. You'll stay the night, of course. You and your friend."

Hunter! Kate stepped back, appalled at her horrible manners. She had left Hunter and Belle standing on the porch during her happy reunion with the Spencers.

She pulled him inside, noting immediately that Belle and Lily had rekindled their friendship begun a few years ago when the Spencers came out to Utah for an impromptu ski trip.

"I'm sorry. Tom, Maryanne, this is Hunter Bradshaw, Taylor's brother. And of course you remember Belle."

She had been a little nervous at their reaction to Hunter but again, she should have known better. Tom reached around her and shook Hunter's hand.

"Mr. Bradshaw. It's a real pleasure. We've heard a lot about you."

Hunter looked a little disconcerted at that information and sent Kate a questioning look.

To her dismay, she could feel herself blush. "Taylor," she explained quickly. "Tom and Maryanne met her when they came to Utah to visit and then she and I drove out here together a few years ago."

"Right."

"Come in, come in," Maryanne said. "I was just getting ready to fry up some chicken. I was making extra for Tom's lunch later in the week so there's plenty for both of you."

"Do I have time to walk the dog first before dinner?" Hunter asked.

"Why, of course," Maryanne answered with Southern politeness. "Will half an hour give you enough time?"

He nodded and Tom grabbed Lily's leash off its hook by the door. "Mind some company?" he asked.

Hunter looked a little uncomfortable at the idea but he shook his head.

"Good," Tom said with a smile. "While Maryanne works her usual magic in the kitchen, you can tell me what brings you both all this way."

Kate watched them go, praying fiercely that Tom wouldn't pull his concerned-father routine and subject Hunter to the third degree.

She watched them walk to the end of the driveway and head west before she followed Maryanne into the kitchen.

The familiar smells and sights in the room seemed to instantly transport her to her teenage years, sitting at the bar, dipping graham crackers in milk and telling

Maryanne about her day while they waited for Tom to come home so he could help her with her Trig homework.

"It's so good to be here," she told Maryanne truthfully.

"Now what's this all about? What are you doing in Florida? And with Taylor's brother, of all people."

Kate took her usual stool at the bar, not sure where to begin. She finally cut to the heart of the matter.

"Looking for Brenda."

"Oh, baby." Maryanne looked up from dipping the chicken pieces in her special blend, her eyes deep and dark with compassion. "What were you hoping to find?"

"Why she did it. Why me instead of some other poor little girl. I had to try to find out. I *had* to. It was Hunter's idea but as soon as he offered to search for her, I knew this was something I had to do."

"Did you find her?"

Kate gripped both hands around Maryanne's ever-present cup of tea. "Yes. She's in a Key West nursing home after a drug overdose a few years ago. She's in bad shape with AIDS-related cancer and the overdose left her with lasting brain damage."

Maryanne frowned. "So you weren't able to find any answers."

She thought of the little they had learned, of those few tantalizing moments when she thought Brenda recognized her and was ready to tell all. "Not what I was hoping for, anyway."

"How did you feel, seeing her?"

Her foster mother was always asking questions like

that, forcing Kate to examine her actions and reactions. She should have been a shrink, Kate thought.

How did winning that geography bee make you feel? Why do you think you made that kind of decision to break curfew? How could you have handled the conflict with your English teacher better?

The third degree used to drive her crazy but now she recognized it for what it was; Maryanne's not-so-subtle method of helping a troubled, confused young girl learn to sort through her wild jumble of emotions to find the truly important ones.

"I don't hate her. I thought I did—from about the third or fourth time she refused to give up her parental rights so you could adopt me, I thought I hated her. You know I did. I expected to feel that hot, familiar weight of it as I walked into her room. But seeing her lying there so frail and worn-out, I felt nothing. Nothing but sadness."

Maryanne appeared to think about this as she added the chicken to the oil. The kitchen was filled with their merry sizzle and delicious scent before she finally spoke.

"You know, the other day I lost my car keys. While I was searching the house for them, I accidentally discovered—to my considerable dismay, you can be sure—that the diamond had fallen out of my wedding ring setting. The big one. I only realized it when I happened to see something glittering on the dresser in the bedroom while I was there searching the room for my keys. If I hadn't been scatterbrained enough to lose my keys in the first place and go looking for them, who knows when I would have realized that diamond was missing and where it would have ended up by then?"

Her gaze met Kate's and she smiled. "Life is funny that way. Sometimes we think we're looking for one thing when, really, what we end up finding is something else entirely. Something we never even realized was missing."

That was something else Maryanne was always doing. She seemed to have a parable for everything, from losing a soccer game to learning the correct way to sort laundry.

"What's that supposed to mean?"

"You think about it. What do you think is more important? Finding out why things happened to you or learning to find peace with it even if you never know the reasons?"

Before she could puzzle this out, she heard the bustle of two men and two dogs returning through the front door.

"Hope that chicken is almost done," Tom said as they walked into the kitchen. "That smells enough to bring a man to his knees. Isn't that right, Bradshaw?"

"Absolutely." A corner of Hunter's mouth quirked up and Kate's heart turned over with love for him.

She may not have found answers or peace on this trip but she had certainly found her own treasure, better than a loose diamond. Too bad she wouldn't be able to keep it.

Chapter 15

Hunter couldn't sleep.

He found that odd, really, because the Spencers' guest room was the most comfortably, cozy space he had inhabited for a long time. With a bed as wide and deep as a mountain lake, crisp, cool cotton sheets and a stack of paperbacks by the bed, he should have been completely content.

But his arms felt empty and familiar restlessness prowled through him.

He missed Kate.

She was the reason he had wandered the guest room for the last two hours, until he knew every inch of it. The discovery wasn't a pleasant one. Though he had only spent two glorious days with Kate in his arms and his bed, the prospect of a night without her left him hollow.

What worried him most was that making love to her wasn't the thing he missed most, but those priceless, peaceful moments he held her while she slept, tenderness a sweet, heavy ache in his chest.

"Damn, I've got it bad," he said out loud.

Belle, curled up on the floor, blinked at him sleepily then snuffled and went back to sleep.

Hunter sighed and wandered to the window again. Outside in the Spencers' backyard, their pool gleamed blue in the moonlight, cool and inviting. If he had brought a suit along he would have worked some of this restlessness off with a good hard swim.

He was almost tempted to go out, anyway, but since he didn't relish the idea of Kate's foster parents wandering out to find him skinny-dipping in their swimming pool, he discarded the idea.

He liked Tom and Maryanne Spencer. They seemed genuinely good people, the kind of grounded souls who calmed everyone lucky enough to wander into their sphere.

On their walk earlier with the dog, he had been sure Tom would grill him, the kind of paternal interrogation a father subjects to any man who drags his daughter across the country.

He braced himself, waiting for Tom Spencer to bring up his prison time—or at least ask if he was sleeping with Kate. But the good doctor only asked about the weather on their trip, what kind of highway mileage his Grand Cherokee got, if they had visited any maritime museums when they were in the Keys.

Only as they turned around and started back toward the house did he ask in a quiet, calm voice how Hunter was adjusting to the world after his incarceration.

Hunter had almost brushed him off with a curt answer but something had compelled him to tell Tom Spencer the truth.

"It's a struggle," he had admitted to Kate's foster father. "But every day seems a little easier."

Tom had smiled and patted him on the shoulder as if Hunter were seven years old. "You're going to be fine, son. Just fine."

The strange thing was, for the first time in a long time, Hunter almost believed him. He kept thinking about Henry Monroe's words earlier in the week, about having a choice to make when he started to go blind.

I could sit there in my house until I died, scared and angry and bitter. Or I could go on living. I decided to go on.

He needed to make that choice, too, but he didn't know how.

Dinner had been enjoyable, he remembered now as he gazed out at the play of moonlight on water. Maryanne's fried chicken had been perfect, crispy and spicy and melt-in-your-mouth delicious. The conversation had jumped all over the place but through it all he had sensed the deep love running like a river through that dining room.

Kate adored them and they obviously returned her affection.

Hunter had never considered himself a touchy-feely kind of person but throughout the evening they spent together he had wanted to grab both Maryanne and Tom in a tight hug and thank them for rescuing a scared, troubled young girl.

With another sigh, he traced a finger down the window. What the hell was he going to do about Kate?

He thought of the courage it must have taken for her to walk into that room at the nursing home earlier that day. It humbled him. She was brave enough to face her fears yet he cowered here, afraid to tell her how much he loved her.

That was the crux of the matter. He had been telling himself since that day on the beach when he realized he had fallen headlong for her that keeping quiet about his feelings was some kind of high-minded, magnanimous gesture. She deserved better, he had told himself.

That hadn't been the issue at all. He faced that now, just past midnight, alone in his room. Really, it all came down to a choice, just like Henry had talked about.

A choice he still wasn't sure he was capable of making.

To reach for Kate and the happiness and contentment that beckoned with her, he would have to let go of all the ugliness, all the hate. There wasn't room in his life and his heart for both.

Was he strong enough to make that choice—to release his anger and bitterness over Martin James and the lives he had taken, the time he had stolen from Hunter—so he could grab hold of something better?

He didn't know. That was the hell of it. So he holed out here in this comfortable guest room, exhaustion seeping through him, more lonely than he had been, even during those dark nights at the Point of the Mountain.

He was just about to give up and toss and turn in the bed for a while when he saw movement out in the lovely yard, a dark shadow slipping out of the house and wandering toward the pool.

Kate.

In the pale, clouded moonlight, he saw she was dressed in a gauzy white nightgown and looked fragile, otherworldly, like something off the cover of one of those spooky haunted-mansion-type novels his sister used to read.

His heart seemed to twist in his chest as he watched her standing by the pool, gazing up at the stars.

The urge to go to her blew through him like a hurricane but he didn't dare. Until he figured out whether he was ready to live again, he would be best to keep his distance.

He would have stayed in his guest room and tried to sleep if the moon hadn't slipped from behind the clouds and captured her features in pale moonlight.

The twist of emotions there broke his heart.

Without taking time to think through the consequences, Hunter made his silent way through the house and out into the quiet backyard.

Kate looked up when he opened the door but said nothing as he approached.

"Nice night," he murmured.

"In a few days we'll be back to single-digit temperatures and whiteouts. I figured I had better enjoy a pleasant night while I have the chance since we won't see one in Utah until June."

"Mind if I join you?"

She gestured to the plastic chaise lounge next to her and they both sat there, gazing up at the stars.

"You ready to talk about things yet?" he asked after a moment.

She didn't say anything for a full thirty seconds. "What time is it?" she finally said.

Disappointment flickered through him at what he thought was another attempt to change the subject.

"About half past midnight."

"It's officially my birthday then."

He stared. "Why didn't you say something? Or the Spencers? They didn't say a word about it all evening. I would have thought Maryanne would have at least whipped up a cake for you."

"They probably don't even know."

"How could they not know it's your birthday?" he asked with a frown.

"December 19 is Charlotte McKinnon's birthday. I only learned that little bit of information after Gage and Wyatt found me. I've always celebrated my birthday on March 16. That's the date on my birth certificate. On Katie Golightly's birth certificate, I should say. I'm three months older than I always thought I was. Funny, isn't it?"

He found the whole thing remarkably unamusing, especially when her last word came out more like a sob.

He couldn't bear it, any more than he could sit by and do nothing. He rose and tugged her into his arms, then sat again with her on his lap.

She stayed frozen in his arms briefly, her spine rigid and her shoulders tight, then she seemed to sag against him. Her arms slid around him and she held on tight while a storm of tears buffeted her.

"I'm sorry," she murmured after several moments of silent weeping. "I'm so sorry, Hunter. I didn't mean to cry all over you again. I feel like all I've done for six weeks is bawl."

Her forced laugh turned into another sob. "I hate this, Hunter. I hate it."

She punched his chest for emphasis and he folded her small fist inside his hand. "I know you do. Anyone would."

"I've always refused to think of myself as a victim. It was important to me. Maybe I went through some ugly stuff when I was a kid. But then, who didn't? I survived it. More than survived it, I've built a good life for myself and I'm doing something I love, helping others. I don't want to feel like a victim but I can't seem to help it."

"You were a victim. You can't change that. You were three years old with no control at all over the situation."

"I thought seeing her today would, I don't know, give me some kind of peace. Closure. But nothing has changed. I still don't know who I am. What I am. I feel like I'm three people wrapped up in one royally screwed-up package. Which is it? Am I Katie Golightly, the poor, pitiful little girl abandoned by her junkie whore of a mother? Or Kate Spencer, M.D., beloved foster daughter of Tom and Maryanne Spencer? And where does Charlotte McKinnon and her family fit into the mix? I just don't know!"

He kissed the top of her head, love and tenderness and compassion thick in his chest. This was it, then. What he had been running from these last few days. His fears seemed insignificant compared to the need to comfort her, to try to ease her pain.

"You're all those things, Kate. All those things and more."

She made a sound of disbelief and he tightened his arms. "I know who you are. You're a smart, compassionate, beautiful woman. All those things you've been through that you want to discount have made you the person you are today."

"A mess?" She meant the words as a little self-deprecating joke but Hunter didn't laugh. Instead, he continued to hold her tightly, gazing at her with the moon shooting sparks of light through his dark hair and an intense expression in his eyes.

"A woman of great courage and strength," he said quietly. "A woman who can't sit by and do nothing when she sees anyone else in pain, whether that pain is physical or emotional."

She drew in a shaky breath, stunned by his words. "Is that really how you see me?"

He studied her, that muscle working his jaw. "Do you want to know what I see when I look at you?"

She nodded, holding her breath as her stomach suddenly jumped with nerves.

"I see a woman with every reason to hate but with this great core of love inside her. A woman who somehow found the strength of character to show the frail, broken-down shell of her kidnapper nothing but compassion and gentleness."

She let out her breath, warmth spreading through her as he went on.

"I've seen so much ugliness in my life, Kate. Parents torturing children, husbands killing wives. It's all part of a cop's life. You learn to deal with it in your own way but it still gets to you, grinds away at your spirit. And then for eighteen months I lived with men who committed crimes heinous enough to put them on death row. Murderers, rapists. Child molesters. The worst of the worst. It's enough to shake a person's faith that there's anything good and decent left in the world."

His arms tightened and she felt the light, feather-soft brush of his mouth against her hair again.

"On this trip, because of you, I've found that faith again. What I saw in that nursing home was beautiful.

The most beautiful thing I've ever seen. And it wasn't just that moment. I saw you show the same loving, healing care to a frightened mother giving birth under less than perfect circumstances and to a frail old man trying to make it to see his granddaughter dance, even though he couldn't see anything at all."

"You helped Mariah and Henry, too," she was compelled to remind him.

"Only because you pushed me into it. On this trip you've made me better than I am, Kate. I don't know if it's because of what happened to you or in spite of it but you're amazing."

He rubbed a thumb over her cheek and the tenderness of the gesture weakened her knees. She wanted to close her eyes and lean into him, to stay right here in his arms.

"You're amazing," he repeated. "How could I help but fall in love with you?"

His words didn't register at first but when they did she jerked her eyes open and jumped to her feet. "What? You *what*?"

He laughed at her stunned reaction. "I know. Shocked the heck out of me, too. I wasn't looking for it but there it is. I love you, Katie Golightly, Kate Spencer, Charlotte McKinnon. Whoever you are, I love you."

She couldn't think, couldn't breathe, could only stand there on a moonlit Florida night and stare at him. "You can't love me!"

"And yet I do."

"How can you possibly, after I dragged you across the country on this wild goose chase and have spent the whole week moaning and complaining about my poor, pitiful life?"

He laughed again and reached for her hand. His fingers caressed hers and sent twirly, twitchy little nerve impulses up her arm. "Oh, I wouldn't say that's all you've done."

Heat soaked her cheeks as she remembered trying to seduce him, as she thought of the passion they shared and her own voraciousness.

The impact of his words finally fully hit her and she sank down onto the chaise lounge again.

"You love me."

"I said so, didn't I? Why is it so hard for you to believe?"

"I never thought I would hear you say that. I...I suppose I can't believe it because I've loved you forever," she finally admitted and had the satisfaction of seeing him blink in surprise.

"You have not."

"Well, at least since the first day we met, when you were sitting in that diner with those cops. I remember it vividly. It was the middle of the night and Taylor and I walked in after studying and you were so thrilled to see her. I never had a brother and seeing how much you obviously adored your little sister was the first thing I loved about you. The more I learned about you, the more I came to love."

He reached for her and kissed her, and the emotion behind it had tears stinging her eyes again.

Several moments later, they were both breathing heavily and her body shimmered with tenderness and desire, all the more acute because she knew they couldn't act on it. Not tonight, while they were guests in her parents' house.

With a groan that told her he was every bit as

aroused as she—and understood it couldn't lead anywhere tonight—Hunter wrenched his mouth from hers.
"We have to stop now or I won't be able to."

There would be other moments, she thought as joy
winged its way through her. Moments when they would
be free to touch and taste and explore. That knowledge
lent an edge of sweet anticipation to her frustration.

"If you loved me for so long," Hunter said gruffly,
"why didn't you say anything?"

She shrugged. "A few reasons. Dru, for one thing.
She was a biggie. You started dating her right around
that time and a few months later she announced to the
world she was pregnant. You were trying to get her to
marry you and I was so angry with her for the way she
acted I wanted to punch out her pretty white teeth."

She grew quiet. "And then she was killed," she said
softly.

"And I was arrested and charged with her murder.
I don't blame you for wanting nothing to do with a
convicted felon."

"That had nothing to do with it! Nothing. I never
once believed you were guilty. You know that. I would
have poured out my feelings at any moment to you but
you didn't even want your sister to visit you in prison.
How could I suddenly show up with some story about
how I was crazy about you? I would have looked like
those desperate women who suddenly claim undying
love for men behind bars."

They were both silent as Kate pondered the amazing twists and turns in their lives that had led them
here, to this moment.

"So what now?" he asked. "I've never done this before so I'm not quite sure what comes next."

She linked her hands through his. Here it was, then, the peace she had traveled across the country to find. They had both been through tough times, but somehow they had managed to come through the other side to find each other.

"Let's go home," she said.

Epilogue

"Are you sure you're up to this?"

Six days later, Christmas Eve, they sat in Hunter's Grand Cherokee gazing out at Lynn McKinnon's cedar-and-glass house, smoke curling from the chimney and Christmas lights gleaming merrily through the fluttery snow.

Full circle, she thought.

Two weeks earlier they had stood together on Hunter's deck while mountain snow swirled around them and now here they were back under the same conditions.

The same weather, maybe. But everything else had changed.

She squeezed his fingers. "Lynn's expecting us. I don't want to hurt her feelings."

"I'm sure she would understand. You're exhausted from all that traveling."

She laughed. "Right. The traveling. That's it."

He looked slightly abashed, which only made her laugh more. They had spent six days on the road, wending their way slowly from Florida to Utah. They probably could have made the journey in half the time barring complications like they encountered on the way east, but neither of them had been in much of a hurry.

They rose late each morning, still warm and sated from a night spent in each other's arms, then drove until they were tired enough—or hungry enough for each other—that they stopped again for more.

How different their return journey had been! With the simmering tension between them gone and their feelings out in the open, Kate had found every moment one of pure delight, whether they were laughing about a bumper sticker on an eighteen-wheeler or watching Belle chase a ball through the snow in Wyoming, where they had spent the previous night.

She loved Hunter more after those six wonderful days than she ever believed possible.

Part of her would rather go home with him and spend this most magical of nights in his arms, at his quiet mountain home where everything had begun.

But she couldn't deny the surprising discovery that her heart beat with eagerness to walk inside Lynn's beautiful home and see again the people she knew waited for her there.

"I'm ready," she murmured.

Hunter climbed out and came around to open her door, then piled his arms with the presents loaded onto the back seat. They had barely had time to stop at her apartment in Salt Lake City to drop Belle off and pick up her stash of gifts. Kate could only be grateful she had been neurotic enough to wrap all but the ones they bought in Florida before she left—and she had paid extra for gift wrap on all those last-minute purchases.

Soft snowflakes drifted around them as they walked up the sidewalk together. Just for old time's sake she stuck her tongue out to catch a few, earning a laugh from Hunter.

Kate freed a hand from the packages she carried to ring the doorbell, and a few moments later Gage's oldest stepdaughter, Gabriella, opened the door, her gamine little face lighting up when she saw them.

"Aunt Kate! Aunt Kate! You're here! That means we can open presents now!"

Aunt Kate. My word. Kate wasn't quite sure how she felt about that one. She didn't have time to sort it out before Gaby raced off, most likely to find her younger sister and partner in crime.

She and Hunter stood in the doorway for a moment, then looked at each other and laughed when no one else came to greet them.

Through the entryway, Kate could hear voices and soft holiday music so she decided just to walk in. She belonged here, after all, whether she was ready to accept that or not.

Laughter and heat and delicious smells assailed them when they walked into Lynn's comfortable-sized gathering room. Pine, roast turkey and some kind of pie—possibly cinnamon apple—were the dominant scents.

No one seemed to notice their entrance and Kate

took the opportunity to study this family she was slowly coming to know.

Wyatt and Taylor were nowhere to be found, but Gage and Allie sat on one of the pair of plump burgundy couches arranged around a river-rock fireplace that crackled merrily. They were holding hands, she saw, as they admired the wrapped presents under the tree with Allie's daughters, who seemed to be pawing through each one for any that might have their names on them.

Kate's gaze found Lynn and Sam standing together in the open kitchen. Lynn wore a holiday-print apron and her lovely face glowed pink. Probably from working in the kitchen all day, Kate thought, judging by the delicious-looking feast spread on the table; then she saw Sam sneak a kiss on the back of his ex-wife's neck exposed by her graceful French braid.

Well, well! This was an interesting development. Sam and Lynn had been divorced since shortly after her kidnapping and neither of them had ever remarried. Wouldn't it be something if they could rekindle their relationship now, after all the years and pain?

As if drawn by radar, Lynn suddenly looked up and found them standing there. She flushed even brighter and stepped away from Sam.

"Kate! You're back."

"Just barely. I only stopped home to drop off my luggage."

"I was so afraid you wouldn't make it in time. Oh, I'm so glad you're here!"

She dropped the wooden spoon she held and rushed forward. Kate barely had time to hand her presents into

Hunter's already burdened arms before Lynn swept her into a cinnamon-scented embrace.

As her mother pressed a soft cheek to hers, Kate waited for the familiar discomfort to pinch her at Lynn's eager affection, but she couldn't seem to find it anywhere. Instead, she returned Lynn's embrace, warm affection bubbling up inside her like eggnog.

Sam joined them and Lynn handed her over to him. Again Kate was startled by the contentment stealing over her.

"Do you want the presents under the tree?" she heard Hunter ask Lynn.

"That would be fine, dear."

He left her side long enough to put their packages along with the rest, to the delight of Gaby and Anna.

"Hunter came with me. I hope you don't mind."

"Of course not!" Lynn assured her. "He's Taylor's brother so that makes him practically one of the family."

And soon he would be more, Kate thought, joy pulsing through her again, but she held that secret close to her heart for now.

"Dinner's almost ready. I'm just taking the rolls out of the oven."

"How can I help?" Kate asked as Hunter rejoined her.

"I've got it. Just sit down and visit with your brothers."

"I see Gage but where's Wyatt? Did we beat them here?"

Lynn gestured absently. "They're around somewhere. Taylor said they had some last-minute presents to wrap. I think they're in one of the bedrooms."

As if on cue, Taylor and Wyatt wandered into the room. Taylor could usually be found elegantly groomed, every hair in place and her makeup beautifully applied. Now, though, her hair looked a little messy, her lipstick a little smudged and her eyes had the glow of a woman who had just been well and truly kissed.

Wrapping presents. Right, Kate thought, hiding her grin as Taylor caught sight of them, her brother and her best friend. She let out a distinctly inelegant whoop.

She slipped from Wyatt's arms and rushed to them, her arms outstretched. When she neared, she came to a dead stop, her eyes wide. Only then did Kate realize Hunter's fingers were entwined with hers, something that had become almost second nature to them in the last six days.

Taylor's gaze shifted rapidly from their joined hands to their faces in turn and then her shocked expression gave way to joy.

She hugged them both hard. "It's about time my brother got some sense," she whispered in Kate's ear when she embraced her.

"Everyone is here at last so we can start dinner," Lynn said. "Sit down, sit down."

"What about presents?" Gaby whined.

Allie shushed her. "Later. I've told you that a hundred times."

"At least," Gage murmured with a fond smile to his stepdaughters.

Everyone took their seats and Kate was grateful to see Lynn must have quickly set an extra place for Hunter—either that or she had suspected all along that Kate would bring him.

When everyone was gathered around the big pine table, Sam cleared his throat. "This is the most wonderful of Christmases. To have everyone together again seems like a miracle."

Everyone's gaze subtly shifted to Kate. A few days earlier she would have squirmed under their attention but now she only smiled.

"Before we say grace," Sam went on, "Lynn and I have an announcement."

He looked as nervous as a boy on his first date, she thought, as her father lifted her mother's hand above the table. "Lynn and I are, um, getting married again. Valentine's Day."

Both he and Lynn looked anxiously at their assembled family as if they thought they had dropped a bombshell on everyone. No one looked particularly surprised, though Kate might have been if she hadn't observed that furtive kiss in the kitchen.

With a sound of disgust, Wyatt reached into his pocket and pulled out a bill, then slapped it onto the table in front of Gage. "There you go. Twenty bucks."

"You bet on whether your parents would get back together?" Taylor asked, her voice outraged.

"No. We both figured out that was a given a long time ago. Gage said Valentine's Day. I thought Mom would hold out for a spring wedding."

Her big, tough FBI agent of a brother pocketed the money, a grin on his handsome features. "What can I say? I'm a romantic."

Wyatt snickered at that but subsided at a stern look from Taylor.

Kate remembered Hunter's proposal the night before when they had been throwing snowballs at each other outside their Wyoming hotel and her joyful acceptance. She thought of sharing the news with her family but decided she wanted to treasure it to herself for a while longer.

She was glad she said nothing when Allie spoke up quietly.

"We have news, too." She reached for Gage's hand. "We're having a baby, due in June."

There were general exclamations of delight at the table.

"We might have a brother," Anna said.

"See, Mama," Gaby added, "I can *too* keep my mouth shut sometimes. I didn't tell anyone, not even Grandma Lynn."

Everyone laughed, but Taylor and Kate both honed in on Allie at the same time.

"Who's your OB?" Taylor asked.

"How is your pregnancy affecting your blood sugar?" Kate asked, concerned over Allie's diabetes.

"Does your doctor anticipate putting you on bed rest for the last trimester?" Taylor asked.

Allie looked a little overwhelmed by all the questions.

"This is what happens when you have two doctors in the family," Wyatt said with a laugh.

"And a nurse," Gage reminded them. "Allie knows how to take care of herself."

"The food's getting cold," Sam spoke up in his quiet way. "You can jabber all you want about babies and weddings while we're stuffing our faces but let's say grace so this feast your mother spent all day working on doesn't go to waste."

Kate smiled a little at Hunter's disconcerted expression when everyone reached around the table to hold hands with those on either side of them, but he reached for Taylor's fingers with his left hand and Kate's on his right.

She was seated next to Lynn and her mother's hand was smooth and soft, though she laced her fingers through Kate's tightly as Sam began to pray.

Her father's prayer was beautiful and heartfelt. He gave thanks for all the blessings the family had seen through the year, for new loves and second chances, and especially for the miracle of their little girl's return to them, after so many years of searching for her.

His voice broke a little at that point and he paused. Kate peeked under her eyelashes to find that tears seeped from both her parents' closed eyes—and even Gage and Wyatt looked suspiciously teary.

She was weeping a little, too, she realized, and her tears dripped even more freely when in his deep, quiet voice Sam gave thanks for those who had cared for her while she was away from them, who had showed her love when her family couldn't.

She thought of Maryanne and Tom, and at that moment she finally realized how truly blessed she was.

How many people had been gifted with two sets of loving parents? When she and Hunter married in a few months, she would have two kind, loving men to walk her down the aisle, two mothers to fuss over her gown and her veil. Even though Hunter's parents were dead, their children would still have two sets of grandparents to love them and spoil them.

She had two sets of parents, two brothers who loved

her, two new sisters-in-law she loved dearly, a pair of beautiful new nieces.

And Hunter by her side, with his strength and his goodness and his love.

She was the luckiest woman in the world.

* * * * *

Also by Patricia Davids

Love Inspired

The Amish Bachelors

An Amish Harvest
An Amish Noel
His Amish Teacher
Their Pretend Amish Courtship
Amish Christmas Twins
An Unexpected Amish Romance

Lancaster Courtships

The Amish Midwife

Brides of Amish Country

Plain Admirer
Amish Christmas Joy
The Shepherd's Bride
The Amish Nanny
An Amish Family Christmas: A Plain Holiday
An Amish Christmas Journey
Amish Redemption

Visit the Author Profile page
at Harlequin.com for more titles.

HIS BUNDLE OF LOVE

Patricia Davids

And whoever welcomes a little child like this
in My name welcomes Me.
—*Matthew* 18:5

Chapter 1

"Hey, wait! Mister, you gotta help us!"

Mick O'Callaghan stopped at the sound of the frantic shout. He turned to see a grubby, bearded derelict emerge from the doorway of an abandoned building, one of many that lined the narrow Chicago street. As the man stumbled down the dilapidated steps, Mick recognized Eddy Todd. Eddy, in his stained and tattered overcoat, was a frequent flyer at Mercy House Shelter where Mick volunteered two days a week.

Staggering up to Mick, Eddy grabbed the front of his brown leather jacket. "Please. You gotta help. She's havin' a baby! I don't know what to do. You gotta help her."

"Take it easy, Eddy. Slow down and tell me what's wrong."

Eddy squinted up at Mick's face, and some of the panic left his watery, gray eyes. "That you, Mick?"

"Yeah, it's me." He kept the old fellow from falling by catching his elbows. The sour odors of an unwashed body and cheap whiskey assaulted Mick. No doubt Eddy had been out panhandling, and some well-meaning Samaritan had given him money for a meal, but he had spent it on a bottle instead.

Eddy regained his balance and tugged at Mick's arm. "Come on. You're a fireman. You can deliver a baby, can't ya?"

Mick cast a doubtful eye at the old tenement. What would a pregnant woman be doing in there? Only broken shards of glass remained in the few windows that weren't boarded over. A section of the roof had collapsed, and debris littered the area. The only signs of life were a few weeds that had sprouted in the sidewalk cracks and struggled to survive in the weak April sunshine. It wasn't the kind of place he wanted to go searching through—especially for an old drunk's hallucinations.

With a gentle tug, Mick tried to coax Eddy away. "Why don't you come down to the mission. Pastor Frank can get you a hot meal. It's meat loaf tonight. You like meat loaf, don't you?"

"Sure, sure, I like meat loaf." Eddy allowed himself to be led for a few steps, then he stopped. "But what about the girl? She shouldn't have her baby in there. It ain't clean, or nothing. Come on, I'll show ya where she is."

Mick studied the building again. What if Eddy wasn't imagining things? He glanced at his watch. Normally, it didn't matter how he spent his days off, but since his mother had moved in for an extended stay after her accident, he tried to make sure she didn't spend much time alone. Tonight was the nurse's night off. Naomi would be leaving in an hour. Perhaps if he hurried, he could check the place out, take Eddy over to the mission and get home before she left.

He turned back to the old man. "I'll take a look, but I want you to stay here," he insisted.

"Sure, sure. I'll stay ri-right here." Eddy nodded, lost his balance and staggered back a step. He wavered on his feet but stayed upright. "You want I should call an ambulance?"

Mick shook his head and hid a smile. "I'll do that if we need one. You just stay put."

Walking carefully up the broken steps, he ducked under crisscrossed boards someone had nailed over the doorway in a vain attempt to keep people out. It took a few moments for his eyes to adjust in the gloomy interior. He faced a long hall with a dozen doors down its length. The first one stood open, and he looked in.

A tattered mattress surrounded by heaps of cardboard boxes lay in one corner. Old clothes, tin cans and trash covered the floor. The place reeked of stale sweat and rancid garbage. As he stepped back, his foot struck an empty bottle of whiskey and sent it rolling across the warped floorboards. Apparently, Eddy had been holed up in there for some time. At least there was no sign of a pregnant woman. Mick turned to leave, but the sound of a low moan stopped him.

It came again, and he moved down the hall to investigate, skirting a pile of broken furniture and fallen ceiling plaster that all but blocked the dark hall. The last door on the left stood open a crack. He hesitated beside it. Four years as a firefighter had taught him caution. Plenty of unsavory characters inhabited these slums, and some of them could be very unpleasant if he'd stumbled onto a meth lab or another equally illegal operation.

Another moan, louder this time, issued from the room. Someone was in pain. He couldn't ignore that. Standing with his back to the wall, he stretched out his arm and eased open the door. From behind, a hand clamped down on his shoulder, and Mick's breath froze in his chest.

"What ya doin'?" a slurred voice wheezed.

Relief surged through Mick as his heart began beating again. He turned and whispered, "Eddy, you scared the life out of me! Didn't I tell you to stay put?"

"Yeah—yeah, you told me, but she's in here. I found some help," he announced and barged through the door.

Mick followed with more caution. Light poured in from a large, broken window on the back wall. It showed a room surprisingly neat and free of the stench that permeated Eddy's lair. It contained little more than a bare mattress where a young woman with short blond hair lay on her side. She wore a simple black skirt and a pale pink sweater with long sleeves. Her splayed fingers covered her small, rounded belly beneath the sweater. A thin wail escaped her clenched lips. This was definitely not a hallucination.

At the sound of voices, Caitlin Williams lifted her head and sighed in relief. Eddy had managed to bring help. She was sorry she had doubted the old guy. The young man with him crossed the room and dropped to one knee beside her.

"Can you tell me what's wrong?" he asked.

Scared out of her wits but determined not to show it, Caitlin said, "I think my baby's coming."

His fingers closed around her wrist, and he stared at his watch. "How far apart are your contractions?"

"Right on top of each other," she panted, trying to stifle a groan as another one gripped her. "You a doctor?"

"No, I'm an EMT. Don't worry, I know what to do."

He sounded so calm, so confident. Maybe it would be okay. Peering up at him, she realized with a jolt that she knew him.

She'd seen him at the nearby homeless shelter where she got some of her meals. Only last week, she had watched him playing football with some of the kids there. He'd caught a wobbling pass and staggered toward the makeshift goalposts with half a dozen of them hanging on and trying to pull him down. His muscular frame had made light work of the load, but it was his hearty laughter that had truly drawn her interest. His rugged good looks and dark auburn hair made him easy on the eyes. At the time, she had thought his face was more interesting than handsome. It had character.

"I know you. At the shelter they called you Mickey O."

A warm smile curved his lips and deepened the crinkles at the corners of his bright, blue eyes. "Mick O'Callaghan at your service. And you are?" A vague trace of Irish brogue lilted through his deep baritone voice.

"Caitlin Williams," she supplied through gritted teeth.

"Pleased to meet you." He laid a gentle hand on her stomach. "When is your baby due?"

"Not till—" Pressing her lips together, Caitlin waited for the pains to pass. "August," she finished.

His startled gaze flew to her face, and her fears came rushing back to choke her. "My baby will be okay, won't it?"

"I'll do everything I can." He reached into his pocket and pulled out a cell phone. He flipped open the lid, then muttered, "Not now."

Caitlin saw the worried look in his eyes. "What's wrong?"

"The battery is dead. Eddy?" he called over his shoulder. "I need you to go get that ambulance, now. And hurry!"

"Ri-right, Mick, sure thing. Um...where should I go?"

"Go to Pastor Frank. Tell him Mick O'Callaghan says to call an ambulance, then bring him here. Can you do that?" Taking off his jacket, Mick spread it over Caitlin and tucked it around her shoulders.

Eddy nodded. "Sure, I can do that."

Mick saw the old man stagger as he hurried out the door. Torn between the need to stay with the woman or make sure that help was called he looked at her and said, "Maybe I should go."

She grabbed his arm. "No, stay, please. Eddy can do it. Stay and take care of my baby."

"Okay, I'll stay." He composed his face, determined to keep her calm. He knew a baby born three months early wouldn't survive unless it waited to be born in a hospital.

Please, Heavenly Father, guide me in making the right decisions here.

Her face tightened into a grimace as she curled forward again. "Something's wrong. It hurts."

"You need to breathe through your contractions, like this." He demonstrated. "Come on, breathe, breathe."

"You breathe. I'm going to scream."

She didn't and he admired her control. "Tell you what, we'll take turns. Every other contraction, I get to scream, and you breathe."

She uncurled and relaxed back onto the mattress. "What have you got to yell about?"

He gave a pointed glance to where she gripped his arm. "You're doing a bit of acupuncture with those fingernails."

She jerked away. "I'm sorry."

"Why don't you hold my hand?" He offered it, but she ignored him and gripped the edge of the mattress instead, and he regretted saying anything.

He had seen this young woman occasionally at Pastor Frank's shelter in the last month. She would show up for the evening meal, but she never stayed long. Like many of the women at Mercy House, she kept to herself. He'd never spoken to her, yet something in her eyes had captured his attention the first time he saw her.

The women who came to Mercy House were mostly single mothers with ragged children in tow or old women alone and without families. Their eyes were dull with hopelessness, desperation and sadness, but life hadn't emptied this girl's eyes—they blazed with defiance.

Up close, their unusual color intrigued him. A light golden brown, they held flecks of green that made them seem to change with the light. They reminded him of the eyes of a cougar he had seen in the zoo. Aloof, watchful, wary. Only now, raw fear lurked in their depths.

Come on, Eddy, don't let me down. Get that ambulance here.

Struggling to hide his concerns, Mick searched for a way to establish a rapport and put her at ease. "Have you got a name picked out for your baby?"

"No. I thought I had plenty of time."

He gave her a wry smile. "I've got names picked out for my kids, and I'm not even married yet."

She arched an eyebrow. "Goody for you."

"A kid's name is important. It's something you should give a lot of thought. Not that you haven't— or wouldn't—I mean," he murmured as he ducked his head.

Caitlin couldn't believe it. This grown man, as big as a house, and probably twenty-five years old was blushing. His neck grew almost as red as his hair. It was sweet, really.

What could she say to someone about to deliver her baby? Things were going to get intimate. Maybe soon. She felt the beginnings of another contraction and reached for his hand. His large fingers engulfed her small ones. Strength and reassurance seemed to flow from him into her, easing her fear. Focusing on his face, she followed his instructions to breathe in and blow out. The pain did seem more bearable.

As the contraction faded, she realized he still held her hand. She pulled away and drew his jacket close, relishing the warmth and comforting scent of leather and masculine cologne. The quiet of the old building pressed in around them.

"So, tell me what names you got picked out," she said at last. "Maybe I'll use one."

He smiled. "For a boy, it'll be William Perry."

"Willie Perry Williams." She tried the name out

but shook her head. "Not a chance. Why would you do that to a kid?"

"Are you joking? William 'The Refrigerator' Perry was the greatest football player in the history of the Chicago Bears."

Her husband had liked football. The thought of Vinnie sent a stab of regret through her heart. He would never see his son or daughter. How she had hoped that he would give up his wild ways once he knew they were having a baby. He hadn't. A high-speed chase while trying to outrun the police ended his life when his car veered off the highway and struck a tree. His death that night had started her down the painful path that led to her current desperate situation.

Within days she had discovered that Vinnie had been gambling away the rent money she worked so hard to earn. The landlord didn't want to hear her sob story. He wanted his money. Three months of unpaid rent was more than she could come up with. She was evicted the day after her husband's funeral. With no money and nowhere to go, she soon found herself living on the streets. The one place she swore she'd never go back to.

She took a close look at her rescuer. Was he the same kind of man? One who would drink and gamble and then lie to his pregnant wife about it? She didn't believe that. Not a guy who liked kids as much as he did.

Managing a little smile, she said, "You don't plan on naming a girl after a football player, do you?"

"No," he answered quietly. "I'll name her after my mother. Elizabeth Anne O'Callaghan."

Amazing! If this guy was any sweeter, he'd rival a candy bar.

Another contraction hit, and his hand found hers. "You got it, that's it. Breathe," he coaxed. "Breathe, breathe. You're doing great."

She curled onto her side and focused on his singsong voice. With his free hand, he began to rub her lower back in slow circles. Okay, she thought, a sweet guy is a good thing to have around just now.

"Is there someone I can call once we get to the hospital?" he asked. "Family? The baby's father?"

She shook her head. "Vinnie, my husband, he's dead. There's nobody."

"I'm sorry."

She bristled at the pity in his voice. Normally, she would have ignored it, but now she couldn't seem to control the emotions that flared in her.

"I don't need your pity. I've had a little bad luck, that's all." She raised up on her elbow to glare at him. "I'll be on my feet again in no time and a lot better off than I was before."

Holding up one hand, he said, "Chill, lady. I wasn't feeling sorry for you."

"You'd better not. I can take care of myself. And I can take care of my baby, too."

"In here?" He gestured around the room. The broken window let the wind in, and strips of dingy wallpaper peeling from the stained plaster waved in the breeze that carried the smells of mildew and rotting wood.

"Lady, I've seen kids living in places like this covered with rat bites and worse. If you think you can go it alone, you're crazy. There's a system to help if you'll use it."

"Why do you care? You want to name your little girl

after your mother, right? You know what I remember about dear old Mom? On my fifth birthday she gave me a Twinkie with a candle in it. Then she left me inside a Dumpster for two days because she was too strung out to remember where she'd put me to keep me quiet while some new boyfriend supplied her habit. Your precious system moved me from one foster home to another when it wasn't giving me back to Mom so she could have another go at me. By the time I was sixteen, I'd figured out living in a back alley was a better deal. Your *system* isn't going to get its hands on my baby. I'll make sure of that."

She squeezed her eyes shut, fighting to hold back a scream as the pain overwhelmed her.

"Okay, you've had it rough," he said gently. "Show me one kid down at the shelter that hasn't. But, if Child Welfare finds out this is where you're living, do you think they're going to let you bring a baby here? I'm just saying stay at a shelter until you find something better. It's not you I'm worried about, it's the baby."

Everyone who'd ever shown her compassion had had their own agenda in mind. Why did she think this guy was any different? Why did she find herself believing he really did care?

"How come you're so concerned about someone else's kid?"

He stared out the broken window for a long moment without speaking, then he looked at her and said, "Maybe because I can't have kids of my own."

She frowned. "I don't get it. What about the names?"

The smile he tried for was edged with sadness. "If I ever marry, I'll adopt children."

"You look healthy to me," she said, giving him the once-over. "What's wrong with you?"

He hesitated, then admitted, "I had a bad case of the mumps when I was a teenager. It left me sterile." He shrugged. "It's just one of those things."

But not a little thing, Caitlin thought as she glimpsed the sadness in his eyes.

"Mick? Mick O'Callaghan?" A shout echoed through the building.

"Last room on the left, Pastor," Mick shouted back.

The sound of someone clambering past the debris in the hall reached them. A moment later, Pastor Frank's bald head appeared in the doorway. "Mick, what are you doing in here? Eddy was raving about you delivering a baby."

His eyes, behind silver wire-rimmed glasses, widened as he caught sight of Caitlin. "For goodness' sake. Are you?"

"Not yet, but we could be. Did you call for an ambulance?"

"I did." The sound of a distant siren followed his words.

Mick turned to her and smiled. "Everything's going to be all right now."

He gripped her hand again. The warmth and strength of his touch made her believe him. He would take care of her and her baby.

Twenty minutes later, two paramedics loaded the stretcher she lay on into the ambulance. Another contraction hit, stronger this time. As she tried to pant through it, the need to push became uncontrollable.

One of the paramedics started to close the door, shutting Mick out.

"Wait," she shouted. "He's got to come with me."

She wasn't sure why she needed Mick. Maybe it was because he truly seemed to care—about her, and about her baby.

She stretched her hand out and pleaded, "Please, Mick, we need you."

The two paramedics looked at Mick. The older one said, "Okay, O'Callaghan, come on. We're wasting time." He motioned with his head, and Mick jumped in. Moments later, the ambulance rolled with red lights and siren.

Mick knew he'd be late getting home for sure now. He would have to call once he reached the hospital. The last thing he wanted was to worry his mother. Yet, for some reason he knew he couldn't let Caitlin go through this alone.

She didn't have anyone. He couldn't imagine what that must be like. Besides his mother, he had two sisters, a dozen nephews and nieces and more cousins than he could count. There were enough O'Callaghans in Chicago to fill the upper deck at Wrigley Field, while this destitute young woman was totally alone.

No, God had set his feet on the path that led to Caitlin today. Mick couldn't believe the Lord wanted him to bail out now. Taking her hand, he smiled at her and said, "You got it now. Just breathe."

The siren wailed overhead. Caitlin struggled to block out the sound as she panted through the contraction with Mick coaching her. Why didn't they shut it off? She couldn't concentrate. She needed to hear his voice telling her everything was going to be okay. And she needed to push.

She was pushing by the time the ambulance reached the hospital. Her stretcher was quickly unloaded and wheeled into the building. People came at her from all directions, yelling instructions, asking for information and giving orders she couldn't follow. All she could do was bear down and push a new life into the world as she clung to Mick's hand like a lifeline.

A sudden gush of fluid soaked the stretcher, and her tiny baby slid into the hands of a startled doctor. "We have a girl," he said. Mick lifted Caitlin's head so she could see.

"She's so small." Dread snaked its way into her soul as they whisked her daughter to a table with warming lamps glowing above it.

"Is she okay? Why isn't she crying?" Caitlin tightened her grip on Mick's hand. So many people crowded around the baby that she couldn't see her. She tried to sit up, but a nurse held her back.

"Your baby's being taken care of."

"Just tell me she's okay. Please, someone tell me she's okay." Frantic now, Caitlin struggled to push the nurse aside, but a sudden, sharp pain in her chest halted her.

She tried to draw a breath but couldn't get any air. Something was wrong, terribly wrong. She collapsed back onto the bed as the crushing pain overwhelmed her.

Long minutes later, they wheeled the baby's bed up beside her. Caitlin turned her head and focused on

"*4 for 4*" MINI-SURVEY

We are prepared to **REWARD** you with 2 FREE books and 2 FREE gifts for completing our MINI SURVEY!

FREE
Value Over
$20!

You'll get...

TWO FREE BOOKS & TWO FREE GIFTS

ust for participating in our Mini Survey!

Dear Reader,

IT'S A FACT: if you answer 4 quick questions, we'll send you **4 FREE REWARDS!**

I'm not kidding you. As a leading publisher of women's fiction, we value your opinions… and your time. That's why we are prepared to **reward** you handsomely for completing our mini-survey. In fact, we have 4 Free Rewards for you, including 2 free books and 2 free gifts.

As you may have guessed, that's why our mini-survey is called **"4 for 4".** Answer 4 questions and get 4 Free Rewards. It's that simple!

Thank you for participating in our survey,

Pam Powers

www.ReaderService.com

To get your 4 FREE REWARDS:
Complete the survey below and return the insert today to receive 2 FREE BOOKS and 2 FREE GIFTS guaranteed!

◄ DETACH AND MAIL CARD TODAY! ►

"4 for 4" MINI-SURVEY

1 Is reading one of your favorite hobbies?

☐ YES ☐ NO

2 Do you prefer to read instead of watch TV?

☐ YES ☐ NO

3 Do you read newspapers and magazines?

☐ YES ☐ NO

4 Do you enjoy trying new book series with FREE BOOKS?

☐ YES ☐ NO

YES! I have completed the above Mini-Survey. Please send me my 4 FREE REWARDS (worth over $20 retail). I understand that I am under no obligation to buy anything, as explained on the back of this card.

194/394 MDL GMYP

FIRST NAME	LAST NAME

ADDRESS

APT.#	CITY

STATE/PROV.   ZIP/POSTAL CODE

Offer limited to one per household and not applicable to series that subscriber is currently receiving.
Your Privacy—The Reader Service is committed to protecting your privacy. Our Privacy Policy is available online at www.ReaderService.com or upon request from the Reader Service. We make a portion of our mailing list available to reputable third parties that offer products we believe may interest you. If you prefer that we not exchange your name with third parties, or if you wish to clarify or modify your communication preferences, please visit us at www.ReaderService.com/consumerschoice or write to us at Reader Service Preference Service, P.O. Box 9062, Buffalo, NY 14240-9062. Include your complete name and address. ROM-218-MS17

© 2017 HARLEQUIN ENTERPRISES LIMITED ® and ™ are trademarks owned and used by the trademark owner and/or its licensee. Printed in the U.S.A.

READER SERVICE—Here's how it works:

Accepting your 2 free Romance books and 2 free gifts (gifts valued at approximately $10.00 retail) places you under no obligation to buy anything. You may keep the books and gifts and return the shipping statement marked "cancel." If you do not cancel, about a month later we'll send you 4 additional books and bill you just $6.74 each in the U.S. or $7.24 each in Canada. That is a savings of at least 16% off the cover price. It's quite a bargain! Shipping and handling is just 50¢ per book in the U.S. and 75¢ per book in Canada*. You may cancel at any time, but if you choose to continue, every month we'll send you 4 more books, which you may either purchase at the discount price plus shipping and handling or return to us and cancel your subscription. *Terms and prices subject to change without notice. Prices do not include applicable taxes. Sales tax applicable in N.Y. Canadian residents will be charged applicable taxes. Offer not valid in Quebec. Books received may not be as shown. All orders subject to approval. Credit or debit balances in a customer's account(s) may be offset by any other outstanding balance owed by or to the customer. Please allow 4 to 6 weeks for delivery. Offer available while quantities last.

▲ If offer card is missing write to: Reader Service, P.O. Box 1341, Buffalo, NY 14240-8531 or visit www.ReaderService.com ▲

BUSINESS REPLY MAIL
FIRST-CLASS MAIL   PERMIT NO. 717   BUFFALO, NY

POSTAGE WILL BE PAID BY ADDRESSEE

READER SERVICE
PO BOX 1341
BUFFALO NY 14240-8571

NO POSTAGE
NECESSARY
IF MAILED
IN THE
UNITED STATES

her daughter's small face. For an instant, all her pain faded away.

Her baby was so beautiful—so tiny—so perfect. But she wasn't moving. Someone spoke, but Caitlin couldn't hear them over the roaring in her ears. Then they pushed her baby's bed out the door. Their faces were all so grim.

"Is she dead, Mick?" Caitlin whispered, terrified to hear the answer.

"No," he answered quickly. "They're taking her to the NICU. It's a special intensive care just for babies. They'll take good care of her there. She's going to be fine."

"Why isn't—she crying?" The pain in her chest made it hard to talk.

"It's because she's so premature," Mick answered. "She has a tube going into her airway to help her breathe, and she can't make any sound with that in."

Caitlin's own breathing had become short, labored panting. A frowning nurse slipped a plastic mask over Caitlin's face and spoke to the doctor. He frowned, too.

Caitlin looked from face to face. She didn't know any of these people. Who would look after her baby?

She gripped Mick's arm, pulling him closer. "Go with her."

He glanced at the E.R. staff, then back to her. "I think I should stay with you."

"I'm fine," she insisted. She forced a smile to her trembling lips. A strange cold was seeping into her bones. "Stay with—Beth. Watch over her for me."

He patted her hand. "Okay. I'll be back soon."

Nodding, she whispered, "Thank you," and watched him hurry out the door.

The nurse beside her claimed her attention. "I need you to tell me your name."

"Caitlin—Williams," she wheezed.

"Are you allergic to any medication? Are you using any street drugs?" Caitlin shook her head at each question the nurse fired at her. The room grew dark around the edges.

So this was what it was like to die. She wanted to cry because she knew what would happen to her daughter now—the same things that had happened to her. It wasn't fair.

"Who is your next of kin?" The nurse continued to insist on answers. Caitlin only wanted to close her eyes and rest, but more people crowded around her, taking her blood pressure, listening to her heart, poking needles in her arm, sticking wires on her chest. They were all frowning.

"Is the man who came in with you the baby's father?" the nurse asked.

"What?" Caitlin tried to focus on the woman's face.

"I said, is that man the baby's father?"

Would Mick see that her daughter was taken care of? She could say he was the father, then he'd have the right to look after her. Would he understand? It didn't matter, she was out of time. She nodded as she whispered, "Yes."

"What is his name?"

"Mick…O'Callaghan." *Don't let her be alone, Mick. Please, take care of her.*

Darkness swooped in and began to pull Caitlin

away. She struggled against it. She needed to stay for her baby.

"We're losing her," someone shouted.

Chapter 2

Mick caught up with the baby as they wheeled her into the nearest elevator. Squeezing in beside them, he stared in amazement at Caitlin's daughter. He'd never seen anything so tiny. Her head was no bigger than the palm of his hand; his little finger was thicker than her gangly legs, yet she was so complete. Downy, brown hair covered her head and miniature wrinkles creased her forehead above arching brows. She even had eyelashes! The tiny spikes lay curved against her cheek. Awed by the wonder of this new life, he gazed at her in fascination. Truly, here was one of God's greatest creations.

Her delicate hands flew up and curled around the breathing tube taped in her mouth.

"No, honey, don't pull on that," a nurse chided as she pried the tiny fingers loose. "Hold Daddy's hand instead," she suggested with an encouraging smile.

Hesitantly, almost fearfully, Mick reached for the baby's hand. Her thin fingers gripped his large, blunt one. Her eyes fluttered open. She stared at him and blinked, then her frown deepened into a scowl. An identical, miniature version of her mother's, and Michael Aaron O'Callaghan fell hopelessly in love.

"She looks like her mom," he said, surprised to hear the catch in his voice. He glanced at the woman beside him. "Will she be all right?"

"She has a very good chance, but there is a long road ahead of her, I'm afraid. I'm Dr. Wright. I'm one of the neonatologists on staff here. Her lungs are much too immature to work properly, so she's going to need help. She'll be placed on a ventilator once we reach the unit." As she spoke, she continued rhythmically squeezing a small, gray bag that delivered oxygen to the baby. "Do you have a name for her?"

"Beth," he answered, "or maybe Elizabeth. Her mother can tell you for sure. When can she come and see her?"

"We'll be busy getting Beth admitted and stabilized for the next hour or so. I'd suggest you wait until then to bring Mom in." The elevator doors slid open, and Mick followed them as they wheeled the baby across the hall and into the NICU.

A flurry of activity began as soon as they entered the large room. At first, it seemed like nurses were scurrying in all directions at once, but it quickly became apparent it was a controlled rush as Beth was placed on a larger bed, and hooked to a waiting ventilator. Within minutes, a jungle of wires, IV poles, tubing and oxygen hoses surrounded her.

Glancing around the room, Mick noted with amusement its peculiar mix of Mother Goose and science-fiction technology. Rows of flashing monitors and digital displays shared wall space with giant nursery-rhyme characters above the open beds and incubators. IV poles held bags of fluid, swaying mobiles and colorful toys.

Dr. Wright spoke as she worked. "We need to administer a medication directly into Beth's lungs to help mature them and start some IVs."

Mick interrupted, "What are her chances, honestly?"

"She weighs barely two pounds, and she looks to be about twenty-six weeks gestation, which means she was born fourteen weeks early. Her chances of survival are good if she doesn't develop any serious complications. Only time will tell."

After the excitement of Beth's admission died down, the nurses let Mick sit beside her bed. He couldn't get over how adorable she looked in spite of the tubes and wires. His heart warmed to her as he watched her with a sense of wonder and fascination. After a while, he glanced at the clock surprised to see how late it was. In the rush of events he had forgotten to call home.

"I'd better go and tell your mother how you're doing. I know she's worried."

He took a last look at the little girl whose arrival had generated so much activity. "Goodbye, Beth. Be well," he whispered, knowing he might never see her again. His mother's voice echoed in his mind, and he smiled. He took hold of her tiny hand. "May God grant you many years to live, for sure He must be knowing, the Earth has angels all too few, and heaven's overflowing."

A nurse across the bed smiled at him as she added medication to a bag of IV fluid. "Are you a poet?"

Sheepishly, he grinned. "It's an old Irish blessing, something my mother always says as a kind of birthday wish."

"It's darling. I'll write it out and put it on her bed. We like to keep personal things by the babies, like toys or photos. Things that help the families connect with their baby."

She reached out and patted his arm. "I'm Sandra Carter. Try not to worry, Irish. She's a fighter, I can tell."

"I hope you're right."

"Hold out your hand." He did and she fastened a hospital wristband around his arm. "You'll need this to get back in."

He fingered the white strip of plastic without comment. He was here under false pretenses, but only because Caitlin had insisted. Still, that didn't quite ease his conscience.

After making his way back to the E.R., he halted on the threshold of the room where he'd left Caitlin. It was empty.

Out at the main desk, Mick spoke to the heavyset woman seated behind it. "Excuse me. Can you tell me where they've taken the woman who just had a baby here?"

"The patient's name?" she asked in a bored voice, continuing to write on the paper in front of her.

"Caitlin Williams."

She laid down her pen, then shuffled through the charts beside her. She located one, flipped it open, then gave him a startled look. "Let me get Dr. Reese to speak with you."

She hoisted her bulk out of the chair and opened a door behind her. "Doctor, there's someone here asking about the Williams woman."

The unease Mick felt intensified when the grave-looking doctor emerged from the doorway. "Are you family?" he asked.

"No. I'm—a friend. Is something wrong?"

"I'm afraid so. Ms. Williams has developed a rare complication of pregnancy called amniotic fluid embolus."

"What does that mean?"

Drawing a deep breath, the doctor continued, "It means during her delivery, some of the amniotic fluid got into her blood stream. Once there, it traveled up through her heart and lodged in her lung preventing her from getting enough oxygen. That stopped her heart."

"She's dead?" Mick struggled to grasp the man's words.

"No," Dr. Reese admitted slowly. "We were able to restart her heart. Ms. Williams is on a ventilator now, but she hasn't regained consciousness. The lack of oxygen can cause profound brain damage, and the embolus can cause uncontrollable bleeding problems. Her condition is extremely serious. She's unlikely to survive."

Unlikely to survive? The phrase echoed inside Mick's head, filling him with a profound sadness. Caitlin was so young. She had a baby who needed her. What would happen to Beth now?

He raked a hand through his hair. "I should have stayed with her. I knew something wasn't right."

"I heard her tell you to go with the baby," the doctor said gently. "These patients often have an over-whelming sense of doom. She knew, and she chose to have you stay with her child. She's a very brave young woman."

"I'm sorry to interrupt," the clerk spoke up. "Doctor, you're needed in room six."

He nodded, then looked at Mick. "I'm sorry we couldn't do more," he said, then hurried away.

"Are you Mick O'Callaghan?" the clerk asked. Mick nodded. The woman pushed several sheets of paper toward him and offered him a pen. "We need you to fill out these forms, and I'll need a copy of your insurance card."

"My insurance card? For what?"

"For your baby."

"No, you don't understand. Beth isn't mine."

"According to Caitlin Williams, she is," the clerk said smugly.

Just then, Sandra and two other NICU nurses rounded the corner and walked past. "Hey, Irish," Sandra said with a bright smile. "I'm glad I ran into you. My shift is over, but I'll be back in the morning. Your daughter's doing fine, but you need to leave us a phone number. We overlooked that detail in the rush of her admission."

She started to leave, but stopped and turned. "Oh, I wrote out your mother's blessing and taped it to Beth's bed. Several other parents have asked for a copy of it. I hope you don't mind." She waved and followed her friends out the door.

"It seems a lot of people think she's your baby," the clerk said with a smirk.

It took a call to his attorney to convince the woman

that unless Mick himself had signed the paternity papers, he had no legal responsibility for the child—something Mick suspected she knew already. After that, he called home to make sure his mother was all right. Surprisingly, his mother's friend and part-time nurse Naomi answered the phone.

"It's about time you called," she scolded.

"I know. I had to take someone to the hospital. I'm glad you could stay. I hope it wasn't an inconvenience."

"I can watch my favorite TV shows here as well as at home. Besides, your mother is good company."

"How is she today?"

"Determined to get up and clean house even with her arm in a cast. I knew it was a mistake for that doctor to take her ankle brace off. The woman has less sense than you."

"Keep her down even if you have to sit on her. And tell her I'll be home in an hour or so."

Knowing that his mother wasn't alone was a relief. After hanging up, he went in search of Caitlin. At the medical ICU, a nurse led him to Caitlin's room. He paused in the doorway. A single bed occupied the small room. He stepped next to it and rested his hands on the cold metal rails.

She looked utterly helpless lying with the sheets neatly folded under her arms and her hands at her sides. A thick, white tube protruded from her mouth connecting her to a ventilator. The soft hiss it made as it delivered each breath made it sound as though the machine had a life of its own. Like a mechanical monster, it crouched there controlling her fate. One breath. She still lived. Another breath. She still lived.

Someone had combed her hair. It made her look

younger, sweeter. The hard edges of streetwise home-lessness didn't show now, only the face of a lovely young woman.

He had promised her that everything would be all right, but he hadn't been able to keep that promise.

The world wasn't full of happy endings; his job, if not his personal life, had taught him that long ago. Only sometimes, like now, when God's plan was hidden from view, he had trouble accepting things which seemed so unfair. Saddened beyond measure, he turned away knowing he could do nothing except keep her in his prayers.

After taking a cab home, he opened his front door and Nikki, his elderly golden retriever, met him with a wagging tail. Mick stooped to ruffle one silky ear. She licked his hand once then padded back to her bed in front of the fireplace, lay down and watched him across the room with calm, serious eyes. He sank onto the sofa and rubbed his hands over his weary face. The clock on the mantel began to chime midnight. He had to be on duty in less than seven hours. He considered pulling the throw over himself and just sleeping where he was, but decided against it. Instead, he rose to his feet and climbed the stairs with Nikki at his heels.

He glanced down the hall and saw that a light still shone from under his mother's door. He walked to the end of the corridor and rapped lightly on the thick oak panel. At her muffled answer, he eased the door open.

Elizabeth O'Callaghan was sitting up in bed reading by the light of a lamp on the bedside stand. She was dressed in a simple cotton robe of pale blue that matched her sharp eyes behind her bifocals. Her long white hair hung over a thick plaster cast covering her

left arm from elbow to wrist, the result of her auto accident. Around her neck she wore a small gold chain
and simple gold cross that glinted in the light when
she moved.

She once told him that the cross had come all the
way from Ireland with her mother. Like her own
mother, Elizabeth O'Callaghan had spent her life praying for the less fortunate. And she hadn't stopped with
simply praying for them.

After his father's death, Mick's mother had worked
to raise her own children and then went on to help other
young women who were alone in the world. Mercy
House had been her idea. Her work, her heart and soul
had started it. With the help of several women and
the local pastor, her work still went on. Mick's heart
swelled with love and pride when he thought of all she
had accomplished. The Lord gave her a strong will, and
she used it to help serve Him.

"Hi, Mom. How's the arm feeling?"

"Not too bad." She wiggled her fingers for his benefit.

"Has Naomi gone?"

"She helped me with my bath then I sent her home.
I'm better now. I don't need a sitter around the clock.
A few more weeks and I'll be able to move back to my
own apartment."

"You can move back when your doctor gives you
the okay and not before."

"I've put you out long enough. A man your age
shouldn't be saddled with caring for a feeble old
woman. You should be looking to get saddled with a
pretty young woman."

"Where am I going to find one prettier than you?"

She grinned at him, laid her book aside and patted

the mattress beside her. "You can't sidetrack me with flattery. I've been waiting up for you. What kept you? Naomi said you had to rush someone to the hospital. Come here and tell me everything."

She sounded like a schoolgirl eager for gossip. He crossed the room in a few long strides and bent to kiss her cheek. "It's a long story."

"I'm not going anywhere and neither are you until you tell me the whole truth and nothing but the truth, young man." She grasped his arm and tugged until he sat on the bed.

"If you insist."

"I do."

"Okay. I was on my way home from Mercy House when an old bum stopped me to help deliver a baby, but we got the mother to the hospital first, and since the baby weighed only two pounds she had to go to intensive care, and the mother asked me to go with the baby and I did, only while I was gone she told everyone I was the baby's father before she lapsed into a coma. Any questions?"

His mother's eyes were wide with stunned surprise. "About a million. Why don't you start at the top and go more slowly."

He grinned and repeated the story with as many of the details as he knew, stopping often to answer her questions. At the end of his tale, he met her sad, concerned gaze and wished he hadn't shared quite so much.

"This woman really doesn't have anyone we can notify?"

"Not as far as I know. It's the only reason I can think of why she would say I'm the father."

"That poor woman. And that poor little baby. Thank

goodness you were there for them. Is there any chance the mother will recover?"

"The doctor didn't think so. I'm not Beth's father but I can't stand thinking of someone so tiny being all alone in the world. Frankly, I'm not sure what to do."

"Why, you do the right thing! And don't be telling your mother that you don't know what that is," she declared. "I raised you better than that."

Mick rose and wished her good-night. On the way back to his room he considered her words. *This time I really don't know what the right thing is. I need Your guidance, Lord. What is it that You want me to do?*

He got ready for bed and lay down, but sleep wouldn't come. Each time he closed his eyes he saw Caitlin's face. He saw her eyes wide with relief when he'd followed Eddy into her room, and he saw them filled with fear for her baby. Such beautiful eyes, closed perhaps forever, yet repeated in miniature, along with her fearsome scowl, in her daughter's tiny face.

He barely knew the woman, but he kept hearing her voice. "Stay with Beth. Watch over her for me." It was the last thing Caitlin had said to him.

Had she sensed that she was dying? Had she been asking him for something more? Was that why she told them he was the father? So her baby girl wouldn't be left alone?

Mick threw back the quilt and sat up on the side of his bed. The light from a full moon cast a glow into the room. Rising, he crossed to the window. Nikki watched him from her spot at the foot of the bed, but she didn't bother to get up.

Pulling the curtains aside, he looked out the second-story window of his home and stared at the shadows of the trees in the park behind his property. It was deserted now, but during the day it would be filled with neighborhood children playing on the swings and slides. On nearby benches, smiling young mothers would follow their play with watchful eyes.

Yet across that park and the railroad yards beyond it, there existed a world those happy children would only know in passing or see on TV. It was a world of intense poverty, where children played in filthy streets and lived in crowded, run-down apartments if they were lucky enough to have a home at all, and where mothers seldom smiled because they worried about where the next meal would come from.

Caitlin came from those streets. If she lived, she'd go back there and take little Beth with her. But if Caitlin died, where would her child go? Into foster care until she was old enough to run away and end up like her mother? Or would she be one of the lucky ones playing in a park like this?

He let the curtain fall back into place. None of the children in the park would ever be his. Facing that fact was more painful tonight than it had ever been. Perhaps because, for a moment, when Beth had grasped his finger and gazed up at him, he had known what it felt like to be a father.

He raked his fingers through his hair. He wasn't responsible for Caitlin or her child, yet somehow the two of them had captured a piece of his heart. He felt connected to them. It wasn't right that they were alone. They needed someone to care about them. They needed him. Before he could change his mind, he crossed the room to the closet where he pulled on a gray wool cable-knit sweater, a pair of jeans and his sneakers, then he headed out the door.

A fine mist fell as he drove down the dark streets. The swish-swish of his wiper blades was almost mesmerizing. Twenty minutes later, he pulled into the parking lot of the hospital. Wondering if he was being a fool, he hurried out of the rain and through the emergency room doors.

At the NICU he showed his wristband, and a nurse answered his questions. Beth was doing as well as could be expected. She invited him in, but he declined. He needed to see Caitlin.

When he entered the ICU and reached her room, he hesitated at the door. What did he hope to accomplish here? Maybe nothing. He pulled a chair up beside her bed. Reaching through the rail, he took hold of her hand.

"Caitlin, it's Mick," he said softly, and gave her hand a gentle squeeze. Glancing at the array of machines and blinking lights around her, he sighed. He didn't know if she could hear him. But if she could, he wanted her to know that she wasn't alone. He began to talk about her baby.

"We're calling her Beth for now. She weighs only two pounds. I know that doesn't sound like much, but she really is a cute, little thing. She looks like you, I think—except kind of scrawny. She has brown hair with a touch of red," he added and smiled. "I don't suppose you're part Irish, are you?"

His words died away in the dimness of the room, and only the sound of the ventilator continued. One breath. One breath.

What should he say? What would a young mother

clinging to life want to know about her child? What would he want to know if it were him? His grip on her hand tightened.

"Your baby is doing fine. The nurses are great. They really seem to care about her. One of them called her a fighter. I guess that means she's going to take after you."

He studied the small hand he held in his large one. Her fingers were long and delicate, but some of her nails were short and ragged. Did she chew them? He knew so little about her, yet she had entrusted him with her baby.

"Girl, do you have any idea how much trouble you've caused me? I don't know why you told them I was the baby's father, unless you thought you weren't going to make it. But I'm not her father, although— well, although I wish I were. She needs her mother— she needs you. You've got to hold on."

He couldn't think of anything else to say. He bowed his head and sought comfort for himself and for her in the words he knew so well. "Our Father, Who art in heaven…"

Lost in a strange darkness, Caitlin searched for a way out. She had to find her baby. She didn't want her daughter to know the terrible, gut-wrenching fear of being left alone—of wondering what she had done that was so bad her own mother would leave her. That was the one promise Caitlin meant to keep. No, she wouldn't leave her baby—not ever.

Pain came again, deep inside her chest. She cried out, but no sound formed in her mouth. Perhaps it was her heart breaking because she missed her baby so. She tried to move her arms but she couldn't. Something or someone held her eyes closed.

A faint voice called her name, and Caitlin struggled to listen. Her baby was fine, the voice said. Had she really heard those words? Joy filled her.

She listened closely. She knew this voice. It was a man's voice. He was praying. The sound of his deep, caring voice saying those simple words brought a sense of comfort unlike anything she had never known.

Then the pain struck again and she began to choke. Somewhere, a shrill alarm sounded.

Chapter 3

Mick paced the confines of the small waiting room outside the intensive care unit where he'd been ushered, and prayed as the minutes ticked by. Was Caitlin's life slipping away beyond those doors? What would become of Beth? Why didn't anyone come and tell him what was going on? Finally, twenty agonizing minutes later, a young doctor appeared. He didn't look encouraging. Mick prepared himself to hear the worst.

"How is she?"

"Stabilized at the moment. She had some bleeding from her lungs. We've managed to control it for now."

"Thank God." Relief caused Mick's tired muscles to betray him, and he sank into one of the blue tweed chairs in the room.

"If it doesn't reoccur—she has a chance."

Mick looked up. "You don't sound very sure of that."

"Her condition is critical. It's best not to hold out false hopes."

"Can I see her?"

"For a few minutes," the young doctor conceded.

In the unit, Mick paused outside Caitlin's door. What was he doing here? Why was he getting involved?

Because she didn't have anyone else.

Stepping up to her bed, he leaned down and whispered, "Don't worry, Sleeping Beauty. I'll see that they take good care of you, and of Beth. You aren't alone. God is with you."

He pressed her hand but got no response. He studied her quiet, pale face. He had called her Sleeping Beauty, and the name seemed to fit. Her heart-shaped face with its prominent cheekbones and expressive flyaway eyebrows coupled with her short hair gave her an almost elfin appearance. What was it about her that drew him so? Was it only because she was alone that he felt this intense desire to take care of her? Somehow, he knew it was more than that.

Crossing to the door, he glanced back. Caitlin's chest rose and fell slightly in time with the soft hiss of the ventilator. One breath. One breath.

"Rest easy. I'll watch over little Beth for you."

As soon as he said the words a deep sense of satisfaction filled him. This was right. This was what he was meant to do.

After leaving Caitlin, he went to see her baby. Beth lay on her side snuggled in a soft cloth nest covered with tiny red and blue hearts. The ventilator tubing and IV lines were neatly organized now, but a daunting array of machines surrounded her bed. Glancing around the unit he saw a number of other parents who like himself had been drawn here in the middle of the night. Most of them stood by beds looking uncertain, their faces a curious mixture of hope and fear, pride and pity.

He pulled up a stool and sat beside Beth. His heart went out to her. She was so little and so alone in the world.

One of her hands moved up to curl around the tube in her mouth, and her brow furrowed in a frown. Gently, he uncurled her fingers and gave her his thumb to grip instead. "You're not really alone," he whispered. "You've got the good Lord and me on your side."

For the longest time, he stared at her tiny face. Each feature so perfect and so new. That she lived at all was nothing short of amazing.

"It's amazing, isn't it?"

The words mirrored his own thoughts so closely that he wasn't sure he'd really heard them. He glanced up and saw a woman seated in a rocker holding a baby on the other side of Beth's bed. She looked old to be a new mother. Her short, dark hair was streaked with gray at the temples and crow's-feet gathered at the corners of her eyes, but she was dressed in a hospital gown beneath a yellow print robe.

"I'm sorry. Did you say something?" he asked feeling bemused, or maybe just sleep deprived.

"I said, it's amazing. They're so perfectly formed even at such an early age."

He nodded. "Yes. I never knew." His throat closed and tears pricked at his eyes. He struggled to regain control and after a moment, he pointed with his chin. "Is yours a boy or a girl?"

Her smile held an odd, sad quality. "I have a little

boy." She lifted the blanket so he could see the baby's face. The features of a child with Down syndrome were unmistakable.

"He has a lot of hair," Mick said, trying to find something kind to say.

She ran her fingers through the baby's long hair. "Yes, he does. It's so very soft," she said almost to herself.

The baby began to fuss. She snuggled him closer and patted him until he hushed. She looked at Mick and smiled. "I wanted to thank you for the lovely saying on your daughter's bed."

Mick glanced at the foot of Beth's bed. His Irish blessing had been written in green ink and surrounded by little green shamrocks drawn on a plain white card and taped to the clear Plexiglas panel. "It's something my mother says."

"It helped me so much."

Smiling gently, he said, "I'm glad."

She tucked her son's hand back inside the blanket. "When I first saw my son—first realized what was wrong with him, I thought it would have been better if he had gone to be with the angels—" Her voice cracked. She blinked back tears when she looked at Mick. "Isn't that terrible?"

Mick found himself at a loss as to how to answer her, but the nurse had come back to the bedside. She dropped an arm around the woman and gave her a quick hug.

"No, it isn't terrible. We can't help the way we feel. Disappointment, fear, sadness—they're all feelings that catch us by surprise when something goes wrong."

"I do love him, you know. It's just that we've waited

so long for a child. I'm almost forty. He was going to be our only one," her voice trailed into silence.

A moment later she patted the nurse's arm. "You've all been wonderful. Thank you. And you." She looked at Mick. "Your mother's saying pointed out to me that God knows what He's doing. My son wasn't meant to be an angel in heaven. He was meant to be an angel here on Earth, like your little girl."

Gazing at Beth's frail form, surrounded by everything modern medicine offered, he could only pray the woman was right.

"You look like death warmed over."

Mick closed the door of his locker and cast Woody an exasperated glance. "Thanks. I could say the same about you."

Towering a head taller than Mick, Woody Mills, a Kansas farm boy turned Chicago firefighter and a close friend, grinned. He pulled his cowboy hat off and ran a hand through a blond crew cut that closely resembled the stubble of the wheat fields he'd left behind. "Tough night?"

Mick nodded. "I never made it to bed."

He wasn't looking forward to staying up another twenty-four hours. Maybe they'd have a quiet shift, and he could grab a few hours in the sack.

"Woody!" They both turned at the sound of the shout. Their watch commander, Captain Mitchell, appeared in the open doorway. "Ziggy needs help in the kitchen. Give him a hand."

Mick groaned, and Woody laughed. "That's right, Mick'O. It's Ziggy's week to cook. So guess what we're having?"

Mick leaned his head against the locker. "Spaghetti. Why can't he cook something—anything—else? He knows I hate spaghetti."

"Then it'll be a good week to go on a diet. Besides, the rest of us like it, so you lose." Still chuckling, Woody left the room.

The gong sounded suddenly and Mick raced for his gear along with the other men. He never found the time that day for a nap or for a plate of spaghetti. Two structure fires kept the company out for most of his shift. It was late the following morning when he found the time to call the hospital to check on Caitlin and the baby.

Caitlin's condition was unchanged, but the news about Beth was less encouraging. She was requiring higher oxygen and higher ventilator pressures, and she'd developed a heart murmur.

"Her murmur is due to a PDA," Dr. Wright explained to Mick over the phone. "It's a condition that often occurs in very premature infants. Before a baby is born very little blood goes to the lungs. As the blood is pumped out of the heart, it passes through a small opening called the ductus arteriosus and goes back to the placenta for oxygen. After a baby is born, this artery closes naturally, and blood flows to the lungs. But in many premature infants, it doesn't close and that's a problem. We can treat her with medication, but if that fails, she'll need surgery."

"Isn't surgery risky for such a small baby?"

"PDA ligation is a routine procedure, but let's not get ahead of ourselves. It may close after the drug is given. I'm optimistic but this is one of the complications I mentioned. I'll keep you informed. Also, our social worker needs to talk to you about signing paternity papers."

It was the perfect opening to admit that he wasn't Beth's father. Only, he didn't take it.

Inside the odd darkness, Caitlin drifted all alone. Sometimes it was as dark as midnight, other times it grew vaguely light, like the morning sky before the sun rose, but never light enough to let her see her surroundings. Voices spoke to her, telling her to open her eyes or move her fingers. She tried, but nothing happened. When the voices stopped, she was alone again.

It was pleasant here. No pain, no hunger, no cold; none of the things she'd come to expect in life. The urge to remain here was overwhelming, but she couldn't stay. She had to find her baby. Once she found her baby she'd never be alone ever again. She would always have someone to love and be loved by in return.

At times, a man's voice came. Deep and low, mellow as the notes of a song, it pulled Caitlin away from the darkness. He spoke to her now, and she knew he was watching over her little girl. Her baby wasn't lost at all.

The voice told her all kinds of things—how much the baby weighed and how cute she was. Sometimes the voice spoke about people Caitlin didn't know, but that didn't matter. Sometimes, he spoke about God, and how much God loved her. He spoke about having faith in the face of terrible things. His voice was like a rope that she held on to in the darkness. If she didn't let go, she could follow the sound and find her way out.

Now his voice was saying goodbye and she hated knowing that he was going away. She felt safe when he was near.

Something soft and warm touched her cheek gently. The fog grew light and pale around her. She opened her eyes and the image of a man with deep auburn hair and a kind face swam into focus for an instant, then the fog closed over her again.

"She opened her eyes!" Excited, Mick stared at Caitlin and prayed he hadn't imagined it.

"What did you say?" The nurse, who'd just entered the room, looked at him in surprise.

"She opened her eyes! She looked at me."

It'd been five days since Caitlin had slipped into a coma, and for the last two days Mick had divided his waking hours between sitting with Beth, whose condition was slowly worsening, and sitting with Caitlin. This was the first sign of any spontaneous movement from her.

"Caitlin, open your eyes," the nurse coaxed. Nothing.

Mick leaned close to Caitlin's ear. "Come on, Sleeping Beauty. I know you're in there. Give me a sign."

Again nothing. The nurse pinched the skin on the back of Caitlin's hand, then lifted her eyelid. Turning to him the nurse asked, "What were you doing when she moved?"

A flush heated Mick's face. "I was getting ready to leave, and I kissed her cheek," he admitted, feeling foolish.

Giving him a sad smile, the nurse touched his arm. "Sometimes we see the things we want to see, even if they're not really there. How is her baby doing?"

Mick glanced at Caitlin's still form and motioned with his head. The nurse followed him from the room. Once outside, he raked a hand through his hair and said, "Beth isn't good. Her heart hasn't responded to the medication they've given her. It looks like she'll need surgery."

"I'm sorry to hear that."

"Are you Mr. O'Callaghan?" Mick turned to see an overweight man with thin gray hair standing in the hall. His ill-fitting, dark blue jacket hung open displaying a wrinkled white shirt stained with a dribble of coffee. He held a scuffed black briefcase in one hand.

"Yes, I'm O'Callaghan," Mick answered.

"I'm glad I finally caught up with you. I'm Lloyd Winston, the social worker for the NICU."

"What can I do for you?"

Mr. Winston glanced at the nurse, then said, "Why don't you come to my office. We can speak in private there."

Mick held out a hand. "Lead the way."

"Have you got a minute to help me change this bed?"

"Sure."

Caitlin heard voices clearly this time—they were right beside her. Cool hands touched her body. She struggled to open her eyes, and for a moment, the blurred forms of two women came into view. Abruptly, they pulled her onto her side, and the movement sent waves of dizziness and pain crashing through her.

"Isn't she the saddest case?"

"No kidding."

"I heard the baby might not make it."

"I heard that, too. Hand me the lotion."

One of them smeared cold liquid across Caitlin's back. Were they talking about her baby? She fought to concentrate.

"My cousin had a little boy that was born prematurely. He's five now, but he's blind and deaf. She feeds him through a tube in his stomach, and he takes round-the-clock care."

"That's awful."

"It's awful to see my cousin tied her whole life to a child who's so damaged that he can't even smile at her. At five, he's hard to move and lift to change his diapers. Think what it's going to be like when he's twenty-five."

My baby's not damaged. She's perfect. Caitlin wanted to shout at them. She wanted to cover her ears with her hands, but her arms were deadweights.

From the moment she suspected she was pregnant, she had wanted a little girl. Her daughter was going to grow up to run and laugh and give her mother a dozen hugs a day. They would have each other forever. Caitlin would never leave her baby hungry, or hurting, or scared and alone in the dark the way she had been treated as a child.

Without warning, Caitlin was rolled to her other side. Her joints and muscles cried out in protest and nausea churned in her stomach. She moaned, but no sound escaped her. Tears formed at the corners of her eyes.

"It's time for her to stay on her left side. Can you help me change the sheets on that patient in room eight?"

The sound of their voices faded away, and Caitlin was alone again, but she was glad they were gone. She didn't want to hear about a child who was deaf and blind. She had to find her own baby.

She concentrated on opening her eyes. Bit by bit, her eyelids lifted and a room came into focus. There was dark blue tiled floor and wallpaper with lines of deep blue flowers running up a pale blue background.

It was a room she'd never seen before. She tried, but she simply couldn't keep her eyes open and the room faded away.

Lloyd Winston's office turned out to be on the same floor as the NICU, and the office was as untidy as the man himself. His desk and file cabinets were piled high with books, forms and folders. Empty foam cups overflowed from the trash can. He cleared off a portion of the desk by moving its contents to a stack on the floor, then sat down. Mick took a seat and waited for him to speak.

Flipping open his briefcase, Winston pulled out a file. "I understand you haven't signed the paternity papers for your daughter. Do you realize that until you do, you're not legally the baby's parent?"

"I understand that," Mick answered. "The situation with Caitlin and myself is a bit—well—unusual." Mick watched the man's confusion grow as he explained how he and Caitlin had met. When he finished, Winston leaned back and pressed his fingertips together over his ample paunch.

"You'd like me to believe that after meeting you for the first time, out of the blue, a woman, who may or may not think she's dying, names you as her baby's father?" His tone held more than a hint of disbelief.

"That's what happened."

Winston leaned forward and stared at Mick intently. "I know that taking on the responsibility of caring for a critically ill infant can be very daunting. It's understandable that you're reluctant to admit to being the child's father."

Mick leveled his gaze at the overstuffed social

worker. "I'm a firefighter. Walking into a burning building is daunting. Trust me. Beth is not my biological child."

The man's eyes widened at Mick's tone. "I see. This certainly complicates things. Dr. Wright tells me the child needs surgery. I'll have to get a court order to make her a ward of the state right away."

Mick frowned. "She has a mother. She doesn't need to be made a ward of the state."

"Ms. Williams's condition prevents her from giving consent for any procedure, and I understand her recovery is doubtful. Since she's incapacitated and you are not any relation to the child, the state must assume care."

"For how long?"

"I beg your pardon?"

"How long will Beth be a ward of the state?"

"Until we can locate a relative. Which we might have done by now if you had come forward with the truth sooner."

"What if you can't locate anyone?"

"If we don't, she'll remain a ward of the state and go into foster care when she leaves here."

A knock sounded at the door, and a nurse from the NICU looked in. "Mr. O'Callaghan, you're wanted in the unit."

Mick shoved out of his chair. "Is something wrong with Beth?" Fear sent his heart hammering wildly.

"I'm afraid so," she said. "Please come with me."

Chapter 4

Mick rushed into the NICU. A crowd surrounded Beth's bed. The monitor above it alarmed as the blip of her heart rate barely moved across the screen. He stopped a nurse hurrying past him, glad to see it was Sandra Carter. "What's wrong?"

"Doctor, the father is here," she said.

"Good." The man in green scrubs looked at Mick. "X-rays show your daughter has suffered a collapsed lung and the air trapped inside her chest is putting pressure on her heart."

Sick with fear and powerless to help, Mick couldn't take his eyes off Beth's pale, gray color. She wasn't moving.

Someone touched his shoulder. Glancing over, he saw Lloyd Winston standing beside him. "They'll do everything they can," he said gently.

"Prep her, then we'll get a chest tube in," the doctor barked orders before turning to Mick. "I understand you have some medical background. Do you know what we're doing?"

Mick nodded. "You're going to put a tube in her chest and suck the air out so her lung can reexpand. Will she be all right?"

"I believe so." Dr. Myers opened a small plastic pack and pulled out a surgical gown. Quickly, he donned it as Sandra poured dark brown liquid antiseptic over the skin on Beth's chest. "Have X-ray standing by, and give her a dose of fentanyl for the pain," he instructed.

"Yes, Doctor. Her oxygen saturation is forty."

"Gloves! Where are my gloves?" he snapped.

"Right here." Another nurse peeled open a package. He pulled them on.

Beside Mick, Lloyd Winston spoke. "You don't have to watch this. We can wait outside," he offered.

"No, I'm fine," Mick answered. How long had her heart rate and oxygen levels been this low? Five minutes? Longer? How much time did she have left before she suffered brain damage? Was it already too late?

As the doctor worked, Mick's gaze stayed glued to the monitor. After what seemed like an eternity, Beth's heart rate climbed to eighty, then one hundred. Slowly, the color of her skin changed from gray, to mottled blue then to a pale pink. One little leg kicked feebly under the drape, and Mick sagged with relief. "Thank You, Lord."

Sandra glanced at Mick and frowned. "Hey, we don't do adults in here. Someone get Dad a chair."

"I'm all right." Mike tried to wave aside her concern.

"No, you're not. You're white as a sheet. Lloyd, take him out to the waiting room."

"I want to stay," Mick protested. What if her other lung collapsed? She could die, he knew it.

"I know you want to stay," Sandra said, "but this isn't something you need to watch. She's not feeling the pain, I promise you that."

"You'll come and get me if…things get worse." Mick stared into her eyes. She nodded and he knew she understood what he was asking.

In the waiting area, he paced back and forth. Ten steps across, ten steps back. The same blue tweed chairs as in the adult ICU sat against the walls. It seemed that all he did anymore was wait—with fear grinding in his gut while doctors and nurses tried to save first Caitlin, and now Beth again.

Please, Lord, let Beth be okay. She's so little. Hold her in Your hands and keep her safe.

Lloyd sat and watched Mick. "Can I get you something?"

"If you have a prayer to spare for her, that wouldn't come amiss."

"Certainly. I have one for her and one for you as well. I've seen a lot a babies get chest tubes. It isn't as serious as you think."

Mick knew better. It was deadly serious, but he couldn't find the words to tell a stranger that he feared Beth might die. Some of what he was feeling must have shown on his face.

"It's okay to be scared," Lloyd Winston said.

Mick sank into a chair beside the social worker. "I know. How do you deal with this kind of pain every day?"

"You said you're a firefighter? Don't tell me you haven't seen some bad things yourself."

Dropping his head to stare at his clenched hands, Mick nodded. He'd seen his share of terrible things—things a man couldn't unsee. There were days when he wanted to quit. If not for the Lord's grace, he might have.

"I expect it's the same for both of us," Winston continued. "We got into our lines of work to make a difference. We stay because, not every day, but some days we do make a difference in people's lives."

Mick nodded, surprised at how well the man understood him. He'd made a snap judgment about Lloyd Winston, thinking the man was an overworked bureaucrat who didn't care. He was wrong. It was evident that Lloyd cared a lot.

Mick's smile faded. "What will happen if Beth doesn't make it? If she dies—what will happen?"

"Usually, the body remains here until the family chooses a mortuary, but in this case, she'll be taken to the city morgue. If no one claims the body after three or four months they'll bury her. The city provides plots for unclaimed bodies."

"What'll happen if she lives, but her mother doesn't?"

"As I said, she'll be placed in foster care."

"No." Mick heard the word, but almost didn't believe he had said it. Was he really considering such a deception?

"I'm sorry, I don't understand." Winston stared at him.

"Beth isn't going into foster care. I know her mother wouldn't want that." *Is this what You want, Lord?*

Was he losing his mind? Saying that Beth was his child was a lie. But Mick couldn't hand her over to strangers—whether she lived or died. Wasn't this what Caitlin wanted? For him to take care of her child if she couldn't? He was adopting Beth with her mother's blessing. His troubled conscience grew quiet.

"I'll sign the paternity papers."

Winston left and returned a few minutes later. Mick took the form and stared at the blank line on the bottom. Signing it would give the child of a stranger his name. Legally, Beth would become his responsibility forever. It would be up to him to make a home for her, to see that she got to school on time for the first day of kindergarten, to see that she had the money to go to college. He'd become responsible for medical bills that could leave him in debt until he was an old man. If she died today, he would plan her funeral.

Was this right? Was it truly what God wanted of him? If he didn't do this, could he live with himself? Could he walk away and go on with his life knowing he had let Caitlin down? He knew that he couldn't.

I'm sorry for this lie, Lord, but I believe in my heart that this is what You are asking of me. Please help me to do the right thing. Bending forward, he scrawled his name on the line.

"Mick, you can come in now." Sandra stood in the doorway.

He leaped to his feet. "Is she okay?"

"She's stable. Come and see for yourself."

He followed her into the nursery. A clear tube stained with droplets of blood protruded from Beth's right side and led to a plastic box below her bed. In its chambers, a column of water bubbled freely.

"It looks weird," Sandra said, "but it doesn't hurt her."

Beth was alive, that was all that mattered to Mick. *Thank You, God. Make me worthy of this gift.*

He slipped a tentative finger beneath the baby's limp hand. She lay pale and quiet, making no move to grip his finger as she'd done before. Sandra pulled a tall stool over beside the bed, and Mick nodded his thanks. Sitting down, he tilted his face to gaze at his baby.

His baby. His daughter. A warm glow replaced the chill in the center of his chest. She belonged to him, legally, if not by blood. How often had he wondered what it would be like? Wondered if he could love an adopted child the same as his own flesh and blood? Now he knew. He'd come to love Beth the first moment she had frowned at him. He loved the way she wrinkled her brow, and he loved her long, delicate fingers. He loved the way she kicked her feet over the edge of her bunting, and the way she fussed until someone changed her diaper when she was wet. He couldn't imagine loving any child more.

As he sat watching her and trying to imagine a future together he saw Beth's face contort into a grimace. She stiffened her arms, holding them out straight. Her whole body twitched. He looked for help. "Sandra, something's wrong."

She came quickly to the bedside. She took hold of the baby's arm, but it continued to jerk. "Let me get the doctor."

She returned with Dr. Myers. "How long?" he asked, watching the baby intently.

"A minute now," Sandra replied.

"You're right. Looks like a seizure. Let's get an EEG

and give her a loading dose of phenobarbital. I'll write the orders."

Mick caught the doctor's arm before he could turn away. "What would cause her to have a seizure?"

"I can't say for sure. We'll have to do some tests. We'll let you know the results as soon as we get them."

Mick stayed with Beth for another hour, then he left the NICU and made his way down to the adult intensive care unit where he waited to be allowed in to see Caitlin. Her nurse for the evening gave him the first encouraging news he'd had since the day Beth was born. Caitlin was assisting the ventilator at times by breathing on her own.

"Does this mean she's waking up?"

The nurse shook her head. "Unfortunately, no. Patients in a coma can often breathe without a vent."

"I see." And he did. If Caitlin came off the ventilator but didn't wake up, she might live in a vegetative state for years.

He opened Caitlin's door and stepped into the dimly lit room. She lay on her side facing the window. Beyond the dark panes of glass, the lights of the city glowed brightly, and traffic streamed by on the streets below. Cars filled with people who had homes and families waiting. Everyone had somewhere to go. Everyone except the woman on the bed.

What he knew of her life had been filled with pain. Had she ever known a safe night in the arms of someone she loved? Would she have a chance for any of those things, or would she live out her life caught between waking and dying, kept alive by tube feedings and overworked nurses?

Pulling up a chair, he sat beside her and took her

hand. "I had to make a choice today, Caitlin. I signed paternity papers. Beth is now legally my child. Our child, I guess. As strange as this sounds, in my heart I feel sure it's what you wanted. It's the only way I can look after her."

He watched the ventilator for a while, but he couldn't tell if it was breathing for her or if she was breathing by herself.

"I'd like to tell you that things are going well for her, but the truth is, she's in a lot of trouble. It was touch and go all day today."

Tears pricked his eyes, and his throat closed around the words he didn't want to say. "I don't know if she's going to make it, Caitlin. And I don't know how I'm going to face it if she doesn't. I love her already—I do."

He wiped his eyes with the back of one hand and drew a shaky breath. "I have to believe she's going to be okay. I have faith, and I've prayed more in the past few days than in any time in my life."

He leaned forward and brushed his knuckles down the soft skin of her cheek. "Lady, you have no idea of the mess you started. I'm not even sure how I'm going to explain this to my family. Frankly, they're going to think I'm certifiable."

"You did what?"

"That can't be legal, can it?"

Mick listened to the protests and objections of his older sisters as they sat at the oak table in his kitchen three days later. He knew they would react this way. That was why he'd called them together, to get the protests over with all at once. Then maybe he could get some sleep.

Beth's lung was healing, but an EEG confirmed she was having seizures. The doctors had started her on a drug called phenobarbital to control them. Soon after that, she had gone to surgery to close her patent ductus arteriosus, and Mick had spent agonizing hours in the surgical waiting room with Pastor Frank and Lloyd Winston at his side for support.

The surgery had gone well, and Beth's condition had finally stabilized enough for Mick to feel that he could spend some time at home. Thank goodness his mother was better and didn't require his constant care. The last few days had seemed longer than a month. He was bone tired, but he needed to get this meeting over with.

"What about this child's real father? Don't you think he has something to say about this?" Mary demanded, crossing her arms over her ample bosom and rattling the lid of a dainty teapot that sat in the center of the table.

Mary was the oldest, and he expected the most opposition from her. He'd often joked that he'd been born with three mothers instead of one. Alice, the sister closest to him in age, was his senior by twelve years. His mother sat at the table with them but she remained quiet.

Mick said, "According to Caitlin the baby's father is dead. She told me when we first met that there isn't anyone."

Mary's frown deepened. "Even so, I can't see why you think you need to be the child's parent. Did you even consider the financial obligation you're taking on? You'll have to support this child until she's eighteen even if her mother recovers."

"I know that."

Mary's lips pressed into a thin line. "And if her

mother doesn't recover? Do you think you can raise a child alone?"

"Yes, I do," he answered with more confidence than he felt. He'd asked himself these questions and more over the past several days. He might not be the best parent in the world, but he intended to give it his best shot.

He looked at each of his sisters in turn. "She's a tiny, helpless baby—so tiny I could hold her in one hand, and she doesn't have a soul in the world to care for her. No one should have to go through the things she is going through alone."

"Will she…will she be right?" Alice asked.

"What do you mean?" he asked.

"Children like this—aren't they—sometimes mentally challenged?"

Mary looked at him with pity. "Oh, Mick, what have you gotten yourself into?"

He wanted to ignore their questions. He knew the possibilities, but it didn't change the way he felt. Beth was his, for better or for worse.

"It's too soon to tell if she will have disabilities," he said. "Tests show she had a small bleed in her brain. A Grade Two, they called it. Some babies do have problems after that, but some do fine. We can only hope and pray she'll be healthy, but it doesn't matter."

"Of course it matters!" Mary's tone was incredulous. "Did her mother use drugs? Is she addicted? Has she been tested for AIDS?"

Mick tried to curb his annoyance. Couldn't they accept that Beth was simply a baby in need of love and affection?

His mother held up her hand. "Hush, girls, and leave him alone. You two don't know how lucky you are to have had healthy babies. No child comes with a guarantee. Only God knows what we will have to face. I've been willing to trust Him all my life and so does Mickey. It's something both of you would do well to try."

He took a deep breath. "If I can't do anything else for her—even if she doesn't make it—I can see that she's not alone in this life."

Mary's gaze fell before his. "But signing paternity papers seems so extreme."

"It was the only way," he said.

Alice lightly clapped her hands. "Great speech. Just the right touch of a plea for maternal understanding. How long did you practice?"

"I think what Mickey is doing is wonderful." His mother rose to his defense. "It's not like he's totally clueless around children. Why, he babysits your kids often enough."

Mary gave a huff. "Watching the kids for an hour or two is not like raising them. And what about your job? You can't simply take off for the next few months."

"I can use the vacation time I've got coming, and I can afford to take off a few more weeks if I have to."

"And when this baby comes home from the hospital? Who's going to watch her when you go to work? You can't expect Mom to take on the job at her age."

"I'm not expecting any of you to take care of Beth. I'll arrange for day care like the rest of the world does."

"You don't always have to be the hero, Mick," Alice said quietly.

"I'm not trying to be a hero here."

"Are you sure?" Mary asked. "First you follow in Dad's footsteps in the same job that got him killed.

And no offense, Mom, but then, Mick insists on moving you in with him after the accident. As great as that is, Mick, I think you're putting your own life on hold. You were only eight when Dad died, but you were determined to be the man of the family."

Mick rose from the table with the pretext of refilling his coffee cup. He'd become the man of the family because, with his dying breath, his father told him he had to.

"My life isn't on hold, and Mom is welcome to stay here as long as she wants."

"Because you promised Dad you'd always look after her," Mary stated.

He whirled around, barely noticing the hot coffee that sloshed over his hand. "Leave Dad out of this!"

"Please, children, don't fight," Elizabeth pleaded.

Mick stuck his stinging knuckles under the tap and turned on the cold water. "Mom is here because we *all* decided it was the best solution. As for my work—I like being a firefighter. It's my life, Mary. Just because I didn't choose a nine-to-five job like your boring businessman husband doesn't mean it's a waste. Money isn't everything."

"As usual, I see you don't intend to listen to anything I have to say. If you wanted my advice, you would have asked for it instead of telling me after the fact. Mother, I hope you can talk some sense into him."

Biting back his retort, Mick turned around. "I'm sorry, Mary. I don't want to argue. I do want your support in this."

"And I can't give it. A child needs a mother and a father. You've got no business trying to raise one by yourself." She rose and headed out the back door, letting it slam behind her.

"You shouldn't have said that about Rodger," Elizabeth chided.

"Oh, pooh." Alice waved her mother's objection aside. "He *is* boring and Mary was the first one to notice."

"No, Mom is right." Mick dried his hands. "I let Mary get under my skin, and then I say something that makes her mad."

"Mary was born mad," Elizabeth added quietly.

Mick and Alice turned to stare at her in astonishment.

After glancing from one to the other, she straightened. "Well, it's true. It's the red hair."

Mick laughed. "My hair's red. Do you say that about me?"

Alice snorted. "Mom has never said an unkind word about you from the day you were born. Frankly, it irked me. Nobody's that perfect."

"Mom doesn't know the half of it," he retorted.

Elizabeth grinned at him. "Don't be too sure about that."

"No," Alice said, "you, little brother, are too good for your own good."

"Would you rather I lie, drink, steal and swear? That's not a very Christian attitude."

"What I'd like is to see you go a little wild once in a while. Skip church on Sunday. The place won't fall down."

"Alice!" Clearly appalled, Elizabeth gaped at her daughter. "Just because you don't go to church on a regular basis is no reason to tempt Mickey to give it up."

Rolling her eyes, Alice asked, "Are you tempted?" When he shook his head, she turned to her mother and spread her hands. "See? All I'm saying is that he needs to have a little fun in his life. He's way too serious."

She rose and crossed the room to stand in front of him. "If you're determined to do this, fine. Just make sure you're doing it because *you* want this, and not because you think this is what Dad would want you to do. Otherwise, much as I hate to say it, I'm with Mary on this."

"Good news, Mick." At the NICU the following morning, Sandra came across the room to greet him. "We pulled Beth's chest tube today. She's doing fine."

"That is good news."

"Would you like to hold her?" Sandra asked.

Joy leaped in his heart. "Of course I would."

Then, just as quickly, his elation took a dive, tempered by a heavy dose of dread. "Are you sure it's okay?"

Smiling, Sandra patted his arm. "I'll be here to keep an eye on her. Have you heard of kangaroo care?"

He shook his head.

"It's where we let parents hold their babies skin-to-skin. We'll lay her on your bare chest and cover her with a blanket. Your body heat will keep her warm, and the sound of your heartbeat will soothe her. Want to try it?"

"Sure."

"Good. We'll be able to do this once a day if she tolerates it, but moving her is rather complicated and that's the stressful part. We ask that you hold her for at least an hour. Do you have that much time today?"

"You bet."

At the bedside, he saw Beth lying curled on her side with both hands tucked under her chin.

"Hey, sweet pea. I get to hold you today. Isn't that great?"

Beth's eyes fluttered at the sound of his voice, and she yawned. Chuckling, Sandra said, "I don't think she's suitably impressed with you."

Sandra indicated a recliner beside the bed. "Okay, Mick, take your shirt off."

He pulled his T-shirt off over his head. Feeling a bit self-conscious, he sat in the chair, still as a fire hydrant, while the nurses transferred Beth. The scary part came when they unhooked her from the vent. Alarms sounded until Sandra laid the baby on his chest, and reconnected her to the machine.

His large hand covered Beth's entire back and held her still as she squirmed in her new environment. She was light as a feather against him. He could barely take in the rush of emotions that filled him. Sandra laid a warm blanket over the two of them, and Beth proceeded to make herself comfortable. She wiggled against his skin, her tiny fingers grasping handfuls of his chest hair.

She felt wonderful, amazing. So real and so precious. A tiny, warm body pressed against his heart. It was everything he had ever imagined it would be and more. He wanted to hold on to this marvelous moment forever. Did Beth hear his heartbeat? Did she draw comfort from the sound? Did she remember the sound of her mother's beating heart?

An intense sadness settled over him, dulling his happiness.

He looked up at Sandra, hovering close by. "It should be her mother holding her for the first time."

"At least she has you. Some children never know a loving touch their entire lives even when they have two parents."

Caitlin opened her eyes to see sunshine streaming in through a wide window that framed a blue sky and fluffy white clouds. Her nose itched. She raised her hand to scratch it then stopped, startled. A padded board and a loop of clear tubing were taped to her hand. Swallowing painfully, she discovered a tube in her mouth.

Bits and pieces of a half-remembered dream danced at the edge of her mind. A deep voice telling her everything would be all right, the wailing of a siren, someone saying, "It's a girl," other voices saying, "blind and deaf."

She tried but nothing settled into place, and her head began to pound. She moved a hand to her belly, seeking the lump that sometimes stirred and kicked. She found only flatness. Had she lost the baby? Cold fear settled in her chest.

The sound of a door opening came from behind her. A moment later, a young woman in a nurse's uniform came around the bed. She stopped short, and her eyes widened in surprise as she met Caitlin's gaze.

"Well, hello. It's nice to see you awake. In fact, it's quite a shock." Taking a small light from her pocket, she leaned over the bed rail and shone it in Caitlin's eyes, checking first one, then the other. Putting the light away she slipped her hand beneath Caitlin's and said, "Squeeze my hand."

Caitlin did, and the woman's smile widened. Gingerly, Caitlin touched the tube in her mouth.

The nurse nodded. "You're on a ventilator, that's why you can't talk. It's been helping you breathe, but I don't think you'll need it much longer. I know you have a lot of questions. Let me get something for you to write on."

Something to write on? No, that wouldn't do. They'd find out how stupid she was. They'd laugh at her. They always did.

The nurse started to turn away, but Caitlin grabbed her. Fearfully, she patted her now flat stomach and waited with dread crawling inside her.

The woman smiled in understanding and grasped Caitlin's hand. "Your baby is here in the hospital, and she's being well taken care of, so don't you worry. We have to concentrate on getting you well enough to go and see her. Okay?"

Caitlin relaxed in heartfelt relief. Her baby was here. She had a little girl, and she would be able to see her. Everything was fine. Just like the voice had promised.

The nurse returned followed by a short, bald man in a white coat. "Welcome back to the world, young woman," the doctor said. "Do you remember what happened?"

Caitlin shook her head, ignoring the pen and paper the nurse laid on the bed.

"I'm not surprised. You've been in a coma. We'd just about given up hope that you'd wake up." Like the nurse, he used a small light to check Caitlin's eyes.

"Mick never gave up hope," the nurse said. "He's been in to see you nearly every day. You're lucky to have a guy like that. Every minute he isn't with you, he's upstairs with your baby. He has the makings of a great dad."

Caitlin frowned as she tried to make sense of the woman's chatter, but the doctor drew her attention when he asked her to follow the movement of the light, then to move her hands and her feet. At last, he straightened. "I'm going to remove the tube in your throat. If you have any questions, go ahead and write them down." He indicated the pad beside her.

Caitlin shook her head. Any questions she had could wait until she could speak for herself.

Caitlin winced as they peeled the tape off her face. When the doctor pulled out the tube, she choked and gasped for air. The nurse put a mask over her face. Quickly, her breathing became easier.

The doctor straightened, and stuffed his stethoscope in his pocket. "Your throat will be sore for a few days, and you'll be hoarse. Let us know if you have any trouble breathing."

"Thanks," Caitlin managed to croak.

"Start her out on ice chips, then sips of clear liquids. Let me know how she does."

"Yes, Doctor." The nurse disappeared out the door.

He patted Caitlin's shoulder. "You're a very lucky woman."

She didn't feel lucky. She felt like a lab rat who'd tested a new poison and found it hadn't quite killed her.

The nurse came back with a foam cup and offered Caitlin a plastic spoon full of ice. Taking it gratefully, she held the cold moistness in her dry mouth, letting it melt and spread to every corner before she chanced swallowing. It was as painful as she expected but the ice felt so wonderful on her dry tongue that she took a second spoonful eagerly.

"This is so exciting," the nurse said. "I just phoned Mick. He's on his way—he'll be here shortly."

Waiting until every bit of the marvelous ice had melted, Caitlin swallowed her second spoonful, grimacing at the discomfort. "Who's Mick?" she managed to croak.

The woman's eyes widened. "You don't remember him?"

Caitlin shook her head, puzzled by the woman's obvious surprise. Pointing to the ice, she asked, "Can I have more?"

The nurse gave her another spoonful. "Are you positive you don't remember Mick O'Callaghan? Think carefully."

"No. Who is he?"

"Your baby's father."

Caitlin choked on her piece of ice.

Chapter 5

"I'm telling you, I don't know anybody by that name." Caitlin tried to hide her exhaustion. Her throat burned from her efforts to talk. She knew her own name; she even knew who the president was, but she didn't know anyone named Mick. So, why was some guy pretending to be her baby's daddy?

The doctor jotted a note on her chart. "Amnesia isn't unusual after a trauma such as you've experienced, but it's usually limited to the time directly preceding the event. The fact that you can't remember a specific person is somewhat worrisome."

"No kidding," she croaked.

"It's best not to try to force your memory. You've been in a coma for ten days. For now, you need rest."

"Ten days?" Caitlin stared at him, aghast. She'd been asleep for ten whole days? How was that even possible? Her daughter had been alone all this time. Who'd been taking care of her? She grabbed his arm. "I've got to see my baby."

"I'm sorry, but you can't get up yet. You've been very ill." The doctor gently removed her hand.

"I want to see my daughter. Let me out of this thing." She shook the bed rails.

"Your baby is being taken care of. If your vital signs remain stable, we'll talk about letting you visit the NICU tomorrow."

Caitlin stared at him. "What's that?"

"NICU stands for neonatal intensive care unit."

Blinding pain stabbed through Caitlin's head. "Intensive care? What's wrong with her?"

"Your baby is very premature. She needs special care to help her breathe and stay warm."

"I've got to see her." Again, she tried to sit up.

The doctor stopped her. "Not today."

"Please?" She hated pleading.

"Perhaps tomorrow," the nurse said.

Caitlin looked down and smoothed the sheet with her free hand, then leaned back and closed her eyes. She wasn't strong enough to fight both of them. Let them think she'd given up. "Okay. I guess I am kind of tired."

The doctor patted her shoulder. "I'm sure you are. Get some rest. Tomorrow will come soon enough."

After a moment, she heard the door close, but the faint sound of movement told her the nurse had remained. She waited. Lying quietly in bed, sleep pulled at her, but she fought it. What if she didn't wake up the next time she drifted off?

Long minutes stretched by until at last Caitlin heard

the door open and close. She chanced a peek. The room
was empty.

Studying the bed rails, she couldn't find a way to
lower them, so she scooted to the foot of the bed. Slipping out the end, she stood and clutched the footboard.
The room spun and tumbled around her like clothes in
a Laundromat dryer.

"What do you think you're doing?"

Startled, Caitlin looked up to see a tall man with
auburn hair and a deep scowl on his face standing in
the doorway. The movement cost her what little balance she had, and she pitched forward.

She would have hit the floor if he hadn't been so
quick. Instead, she felt herself swept up and cradled in
arms that were as strong as they were gentle.

"Easy does it. You're okay, I've got you."

She kept her eyes closed to shut out the sight of the
spinning room as the last of her strength drained away.
She knew that voice. It haunted her dreams.

Mick stared at the pale slip of a woman in his arms.
Her full lashes, tipped with burnished gold lay fanned
against her high-boned cheeks. They fluttered for a moment, then lay still. An ugly, red mark left by the tape
that had held her ventilator tubing marred her fair skin.

Sleeping Beauty was awake. He was glad for Caitlin's recovery, but his dreams and plans for Beth had
died a quick death when he got the phone call. Oh, he
intended to remain a part of her life—a big part. But
just how much depended on the woman he held.

Caitlin stirred in his arms, and he noticed the thin-
ness of her body beneath his hands. She felt delicate
and fragile. During the past week and a half, she had
lost weight she didn't have to spare. The thought roused

feelings of pity. How had someone so small and exquisite survived in the harsh, violent world of Chicago's slums?

And how could she take care of Beth in that same brutal environment? The thought of what might happen to them sent chills down his spine. He'd seen enough worst-case scenarios to know the odds were stacked against them.

Caitlin gathered her strength as she rested for a moment with her cheek pressed against the crisp material of the man's shirt. It held a clean, fresh smell, but beneath that scent was a deeper more disturbing one—a masculine essence.

"Next time wait until someone is here to help before you get up." Deep, mellow and scolding, the voice from her dreams rumbled up from the chest beneath her ear. She chanced opening her eyes. The face above her was handsome except for the frown etched between his deep blue eyes. Handsome and vaguely familiar. She stared at him feeling both puzzled and disturbed.

"Mick, what on earth happened?" The surprised question came from the nurse who hurried into the room. "Is she hurt?"

"I don't think so."

"Let's get her back into bed. What was she trying to do?"

"I haven't the faintest idea."

Caitlin's dizziness eased, but her pounding headache didn't. Still, she kept her gaze fastened on the face of the man who laid her gently on the bed. So this was Mick, the guy claiming to be her baby's father. There was something familiar about him—but she couldn't put her finger on it.

The nurse checked Caitlin's IV, then wrapped a blood pressure cuff around her other arm. "I had hoped that seeing you might jar her memory."

"Stop talking about me like I'm not here." Caitlin eyed the man beside the bed. He rubbed his hands on the sides of his jeans then thrust them into his front pockets and avoided looking at her. Why was he saying he was her baby's father? What did he want?

The nurse seemed satisfied with Caitlin's blood pressure. She folded the cuff and tucked it in its holder above the bed.

"Betty, could I talk to Caitlin alone?" Mick asked.

"Of course. I'll be right outside if you need me." The nurse flashed him a sympathetic smile, patted his arm and left.

So he was on a first-name basis with the nurses. The knowledge made Caitlin uneasy. What was his angle? She waited until the door closed. Arching one eyebrow, she said, "Okay, Mick—jar me."

He pulled a chair up and sat beside the bed. Clasping his hands together, he stared at them for a long second, then met her gaze. "What's the last thing you remember?"

She tried to concentrate, but her headache pounded away inside her skull. Trying to remember only made it worse. She struggled to keep her face bland. It never paid to let others see your weakness. "I remember thinking I was in labor."

"You called out and Eddy came."

"That's right," she admitted slowly. "He said he'd get help, but I had my doubts."

A small grin lifted the corner of his lips. "I guess we both underestimated him."

It was his smile that triggered her memory. Oh, yes, she knew him now. She had sketched him once, tried to capture his powerful body and his gentle manner that was so at odds with his size. She had caught that unique quality with limited success. Maybe because gentleness was something she knew little about. "I've seen you at one of the shelters."

"I try to get over to Mercy House once or twice a week."

"Eddy brought you to my room, and you stayed with me until the ambulance got there. You came with me. The siren was so loud. What happened after that?"

"You had your baby in the emergency room."

"I don't remember," she whispered.

"You told me to go with her when they took her to the nursery, and I did. Apparently, before you passed out, you told them I was the baby's father."

Caitlin resisted the urge to believe him. "Why would I do that?"

"The doctor said that women who have an embolus like you did—they know something is wrong. If you thought you were dying, maybe you didn't have anyone else who could take care of her."

He was telling the truth. Somehow she knew it, but she couldn't remember. What kind of mother forgets the birth of her own child?

No! She couldn't think like that. She was going to be a good mother. Sitting up, she ignored the pain and dizziness that came back as she swung her legs over the edge of the bed. "I have to see her."

"Whoa!" He grasped her shoulders. "You almost wound up on the floor the last time you tried this."

She struck his arm away. "Get your hands off me."

"Hey, I'm trying to help. Do you *want* to fall on your face?" His voice rose in response to hers.

"What I want is for you to get away from me," she shouted.

The door opened and the nurse entered, followed closely by the doctor who had examined Caitlin earlier.

"Oh, no you don't," the nurse chided. She quickly slipped her arms under Caitlin's legs, lifted them back onto the bed and pulled up the rail, killing Caitlin's hopes.

Angry and frustrated by her own helplessness, Caitlin shook the bed rails again. "Put this thing down! You can't keep me away from my baby!"

The doctor spoke up. "Ms. Williams, you must calm down."

Mick listened to the outburst that followed in stunned disbelief. Sleeping Beauty was awake, but this was no princess. And she wasn't behaving the way he had imagined Beth's mother would act. He should have known better. The woman had spent her life on the streets. Why had he expected something different?

The doctor grabbed Caitlin's swinging arms and held them still. "Nurse, give her ten milligrams of Valium IV, *stat.*"

"No!" Caitlin's voice rose to a shriek. The fight drained out of her. "No drugs. Please—I'll be good. I will. Only, no drugs," she pleaded.

Her gaze fastened on Mick. Those wide, beautiful, tawny-gold eyes begged for his help again, he knew it without her saying a word. How did she do it? When her defenses were up, he couldn't read a thing in her eyes, but now they spoke volumes, like the time he'd found her in labor.

Mick laid a hand on the doctor's shoulder. "Sedating her won't be necessary."

Releasing his grip on her now limp hands, the doctor straightened. Caitlin remained quiet. Staring at Mick, she nodded slightly then closed her eyes in defeat.

"Outbursts like this can't be tolerated," the doctor began.

Mick spoke up. "Don't worry, it won't happen again. Will it, Caitlin?"

Her eyes snapped open and for a moment, defiance glared out at him, but it quickly disappeared. "No, it won't happen again," she answered meekly.

What a chameleon she was. He almost laughed. Instead, he said, "Ms. Williams is obviously distraught over her desire to see her daughter. I'm sure she would rest better if she could see her baby, even for a few minutes. I could take her."

Rubbing his arm where Caitlin had landed a blow, the doctor considered the request. "I'm not insensitive to her concern, and she certainly appears stronger than I expected. I'll have one of the nurses accompany you. But just for a brief visit, then she comes directly back here."

"Understood," Mick agreed. Caitlin remained silent. Did she have enough strength to tolerate the trip? Perhaps it wasn't wise to risk taking her to the NICU.

Suddenly, her hand shot out and gripped the doctor's arm. "Thank you," she whispered hoarsely. Her eyes brimmed with unshed tears as her gaze fastened on his face.

The doctor patted her hand. "You win this round, but don't expect to win every one. I pack a mean left hook, myself."

A slight smile trembled on her lips as she nodded.

With Betty's help, Mick swaddled Caitlin in a blanket and carefully lifted her into a wheelchair, then with the two of them managing the IV pole and pumps, they made the trip down the hall to the elevators. He watched with renewed concern as Caitlin slumped lower in the chair when the elevator door closed. He touched her shoulder. "Are you okay?"

Caitlin battled the nausea threatening to overwhelm her as the elevator rose, but she straightened at Mick's touch and managed to answer, "Sure."

If she admitted to anything different, showed any sign of weakness, she knew he'd take her back to her room, and she wouldn't see her baby. Her head alternated between piercing pain and reeling dizziness. If she had tried to walk she never would have made it.

He rattled on about the NICU, but she couldn't listen. It was all she could do to keep from falling out of the wheelchair.

The bell chimed for their floor and the doors parted. "This is it," Mick announced.

Anticipation lent Caitlin added strength. Her baby was here.

Mick maneuvered her through a set of wide doors. A young couple stood washing their hands at a large sink. Mick waited until they were finished, then he pushed Caitlin up to the sink. He patted a sign on the wall beside her.

"The directions for working the sinks and for washing your hands are right here. You have to do this every time you visit. I'll let them know you're here." He stepped over to a sliding glass window and spoke with a woman seated at a desk behind it.

Caitlin stared at the gibberish on the wall. Now what? She searched for a way around her problem. There was always a way. Leaning back, she turned her friendliest smile on the nurse waiting beside her and held out her arm with its IV board. "I can't get this wet, can I?"

"It says to use the germicidal foam. Let me help you."

"Thanks." Caitlin waited while the woman applied a white foam that looked like whipping cream and smelled like alcohol.

Mick came back at that moment. "Let me get scrubbed, then we can go in."

Caitlin watched closely. She could remember how to do just about anything if she saw it done once. He pulled a small package from a holder on the wall. Opening it, he used a funny little stick to clean under his nails, then he scrubbed up to his elbows with a brush. He kept glancing at a clock over the sink. After three minutes, he rinsed and dried off with paper towels. She could remember that.

Betty held the door open as Mick pushed Caitlin through and said, "I'll wait downstairs until you're done. Give me a call when she's ready to come back."

He agreed then maneuvered Caitlin's wheelchair into a large room, and her heart began to race. At last, she was going to see her baby. But in the room lined with babies in beds and incubators, Caitlin suddenly realized she didn't know which baby was hers.

She had no idea what her daughter looked like. She wouldn't know her own child! They could show her anyone's baby, and she would have to believe them.

A nurse came across the room and stopped beside Mick. "Is this Beth's mother?"

"Yes," Mick said, "Caitlin, this is Sandra, Beth's primary nurse."

Bewildered, Caitlin glanced from one to the other. "Who's Beth?"

The nurse frowned slightly and looked at Mick. He knelt beside Caitlin. "Beth is your baby's name."

"You named her? Who gave you that right? Where is she?"

"She's down here." The nurse led the way, and Mick pushed Caitlin's wheelchair down the length of the room.

Caitlin stared at the infants in the beds as she passed them. Some were tiny, smaller than any babies she'd ever seen. Black, white, crying, sleeping, there had to be thirty of them here, at least. A mother seated in a rocker was smiling at the child she held. A couple waited as a nurse opened the front of an incubator and carefully lifted their baby out, trailing a tangle of cords. Monitors lined the walls above the beds. An alarm sounded somewhere, then another and a nurse hurried past them to a bed at the far end of the unit.

Mick stopped beside a flat bed with clear plastic sides and a warming lamp glowing overhead.

"This is your daughter," the nurse said, opening the side of the bed. Mick edged the wheelchair closer.

Shock, disbelief and confusion swirled through Caitlin as she stared at the tiny infant on the bed in front of her. She was so small!

The baby lay on her back with her scrawny arms folded against her chest, and her hands resting beside her cheeks. A white bandage covered most of her right side. Wires ran from small patches on her chest and legs. Thick tape across her cheeks held a breathing tube

in her mouth. Clear tubing tied into her shriveled umbilical cord led to IV pumps beside the bed. Her long
legs looked like they belonged on a frog. She didn't
look anything like Caitlin had imagined she would.

Had she caused this? She didn't smoke, didn't do
drugs. She'd tried to eat right, but the stuff at the soup
kitchens wasn't always that healthy. Once, she'd even
shoplifted a bottle of vitamins. If only she'd gone to the
free clinic again and gotten another checkup, maybe
they would have prevented this. What if it was her
fault, and now her baby was suffering because of it?

Caitlin waited to feel joy, happiness, love—all the
things she had known she would feel when she first saw
her baby—all the things she wanted desperately to feel.

Instead, she felt guilt and grief. In the dreams she
had cherished for months when she was cold and hungry and alone, she had imagined a plump, sweet-
smelling baby she could hold close to her heart. Nothing like this.

Caitlin looked up at the nurse. "Are you sure this is
my baby?" she asked, then cringed. How stupid did that
sound? What mother wouldn't know her own child?

The nurse smiled. "I'm sure she's yours. We put an
identification band on her right away. Both you and
Mick have one with the same number on it. See? Has
she changed a lot since she was born?"

"I never saw her. At least, I don't remember if I did."

They were waiting for her to say something else,
Caitlin sensed it. But what could she say when there
was nothing but emptiness and sorrow inside. Was this
the way her own mother had felt? *Please, don't let that
be true.*

She managed a smile, but she felt as if her face would crack. "Will she be okay?"

"We're doing everything we can. She has a good chance."

A good chance. To live? That meant there was a chance she could die. Coldness settled over Caitlin and she shivered. An alarm sounded. She looked at the monitors, but she couldn't tell anything from the glowing numbers.

Mick touched her arm. "It's another baby."

When Sandra left to answer the alarm, he pulled up a chair and sat beside Caitlin. "I know she's tiny, but she's really cute, don't you think? Her hair looks like it may be red. She weighs one pound, twelve ounces today."

Caitlin couldn't listen to him. Why didn't he shut up? His babbling made her headache pound harder than ever. She wanted to concentrate on the baby—her baby. The tiny face swam out of focus, and Caitlin realized tears had filled her eyes.

"You can touch her," Mick offered.

"She's so little. What if I hurt her?"

"You won't."

Cautiously, Caitlin extended her hand and lightly stroked the baby's downy hair. Moving her fingertips to a miniature arm, Caitlin marveled at the softness of her baby's skin as she stroked its length. The baby jerked once and kicked out with her legs. Her tiny face screwed up, and she began to cry, but no sound came from her. Caitlin snatched her hand away. "What's the matter with her?"

Mick stood and cupped his hands across the baby, quieting her with soft words. He looked down at Caitlin. "Don't stroke her, just hold her like this. My little girl likes to be contained. Her skin is too thin and sensitive to stroke."

Caitlin's fright turned to anger as she listened to his lecture. He didn't have any right to be here. Maybe she had asked for his help once, but he had no business saying the baby was his.

Sandra came back to the bedside. "Very good, Mick. You're reading her signals."

"Signal? I don't understand." Caitlin glanced at her in confusion.

"Preemies have their own type of language. Body language, really. We have some wonderful handouts that explain all about it. Mick's been doing his homework. I wish all of our fathers took as much interest in their babies as he does."

"There's still a lot I don't know," he admitted. "I did pick up some books on parenting in the NICU. You can borrow them if you'd like," he offered Caitlin.

"Sure." She wouldn't admit to *him* that she couldn't read. Reading didn't make a good parent. Only love did that. Her stabbing headache made it hard to concentrate. She fingered the loose, white plastic band on her arm. Here was the only proof she had that this tiny person belonged to her and she couldn't even read it.

Nothing seemed real. Maybe if she held her baby this void she felt would fill with something—anything.

She turned to the nurse. "I want to hold her."

Sandra shook her head. "I'm sorry, Mick has already held her today. Tomorrow you can."

Mick had held her. Mick had named her. Mick, Mick, Mick. Caitlin wanted to scream. This man, this stranger, was stealing her baby. His touch, his voice gave her daughter the comfort her mother should give her. The nurse smiled at him like he belonged here. Caitlin couldn't bear to watch a moment longer.

"Take me back to my room."

"Oh, Ms. Williams, that doesn't mean that you can't stay and visit with her." The nurse laid a hand on Caitlin's shoulder, but Caitlin shrugged it off.

"I want to go back, now!"

"But you've barely touched her," Mick said. He took Caitlin's hand and laid it on the baby, covering it with his own. "Hold her like this with your hands cupped around her. It makes her feel safe."

The baby squirmed. Maybe she didn't want her mother touching her. Why would she? Her mother was a stranger. None of this was right. He was making it all wrong.

"Let go of me!" Caitlin jerked away from him, but her armband caught on something. A shrill alarm pierced the air.

Panic and fear crashed over her. "What did I do?"

Chapter 6

"I need some help," Sandra yelled. Within seconds, two other nurses were at the bedside. One of them pulled Caitlin away from the bed.

"What's wrong? What did I do?"

"You pulled out a line that was in an artery. We have to stop the bleeding."

"I didn't mean to. It must have caught on my armband. Is she okay?" Caitlin looked from face to face, desperately wanting to be reassured, but everyone was intent on the baby. No one answered her.

"Please, is she okay?"

Mick took her hand. "We need to let them work."

Caitlin focused on his stern face. "It was an accident."

"I know."

"I wouldn't hurt my baby. I wouldn't." Yet, she had, just by touching her.

Sandra spoke to Mick, "I'm afraid you'll have to step out."

"Sure." He turned Caitlin's wheelchair toward the door.

"No, wait! Let me stay." Caitlin couldn't bear to leave. She needed to know her baby was okay.

"We're in their way. We have to give them room to work." He spoke quietly, but his tone brooked no arguments.

Caitlin swallowed her protests and allowed him to wheel her away. She slumped in the chair and covered her face with her hands. A vast weariness pressed down on her, leaving her to feel strangely disconnected. Nothing was the way she had dreamed it would be. Nothing was right.

Mick pushed Caitlin out into the waiting room. He tried not to feel resentment toward the woman seated in front of him. It had been an accident, he knew that, but Beth was so small. He and the nurses always took special care with her lines.

Sitting on one of the chairs, he folded his hands on his knees. "They'll let us know when we can come back in. Sandra's really good about that."

"I want to go to my room." Caitlin's voice was flat, emotionless.

"What happened was partially my fault." He laid a hand on her shoulder in an effort to comfort her, but she flinched away from him.

"Take me to my room." Her words were little more than a strained whisper.

"Sure." He pushed her back to the ICU, managing both her wheelchair and IV pumps with difficulty.

Several nurses stood at the desk chatting, but Betty hurried forward with a bright smile when she caught sight of them. "What'd you think? Is she as cute as Mick is always telling us?"

Caitlin didn't say anything. She sat unmoving with her head bowed. Mick caught Betty's eye. "I think we overdid it."

Betty shot him a puzzled look, but took her cue from him. She patted Caitlin's arm. "You look exhausted. Let's get you back into bed." She beckoned to the other nurses. They wheeled Caitlin into her room and closed the door.

A few minutes later, Betty came out.

"How is she?" he asked.

"Withdrawn, but physically fine as far as I can tell. What happened?"

"She accidentally pulled out Beth's arterial line."

"Oh, my. Is the baby okay?"

"I think so. I don't understand it."

"What?"

"Caitlin. She didn't seem happy to see the baby. She seemed more shocked than anything, although I explained what she would see when I took her there. She seemed so remote, so cold. It wasn't how I expected a mother to act."

"Maybe she was frightened," Betty offered. "And rightly so. A baby as premature as hers can be a scary sight."

"Shouldn't a mother be attached to her baby no matter how tiny it is? Isn't that how it works?"

"Honestly? Not for everyone. Especially mothers of premature babies. They're afraid the child will die and they shy away from the pain they think they'll feel. Given time they come to love their baby as much as any mother does. But sometimes—well—not every woman is cut out to be a loving mother."

The door to Caitlin's room opened as the other nurses came out. One of them closed it behind her, but not before Mick caught a glimpse of Caitlin. Pale and still, she lay curled on her side.

Betty gave Mick a sympathetic pat on the arm. "Give her some time. She's been through a terrible ordeal."

Inside the room, Caitlin blinked rapidly to hold back her tears. Crying never did any good. It only showed others your weakness. She'd heard the nurse tell Mick some women weren't cut out to be mothers. They had been talking about her. She should have resented their judgment, but she didn't. They were right.

She wanted it to be different. She wanted a baby to love and cherish. Instead, her child cried at her touch and quieted at the touch of a stranger. As tiny as she was, did Beth know that her mother would hurt her?

Caitlin never wanted to hurt anyone. Okay, maybe Vinnie after she discovered he'd stolen every cent she had managed to save. After she found out how he'd lied to her. But he was already dead and nothing could hurt him. She was the one left to suffer for his deeds.

She turned over and faced the wall, determined to ignore the pain of Vinnie's betrayal as well as her fierce headache. If only she had stayed asleep, then her baby would still be safe. How was she? Would anyone let her know?

Closing her eyes, Caitlin waited for sleep to come. She welcomed the thought now. There was no pain in sleep, no fears. Maybe she'd never wake up again. Maybe that would be best.

Was that why her own mother had sought to stay in a drug-induced stupor? For the first time in her life, Caitlin felt the stirrings of sympathy and understanding for the woman who had caused her so much pain.

The room lay shrouded in darkness when Caitlin awoke. Sleep hadn't sent her back into the gray world where she had existed before. Instead, she had to face what she had done. Her headache had lessened, but it was still there, promising to mushroom again if she moved her head. A rustling sound came from behind her. She knew who was there. She'd known the moment she opened her eyes. "How is she?"

Please, please let her be all right.

"She's doing okay, now," Mick answered. "They've given her a transfusion."

Caitlin whipped her head around. "Isn't that dangerous?" She'd been right about the headache.

"There's a very small risk, but they didn't have much choice. Look, I'm sorry about what happened. You weren't up to it. I should have listened to your doctor."

Caitlin turned back to face the wall. It was easier to talk if she didn't have to see him. In the darkness, his voice seemed more like the voice in her dreams, the one who had promised her everything was going to be all right. Only that had turned out to be a lie, too. She bit her lip to stop its trembling. "I didn't mean to hurt her."

"I know. There's so much stuff to be careful of. You weren't used to it. Tomorrow will be better, less overwhelming. If she's doing well, you can hold her."

What if she did something else, something worse? Torn between the need to hold her baby and her deep-seated fear of harming her, Caitlin made a decision that broke her heart. "I won't see her tomorrow."

An uncomfortable silence filled the room.

"Well, as soon as you're feeling better," Mick said.

She ignored him. Why didn't he leave? Why couldn't she open her mouth and send him away?

Because she wanted him to stay. He was a link to her child. And maybe she wanted him to stay because she felt something different when he was near. She felt safe. It was a feeling she didn't dare trust. "You named her Beth, right?"

"Elizabeth Anne, actually, but everyone calls her Beth."

"After your mother?"

"Yes. When she was born, you said, 'Stay with Beth.'"

"I don't remember."

"I didn't know what else to call her. 'Hey You' seemed a little impersonal."

She smiled slightly. His voice was so beautiful—deep, expressive, soothing. Just the sound of it made her headache better. No wonder the baby responded so well to him.

"Elizabeth Anne," she tried the name on her tongue. It sounded regal. It was a big name for such a tiny person. "I guess it's as good a name as any," she conceded.

The silence lengthened. She waited for him to make some excuse and leave. She'd spent so much of her life alone. Funny that she dreaded it still. At least her baby hadn't been alone. Mick had been there for her. She began to remember bits of things he'd said and done when Eddy brought him to her room.

Caitlin tried to swallow the lump that pressed up in her throat. She wanted to thank him, but she couldn't find words to express the way his voice—his very presence had given her an anchor when she'd been so lost.

She closed her eyes and struggled to shut away the feelings this man aroused in her—feelings of caring and tenderness, feelings that threatened to overwhelm her only because she was still so weak. She didn't need an anchor now, and she didn't need him. She needed to be strong. Only the strong survived on the streets. She couldn't afford to depend on anybody but herself.

In the past, she had depended on others, but they always let her down. She wouldn't forget that fact. Not after her mother—not after Vinnie. Everybody had an angle, only some were harder to figure out than others.

She drew a deep breath, then turned over to face him. "What are you getting out of this?"

His eyes widened at her tone. "I don't understand."

"You've got nothing better to do than hang out at the hospital with a woman in a coma and someone else's kid?"

"Beth is a very special child."

Caitlin resented the determined pride she heard in his voice—something that she should feel, but didn't. Maybe she wasn't cut out to be a mother. She certainly hadn't had a role model to follow. "You can't have kids, right?"

"That's true."

"So you thought you'd take mine?"

A frown creased his forehead. "It's not like that."

"Oh, yeah? Well, what was it like—exactly? You've been telling people you're her father. That's a lie."

"You're the one who said it." His tone grew defensive.

"So you tell me."

"Look, there are some things we need to discuss, but I don't think now is the time. You're getting upset."

"No kidding!" She turned away again. "You're giving me a headache. Take a hike, why don't you?"

Even as she spoke, she hoped he'd ignore her words, hoped desperately that he would see through her act and stay. She was so tired of being alone.

Mick stared at her back in the dim light from the window. He didn't know if he wanted to shake her or gather her in his arms and comfort her. Maybe both. One moment she was like a lost child, the next minute she was a sharp-tongued shrew. Which person was the real Caitlin?

"You're tired," he said. "We'll talk later."

"Whatever."

Opening the door, he paused and cast one last glance at the rigid figure on the bed. He heard a muffled sob and saw her wipe at her eyes. Softly, he closed the door and left.

The next day, Mick stood in the deserted street and stared at the crumbling facade of the abandoned building where he'd first found Caitlin. The boards that once crisscrossed the door lay on the sidewalk where the ambulance crew had tossed them in their hurry to get their gurney inside; otherwise, nothing had changed. This was the last place he had any hope of finding out something about Caitlin.

Pastor Frank knew nothing of Caitlin's history. Like a lot of the homeless, she came and went at the shelter with barely a word.

With a little more digging, he'd found a small newspaper article about the death of Vincent Williams. A visit to Harley's Diner, the place Vinnie was accused of robbing, yielded only the information that Caitlin had worked there, but that she had been fired after the incident. He was able to track down where she lived from their records, but the landlord of the run-down apartments would only say that Caitlin had been evicted the same week her husband died. The man didn't know and didn't care where she went. As far as Mick could tell, after that Caitlin had ended up here.

Inside the old building it was cool, dark and smelled of mold where the rain had dripped in from the sagging roof. He passed Eddy's room and glanced in. It was empty.

After making his way around the debris in the hall, Mick opened the door to Caitlin's room and stepped inside. The same mattress lay in the corner. Three cardboard boxes sat beside the bed and a few clothes hung from nails in the wall.

Dropping to one knee beside the mattress, he noticed a small black purse tucked between two boxes. He picked it up and dumped out the contents onto the bed.

A gray vinyl wallet held six dollars and eighteen cents, but no ID and no pictures. A tube of lipstick and three books of matches were the only other things in the purse. All of the matchbooks were from the Harley's Diner where Caitlin had worked busing tables and washing dishes.

Mick turned his attention to the boxes. The first one contained a few cans of food. The next one held some clothes, and nothing else. The last carton said Sunkist Oranges. Did she like oranges or had the box simply been handy? He opened the lid.

A baby blanket lay on top. Neatly folded, the downy

soft square was covered in pastel-colored hearts and teddy bears. A second blanket, white and trimmed with yellow lace, lay under the first one. He set them carefully aside. Next he drew out a pink sleeper and small pair of white knit booties with tiny blue bows and laid them on the blankets.

Caitlin had obviously wanted her baby. Except Mick knew wanting a child wasn't enough. Perhaps Beth's premature birth had been a blessing in disguise. The Lord moved in mysterious ways. Now she would never live in this dump. She'd never be homeless or hungry or cold. Now she had Mick O'Callaghan to look after her.

The rest of the box held only papers. He took a closer look. They were sketches.

Rising, he carried them to the window and sat on the sill. One by one, he held the drawings up to the light.

Eddy stooping to pet a scrawny cat. A thin woman clutching a small child in her arms. Pastor Frank holding a cup to the lips of a frail, elderly woman. Somehow, the strokes of the pencil had captured the warmth in Eddy's gesture, the fear on the face of the young mother and the gratitude in the old woman's eyes.

He leafed through several more sketches; they were mostly of children—kids from the shelter and from the streets. Then the next drawing stopped him cold. He was looking at himself.

He had a football in his hands and three small defenders were putting a stop to his run by hanging on to his legs. The details in the picture were incredible. She had captured the boys' determined expressions perfectly, but the gentle look of happiness on his own face surprised him the most.

He thought back to that day. He had glimpsed Caitlin in the shadow of the building watching the game, but he didn't remember seeing her with a drawing pad. He stared down at the sketches in amazement. Could she have drawn these detailed images from memory?

He looked through over a hundred sketches that Caitlin had drawn. At the bottom of the box, he found a single photograph bent in half. Picking it up, he unfolded the picture and gazed at a small blond girl standing beside a young woman with dark hair. The child was Caitlin, he was sure of it. Was the tired-looking woman with a cigarette dangling from her lips Caitlin's mother? The white line of the folded picture separated the mother and child, perhaps just as her mother's addiction had separated them in real life.

A scraping noise reached him, and Mick's head snapped up. Something heavy was being dragged down the hallway. A moment later, the door swung wide, and an overcoat-clad figure backed into the room, muttering loudly. "Ya stupid piece a junk. I should a left ya for the garbage truck."

"Eddy, what in the world are you doing?"

The old man spun around, his eyes wide and startled. "Sheesh, Mick, ya scared the livin' daylights out of me."

"Sorry. Can I give you a hand with that?" Mick offered, leaving his place on the windowsill after he replaced the photo and the sketches in the box.

Eddy's face brightened and a nearly toothless grin appeared. "Look what I found fer Caitlin." He pulled an ancient, enormous baby carriage through the doorway.

"Pastor Frank told me she had a baby girl. She don't have no place to keep a baby in here, so I got her this. Pastor Frank said I was a real hero for gettin' her help that day. He said without me, her baby woulda died fer sure. Ain't that somethin'? I mean—him sayin' I was a hero?"

"It's nothing but the truth, Eddy."

"You—you think I was a hero, too?"

Mick patted the small man's shoulder. "I know you were the hero that day."

Eddy's smile faded, and his face grew somber. "I ain't never amounted to nothin' in my whole life. Not like you, bein' a fireman and all. I been a drunk and a bum…since I was born, I reckon, but I did somethin' right for once, didn't I?"

"You sure did."

Eddy wiped at his eyes with the back of his dirty, tattered sleeve. "What are you doin' here?"

Mick glanced around the dingy room with its peeling plaster and sagging ceiling. "Caitlin is pretty sick. I was hoping to find out if she had any family or friends, anyone I can notify."

Eddy scratched his head. "Not that I know of." He pushed the baby carriage across the room. The thing bobbed and wobbled on a bent front wheel.

"How about the baby's father? Did she ever tell you anything about him or his family?" Mick probed.

"Yeah. Let me think."

Mick waited impatiently. "It's important, Eddy."

"Oh, I know. She said he was a case of bad judgment."

"That's it?"

"She ain't much for talkin'."

"Take a look at these sketches and see if you recognize anyone who might be a friend of hers."

Eddy took them and held them out at arm's length. "I don't see so good anymore, Mick."

Battling back his frustration, Mick nodded and took the drawings from him. "Okay, Eddy. Thanks for your help."

"Pastor Frank said the baby's gonna be in the hospital a long time on account of her being so small. That true?"

"Yes, she only weighs about two pounds. It's going to take her a few months to get big enough to go home."

"Do ya—do ya think I could come and see her? Like a visitor, I mean? I'd like to do that."

Mick looked at Eddy's grubby clothes and at his beard with wine stains and bits of food clinging in it. The smell of his unwashed body was overpowering, yet his face held such hopeful longing. How could Mick tell him no without crushing the pride that Eddy had found for the first time in his life?

"She's too tiny to have visitors yet," he said gently.

"Oh." The hope on Eddy's face drained away. Looking down, he brushed at the front of his clothes. "Sure, I understand."

Mick couldn't let the man think he wasn't good enough to see the baby whose life he had helped save. "But she's getting bigger and stronger every day."

Eddy looked up. "She is?"

"I'll tell you what. You check in with Pastor Frank. When she's big enough to have visitors, he can bring you to see her."

"Honest? You mean it? Ah, Mick—" Eddy's voice broke, and he turned away to busy himself straightening up the leaning pram.

After a moment, he said, "I clean up pretty good, Mick. You'll see. She won't be ashamed of me."

Mick blinked back the tears that threatened his own eyes. "How could she be ashamed of the guy who saved her life?"

Mick gathered up Caitlin's things. A sketch fluttered to the floor and he bent to pick it up. It was a portrait Caitlin had drawn of herself. Her pixielike face and wide eyes stared back at him, but like Caitlin herself, the sketch gave him no answers.

He had to admit that holding her in his arms had stirred his protective instincts and made him aware of her as a woman, but who was she really? He'd invented a persona for her when she'd been unconscious, he realized, and now he was disturbed to discover it didn't fit her at all.

Where was the vulnerable, desperate woman he'd taken to the hospital? The woman he'd begun to care about? He wasn't comfortable with the Caitlin who had emerged yesterday. Her refusal to see the baby again disturbed him deeply.

There were unfit parents in the world, he knew that. In his line of work he'd met men and women who neglected and abused their children. He simply didn't want to believe Caitlin was one of them. Even if she was the best mother in the world, she didn't have a job or a place to live. She couldn't take care of herself let alone a baby. She needed his help. She needed him.

The doctor listened to Caitlin's chest, checked her eyes, peered down her throat, had her squeeze his hands and finally hit her knees with a little, red rubber hammer. Without comment, he took the chart from the end of her bed and leafed through it.

He gave her a pointed look over the top of his glasses, then snapped the chart shut. "You're making a remarkable recovery. A week ago, I wouldn't have believed it was possible. How would you like to move to the maternity floor? You'll be closer to the NICU."

"I'd like that." Caitlin struggled to keep her elation from showing. She'd be closer to her daughter. Closer, but not close enough to cause any more problems.

"Good. If you keep up this progress, I'll have to let you go home in a few days."

Caitlin twisted the edge of the covers in her hands. Home? Where would that be? A crowded shelter or maybe the building where Mick had found her? Some choice. Neither one was a fit place to take a newborn.

If only Beth had waited until August to be born. Caitlin had planned to earn enough money selling her sketches to tourists down on the Navy Pier over the summer months to be able to afford a place to live. She'd made a few bucks in the past two months, but not many people wanted to sit for portraits when the cold north wind was whipping off the lake.

No matter, she'd manage somehow—she always had—but she hadn't had a baby to look after. How was she going to pay the hospital bills, or find a job or someone to look after the baby while she worked? She forced those fears to the back of her mind. She couldn't dwell on them or she'd go crazy.

"Feeling hungry?" the doctor asked.

She shrugged. "I could eat."

Turning to the nurse, he said, "Betty, pull that IV and start her on a general diet."

"Yes, Doctor."

After he left, Betty said, "This is great. Now you'll be right down the hall from the NICU. Let me get you a menu. You can choose something for dinner tonight besides Jell-O."

There didn't seem to be any end to the things they wanted her to read in this place. If she wasn't careful, they'd discover the truth. She hated the way people treated her when they found out. She hated being stupid.

"I don't see how you expect me to read anything without my glasses." It was her oldest line.

Betty's eyes widened in surprise. "I didn't know you wore any. Maybe they're in the things that came from E.R. with you." She opened the closet and began searching through a large, white plastic bag marked with the hospital's logo. "They don't seem to be here. Are you sure you had them with you?"

"I was unconscious, remember?"

"Why don't I give Mick a call? Maybe he has them."

"No! I mean, don't bother. I'll manage."

"Perhaps I can read you the choices and mark them for you. Will that work?"

"Whatever." Caitlin stared at the window. She didn't like acting this way, but she had discovered early on that if people didn't like her, they left her alone. When she was alone, she didn't have to watch what she said or did.

"It's no trouble. Let me take your IV out. The sooner that's done, the sooner you can move out of here."

Caitlin held up her arm. "Knock yourself out."

Two hours later, Betty helped her out of a wheel-chair and into her new bed on the maternity floor. As she watched the woman prepare to leave, Caitlin realized that she would miss the cheerful, little nurse. Betty had been nothing but kind even when Caitlin had been deliberately rude. As the nurse maneuvered the empty chair toward the door, Caitlin called out, "Hey, Betty." She looked back and Caitlin managed a smile. "Thanks. For everything."

Betty grinned, then surprised Caitlin by crossing the room and enfolding her in a quick hug. "Good luck, honey. I'll keep you in my prayers," she said, and then she hurried out the door.

Caitlin tried to swallow past the lump that rose in her throat. She wasn't used to people being kind to her.

Somewhere down the hall a baby was crying. But not her baby. Her baby was barely clinging to life. Every time she heard that sound, she'd be reminded of what she didn't have. Of what she had missed out on.

A new nurse came and took Caitlin's temperature and checked her pulse, then offered to take her down to the nursery. Panic exploded through Caitlin. What if she did something else that hurt the baby? "No. I—I want take a nap. I've got a headache."

It sounded lame, but it was no lie—the pain behind Caitlin's eyes never let up. The nurse gave her a puzzled look but didn't push the issue. After the woman left, Caitlin stared at the wall as thoughts of her daughter ran around and around in her mind. As the shadows of evening lengthened, Caitlin's feelings of inadequacy and guilt grew. Beth needed a breathing machine, and IVs. She was hooked to wires of every kind. She needed doctors and nurses with her now, not a mother who had failed at everything in life. Not a mother who couldn't even keep her safe until the right time to be born.

Caitlin's throat tightened at the thought and she began to sob. Turning over, she muffled the sound in her pillow.

If only Mick were here. She longed to hear his voice telling her that everything would be okay. She pressed her palms to her aching temples. Why should she crave the comfort of a man she barely knew? She didn't need anyone to take care of her. She had always taken care of herself. Always!

Confused, frightened and weary, Caitlin stayed in her room and slept fitfully as the night slowly crawled by. Her breakfast tray arrived, but it sat untouched on her bedside table until someone came and took it away.

Occasionally, a nurse came to check her temperature and her pulse or with an offer to take her to the NICU. Caitlin ignored them, and for the most part, they went away. The more persistent ones she brushed off with rude remarks. They left, too, and that was what Caitlin wanted. She wanted to be left alone.

Mick snapped his locker shut and glanced at the clock. Twenty-three hours and thirty minutes until he could see Beth and Caitlin again. It was his first day back on the job since he'd signed paternity papers. Already he missed visiting Beth, but at least Caitlin would be with her.

When he had called the hospital yesterday afternoon

he'd been informed that Caitlin had been moved to a floor adjacent to the neonatal unit. He heard the news with mixed emotions. He was happy Caitlin was improving, but where did that leave him?

Woody stopped and leaned on the locker next to him. "Is it true?" his friend demanded.

"Is what true?"

"That you had a baby and that she's really sick?"

"Who told you?"

"Captain Mitchell let it slip. So, it is true! Why didn't you tell me? What's wrong with her?"

"She's premature—she only weighs two pounds. She's doing okay now, but it was touch and go for a while. She'll be in the hospital for several months."

Woody punched Mick's shoulder. "You dog! I didn't even know you were seeing anyone. So, who's the mother?"

Mick rubbed his arm. "I'm not sure that's any of your business."

"I'm your best buddy. You can tell me anything. Do I keep secrets from you?"

"Sometimes I wish you would."

Mick debated whether he should explain that Beth wasn't really his child. And what could he say about Caitlin?

"Is she a fox?" His friend probed for more information.

"She's pretty, if that's what you mean. Her name is Caitlin Williams. We met first at Pastor Frank's place."

Woody's disbelief was almost comical. "Then she's definitely not a fox. The only fox in the church I went to as a kid was the dead one on the collar of the old dame that sat in the pew in front of me."

Mick shook his head. "There is a lot more to church than checking out the girls. Are you still cruising the art galleries looking to pick up classy chicks?"

Woody grabbed Mick's arm and cast a quick look around. "Hey, watch it, will you? I'd never live it down if these guys found out."

"Being an art lover isn't a crime."

"Yeah, right. The only art that's appreciated around here is the picture of the swimsuit model on Ziggy's calendar. These guys wouldn't know the difference between a Picasso and a piccolo."

"Your secret is safe with me."

"It had better be. And speaking of secrets, tell me more about this woman. I didn't know you were dating anyone."

"We were never exactly together." He shook his head. "It's a long story."

"In other words, it's none of my business."

"It's not that." Taking a deep breath, Mick said, "It's that she's decided she doesn't want me involved. She doesn't want my help. Have you ever met a woman who makes you feel like you don't know which side is up?"

"Often. It's what they do."

Mick grinned. "No, this is something more. I really care about this woman, but I can't figure her out."

"No one can figure out women."

"You're being a big help."

"Mick, you can't make her let you into her life unless you take her to court and get a custody agreement to share the kid. How many of those relationships turn out friendly? Either she's still interested in you or she isn't. Decide how far you're willing to go before you're in over your head."

Wasn't he already in over his head? Mick crossed his arms and leaned back against his locker. "I know I can't risk driving Caitlin away and losing Beth, too."

It was a little after one o'clock in the morning, and Caitlin had been in her new room for nearly two days before she faced the fact that she couldn't make herself stay away from Beth any longer. Gathering her courage, she walked down the hall to the NICU.

Her legs felt like rubber, but she forced herself to go on. How long would this weakness plague her? Out on the streets, weakness made a person an easy target. She'd learned the hard way that she had to look strong even if she wasn't.

She scrubbed her hands and arms as she had seen Mick do, then showed her ID band to the unit clerk. The woman opened the door and Caitlin walked into the nursery. A gray-haired nurse came up to her with a bright smile and asked, "Can I help you?"

"I'm Caitlin Williams. I'd like to see my daughter."

"Ah, you're little Beth's mother. It's nice to meet you. I'm Phyllis, and I'm her nurse tonight. She's doing very well."

The nurse led the way to Beth's bedside. Once there, she lowered the Plexiglas panel and pulled up a chair so Caitlin could sit down. Beth lay on her side in a U-shaped roll that kept her arms and legs tucked close to her body.

"Has anyone explained our equipment to you?" Phyllis asked.

Caitlin shook her head. She still couldn't get over how small and how totally helpless her baby looked.

"Okay, I'll explain it all, but you only need to remember one thing."

Caitlin's gaze flew to the nurse's face. "What's that?"

The woman smiled warmly. "All of this equipment belongs to the hospital, but Beth belongs to you. Our job is to take care of her until she's ready to go home, but we can't replace you. Your job is to love her."

Caitlin bit her lip and nodded. It sounded so simple.

The nurse patted her arm. "Good. This machine is a ventilator, and it's helping her breathe. You and I breathe twenty-one percent oxygen in the air around us. Beth is getting thirty-two percent oxygen. The monitors tell us her heart rate, how fast she's breathing, and how well she's using the oxygen we're giving her. It will also tell us if she needs more."

She indicated the small clear tubes taped to the baby's stomach. "These are her IV lines. One is in an artery in her umbilical cord and the other one goes into a vein."

"The first time I was here, I pulled one of them out," Caitlin admitted.

"Yes, I know." The nurse laid a hand on Caitlin's shoulder. "It was a very unfortunate accident. In the twenty years I've been working in this NICU, it's only happened a few times."

Surprised, Caitlin glanced up. "You mean someone else did it, too?"

"Yes, and they were just as scared as you were. I

know things seem overwhelming, but try not to focus on the equipment. Focus on your baby. Talk to her. She's heard your voice all these months, and she'll know it now. She knows your smell and your touch. Really, she does. Babies are amazing people. Now, I'll leave you two alone." The nurse started to move away.

"Can't you stay?" Caitlin called after her, frightened at the idea of being left alone with her baby.

"I have other babies to take care of. I'll be right over here." She indicated an incubator down the aisle. "Just sing out if you need something."

Caitlin nodded, but couldn't quell her sense of fear. She stared at her baby. Now what?

Chapter 7

Caitlin stared at her daughter. Talk to her about what? Beth stretched in her sleep and stuck one foot in the air. Carefully, Caitlin reached for it. Five tiny toes spread wide apart then curled tight as she touched them. Leaning closer, Caitlin saw the baby's second toe was longer than her big one.

She's got my feet!

"Beth with the funny toes is mine," Caitlin whispered.

A sudden flood of emotion took her breath away. It tightened her chest until she could barely breathe. Her baby's foot was warm and real in her hand. For the first time, she felt connected to her child. The rolling, kicking, belly-heaving lump had turned into a person with feet like her mother's.

A profound sense of wonder grew into a joy unlike anything she had ever experienced. Suddenly, she had to know everything about her child. She studied Beth's thin legs and knobby knees. She had Vinnie's knees.

"Well, if you had to get something of your dad, his knees aren't such a bad thing."

Pity for Vinnie skirted the edge of Caitlin's happiness. How could something so wonderful have come from something so wrong?

The baby stirred and captured Caitlin's attention once more. The diaper, small as it was, almost swallowed her. Her arms were as lanky as her legs. And was that hair on her back? It was! Fine, downy hair covered the baby's shoulders.

"You look like a cross between a monkey and a frog, you poor little thing."

The tape that held the ventilator tubing in place hid part of the baby's face, but Caitlin intently studied the rest. She saw a small pointed chin and flyaway eyebrows, and wrinkles on a wide forehead. Her soft cap of hair held a hint of red just as Mick had said.

Sitting motionless, gently clutching her daughter's foot, Caitlin's gaze poured over every inch of her baby. Wonder, fear and a deep happiness stirred inside her. This was her daughter—her child for a lifetime. The knowledge made her want to shout with joy. For the first time in years, she felt maybe God was on her side after all.

If You're listening, God, thanks for saving my baby.

Her elation faded and doubts pressed in. How would she take care of such a small and frail person? Would she repeat the mistakes that Dotty, her own mother, had made?

Dotty hadn't been able to care for herself, let alone a child. Caitlin lost count of the times her mother tried to get straight. Each and every time, Caitlin hoped and prayed and promised God anything if only He would help her mother stay off drugs. Each and every time her mother failed, Caitlin knew it had somehow been her fault. She hadn't been good enough. She wasn't smart enough, or quiet enough, or neat enough.

After she had been taken away from her mother, she went through a string of foster homes. There were a few bad homes, but there had been more good ones— ones with people who cared about her, and whom she cared about in return. The best one had been the Martin family. She lived with them for almost the whole year when she was eight.

The Martin family took her in and treated her like she was somebody special. They went to church and took Caitlin with them. They prayed together and they talked about loving each other and loving God. Caitlin found it odd at first, but after a while it began to comfort her, knowing that God was looking out for folks.

But in the end He didn't let her stay with the Martins, either. No matter how hard she prayed, she was still sent away. Once more she went back to Dotty during one of her sober, repentant spells. If God heard any of Caitlin's prayers after that, He didn't show it.

Dotty claimed to want and love Caitlin, and maybe she did, until life became too difficult, until her cravings for drugs pushed aside her need to be a mother. Then Caitlin was neglected and forgotten again.

It wasn't long before Caitlin understood that her mother was never getting straight, and she knew that God didn't care.

So, Caitlin stopped caring about being good, or neat or smart. Surviving became her goal. She never allowed herself to depend on anyone ever again. Not until Vinnie had she let another person get close. And what a fool she had been over him.

Oh, he was good—she gave him credit for that. He was as smooth a liar as she had ever met, and she had met some great ones. He'd studied her and found a weakness she hadn't even known she possessed. He made her feel needed.

He had pursued her with a single-mindedness she mistook for love, but she refused to follow in her mother's footsteps. She insisted on getting married. To her surprise, Vinnie agreed. Things were good at first, but it wasn't long before he started to stray.

Afterward, he made a great show of being sorry and begging her to forgive him. The sad part was that she did. She believed him when he said he was paying the rent and putting the meager paycheck she earned into a savings account. She signed them over to him every Friday evening without hesitation.

Then, one Friday night, it wasn't enough. That night Vinnie robbed the diner where she washed dishes and he died in a car chase with the police.

Now, she didn't have money or a place to live. She didn't have a job or much hope of finding one, but she had a baby.

A beautiful, baby girl. She had someone to love and cherish—someone who would love her in return. She touched Beth's cheek with her fingertips. The baby opened her eyes and blinked. Caitlin smiled and leaned toward her.

"Hello, Beth," she said softly. "We haven't really met, yet. I'm your mother."

Phyllis stopped by again. "Would you like to hold her?"

"Could I?" Excitement sent Caitlin's pulse racing. "I'll be real careful."

"I know you will. Let me get someone else to help."

"What do I do?"

"Just relax and enjoy her."

Caitlin tried, but she was so nervous her hands shook as two nurses transferred the baby from the bed and laid her on Caitlin's chest. At the feel of her baby's small, warm body next to hers, Caitlin's heart expanded with a wealth of emotion so overwhelming it stunned her. She laid her cheek against Beth's head and longed to curl around her, to draw her even closer and hold her so tight that nothing could ever hurt her again.

Caitlin's whole world narrowed to the child she held. Her very own wonderful, wonderful child.

She had no idea how long she held Beth. It wasn't until the nurse came back and asked her if she was tired that Caitlin realized she was.

"A little," she admitted after glancing at the clock and seeing it was almost five in the morning. She was tired, but content for the first time in a long, long while.

They moved Beth back to the open unit and Caitlin's sense of helplessness returned. She could hold her child, but Beth needed nurses and machines. Caitlin rose stiffly from the rocker.

"Let me call your nurse and have her take you back to your room," Phyllis offered.

"No, I can manage."

"Are you sure?"

Caitlin nodded. She had to regain her strength, and she couldn't do it by letting others take care of her.

"All right." Phyllis turned away, then paused and looked back at Caitlin. "I meant to ask you earlier if you were planning to nurse her?"

Caitlin frowned. "I wanted to, but I can't now, can I?"

The nurse's smile was indulgent. "Of course you can. I'll get you a pump and show you how to use it. You'll need to start pumping every three to four hours. If you do that, your milk should come in again. It'll take a while, and you'll have to be faithful about pumping, but when Beth is ready to start feedings, you should have something to give her. We'll store what you pump in our freezer. That way, we can have milk for her even when you can't be here.

"Mother's milk is the best thing for her. It's easiest for her to digest, and it has antibodies that will help her fight off infections. She'll have to be a lot bigger and off the ventilator before she can actually try to nurse, but she'll get there."

Suddenly, Caitlin's feelings of helplessness eased as she realized this was something that no one else could do for her child—not Mick, not the nurses, no one. Mother's milk was best and it was something only she could provide. Elation filled her. "I'll do whatever it takes."

"Good. I'll get you a kit."

The nurse left, and Caitlin smiled as she tucked Beth's foot back inside the roll. A small arm shot up and waved in the air in response. Caitlin grasped the hand and felt tiny fingers clutch hers in return. Waves of warmth flooded Caitlin's heart. Her baby did need her, and somehow, she would find a way to take care of them both.

* * *

Mick left the firehouse as soon as his shift was over and drove straight to the hospital. Fortunately, it had been a quiet shift, and he'd managed to get a few hours of sleep. Now he had forty-eight hours until he had to be back on duty and he planned to spend a lot of that with Beth, and hopefully Caitlin.

At the NICU, he was pleased to see that Beth had Sandra as a nurse again. It made him feel like he had a friend taking care of Beth.

"How's she doing?" he asked, pulling a stool close to the bedside.

"Hey, Irish. We've missed you around here."

"I had to go back to work."

"I understand. Beth is doing well. She even gained a little weight. About a quarter of an ounce."

"How did Caitlin do?"

Sandra's smile faded. She turned away and began to straighten some papers on the bedside stand. "Ms. Williams didn't come in when I was here yesterday."

Mick frowned. "She didn't? I was told she was moved to the maternity floor. Isn't that just down the hall from here?"

"Yes, it is."

"And Caitlin didn't visit at all? Maybe she isn't feeling well. I should go check on her."

"I heard in report that she's being released the day after tomorrow."

"That soon?"

Sandra eyed him intently. "You didn't know? I assumed she was going home with you."

Mick avoided her gaze. He didn't want to get into a lengthy explanation. "Caitlin and I aren't together."

"I'm relieved to hear it."

"Why?"

"You don't seem like the kind of guy who'd put up with a person like her."

"I don't know what you mean."

"She's been pretty rude to some of the staff."

"I know she's got a mouth on her."

"Well, her nurses offered to bring her in several times, but she flatly refused to come. Apparently, she was none too nice about it."

"She refused to see Beth? In the ICU we had to all but tie her to the bed to keep her from coming here."

"We have to be concerned when a mother shows signs of detachment from her infant. If Ms. Williams doesn't begin to visit regularly, we'll have to inform our social worker."

"I don't know what to say." Mick cupped his hands carefully around Beth's body. She squirmed a little, then lay still. She was so adorable. He knew he'd never tire of watching her.

Sandra covered Mick's hands with her own. "Beth is such a little darling. It's good to know that she has at least one attentive parent. I've seen a lot of fathers go through here, but I've rarely seen one as loving and as devoted as you."

"My—don't you two look cozy."

Mick's head snapped around. Caitlin stood a few feet away watching them with narrowed eyes. If anything, she looked even paler than the last time he'd seen her. Dark circles under her eyes made her face look pinched and worn.

Sandra removed her hands from Mick's. "Good morning, Ms. Williams. It's nice to see you."

Mick stood and offered Caitlin the stool. "I just came in to say good morning to Beth, and Sandra was kind enough to update me on her condition."

"How sweet. Maybe she'd like to update me, too."

"Of course." Sandra's smile was cool. "Beth gained a small amount of weight, about a quarter of an ounce, and her oxygen is at twenty-seven percent."

Caitlin sat down and gently took one of Beth's hands in her own. "That's less than when I was in earlier."

Puzzled, Mick glanced from Sandra to Caitlin and back. "Sandra, I thought you said Caitlin hadn't been in?"

"I guess I was mistaken."

Caitlin gave her a pointed look. "I guess you were."

"I didn't see you yesterday or the day before, and I wasn't told in report that you'd been in." With that, she left the bedside.

Caitlin watched her go. "That woman doesn't like me."

"But she's very good with Beth."

"I guess that's what matters, isn't it?"

The scent of Mick's crisp aftershave soothed Caitlin's headache. Everything about him was soothing. His voice, how he cared for Beth. She had to remind herself that he wasn't for the likes of her. He'd be interested in smart women, someone like Sandra. Not someone too stupid to read.

She should concentrate on Beth, not her feelings for Mick. Her baby was the one who was important. They had missed too much time together already. He was a distraction she couldn't afford. It would be better if he left before she found herself hoping for something more from him.

She said, "Thanks for stopping by, but don't let us keep you."

Mick shifted from one foot to the other beside the bed. Caitlin gave him a dismissive glance. "What?"

"There are some things we need to talk about."

With an exasperated sigh, Caitlin swung around on the stool to face him. The sudden movement sent dizziness sweeping through her, but she managed to stay upright with a tight grip on the bed.

"Mick, thanks for getting me to the hospital and for watching over the baby while I was out of it, but I'm fine now. You can go. You've done your job like a good little Boy Scout."

He glanced around the unit, then leaned close to her. "It isn't that simple."

She leaned away from him, away from the desire to rest her aching head against his strong chest the way she had when he held her in his arms. "It is that simple. I'm her mother. You're just some guy who happened by. Thanks for the help, but we'll be fine on our own now. I think it would be best if you didn't come around anymore."

"Why?"

For a lot of reasons that she couldn't say aloud. She didn't want to feel this longing that possessed her whenever he was near. She didn't want to hear the voice that wove its way through her dreams with whispered words of reassurance and caring and made her believe that everything would be okay.

He wasn't part of her life. He donated a few hours of his time each week to play with the kids at the homeless shelter—he didn't live there. He didn't belong to the world that Caitlin struggled to survive in. He was a fantasy, a fairy tale, a glimpse of the kind of life she could only dream about.

Sandra came back to the bedside with a new bag of IV fluids and began to change the old one. Caitlin addressed her. "Is it true that only a parent can decide who's allowed to visit a baby in here?"

"Yes, that's true," Sandra answered.

Caitlin indicated Mick with a jerk of her head. "I don't want him in here anymore."

Obviously puzzled, Sandra glanced from one to the other.

"Caitlin, please," Mick pleaded. "Let's talk about this in private."

"There's nothing to talk about."

Sandra laid down the bag and tubing. "I can't keep Mick from seeing Beth. A father has the same legal rights that a mother does, whether they are married or not."

"He's not her father."

"I was told—"

"I don't care what you were told." Caitlin's headache mushroomed and her dizziness worsened. She saw Mick's eyes narrow as he stared at her. She couldn't let him see how weak she was. She summoned up the strength to glare at him and keep her voice level. "I'm telling you he's not her father."

"Sandra, can you excuse us?" Mick spoke quietly, his gaze never wavering from Caitlin's face.

"I'm afraid not. I'm going to have to ask you to take this outside the unit. The relationship between you two is not my concern, but Beth's welfare is. Babies are very susceptible to our emotions, and I won't allow you to upset my patient."

Glancing at the woman's set face, Caitlin felt a grudging measure of respect for her. "Fine. Whatever."

Caitlin stood, and Mick's hand quickly closed around her elbow to help steady her. For a moment, a surge of something she couldn't define raced through her blood at the warmth of his touch. If only she could lean on him.

Don't do it. He'll just let you down when you don't expect it. Hadn't she learned anything? No one was going to take care of Caitlin, except Caitlin. She twisted away from him, and keeping her back straight, she walked out of the unit and down the hall to her room. Once inside, she sank gratefully onto the side of her bed. The simple walk had left her exhausted.

"Are you all right?" he asked.

"I'm fine," she lied. "I don't know why you're still hanging around. What part of *go away* don't you get?"

"I wanted to make sure you were okay."

"Save your pity for the kids at the shelter. Beth and I are going to be fine on our own." She was so tired. If only he would go. She didn't want to say things that would hurt him.

Mick shoved his hands into his pockets and turned away, but he didn't leave. He crossed the room to stare out the window. Something was eating at him, she could tell by the tense set of his shoulders. After a moment, he turned to face her.

"It isn't pity that I feel for Beth. I've grown to love her. The kind of love a father has for his child. I don't know how else to tell you this except to say it flat out. When Beth needed surgery and it looked like you weren't going to recover, I signed paternity papers. Beth is legally my daughter."

Chapter 8

Caitlin shot to her feet, anger lending her a surge of strength. "You can't take her away! She's mine! She's my baby!"

"Calm down." Mick seemed unfazed by her outburst.

"Don't tell me to calm down!"

"Yelling isn't going to help anything. Let me explain."

"Oh, I already know what's going down. You're trying to steal Beth from me."

He regarded her with a steady gaze. "I'm not trying to steal anything. I'm trying to do what's best for her."

"*I'm* what's best for her," Caitlin shouted, advancing toward him. "*I'm* her mother, and *I* can take care of her."

"How?"

His quiet question drove the fight out of Caitlin and left her reeling. She backed away until her trembling legs touched the bed. She sank onto the edge of the mattress.

She didn't know how. Looking down, she saw her hands were shaking. She clutched them together until her knuckles grew white in an attempt to hold them still.

"By the time Beth leaves this hospital her bill will be close to two hundred thousand dollars. Do you have it stuffed in a sock somewhere, because I didn't find it in your purse or your boxes?"

He'd looked through her things, through her sketches and her few pitiful possessions. She felt sick inside. "You had no right to do that."

"I was trying to locate some family or friends."

"I told you, there isn't anyone. I'm all she has. I'm all she needs."

"Caitlin, no one should have to live the way you were living. I want to help. I've put Beth on my insurance. Her care here will be covered, all but a few thousand dollars. I'll take care of that."

"I don't want your money."

"It's not for you, it's for Beth."

Caitlin stared at him a long time without speaking. He met her gaze without flinching. Was he sincere? People she trusted had fooled her in the past. She watched his face closely. "What are you getting out of this?"

"I get to know that Beth isn't going to be destitute, that she isn't going to be living in a shelter, or a slum, or worse."

"I don't need your help." Her defiance was an act she prayed he couldn't see through.

"That's not the way I see it." He leaned a hip against the windowsill and folded his arms. "According to her doctor, Beth will be here for at least another two months. If, by the time she's ready to be discharged, you have a job and a decent place to live, I won't do anything except provide support payments. I'd like to think we can work out a schedule for visitation."

And if she didn't have those things? Fear, cold and deadly, crawled over Caitlin. Her stomach clenched in a painful spasm, and bile rose to the back of her throat. He couldn't take her baby from her, could he?

"You aren't her father. There's some kind of test that'll prove it."

"You mean a paternity test? One can't be done without my consent. I've signed a legal paternity paper. I can even produce witnesses from the E.R. who'll swear that *you* said I'm her father."

"I'll say I lied."

Mick watched with concern as the color drained from her face. He was going about this all wrong, but the woman knew how to push his buttons. She couldn't take care of Beth without help. He had to make her understand that.

"Social services won't let you take a baby back to the squalor you were living in. I can provide everything she needs."

"I see you've thought this through." She managed to hold her head up, and he admired her control, but she couldn't stop the quiver in her lower lip.

"I'm serious about seeing that Beth is well taken care of. I love her like she was my own child."

"And this is how you show it? By threatening to take her from her mother?"

"I'm not threatening you. I want to give Beth a decent life. She would have died if she had been born out there. You barely survived. Is that what you want for her?"

"No." She pressed a hand to her trembling lips.

Suddenly she wavered, and he crossed the room in three long strides to reach out and steady her. He'd been too hard on her. He should have found an easier way to make her see that she had to accept his help. "Are you okay?"

"I'm going to be sick." She bent forward.

Mick held on to her, preventing her from tumbling off the bed. Bracing her against his side, he reached for the call light. "Easy," he coaxed. "I'll get you some help."

When her spasms passed, he helped her sit up and lie back in bed. Her face resembled white marble with pale blue veins the only color in it. He was ready to rush out into the hall and grab the first nurse he saw when Caitlin's eyes fluttered open.

Slowly, she focused on his face. "I messed up your shoes."

"I think maybe I deserved it."

"You did." She closed her eyes again.

"I'm sorry I upset you. We can talk about this later."

Her eyes snapped open, and her gaze bored into his. "There's nothing to talk about. She's my child, not yours."

The intercom on the wall over the bed clicked on. Someone said, "May I help you?"

"Yes," he answered. "Miss Williams has just been sick. Could you send a nurse in?"

"Someone will be right there" came the clipped reply.

Caitlin turned her face away from him. Stubborn,

irrational, pathetic—every word fit the pale young woman in front of him, but the image that stuck in his mind was that of a wounded lioness snarling in defense of her cub. Maybe it was the color of her eyes or the fierce determination beneath her words. Whatever it was, he knew he would have a fight on his hands unless he could convince her to accept his help.

He waited in awkward silence for the promised help and breathed a sigh of relief when a nurse finally entered the room. He stepped back from the bed. "I'll wait outside."

Caitlin made no comment, and he left the room with the sinking feeling that he had failed miserably at presenting his case. Instead, he was afraid he had left exactly the opposite impression.

After locating a public restroom, he cleaned his shoes as best he could, then returned to wait outside Caitlin's door. It opened at last, and the nurse came out. He moved to pass her, but her arm shot out blocking his way.

"I'm sorry. Ms. Williams has requested that you not be allowed back in."

Caitlin obviously wasn't willing to listen to reason.

"All right, I'll leave," he told the waiting nurse. "Do you have something I can write a note on?" He took her pen and notepad and wrote out exactly what he intended to do. He offered to help Caitlin find a job and a place to stay. His only aim was to help her get back on her feet.

Caitlin listened to the muffled voices outside her door. If only he would go away. She never wanted to see his face again. In the dark interior of the crumbling building where she had labored in pain, Mick had ap-

peared like a movie hero. His voice had been soothing and calm, his hands had been strong and gentle.
She had dared to trust him because there hadn't been
anyone else. Now, he could take away the only good
thing that had ever come into her life. An overwhelming sense of betrayal brought a fresh rush of tears to
her eyes.

Dashing them away with both hands she vowed
they would be the last ones she ever shed over Mick
O'Callaghan. She had to be strong now—strong enough
to keep her baby. When the time came, she and Beth
would disappear before Mick could stop them. The
first thing she had to do was to get out of this hospital.

The door opened, and the nurse came back into the
room. "Has he gone?" Caitlin asked.

"Yes. He wanted you to have this." She held out a note.

After a second of hesitation, Caitlin took it. Opening the folded piece of paper, she stared at the dark,
bold lines marching across the page and desperately
wished they made sense to her the way they made
sense to everyone else. Crumpling the message, she
tossed it toward the trash can. It didn't matter what he
had to say. She wouldn't let him or anyone else take
her baby. Ever!

Caitlin waited, but the anger she hoped would burn
away the memory of Mick's deep, soothing voice didn't
materialize. The ache of his betrayal remained, but she
couldn't hate him.

Beneath the pain caused by his words, she saw the
truth in what he said. He only wanted what was best
for Beth. Maybe she couldn't take care of her baby.

No, she wouldn't accept that. Flinging aside the covers, she forced her weary body out of bed. "I'm going to the nursery."

The nurse moved to help. "Are you sure you want to get up?"

The room swam around Caitlin, and she clutched the side of the bed to steady herself. "I'm fine. Really."

She even managed a smile. She couldn't allow anyone to see how sick she was. She had to get dismissed from this place.

"Excuse me, but are you Ms. Williams?"

Caitlin turned to find a man in an ill-fitting suit standing in the doorway.

"I'm Caitlin Williams," she answered.

The man seemed distracted as he searched through papers in the folder he held. His face brightened when he located what he was looking for. "I'm Lloyd Winston, the social worker for this unit."

On a scale of one to ten, that statement dropped the man to a quick zero in her books. Had Mick already set the ball in motion to get custody of Beth? She tried to hide her sudden fear.

He closed the file and smiled at Caitlin. "I see here in your doctor's note that he plans to dismiss you tomorrow. I understand that you are currently without a place to live. Tell me, where do you plan to go once you're discharged?"

"Out of here."

"That's your only plan? Well, perhaps I can help. Let me see what shelters have openings."

Mick maneuvered his SUV through the Saturday afternoon traffic with less than his usual care. He was furious.

Lord, help me. I know I shouldn't pass judgment on Caitlin, but she is deliberately making things harder.

She had been dismissed from the hospital, and the only information he could get was that she had gone to a shelter. Apparently, she'd asked Winston not to disclose which one.

Cutting sharply in front of another car, Mick ignored the irate honking behind him and took the off-ramp. Ten minutes later he pulled up in front of his home.

His mother and Naomi stood at the curb pulling shopping bags from the trunk of a gray sedan. The women smiled when they caught sight of him.

"You're just in time. Make yourself useful." His mother held out a bag. He took it, picked up another, then followed the women into the house.

Once inside, he placed his bags on the kitchen counter. Naomi began putting the contents away. "We haven't seen much of you lately, Mick."

"I've been at the hospital a lot. Did you miss me?"

She chuckled and batted his arm. "Of course I didn't, but your mother did."

"Nonsense, Naomi, I'm a big girl. I can spend a few hours without someone hovering over me. How's the baby doing?"

"Better. Dr. Wright said she'll begin trying small feedings tomorrow. It's definitely a step in the right direction."

His mother nodded. "Good. And how's the baby's mother?"

"She's a royal pain." He glanced at her. "Sorry."

Elizabeth gazed at him for a long moment. "I'm surprised to hear you admit as much. For a while I thought you were developing an infatuation for her."

He looked away from her intense scrutiny as he shifted uneasily. "It's not like that. It's just that she needs so much help, but she won't admit it."

Naomi shut the cupboard door with a crack. "Maybe it's because her house isn't on fire."

He looked at her sharply. "What do you mean?"

"It seems to me that you're way too eager to dash in and try to save her."

"And that's a bad thing?"

"Of course, it isn't," his mother interjected.

"Unless the person you're trying to save knows the house isn't burning," Naomi added.

"You think she doesn't want my help because she doesn't believe she needs it?"

Naomi leaned against the counter and crossed her arms over her thin chest. "Look at it from the poor girl's point of view. She asked for your help when she was in labor, didn't she? And she accepted the help you offered?"

"Yes."

"If you're right, and she named you as her baby's father only when she thought she was going to die, it stands to reason that now that she's recovered, she feels that she doesn't need your help anymore. I think you should respect her wishes. You can't force people to accept help if they don't want it."

"But she's destitute. How is she going to take care of Beth if she doesn't have a job or a place to live?"

"Surely she has family or friends she can stay with?" Elizabeth suggested.

"Not that I could locate."

"Did you ask her?" Naomi demanded.

"Sort of," he admitted slowly.

"And did you give her a chance to answer, or did you charge ahead with your plans for her 'rescue'?" With both hands she made quotation marks in the air.

"Maybe I was a little forceful, but I care about Beth."

His mother moved to cup his cheek with her free hand. "You're a very caring man. I'm sorry things didn't work out the way you hoped."

"I can't let Caitlin take Beth and vanish."

"Wait a minute." Elizabeth held up one hand. "Caring for a child who's alone in the world is one thing, but getting involved in a custody dispute is a whole different kettle of fish."

"My choices are do nothing and let Caitlin disappear into those stinking slums with a helpless baby, or I make sure that doesn't happen. God put me in Beth's life for a reason. I'm not turning my back on her."

He rose and headed for the front door, more disappointed than he cared to admit.

She caught his arm and stopped him. "Mick, you can't save every destitute child you see."

"I can save Beth. She's going to be part of my life. Why is it so hard for everyone to accept that God wants me to care for this child?"

Elizabeth pulled her hand away. "It may be what the good Lord wants. But I think you need to be very sure this isn't just about what Mick O'Callaghan wants."

Caitlin stood and listened to the hawk-faced matron in charge of the women's dorm at the Lexington Street Shelter.

"Your bed is the last one on the left. There's no smoking and no drinking. Keep a close eye on your valuables—we're not responsible if anything gets sto-

len. There are twenty-two women and children on this
floor and one bathroom, so don't hog it. We provide
two meals a day. Breakfast is at 7:00 a.m. sharp. Supper is at six. If you're late, we don't hold anything for
you. Any questions?" She folded her arms and waited.

Caitlin shook her head. "I've stayed here before.
I know the rules." She stared down the long, narrow
room. She'd stayed here once during the coldest nights
of winter when she had been sixteen, scared and out
of food. It wasn't a pleasant memory.

This time, she wouldn't be leaving after a few meals
of thin soup and a break in the weather. The hospital
social worker had arranged for her stay here so that she
could be near a phone in case Beth's doctor needed to
contact her. It had been the closest shelter with room
to take her on such short notice.

She moved down the crowded room lined with
narrow beds toward the one the matron had indicated. The place reeked of unwashed bodies. A worn-
looking woman rocked and hummed to a little girl of
about three. The child was whining that she was hungry. Loud snoring came from beneath a heap of blankets on a bed in the middle of the room while a teenage
girl paced the small space in front of the room's only
window with her arms clasped tightly around herself.

Caitlin sat on the thin, blue-striped mattress of the
last cot and looked around. She was alone again no
matter how crowded the room was. Leaning down,
she slid a plastic bag with her few belongings underneath the bed. The crackle and rustle of papers made
her frown.

The nurses at the NICU had made sure that she had
plenty of information when she was discharged—all

of it in writing. Neat little brochures on colored paper that were useless to her. She had wanted to ask questions, but the staff had been so busy with admissions that she had simply been handed the papers and hustled out the door.

A harsh, racking cough interrupted the soft humming of the young mother. After a few moments, she began to sing in a trembling and off-key voice. "'Hush little baby, don't say a word. Mama's gonna buy you a mockingbird.'"

She didn't seem to know the rest of the song because she repeated the same lines over and over again. Lying on her side, Caitlin faced the wall and listened to the senseless song.

"Hush little baby, don't say a word."

Was Beth crying now? Did she miss her mother's touch, her voice? Would the nurses pay as much attention to her now that they were busy?

A hollow place had formed in Caitlin's heart when she walked out the hospital doors without her daughter. It grew now into a vast emptiness that ached like a gnawing hunger. She missed her baby—missed the smell of her and the feel of her. She had left her baby behind. It didn't matter that she hadn't had a choice.

Maybe Mick would be with Beth tonight. He did care about her, Caitlin knew that. Yesterday, she had been scared and angry. That made her determined to prove that she could care for Beth by herself. But now, miles away, Caitlin could only hope Mick would ignore her angry words and stay with the baby. Beth didn't deserve to be alone. No child did.

How many times had Caitlin huddled, cold and hungry, while her mother was gone for days on end? Back

then, Caitlin had dreamed that her father would somehow find her and take her away with him. The man
in Caitlin's imagination had been a man like Mick—
tall and strong, and sure of what was right. But no one
ever came.

Mick claimed he wanted to be a father to Beth, but
for how long? How long before he couldn't find the
time for a kid who wasn't really his? Life had a way
of dulling even the best of intentions. She didn't want
Beth wishing for some imaginary daddy, or worse yet,
pining for someone real who never came around.

Caitlin would be all that Beth needed. If Beth had a
mother who loved her and cared for her, she wouldn't
miss having a dad.

Closing her eyes, Caitlin tried to shut out the sounds
and the smells around her and recall Beth's face. She
pictured her tiny hands and feet. She pictured the way
Beth's mouth widened into an O when she yawned,
the way her eyebrows arched perfectly in the center.

Caitlin's fingers itched for her pencils and drawing
pad. If only she could put the pictures in her head down
on paper, then maybe she wouldn't feel so alone. She'd
have something of Beth to keep beside her.

But she didn't have her sketchbook anymore. Her
sketches, her baby's clothes, everything that she owned
had been left behind in the building where Mick found
her. Someday she would make her way back there, but
she held little hope of finding her things undisturbed.

The next morning Caitlin rose from a fitful, night-
mare-haunted sleep where she searched through garbage cans and dark alleys for a baby she could hear
crying but couldn't find. At breakfast, she forced down

a bowl of lukewarm oatmeal before she gathered her few possessions and walked the long miles back to the hospital.

At the nursery, she went directly to Beth's bed. Only when she saw for herself that Beth was okay did Caitlin relax. She touched her daughter's hand and gazed at her beautiful face. "Morning, jelly bean. I told you I'd be back."

"Jelly bean—that's cute."

Caitlin looked up to see Mick standing a few feet away. Her foolish heart took an unexpected leap of joy, and she almost smiled before she remembered to be angry with him.

He moved to the bedside. "The nickname fits her. She's little and she's sweet."

Caitlin turned her attention to the baby, determined to ignore him. "What do you want?"

"I won't stay long," he said. "I just wanted to apologize for upsetting you. I was wrong."

"No kidding."

"Look—" his exasperation came through in his voice "—I want you to know I'm sorry for trying to strong-arm you. You don't want my help, that's fine. Where you go and what you do is none of my business. My concern is for Beth. I'm only going to ask you for one thing."

She slanted a look at him. "What?"

"While she is in the hospital, I'd like to continue to visit her."

"You're asking my permission?"

He thrust his hands in his pockets and looked down. "Yes. You're her mother, and I'm just some guy who happened by."

Caitlin mulled over his change of heart and wondered what had prompted it. Did this mean he wasn't going to try to take Beth away from her? She was almost afraid to believe him. "And what if I say no?"

He leveled his gaze at her. "I'll respect your wishes."

She studied his face and saw the uncertainty in his eyes, saw the tenseness in the set of his shoulders. He was waiting for her to tell him to get lost.

But he wasn't just some guy who had happened by. She hadn't dreamed the voice she had heard in the darkness. It had been his voice. And he'd stayed with Beth when the baby needed someone the most. He'd given his mother's name to the child of a total stranger. Some guy passing by didn't do all of those things— only someone who truly cared about Beth.

Doubts clamored inside Caitlin's head warning her not to trust him, but faced with his kindness and sincerity, she chose to ignore them. "I guess it would be okay."

Hope brightened his eyes. "Thank you. This means a lot."

Caitlin turned her attention back to the baby and prayed she hadn't just made the biggest mistake of her life. "I'm doing it for her, because I can't be here as much now."

"I understand. Now that I'm back at work, I won't be able to be here as often as I'd like, either. Look, I don't know where you're staying, but if you ever need a ride here or anything, just say the word."

"I take the bus." She didn't want to admit to him that she couldn't even afford bus fare. "Getting here at night is hard. If you could spend time with her then, that would be nice."

If he came at night, she wouldn't have to see him. She wouldn't have to pretend she didn't long to hear his voice or to feel the touch of his hand.

Her grudging permission sent a wave of relief through Mick. He sat next to her and struggled to separate the feelings running through him. It was more than happiness at getting to see Beth again. A lot of it had to do with seeing Caitlin.

He liked being near this woman, he liked the sound of her voice, the way the light changed the color of her eyes. He liked the soft curve of her ears and the way she tucked her hair back when she was nervous.

An alarm sounded and he scanned the array of monitors to see which one it was. Beth's nurse reached up to silence the one that monitored the oxygen level of her blood. It was then he noticed how much oxygen she was getting.

"She's up to fifty percent," he said. "She hasn't been that high before."

"Hasn't she? Let me check her chart." He waited impatiently for her to confirm what he already knew. "You're right," she said. "I'll let Dr. Wright know."

"What is it? What's wrong?" Caitlin demanded. Her hand closed on Mick's shoulder in a death grip. He covered it with his own in a gesture of comfort as they waited for the doctor.

Dr. Wright came to the bedside and quickly checked the baby over. "She is needing more oxygen and her heart rate is up as well. That has me a bit worried. She may be getting sick."

"But how could she get sick in here?" Caitlin asked, clearly worried and perplexed.

"Babies like Beth have a very poor immune system. No matter how careful we are, we can't prevent every illness. We'll draw some blood work and that will tell us more."

"But she'll be okay, won't she?" Mick asked. The pounding of his heart was so loud he thought he might not be able to hear the doctor's answer.

Please, Lord, Beth has been through so much already. Isn't it time she caught a break?

Dr. Wright smiled. "If her blood work shows any signs of infection, we'll start her on antibiotics. Unfortunately, this isn't all that unusual. Remember, Beth has a long road ahead of her. We have to take it one day at a time."

Caitlin noticed then that Mick's hand covered hers where it rested on his shoulder. She pulled away from him, but she missed the comfort of his touch.

After the doctor left the bedside, Caitlin cupped her hands around Beth the way Mick had shown her the first time she saw her daughter. Mick had taught her so much. Sudden tears stung Caitlin's eyes and her throat tightened as regrets welled up out of nowhere. She wasn't surprised that he noticed.

"Caitlin, what's wrong?"

"It was so hard at first."

"What was hard?" he asked gently.

"All of it. Knowing you named her, knowing you held her first. I resented the way you seemed so at ease with her while I was scared to even touch her. It was like she didn't even need me."

"You're her mother, of course she needs you."

"The first time I came in here, I didn't even know which baby was mine. What kind of mother doesn't know her own child?"

"Maybe one who was unconscious for days, one who almost died? Don't beat yourself up over the things you can't change."

"I'll always feel I missed the most important moment of her life—and of mine."

She couldn't believe she was telling him these things. Yet looking into his bright blue eyes filled with compassion and understanding, she knew that there was something about this man that drew out a part of herself that she had never wanted to share with anyone else. His voice, his touch, they made her feel something that she had been missing her whole life. He made her feel safe.

She looked away, afraid he would read in her eyes just how much she longed for the comfort of his touch.

Mick reached across the space between them and placed the tips of his fingers under her chin. Gently but firmly, he turned her face back to his. "You did miss out on something special. You have a right to feel cheated. But what's important is how you go on after life hands you a raw deal. Remember that God never gives us more than we can bear."

"The Guy has got way too much confidence in me."

Mick smiled. "No, I don't think so."

"You really believe that stuff? About God, I mean."

"I really do."

"Well, I don't. He's never given me an even break."

"He gave you Beth."

"Yes, He did. I can't believe how much I love her."

"That's the same way God loves you. It's hard to have faith, I know. But once you find it, once you real-ize how much God loves you, then all things are bearable. Don't look for God with your eyes, Caitlin. Look for Him with your heart."

"You make it sound so simple."

"It is."

She wanted so badly to believe him, but instead she shook her head. "Maybe God loves you, but He doesn't love me."

Chapter 9

A few days later, Caitlin stifled a groan, picked up her spoon and stirred the thin oatmeal in the orange plastic bowl in front of her. She forced herself to swallow a bite.

Between the chills and the sweats and her aching body, all she wanted to do was sleep, but her rest had been fitful at best. The shelter was noisy even at night with so many women packed into one room, and her bed, the one closest to the only bathroom, guaranteed she heard the gurgling and clanking pipes every time it was used.

She took another bite of her unappetizing fare and almost gagged. Oatmeal wasn't her favorite food even when her stomach wasn't doing flip-flops. She forced down a third spoonful. She had to keep up her strength so that she could be with her daughter.

Beth wasn't doing well. She'd had another seizure and had been started on another round of antibiotics. It seemed like she took one step forward and fell back two. The last few days had been really rough.

Sometimes, Caitlin wondered if it was wrong to put Beth through so much pain. She wondered if it wouldn't have been better if... *If she hadn't lived.*

The terrible thought tormented her each time Beth underwent yet another round of painful tests—each time she watched sobs rack her daughter's tiny body when she was poked for blood or another IV. Because Beth was still on the ventilator, she couldn't make any sounds. Somehow, the silence of her crying made it all the more gut-wrenching to watch, and Caitlin's burden of guilt grew heavier.

If this is Your plan, God, it stinks.

Mick had faith. It was plain for all to see, and Caitlin was moved by his devotion, but she couldn't find it in her heart to accept a God who would let a tiny baby suffer.

Mick entered the nursery late that afternoon and made his way to Beth's bedside. Sandra, seated in a rocker across the aisle, fed a chubby infant with thick black hair. Arching one eyebrow, she said, "I'd say good afternoon, but from the looks of you, I'd guess it hasn't been."

"Do I look that bad?"

"Worse. Bad day at work?"

"Yeah, bad three days. I took an extra shift so one of the guys could spend some time with his family on Memorial Day. I forgot how much I hate working holiday weekends."

He sank onto a stool and gently took Beth's hand in his. His heart lightened as her fingers closed over his in a soft grip. Just seeing her made the whole crazy world seem better. He hadn't been in for four days and now that he was, he couldn't believe he'd stayed away so long.

At his last meeting with Caitlin, he'd had a glimpse of just how much she loved Beth. He had begun to think that he'd been wrong about her. Maybe she could get on her feet and take care of Beth, too. He prayed often about what he should do. Still, the answers he sought continued to elude him.

Stepping out of the role of a father was proving to be harder than he had expected. So was not seeing Caitlin. For some reason, she had taken to haunting his dreams at night.

"Want to talk about it?"

For a second, he thought Sandra was asking about his nocturnal visions, but before he blurted out his confession, he realized she was asking about his job.

"No, not really," he answered with a shake of his head. He didn't talk about the car wrecks and the bad fires, the ones with lives lost. For now, he wanted to put his job out of his mind and concentrate on the little wonder in front of him. "How's my girl doing?"

"About the same today. We've stopped her feedings again."

Mick pinned Sandra with a steady stare. "This isn't usual, is it?"

"Every baby is different. There is no 'usual.'"

He turned his attention to Beth. Her color didn't seem right. He glanced at her oxygen reading and was relieved to see it was normal. Maybe he was being paranoid. Three days and nights of pulling bleeding people out of mangled cars up on the Eisenhower Expressway and taking bodies out of smoldering houses tended to make a guy feel that nothing turned out right. Beth was going to be fine. He had to believe that. "Is Caitlin here?" he asked.

"You just missed her."

Something in Sandra's voice made him glance sharply at her.

"What's wrong?"

"The staff has noticed a change in Caitlin's behavior."

Mick sent her a tired, amused smile. "What? She's turned sweet all of a sudden?"

Sandra grinned at his teasing. "That *would* be a change." Her smile faded. After tucking her charge in, she pulled her rocker over beside Mick. "Have you seen her lately?"

Mick stared at Sandra's concerned face. "No. Not for several days. Caitlin and I agreed it would be best to divide our time so that Beth usually had one of us here. Caitlin comes in the daytime, I come in the evenings when I'm not working."

"Caitlin has been here every day, I'll give her that, but she has started coming in later and not staying as long. One nurse reported that she thought Caitlin was strung out. She could barely keep her eyes open. She slept in the chair beside the baby for most of the time she was here."

Mick found himself coming to Caitlin's defense. "Maybe she's just tired. It's got to be hard getting here every day. Have you suggested she take a day off and get some rest?"

"Of course we suggested that."

"And?"

"And you know Caitlin. She didn't take the suggestion well. She said she was fine in a tone that sounded more like 'Mind your own business.'"

"Maybe I should talk to her."

"There's something else. Several of the mothers in the unit have reported that they have had money taken from their purses."

"And you think Caitlin had something to do with it?"

Sandra nodded at the baby across the way. "Both mothers have babies near this bed, and both of them were here the same time Caitlin was. Does Caitlin use?"

"You mean drugs? No."

"Are you sure?"

Was he? Caitlin had grown up a street kid. Drug use was common among them, he'd seen it often enough. Even if she hated the fact that her own mother had been an addict it didn't mean that Caitlin didn't have the same dependency.

Sandra must have read the doubt in his eyes. "Caitlin's behavior hasn't been sterling at the best of times, but this change makes us very suspicious. Having a sick baby is a terrible strain on any mother. Many of them feel tremendous guilt."

"What will you do?"

"We've already done it. When Caitlin came in today, we had security take her to the lab for a drug test."

"She consented to that?"

"She was…how shall I put it…very verbal in expressing her opinion of us, but she went."

"When will you have the results?"

"Tomorrow afternoon at the latest. But, Mick, her results will be confidential. I'm stretching it just tell-

ing you that we're having her tested. We won't be able
to tell you the results, one way or the other."

He tightened his grip on Beth's hand. "What will
happen if Caitlin's drug test is positive?"

"If she is using, she won't be taking Beth home."

Caitlin didn't know how much longer she could
keep walking four miles twice a day. Instead of getting strong she seemed to be getting weaker. Today
she hadn't been able to drag herself out of bed until
almost noon.

She braced herself before she entered the nursery.
Would her drug-test results be back or would she be
subjected to another day of frigid stares and barely
concealed dislike by the staff? She looked forward to
the apologies they would have to give her when her
results showed she was clean. A person couldn't act
a little tired without some snoopy nurse jumping to
wild conclusions.

In the nursery, Dr. Wright stood beside Beth's bed.
For a moment, their images swam in front of Caitlin's
eyes, and she grabbed the back of a nearby chair to
steady herself. When she looked up, the doctor was
staring at her intently.

Caitlin straightened and moved within a foot of the
woman. "I'm clean, right?" she demanded.

The doctor had the grace to look shamefaced. "Yes.
I'm sorry we had to put you through that, but Beth is
our primary concern."

Caitlin scanned the faces of the nurses around the
unit who were watching with undisguised curiosity.
"Did you hear that? I'm clean."

The women quickly busied themselves with other

tasks, but Caitlin was satisfied that they all knew they had misjudged her.

Dr. Wright laid a hand on Caitlin's arm. "There's something else we need to discuss."

Caitlin's elation died a quick death. "What?"

"Your lab work showed a high bacteria count in your milk. Have you been running a fever or having chills?"

"I'm a little tired, that's all."

"I'm afraid it's more than that. If you are sick, you shouldn't be visiting the baby. You can make her sick just by touching her. And we can't be giving her your milk. We'll have to discard what you've brought in." She took the small bottle from Caitlin's hand and tossed it in the trash. "I'm sure all of this was explained in the handouts we gave you when you went home. Do you have a doctor you can see?"

Caitlin shook her head.

"I'll write you a prescription for some medication. I want you to take it as directed and I'm afraid you'll have to wait forty-eight hours before coming in to see the baby again."

Dr. Wright scribbled something on a small square of paper and placed it in Caitlin's hand. Her fingers closed around it, but nothing registered except that she had hurt Beth again. Suddenly, she had to get away. She pulled away from the doctor's steadying hand. Somehow, she stumbled out of the nursery and down the hall to the elevators. Gasping for air, she leaned against the wall as she waited for the doors to open.

How could she have been so stupid? She had tried to ignore her own illness, and she had made Beth sick. The elevator doors slid open and Caitlin stepped in. Thankfully it was empty. As the doors closed, she wished they would stay shut forever. If only she could be trapped in here. Then she couldn't harm her baby.

Her ignorance had caused Beth to be stuck with needles countless times. The information was in the colorful pieces of paper Caitlin had been sent home with—only she was too stupid to be able to read them.

The elevator didn't keep her trapped, instead, it opened at the main lobby where people were coming and going as if nothing were wrong. With weary steps, Caitlin made her way out the main door. The gloom of the overcast evening had deepened into a premature darkness and rain had begun to fall. Without a thought, she walked out into the cold mist.

Mick pulled into the hospital parking lot and turned off his engine. A thin drizzle had begun to fall earlier, and it continued lightly but steadily into the evening. Through the speckled windshield he spied Caitlin leaving the building. She was late tonight.

She didn't even have a jacket on, he noted, only a thin sweater. Hunching her shoulders, she left the protection of the hospital entrance and stepped out into the rain walking toward the bus stop. She'd be drenched in no time if she intended to wait at the curb in this stuff. Didn't she have any sense? He had half a mind to drag her into his car and keep her dry until the bus came by. Glancing down the street, he saw the bus turn the corner, and he realized that wouldn't be necessary.

Stepping out of his vehicle, he made a dash across the parking lot and stopped under the cover of the hospital's wide portico. He wanted to spend an hour or so with Beth before he called it a night. He cast one last glance at Caitlin. The bus stopped and opened its doors, but she walked past as if she didn't see it. What in the world was she up to now?

Sandra's suggestion that Caitlin had been strung out during her last visit sprang to his mind. He didn't want to believe it, but Sandra's concern had him almost convinced. If Caitlin was using drugs he had to know. He had to have proof. Unsure of exactly what he intended to do, he stepped out into the rain and began to follow her.

The bus belched a cloud of dark smoke as it pulled away, and the sound of Caitlin's harsh coughing reached Mick as the roar of the engine faded away. She wrapped her arms around herself as though she were chilled, but she never raised her head as she made her way across the street and continued down the dark sidewalk.

The streetlamps made pools of silvery liquid light in the rain, but Mick avoided them as he followed Caitlin. He didn't want to be spotted if she looked back. After a few blocks, the lights grew fewer.

He followed discreetly, trying not to attract attention. After a while, he realized no one cared. The few people he met hurried past with their heads down, or they hunched beneath umbrellas or newspapers held up to shield them from the drizzle.

After nearly two miles, the sidewalk became busier, and Mick closed the distance between himself and Caitlin as she continued into a district known for its unsavory activities. If she was looking for an easy place to score drugs, she was headed in the right direction.

He moved past the peep shows, novelty shops, bars and adult bookstores without a second glance. He was afraid of losing sight of Caitlin.

Up ahead of him, she slowed her steps then stopped. She sank onto an empty bench near the street corner and slumped forward with her head bowed. Mick stopped as well. Turning, he pretended to gaze at the jewelry displayed in a brightly lit pawnshop window while he covertly glanced toward Caitlin. What was she waiting for? Was she meeting someone? A dealer, maybe? Mick started to move closer when a gray car with a dented fender pulled to a halt at the curb in front of the bench.

The driver leaned across the seat and rolled the window down. "Hey, baby! You wanna party?"

Caitlin raised her head to stare at the man. Suddenly, Mick thought he'd be sick. His hands balled into fists. Was that how she had survived on the streets? He didn't even want to think about the answer. He started toward her.

"Get lost, creep!" At the sound of her sarcastic voice, Mick skidded to a halt.

Caitlin stood and walked on, pulling her thin sweater tight once more. The rain plastered her hair to her bowed head. Mick had never felt more ashamed of himself than he did at that moment.

At the corner, she turned and headed down Lexington. It was then that Mick thought he knew where she was going. The Lexington Street Shelter was about six blocks farther on. Had she been walking all this way to see the baby every day?

She paused at the side of an old brick building and reached out a hand to steady herself. Without warning, she crumpled to the pavement.

Mick broke into a run. Darting across the rain-filled street, he dodged a taxi and almost bowled over a man waiting at the crosswalk. Ignoring the indignant shout behind him, he raced to the fallen woman and dropped to his knees beside her. Her eyes fluttered open as he lifted her by the shoulders. "Caitlin, are you all right? Caitlin, answer me!"

"Mick? What are you doing here?"

"Never mind that. Are you okay?"

"I think so." She raised a trembling hand to the back of her head and winced. Lowering her hand, she stared at the blood smeared across her palm. "Or maybe not."

"Let me see."

"It's nothing."

"I'll be the judge of that." Easing her head forward, Mick probed her scalp with hands that were less than steady. He located a knot, but it was too dark to see the damage.

"You've got a goose egg. It doesn't feel like a bad wound, but I can't tell for sure. Can you stand?"

"I think so." She made an effort to rise.

He helped her up and steadied her once she gained her feet. She bowed her head and leaned heavily against him. He wrapped his arms around her and held her close. The feeling of her safe in his arms brought a rush of gratitude.

Thank You, God, for prompting me to follow her.

The trembling woman he held was so slight that he thought a single gust of Chicago's notorious wind might blow her away. She lifted her face to gaze at him. Possessed with the need to keep her safe, Mick bent his head and covered her trembling lips with a gentle kiss. For a second, she seemed to melt against him and it felt so wonderfully right. Then she stiffened and pushed away.

Pulling back, Mick stared into her eyes now wide with surprise. She bit the corner of her lip and looked away. A tremor shook her slender body.

"We need to get you out of this rain." Mick took a firm grip on her elbow as he led the way out of the alley and back toward the busy street. Within minutes he had flagged down a cab.

Caitlin gave the cabby the address of the shelter, then lapsed into silence in the back seat. Mick pulled off his jacket and tucked it around her. It was damp, but it still retained some of his body heat and he didn't have anything else to offer. He considered putting his arm around her, but thought better of it. The kiss had been a mistake. While she hadn't protested his embrace, she had clearly been surprised by it and perhaps even a little frightened. Adding to her fright was the last thing he wanted.

When the taxi pulled up to the curb in front of the shelter Caitlin handed him his jacket. "Thanks, Mick."

She opened the door and stepped out, but he was close behind her. After telling the driver to wait, Mick took her arm and hustled her toward the door of the building.

Once inside, he halted in the lobby lit by a single bulb in a bare socket in the ceiling. The place was packed with men and women sitting and lying around the perimeter of the room. The rank smells of unkempt bodies and dirty, wet clothes laced the thick air.

Ignoring the squalor around him, Mick took Caitlin by the shoulders. "Let me have a look at your head. I'm not going to leave you here if you should be in an emergency room."

Wordlessly, she turned around. Her meekness sent

a small jolt of worry through him. Once he was satisfied it wasn't a deep cut he pulled her around and took a closer look at her eyes. Her skin that should have been cold from the damp rain was hot to his touch.

"I'm fine, Mick, don't fret." Her voice, so timid and soft, sent alarm bells ringing in his mind. This wasn't right. It wasn't the Caitlin he knew.

"You don't look fine. You look like a drowned cat. What you need is a hot bath, dry clothes and a filling meal," Mick stated firmly.

"That's just what I'll do, Mick. You don't have to hang around."

"Ha!" said a woman seated on the floor of the lobby. "They ain't got a tub here, only a drizzling shower and the water ain't never hot."

Mick frowned. "You've got to be kidding." Glancing around at the ragged men and women lining the room, he knew she wasn't. Not all of the shelters in town were as well-equipped or as well-funded as Mercy House.

"She can't get nothin' to eat, neither. They done served the last meal, and the kitchen ain't open again till morning."

Suddenly, the pieces began to fall into place. Caitlin wasn't using drugs, she was exhausted and undernourished.

"Mick, I'll be fine. I'll go right to bed. All I need is a little sleep." Even as she spoke, Caitlin's knees buckled and she would have fallen if he hadn't scooped her up.

"You aren't fine, and you aren't staying here." He and the nurses had misjudged Caitlin badly. Her only crime was that she didn't know how to ask for help. He turned and carried her toward the door.

"Where you takin' her?" the woman called after him.

"To my place. I'll bring her back when she's able to take care of herself."

"They won't hold her bed. If she ain't in it by ten, they'll give it to somebody else."

"Let them!" The door closed behind him with a bang.

Chapter 10

The taxi driver cast Mick a puzzled look when he deposited Caitlin in the back seat and climbed in beside her, but didn't make any comment. As the cab pulled away, Caitlin's head lolled to Mick's shoulder, and this time he didn't hesitate to drape an arm around her and pull her close.

"I don't want to go home with you," Caitlin said. A shiver coursed through her.

"I'm not giving you a choice." Mick glanced at her, but her eyes were closed, and she missed the amusement that curved his lips into a smile. He was relieved to hear some defiance creeping back into her voice. She attempted to sit up, but Mick pressed her back against his chest. It felt right to hold her close. For now, it was enough to know that she was safe.

All too soon, the cab pulled to a stop in front of

Mick's home. He paid the driver, then gently lifted Caitlin from the car.

"I can walk," she protested weakly.

"So can I," Mick countered.

"I mean, you don't have to carry me."

"I want to."

"Oh."

That silenced her, or maybe she was simply too exhausted to put up more of an argument. On the porch, he set her feet down long enough to locate his keys and unlock the door, but he kept a firm grip on her with one arm. When the door swung open, he scooped her up and carried her inside.

Nikki gave a woof of a greeting from her spot by the fireplace. Mick lowered Caitlin to the sofa. With a quick tug, he pulled the worn, fuzzy throw emblazoned with the Chicago Bears logo from the back of the couch and swaddled it around her. Nikki rose and ventured across the room.

"You have a dog?"

Mick didn't understand the wistful tone that filled Caitlin's voice.

"This is Nikki. She won't hurt you."

Wagging her tail in greeting, Nikki sat down and promptly laid her head on Caitlin's lap. One of Caitlin's hands crept out from between the folds of the blanket to stroke the dog's head. "She's beautiful."

Mick patted the dog's side with a quick thump. "She's a good old girl. She wouldn't hurt a flea. I'm sure she'd hold the door open for a burglar and then lick his face just to show him how happy she was for the company."

Why was he standing here babbling about the dog?

The woman on his sofa looked ready to keel over. He frowned. "When was the last time you had something to eat?"

"I don't know."

"Today? Yesterday?"

She didn't answer. He turned and headed for the kitchen. He searched through the cabinets until he located a box of instant soup. It would be fast and it would warm her up. He poured the powdered broth and tiny noodles into a thick white mug, then put the kettle on to boil. When the kettle began to whistle, he filled the cup, cooled it with an ice cube and carefully carried it in to Caitlin.

She was where he'd left her, only her head was lying back against the sofa. The fingers of one hand were still threaded through the long fur of Nikki's ear, and the dog watched her with adoring eyes. Nikki shifted her gaze to Mick as he came into the room, but she didn't move until he nudged her aside with his knee. Gently, Mick laid a hand on Caitlin's shoulder. "Wake up."

"Go away," she said without opening her eyes.

"No. Come on, sit up a minute."

"I said, go away."

"And I said, no."

She peeked out from under one lid. "You're a mean man."

"I know, but I have my good points."

"Name one."

"I've got a cup of hot soup here."

Both her eyes shot open. "That would be a good point."

"Think you can drink this before it gets cold?"

She reached out with both hands. "Even if I have to fight the dog for it."

Mick chuckled, but he didn't miss how her hands shook before they closed around the mug. "Don't worry, Nikki is a picky eater. I'm afraid instant chicken noodle soup is beneath her notice."

Caitlin took a tentative sip, then a longer one. With a murmur of appreciation, she licked her lips as she clutched the mug close to her chest and bent her face to inhale the fragrant steam. "Her loss. This is good."

"I'm glad you like it."

"It's fantastic," she murmured as she raised the cup to her lips and took another sip. She gripped that mug like it was the last meal she was ever going to get. He could make sure that it wasn't, and he could see that she had a decent place to live as well.

He had plenty of room here. He practically rattled around in this big, old house when he was home— which wasn't all that often. Somehow, he'd convince her to stay here. He owed her that much for his unjust suspicions. She wasn't going to get back on her feet staying at that run-down shelter. She needed help. He intended to see that she got it. "I'm going to let my mom know you're here."

"I already know." He looked up to see his mother descending the stairs. "I heard voices and came to see what was going on."

She crossed the room, took a seat beside Caitlin, and held out her hand. "Hello. I'm Elizabeth O'Callaghan. You must be Caitlin."

Caitlin nodded as she took the offered hand. "My daughter is named after you."

"I know. I'm quite flattered. My dear, you are soaking wet. Mick, why don't you run a bath for our guest."

He smiled. "That was next on my list."

"I don't want to be any trouble."

Caitlin's feeble protest caused his mother to grin. "It's no trouble at all. I'll find something you can change into. Don't just stand there, Mick. Get a move on."

Caitlin giggled. "So this is where he gets it."

Elizabeth gave her a puzzled look. "Gets what?"

"His tendency to boss people around."

Mick chuckled as he followed his mother up the stairs. He called over his shoulder. "You might think I'm bossy, but you have just met the master."

After adjusting the temperature of the water pouring into the ancient claw-footed tub that occupied the house's only bathroom, Mick straightened. His young nieces always insisted on a tub full of bubbles with their baths. Would Caitlin like that? If she hadn't had anything but lukewarm washups at the shelter since she was dismissed from the hospital, he was pretty sure she might.

Turning, he surveyed the room. The last time Mary's kids had slept over, he had picked up a box of bubble bath at their insistence. He finally discovered the slightly battered box under the sink. He shook out a bit of the powder under the running water and a few bubbles began to form. It didn't seem like enough. With a shrug, he emptied the rest of the box in the tub and headed downstairs to get Caitlin.

She was asleep again. The empty soup cup dangled precariously from one hand while her other hand lay on Nikki's head where the dog had curled up on the sofa beside her.

"Get down, mutt," he grumbled softly. Nikki ignored him as usual. Mick bent and scooped Caitlin up in his arms.

Her eyes fluttered open. "You kiss nice."

He didn't know how to respond to that so he said, "Your bath is ready."

He started up the stairs and noticed how pleasant it was to carry this woman in his arms.

"I don't need a bath," she grumbled.

"Would it be ungentlemanly of me to say, yes, you do?"

Her tired eyes settled into a frown. "I don't stink."

"I never said you did."

"You said—"

"I said you need a bath. You've been soaked to the skin and chilled to boot, and a hot bath is exactly what you need."

"Okay. But I don't stink."

"No, you don't," he agreed, and hoped she didn't notice the amusement in his voice. He pushed open the bathroom door and stopped.

"Awesome!" she said in amazement.

Mounds of foam filled the tub and lazy sheets of it slid over the side to pool on the floor. Quickly, he deposited her on the toilet seat and turned off the water, feeling like a first-class nitwit.

"I thought you'd like a bubble bath. It's just Mr. Bubble—that's all I had. My niece left it here. I know my sisters used to use some kind of scented foamy stuff that smelled like lilacs or gardenias or some such flower." He realized he was babbling like an idiot and stopped talking.

"This is just like in the movies. I always wanted to do this."

He frowned at her. "You've never taken a bubble bath?"

"Not that I remember."

She didn't seem to realize how pathetic that simple statement sounded. What a hard, bare life she had lived. He rubbed his palms on the sides of his jeans. "Well then, I'm sure you'll like it. Just don't fall asleep and drown. I'll wait outside the door and you can hand me your clothes. I'll toss them in the washer for you."

She cast a suspicious look in his direction.

"Don't worry, dear," his mother came in behind him. "I have a robe you can wear. Go on, Mick. Shoo."

He retreated and closed the door.

A few moments later, it opened a crack and his mother dangled Caitlin's clothes out by one hand. He took them and beat a strategic withdrawal to the laundry room in the basement. He tossed her skirt and hose into the washer, but paused as he stared at the sweater in his hands. A few drops of blood speckled one shoulder.

It was frighteningly easy to imagine Beth living a life with Caitlin, and he shuddered at the thought of what she would endure if that happened. Caitlin deserved his help. Because if she didn't get it, Beth might be with her the next time she waited in the lobby of a crowded shelter to find out if there would be a bed for the night. And if there wasn't room, Beth would sleep with her mother in a doorway, or alley, or on a grate to keep from freezing to death in the winter.

No, Beth wasn't going to live like that. He would make sure of it. He started to toss the sweater in with the rest of the load, but a piece of paper fell out of one of the pockets and landed at his feet. He made a quick search of both pockets, but he didn't find anything else.

Bending down, he picked up the paper and smoothed out the small, damp note. With a muttered oath, he hurried back upstairs. He knocked on the bathroom door and didn't get any answer. "Caitlin, I need to talk to you."

"Just a moment," his mother answered.

He heard the sound of the shower curtain sliding on the rod, then his mother called out, "You can come in."

He pushed open the door. The gray-and-white-striped shower curtain hid most of Caitlin. All he could see was her head as she leaned against the back of the tub. His mother sat on a small vanity stool beside her. Caitlin opened her eyes and smiled sweetly.

"This is totally awesome." She lifted her palm filled with a small mountain of suds and blew. Bubbles danced through the air. "Can you imagine being able to do this every day?"

Having soap and hot water was something he never gave a second thought to, but with a simple question, she changed all of that. He held out the note. "I found this in your sweater pocket."

"What is it?" She frowned at the paper as if she'd never seen it before.

"Caitlin, this is a prescription for antibiotics for you written by Dr. Wright."

All at once, huge tears began to stream down her face. Alarmed, Mick said, "What's wrong?"

"I never meant to hurt her. I'm so sorry." With that, she broke into hysterical sobs.

"It's all right." The force of her uncontrolled weeping was so unlike the tough and resourceful woman he knew that he began to fear she would do herself physical harm.

"Let me handle this," Elizabeth said as she pushed him out the door and closed it in his face.

Finally, his mother called for him to come in. He opened the door and saw Caitlin wrapped in a long, thick robe and slumped against his mother on the edge of the tub. Elizabeth held her awkwardly with her one good arm.

"Can you carry her to the spare bedroom, son?"

"Of course." He slid his arms around Caitlin and lifted her easily. In the bedroom, he sat down on the edge of the bed where he held her and rocked her and murmured words of comfort until the storm of her weeping abated. She kept repeating that she was sorry. Sorry for what, he couldn't make out.

He looked at his mother, hovering beside him and said, "She's on the verge of exhaustion. This can't be good for her."

"She needed sleep more than anything else, but we can't put her to bed in a damp robe. I'm not sure I can get her into one of my nightgowns by myself."

Gently, he laid Caitlin down on top of the coverlet and went to his room. From his chest of drawers, he pulled out a button-down pajama top that would have to suffice for a nightgown and returned to her room. He paused beside his mother in indecision. "Can you manage this?"

"Yes, this will work. I'll call if I need you." She took his shirt.

He was sitting on the side of the bed when his mother joined him a short time later.

"She's more than exhausted, Mick. The woman is sick."

"I know." He held out the crumpled prescription.

"Has she been seeing the baby?"

"Every day. I'm guessing that's why Beth is sick, too."

He picked up the phone and dialed the number for the NICU.

"This is Mick O'Callaghan," he said tersely when the unit clerk answered. "I need to speak with Dr. Wright, immediately."

A knocking sound woke Caitlin from a pleasant dream. She opened her eyes and stared at an unfamiliar room with walls painted a delicate shade of rose. Across from her, white curtains billowed from an open window. Beyond she could see the branches of a huge tree silhouetted against a blue sky. Beside the window, a large purple toy cat stared at her from a rocking chair. Another knock sounded. It came from behind her. She turned over and winced. Every part of her body ached.

A door opened and Mick peeked around it. He stepped into the room looking uncertain and wonderfully handsome. "How are you feeling?"

"Kinda…confused."

"I'm not surprised. You've been asleep for thirty hours."

He crossed the room in three strides. She flinched when his hand shot toward her, and he froze. "I'm not going to hurt you. I only want to make sure your fever's down. May I?" Slowly, he extended his hand and touched her forehead.

She remembered now, she remembered everything—the doctor telling her that her milk had made Beth sick, Mick's rescue, meeting his mother. He had brought her to his home. What else had been real and not part of a dream? Had he really kissed her?

Embarrassment flooded her, but she couldn't help thinking about kissing him again.

"I'm fine." She turned away from his hand.

"You're better, but not fine. Look, I've got to get to work. I won't be back until tomorrow morning. Mom is here and my number is on a pad by the phone in the kitchen if you need anything. Make yourself at home. Fix yourself whatever you'd like to eat. I'd like you to consider staying here for a while. My mother will be here as well."

"How come a guy your age still lives with his mother?"

He laughed. "I don't normally. Mom was injured in a car accident two months ago. I'm sure you saw the cast on her arm."

"Yeah, I wondered about that."

"Her doctor didn't want her staying alone. My sisters both have jobs that require them to travel. I work one day and get two days off. Having Mom stay with me seemed like the best solution. She has a nurse that comes in while I'm gone. You won't be expected to take care of her if that's what you're worried about."

"I wasn't thinking about that. I'd like to repay your kindness, but I'm not sure I can stay here."

"It's only until you're well. You don't have to make a decision today. Just tell me you'll think about it."

Soft bed, clean sheets, a room to herself—or back to the shelter—oh, hard choice! "Okay, I'll think about it."

He nodded, then started to leave the room, but as he opened the door, he turned back. "Oh, I left your medicine on the bathroom sink. Dr. Wright said to take one pill morning, noon and night. Your pump is in there, too."

He looked down, and Caitlin saw his dog wiggle past him into the room. She trotted over to the bed with her tail wagging and pressed a cold, wet nose into Caitlin's hand.

Caitlin pulled her hand away and crossed her arms, then turned to stare out the window. She didn't want Mick to see the tears that threatened once more. "I don't need a pump."

"Sure you do."

"Didn't the good doctor tell you my milk is what's been making Beth sick?"

He didn't answer her, but a moment later, she heard him pull a chair next to the bed. "Caitlin, look at me."

She couldn't. She couldn't let him see how much it hurt to fail at the one thing she wanted so desperately to do for her baby. Gentle fingers cupped her chin and pulled her face toward him. She couldn't look him in the eye, so she fastened her gaze on the top button of his dark blue shirt.

"Dr. Wright told me it was possible that the infection you have may—*may*—" he emphasized the word again "—have made Beth sick. But she also said babies who are on formula, even babies that haven't been fed, can have the same problem."

She looked into his eyes. "Honest?"

"Honest."

"But they threw my milk out."

"I know." He pulled her close and wrapped his arms around her, and she rested her cheek against his shoulder. His touch said without words that he understood how much that had hurt.

"Once you're better, you can start saving your milk again. As soon as Beth is ready, they'll give it to her."

"What if it makes her sick again?"

"It won't."

She straightened, pulling away from him. "But if it does?"

"Then we'll cross that bridge when we come to it. The main thing now is to get you well. There's plenty of food in the kitchen. You need to eat and put some flesh on your bones." He tweaked her nose. "You're way too skinny."

She sniffed once and rubbed her nose with the back of her hand. "I'm not skinny."

"You're skinny, skinny, skinny."

She tried to hold back her smile, but lost the battle. "You're a mean man."

"As I pointed out before, I have my good points."

"I don't see any soup, so I guess you'll have to name one."

"I kiss nice. You said so yourself."

Before she could think of a comeback, he rose and left the room, closing the door behind him. Nikki put one paw on the bed and whined for attention. Caitlin reached out to pet the dog.

"If I said that, I was delirious." Maybe she had been, but it was the truth.

Tossing the covers aside, she sat up on the side of the bed and glanced down at the green-and-white-striped pajama top that more than covered her. She vaguely remembered Mick's mother putting it on her. A soft warmth stole over her at the memory. These people were gentle and kind. She wasn't exactly sure what to make of them.

She stood and felt the hem of his shirt drop to her knees. Grinning, she raised her arms and flapped the sleeves dangling a good six inches past the end of her hands. The door opened after a gentle knock. Caitlin paused in midflap as Mick looked in again.

"I almost forgot—" Whatever he started to say dissolved into a hearty laugh.

She dropped her arms to her sides and scowled at him.

He held up one hand. "I'm sorry. It's just that it's a pretty silly getup."

She planted her hands on her hips. "It's your shirt, not mine. If anyone here has bad taste in sleepwear, it's you."

He flushed. "I came back to tell you my mother left a few things for you to wear. They're in the closet along with your clothes. She said to keep what you like, she doesn't wear any of them anymore."

He hesitated a moment, as if he intended to say something else, but instead he closed the door. Caitlin waited, but this time the door stayed shut.

His kindness to her was something she didn't quite know how to deal with. He was kind to everyone, she reminded herself. He was kind to the kids at the shelter, to scared women in labor and even to old bums. The feel of Mick's strong arms holding her might tempt her to believe it had been something more, but she wasn't stupid. Besides, he was way out of her league. A man like him could have the pick of any number of women. Smart women, women with class. Not someone like her.

Out of curiosity, she crossed the room and opened the closet. A plush pink bathrobe hung from a hook on the back of the door. She fingered its softness. A half dozen outfits hung from hangers on a wooden rod. One was the black skirt and pink sweater she'd been wearing for weeks. She pushed it aside. "If I never wear this again, it'll be too soon."

Instead, she reached for a pair of raspberry red sweats that looked like they might fit. When she pulled the top off the hanger, she noticed it still had a price tag attached. She checked the others. They all did.

Caitlin looked at the dog sitting at her side. "Keep what I want because his mom doesn't wear them anymore? One or both of them are very poor liars."

Nikki whined and gave a small woof.

"I'll take that to mean you agree."

Looking for her shoes, Caitlin spied a familiar orange crate on the floor. With a glad cry, she dropped to her knees.

"My baby clothes, my sketchbooks, it's all here." She lifted the baby blanket from the box and held it to her cheek. Mick had saved her things. There was no way she would ever be able to thank him. Sitting back on her heels with a happy smile, she lovingly replaced the blanket. There was no way she was going to lose them again. Jumping up, she pulled off a pink-striped pillowcase from the pillow on the bed and stuffed her treasures and new clothes inside.

Her stomach growled, reminding her that she hadn't had anything to eat except broth for the past two days. She dressed in the soft sweats, then with pillowcase in hand, she opened the door of the room and stepped out into a narrow hall. The dog slipped past her, and Caitlin followed the animal downstairs.

Nikki made a beeline for the kitchen. She stopped in front of the refrigerator and raised a paw to scratch at the door.

"My thoughts exactly," Caitlin agreed. Pulling open the fridge door, she stared in amazement at the food that crammed the shelves. "Awesome!" She looked at the dog. "He did say to fix myself anything I wanted, didn't he?"

Nikki answered her with a short, sharp bark.

"That was a definite yes." Caitlin reached in, pushed aside a bag of oranges, a jug of milk and a carton of eggs to pull out a round pan. "I don't know about you, but I want some of this pie."

She made a quick check of the cabinet drawers, located a fork, then plopped on a chair at the table. The first giant bite of whipped topping and chocolate cream pie straight from the pan was the best thing she had ever tasted. The second bite was every bit as good. Only when the pan was half-empty did she pause long enough to take a closer look at her surroundings.

It was hard to imagine having all this space and not having to share it with somebody. She ran a hand over the smooth surface of the table. She'd never eaten off anything so fine, not even when she'd been in some of her good foster homes.

A delicate teapot sat in the center of the table. Her eyes widened as she reached for it and turned it over. She had learned a thing or two about good junk in her years of scrounging in garbage cans and Dumpster diving for food and stuff to sell.

"Do you see this?" she asked the dog in astonishment. "This little green crown means this is valuable. I could get twenty, maybe twenty-five bucks easy for it at a pawnshop."

"Nikki is smart for a dog, but I don't think she can

read labels." Elizabeth stood in the kitchen doorway dressed in a pale blue robe and slippers.

Caitlin flushed with embarrassment and looked down. She couldn't read, either—she was no smarter than the dog. Replacing the teapot with care, she said, "I wasn't going to steal it."

Elizabeth came to the table and laid a hand on Caitlin's shoulder. "It never occurred to me that you might. But if you like it, you're welcome to have it."

"No, thanks. I'm not much of tea drinker."

"Maybe that's because you've never had someone make you a *good* cup of tea. Sit there and I'll fix you some Earl Grey with honey and cream. I promise you'll love it." She headed to the stove and picked up the kettle.

Caitlin jumped up. "Let me do that."

Elizabeth shook her head. "No, I can fix tea one-handed. Naomi will be here any minute. She'll spend the day fussing over me and scolding me. This may be the only chance I get to do something for myself. Please, sit down."

"Okay. If you're sure." Caitlin sank into her chair again. "I'd like to do something to repay you for these clothes."

"Your clothes? I don't understand."

"Mick said you wanted me to have these because they didn't fit you. Only you forgot to take the price tags off."

Elizabeth gave a bark of laughter. "It wasn't me. I can't believe my son went shopping for women's clothes. What else did he buy?"

"I have them right here." She touched the pillowcase with one foot.

"Wonderful. You can show me what he bought later this morning. When we've finished our tea I'll give you a tour of the house. Would you like that?"

"If you think Mick won't mind."

"Of course he won't. Besides, if you plan on staying for a while, you'll need to find your way around. Do you plan on staying?"

"I don't know. It feels kind of weird living in someone else's house as an adult."

"I have to agree with that. It was wonderful of Mick to let me stay here after my accident, but I do miss my own space. I thought the pillowcase meant you were on your way out."

"No. I just don't want to lose my stuff again. I was really lucky to get it back this time."

Elizabeth's eyes filled with understanding and sympathy. "It must be difficult to keep the things you love living on the streets."

Caitlin shrugged. "People will steal anything of value. You can't blame them. Some of them have nothing. They don't know any other way to survive."

"It's the sad truth. Keep your things close if it makes you feel better and keep the pillowcase. I never did like that pattern, anyway."

"Thanks."

"Good. Now, the plan is tea and a tour. I have to warn you, Mickey is not a great housekeeper. Dust bunnies abound under his furniture. Once I have two good hands again, I'm going to make a clean sweep of things."

Caitlin brightened. Here was a way she could repay some of their kindness. "I've got two good hands. Show me where the broom is and I'll get rid of them for you."

"You've been sick. Mickey would skin me alive if he knew I'd put you to work your first day out of bed."

"We won't tell him. If he's like most men, he'll never notice that the place has been cleaned."

Elizabeth pressed her one good hand to her lips and chuckled. "My dear, I do believe I'm going to enjoy having you around."

Mick pulled into his drive the next morning, turned the engine off and remained sitting behind the wheel. Was she still here, or had she taken off? He shouldn't be surprised if she had. He couldn't believe how much he wanted her to stay.

He walked around to the front, picked up the morning copy of the *Tribune* from the steps and quietly let himself into the house. Nikki wasn't in her usual place, and that gave him his first bit of hope.

He checked the kitchen. No Caitlin and no dog. He stopped at the foot of the stairs and called out. Only silence greeted him. Where was everyone?

He climbed the stairs and after knocking twice, he opened the door to the guest room. It was empty, the bed neatly made. He checked the closet. The clothes he'd bought and all her things were gone.

Chapter 11

Mick struck the closet doorjamb with the heel of his hand in frustration. He wanted her to be here. He wanted her to stay more than he cared to admit. She was sick, broke and alone in the world. She needed his help, but every time he tried to give it, she threw it back in his face. Why did he keep trying?

He knew Beth was part of it, but it was more than his attachment to the baby that drew him to Caitlin. Caitlin was like a song in his head that wouldn't go away. The more he tried to ignore it, the more he found himself humming the same tune over and over. His attraction to her didn't make sense. They had almost nothing in common. She didn't even share his faith.

The sound of a dog barking followed by a burst of girlish laughter reached him through the open window. He rushed to look out. Caitlin lay stretched out in his hammock in the backyard. One bare foot hung over the side, and she swung herself back and forth with an occasional push. She held one of Nikki's favorite toys and laughed at the dog's antics as Nikki bounced up and down waiting for her to throw the ball.

Mick's heart gave a leap of joy that he couldn't ignore or explain away. She was here.

He sank onto the chair beside the window, knocking aside the stuffed cat. Reaching down, he picked up his niece's toy and stared blankly into its glass eyes. If it started talking he wouldn't be as surprised as he was by the realization that he was falling in love with the woman outside.

When had it happened? He certainly hadn't been looking for a relationship, had he?

Caitlin's laughter rang out again and drew his gaze. Nikki was trying to crawl into the hammock and was making a serious attempt to lavish doggie kisses on Caitlin's face. His Sleeping Beauty was awake, and she was even more beautiful in the bright light of day.

Her giggles eased the doubts clambering in Mick's mind. He'd rarely seen her smile, and this was the first time he could recall hearing her laugh. It felt good to see her happy. Perhaps that was why God had brought her into his life.

Her life had held little happiness, but he'd never heard her complain. Instead, she faced it with a belligerent determination and a resilience he could only admire. Was it any wonder that he was attracted to her?

So what are you going to do about it, Mick'O?

He didn't have a clue. No, that wasn't quite true. He knew one thing for sure. He wouldn't do anything to hurt her. She had been hurt far too much already.

For now, she was safe and happy, and he didn't want to jeopardize that. Caitlin was as wary as a feral cat and just as likely to disappear unless he could gain her trust.

Mick put the purple cat back on the window ledge. He had a lot of soul-searching ahead of him. *Please, Lord, show me what I need to do to help her.*

He left the spare bedroom and went downstairs to the back door. From there, he watched Caitlin playing with Nikki until the dog spotted him and came loping toward him. Caitlin picked up a stuffed pillowcase from beside the hammock and followed.

"You're home," she said with a smile that turned his heart upside down.

"I am. Any problems while I was gone?"

"Not a one. Nikki and I had a great time, didn't we, girl?"

"I'm glad. You look better. How are you feeling?"

"Less like a drowned cat all the time."

"Good. Where is my mom?"

"Naomi took her shopping. They should be back in an hour or two. Your mom had a list of things she thinks I need."

"Does that mean you're planning to stick around? I thought maybe you were on your way out." He pointed to the bag she carried.

"It's just my stuff. I don't want to lose it again."

"I think it would be safe up in your room."

"I guess it would. I'm just not used to leaving my stuff unguarded, that's all."

"If that's the way you feel, I've got a duffel bag that might work better than a pillowcase."

"That would be great. Thanks."

"So, you do plan to stay."

"I'm not an idiot. This is better than any shelter. It'll do until I find a place of my own. Besides, Nikki needs someone to play with when you're gone. Don't you, girl?" She leaned down to pat the dog.

It was the answer he wanted and his heart took flight.

Straightening, she threw a punch at his midsection. "Right now, I'm starved. I hope you can cook because I hate cooking. Besides, I'm no good at it, and all the pie is gone."

He'd never seen her this accommodating. He'd half expected a bitter battle just to get her to spend another night here. "I don't cook much myself, but I guess we'll get by."

"Fast food is fine if you want to treat me to Mickey D's. Hey, I can eat at Mickey O's or Mickey D's."

Surprised, he gaped at her. "Was that a joke?"

She frowned. "Yes. It wasn't that bad."

"Not at all. Sometimes, I'm a little slow after I've been at work for twenty-four hours. How about some bacon and eggs?"

"Sounds great. I can make the tea. Did you know you should always warm the pot first? I like the orange kind better than the Earl stuff, but please don't tell your mother I said that."

Bemused, he said, "Do you think if Prince Charming had known that Sleeping Beauty had a multiple-personality disorder he would have kissed her, anyway?"

"Huh?"

"Never mind." He held the door open. "After you."

She flounced past him into the house. He followed

her to the kitchen and watched as she put the kettle on, then slid into a chair at the table. She ran a hand through her short hair. "You got a nice place here. It's kind of big for one guy, isn't it?"

He pulled the eggs and bacon from the fridge and carried them to the stove. "A little, but it suits me. There's always plenty of room when my family comes to visit."

"Your mom is really sweet. I'm not sure if I should ask, but what happened to your dad?"

"He died when I was eight. He was a fireman, too. How about your parents?"

"Mom OD'd a few years ago. I don't know who my dad was."

"Any brothers or sisters?"

"Nope. I always wanted a sister, though."

"Great! I'll give you one of mine. I've got two."

"Was that who helped you buy my clothes? Did you know you forgot to take the tags off?"

He sent her a sheepish glance. "I guess I was too worried about getting them into the closet without waking you."

"Why say they belonged to your mother?"

"Because I thought you might refuse them if you thought they were from me. I don't know if anyone has mentioned this, but you can be stubborn at times."

She shrugged one shoulder. "I need clothes, and these fit pretty good," she acknowledged, rubbing a hand down her denim-clad thigh.

"I see that. I was afraid the jeans would be too small."

"How'd you know what size to get?"

He propped one hand on his hip. "Having sisters

gives one a sense of fashion, darling. Actually, I took your skirt with me and let the saleslady make an educated guess."

"Be sure and tell your mom that. I think she was worried that you knew how to buy women's clothes."

"I think I'll let her wonder about that one."

Her giggle did his heart good. "How do you like your eggs?" he asked.

"Cooked, but not burnt."

He turned to the stove. "Cooked, but not burnt it is. In fact, hand me some mild cheddar, not the sharp, and some Tabasco sauce from the fridge. I'll make you Mickey O's famous Scrambled Eggs O'Callaghan."

When she didn't answer, he turned back. A frown had replaced her smile. "What's the matter?"

She jumped to her feet. "Get it yourself, what am I, your servant? Anyway, I—I've got to go to the bathroom." She fled from the room.

"I guess you do," he said to the empty air.

The eggs and bacon and tea were ready by the time she came back. He set a plate in front of her, then sat down, bowed his head and said grace. Caitlin didn't participate, but sat quietly until he finished. She ate, but she remained subdued. She answered his questions with monosyllables and none of his jokes brought back her smile.

"Are you feeling okay?" he asked at last.

"I'm fine. Thanks for breakfast." Her voice held a sharp edge to it. She carried her plate to the sink.

"I can clean up," Mick offered, wondering how he had offended her.

"No, I do my part."

"Would you like to go to the hospital when you're done?"

She spun toward him. "Oh, yes."

He nodded. "Let me grab a quick shower, and we can go."

"Don't you need to get some sleep?"

"I was able to grab a few winks at work. I thought I'd take you to the hospital and let you spend some time with Beth while I came home and pulled in a few more z's."

"That would be great." Caitlin paused, then added. "Your job is a tough one, you must love it."

It blew him away that this woman could see how he felt about his work when his sisters, who knew him so much better, still didn't understand.

"I think it's the calling God chose for me. I can't imagine doing anything else. Of course, my family thinks I'm nuts."

"But you said your dad was a fireman."

Mick nodded and stared at his plate. "He died on the job."

"I'm sorry."

He nodded without looking up. "I was eight, but I remember it vividly—the men at the door, my mother's weeping, the race to the hospital, the smell of charred flesh in the burn unit."

She slipped onto the chair beside him and covered his hand with her own. "Did you get to see him before he died?"

"I did."

"Was it terrible?"

"His face wasn't burnt. One of his arms was covered in a thick bandage. They had a kind of tent over the rest of him. He was conscious, and he said he wasn't in much pain. I think the hardest part was my mother's crying. For him, too. He told me I would be the man of the house and that he expected me to take care of her. I didn't have the slightest idea how I could do that, but he made me promise, and I did."

"That wasn't fair."

He looked at her then. Her eyes were full of sympathy, as if she knew what that vow had cost him. "Maybe it wasn't, but I did my best to keep that promise. He died the next day. I never wanted to be anything except just like him."

"Well, you are. You're a fireman."

"I don't mean the job. I wanted to be the same kind of man he was. He was the best dad a kid could have. He always had time for me. We played catch, we went fishing, we took in the ball games—he was always there for me. I wanted to be the same kind of father. But it didn't work out that way." Mick voiced the death of his dreams in a matter-of-fact tone that bore little resemblance to the state of shock that he had been in when he endured his doctor's explanations of sterility.

Sterile—the word changed his life. It made him less than a man, and he knew then that he would never be like his father. In time, he came to grips with the knowledge, even learned to accept it as God's will.

"But you can adopt, right?" Caitlin asked.

How many times had he heard that platitude from his family? He forced a smile and nodded. "Sure, I can always adopt."

"Your mother never remarried?"

"No, she never did." He was glad to change the subject.

"How did she take it when you decided to be a fire-fighter?"

"My sisters didn't understand, but Mom was proud of me. The fact that I wanted to be like him made her very happy."

"That was lucky."

"Lucky? Why?"

"Because it turned out to be a job you love."

He nodded and gave her a small smile. "You're right. I could have done it to please her and then been miserable."

"Did you?"

"Do it to make her happy? Maybe."

"Are you still trying to make her happy?"

He frowned. "What do you mean?"

"Taking me in, naming Beth after her, taking responsibility for a baby that isn't yours."

He studied her face a long moment. "Caitlin, I try to live my life the way I think God wants me to live it. Do you know what that means?"

"Kind of. But I don't believe in all that stuff."

"What do you believe in?"

"Not much. Life stinks and then you die. That's it."

"That doesn't leave much room for hope, or love or kindness."

"Sometimes that stuff comes along, but you can't count on it. If you do, people let you down. I count on me and no one else."

"You can count on God, Caitlin. He loves you no matter what you think. And you can count on me. Please believe that."

"Aren't we going to the hospital?"

It was obvious she wanted to change the subject. "Sure. As soon as I wash up."

In the bathroom upstairs, he braced his hands on the sink and stared into the mirror. He rarely talked about his father, but it was easy to talk to Caitlin. She had endured a childhood far tougher than his, and maybe that created a bond between them. She was a homeless waif, but he saw the potential for so much more in her.

A frown creased the brow of his reflection in the mirror. He had told her a great deal about himself, but she had shared almost nothing about herself. She was willing to accept a place to live but he sensed that she still didn't trust him.

Would she learn to? Perhaps if he gave her enough time. If she didn't, he stood to lose more than the growing affection he felt toward her. He stood to lose both her and Beth.

Caitlin stood beside Beth's bed and waited. The baby lay on her back with her arms limp at her sides. Sandra listened to her with a stethoscope.

"How is she?" Caitlin asked when Sandra pulled the instrument from her ears.

"About the same, except she's up to sixty percent on her oxygen."

"Her color doesn't look so good. What does Dr. Wright say about it?"

"She says we need to keep a close eye on her, but we're doing everything we need to do. This happens sometimes when these little babies get sick."

"Can I hold her?"

Sandra laid a hand on Caitlin's shoulder. "I don't

think it would be a good idea. She hasn't tolerated much today."

Caitlin nodded. She would do whatever the nurses and doctors thought was best. She'd learned her lesson. Guilt, she found, was harder to get rid of than head lice.

"You're looking more rested," Sandra said.

"Thanks, I feel better."

Pulling a chair close, Sandra sat beside Caitlin. Two other nurses who often took care of Beth came over and stood behind her. Caitlin tensed. What was going on now?

Sandra reached out and covered Caitlin's hand with her own. "We want to apologize."

"For what?"

"I think you and I got off to a bad start. Mick told me how sick you've been, and how you'd been walking all the way from the Lexington Street Shelter—"

"Sometimes Mick talks too much."

"In this case, I don't think so. As nurses, we should have noticed you were sick. You and I weren't on friendly terms and that led me to believe the worst about you. I'm sorry."

"I'm sorry, too," one of the women behind Sandra added.

"So am I," the other one chimed in.

Caitlin met Sandra's gaze. "It wasn't your fault. I should have told someone I wasn't feeling well. If I had, Beth wouldn't have gotten this sick."

"It wasn't entirely your fault. We take part of the blame. Anyway, we wanted you to know how sorry we are."

Caitlin swallowed the lump that formed in her throat. These women had taken care of her baby day and night for weeks. She resented them for being the ones Beth needed. Sometimes, she even felt that they were trying to replace her as Beth's mother, but the truth was, without them Beth wouldn't be alive.

"If you have any questions, about anything, please know that we'll be glad to answer them," Sandra continued. "Our job is to see that Beth goes home with you as soon as she can."

Caitlin nodded but didn't trust herself to speak. It seemed that all she wanted to do anymore was cry. She wasn't used to people being nice to her.

The nurses left to attend to other babies, and Caitlin drew her chair closer to Beth's bed. She kept one eye on the baby's oxygen saturation monitor. A drop in that number was often the first clue that Beth wasn't tolerating touch or sounds near her.

"Hey, jelly bean, how are you? I'm sorry I haven't been in, but I've been sick myself. I sure missed you." Caitlin grasped Beth's hand but it remained limp.

"I know you don't feel good. Mick says hello. He wanted to come up—I could tell—but he said he thought we needed some time together—just you and me.

"I'm staying at his place with him and his mom. He's got a big house with a yard right beside a park, and he's got a dog."

He had all the things that Caitlin had dreamed of having. All the things she wanted to give Beth.

"The place you and I get won't be fancy, but it'll be decent, and I'm going to tell you every day how much I love you. So, you have to get better."

Sitting back in the chair, Caitlin was content to watch Beth sleep and study her face. She was so beautiful. Caitlin had heard that mothers always thought their own kids were the cutest, even the ones who had ugly kids, but until now, she hadn't understood how that was possible. Beth was beautiful in so many special ways. Suddenly, Caitlin had to sketch her.

After telling Sandra that she would be back, Caitlin went to the parent's check-in room and pulled the duffel bag Mick had given her from one of the tall, narrow lockers. She unpacked her sketchbook, then stuffed the bag in again. Back at Beth's bed, Caitlin flipped her drawing pad open and began to transfer her baby's most beautiful features to paper.

First she sketched Beth's fingers, the long, delicate way they lay cupped on the bed. Then her pencil mapped out the faint frown lines on Beth's brow and the gentle arch of her eyebrows. Soon a picture of her baby's face emerged, but at the mouth, Caitlin paused. She'd never seen Beth's mouth without the ventilator tube and the thick mustache of tape that held the tube in place.

Smiling at her daughter, Caitlin said, "I guess that part of you will have to stay a mystery." Reluctantly, she added a small part of the equipment that was so alien and yet so much a part of her child.

"You draw beautifully."

Caitlin looked up to find a young woman standing at her shoulder. "Thanks. It helps having a pretty model."

"Are you a professional artist?"

"Not hardly."

"You could be. I've often admired the poem she has on her bed. It helps me keep faith that my little boy will get better." The woman pointed to the card with green shamrocks around its border.

Caitlin had noticed the card the first time she had

come to visit, and she had wondered what it said, but she couldn't bring herself to ask. Instead, she said, "Which one is yours?"

"Jacob is in the last bed on this aisle. He weighed almost the same as your daughter when he was born."

"Is he doing okay?"

"Pretty good. He got off his ventilator today. It's the second time they've tried him off. Last time, he went a day before he had to go back on."

"That's good. Beth has never been off hers."

"She will. Well, I'd better go. It's time to feed him. I like to hold him when he gets fed even if it's just by tube. It's not like I can do much more for him yet."

"I know what you mean." Their gazes met and Caitlin nodded. She knew about feeling useless, about not being able to do a single thing that would ease her baby's way. She recognized that same emotion in this mother's eyes.

"I'll let you get back to your drawing," the woman said and walked to her child's bed. Caitlin watched as the nurse moved Jacob to his mother's arms and attached a syringe with milk in it to his stomach tube. The look on his mother's face was pure happiness as she held him close.

Glancing around the unit, Caitlin realized she wasn't the only mother riding the emotional roller coaster of having a baby in the NICU. Some mothers were proudly showing their infants to visitors, one sat silently staring into an incubator and a few others leaned over the sides of their children's open units to try to be close to their babies. Nurses moved between the beds with a smile or a word for the parents, who like

Caitlin, were learning to take one day at a time, and to measure success in a few ounces of weight gained.

Later, when Jacob's mother was leaving, she stopped beside Caitlin again. "I know it's a lot to ask, but could you sketch a portrait of my baby? I'd be happy to pay you for it."

"I don't know. You can take pictures in here, I've seen people with cameras."

"I know. We've taken lots of them, but your drawings… I don't know…they're so soft." She reached down and touched the page Caitlin was working on. "All that's here is your baby. In a photograph, all the equipment, all their stuff, it's always in the picture."

Caitlin turned over the idea in her mind. She could use the money, but somehow, it didn't seem right to take advantage of a mother with a sick child. "I'll think about it," she said.

"If you decide that you want to, I'll let Jacob's nurse know that you have my permission."

"Good point."

The woman smiled and leaned closer. "They are sticklers, aren't they? I know their hearts are in the right place, but sometimes, I have to wonder whose baby he is—mine or theirs?"

"Let me get this straight." Woody moved a chess piece, then leaned back in the black leather chair beside the game table in his apartment. His stark white walls held numerous landscapes done in watercolors and oils in every size. "You aren't the father of this baby. But instead of letting Caitlin go her own way, you keep tabs on her and wind up taking her home with you."

"She was sick and walking all the way from the

Lexington Street Shelter to the hospital." Mick studied the board and made his move. His heart wasn't in the game. He was here because Woody was the one person he could talk to who wouldn't judge or offer unwanted advice.

"I get that part." Woody moved a knight to block Mick's next play. "Wow! No wonder you didn't tell me the whole story when I asked. Now that she's better, why is she still staying with you and your mom?"

Mick reassessed his strategy and moved his queen. "She doesn't have anywhere to go. She's homeless, remember?"

"So you are going to take care of both of them. Mother and child. A ready-made family."

"I didn't plan it that way."

"I know that. You never look more than four moves ahead when you play this game, why should your life be any different?"

"Now you make me sound likc a fool."

"Not a fool, Mick. Just a guy who leads with his heart instead of his brain." He countered Mick's move. "Check and mate."

Mick studied the board. Woody was right. About the game and about Mick's tendency to follow his heart. He sat back and looked at his friend. "What would you do in my shoes?"

"Buy a bigger pair. Your boots are two sizes smaller than mine."

"You know what I mean." Mick reached down and moved the chess pieces back to their starting positions.

Woody began to line his up as well. "I can't help you with this mess, buddy. If the child was yours, I'd say you have every right to be part of her life. But this? I know you thought you were doing the right thing, but I'm not so sure. I guess you'll have to find out what it is that you really want and then go from there. If you like this woman as much as you say, get to know her better. If she can take care of Beth, give her some room. If she can't—you've got to do what's best for the kid. You and I have both seen the downside of situations like that."

"I know we have."

"And what's the most common thing friends and neighbors say when we find a neglected or abused kid in a home?"

"They say 'I knew something was wrong.' Or 'I wish I'd done something sooner.'"

"Don't let that be you, Mick'O. Don't let that be you."

The next morning, Mick looked up from the potatoes he was peeling at the kitchen sink. "Mind if I ask you a personal question?"

"Shoot," Caitlin answered.

"Do you like celery in your stew or will it be okay if I just add potatoes and carrots?"

She looked up from the sketch she was working on and cocked an eyebrow. "That's your idea of a personal question?"

"You don't think like or dislike of celery is personal?"

"Not hardly."

He carried his pan of stew makings to the stove, then faced her. "Okay, a personal question. Where did you learn to draw like that?" He indicated the sketch pad on the table in front of her. A remarkably detailed picture of Nikki asleep on the kitchen tiles was taking shape.

"I sort of picked it up."

"You're good. I thought you might have had professional training or art courses in school."

"No." Caitlin flipped the paper over and began another series of quick strokes with her pencil. "In school, I was always in trouble for doodling instead of doing my work."

"Surely one of your teachers recognized your talent?"

"Nope."

"I can't believe that."

"Maybe it was because my teachers were my main subjects." She held up the pad. It was a picture of him, but with a carrot for a nose and celery stalks for teeth in a wide-mouthed grin.

Mick chuckled. "I can see where that might have gotten you in trouble." He glanced at his watch. "Did you remember to take your medicine?"

She pulled the vial from her pocket and shook it. "Yup." Suddenly she looked serious. "Mick, why are you doing this?"

He turned back to the stove and set the fire to a low flame before he glanced at her again. "Because I like stew, and it's one of few things I can cook well."

"I don't mean the food. Why are you letting me stay here? I can't figure out your angle."

"Do I have to have an angle?"

"Does a rat have a tail?"

"Only if it's a four-legged one."

"True." She laid the pencil down and stared at him. "I don't know what you expect in return, but I'm not *that* kind of girl."

He straightened in astonishment. "I never thought you were. Do you honestly think I'm the kind of man who'd demand something like *that* in exchange for a place to stay?"

She gathered her sketches, picked up her duffel bag and stood. "Nobody gets something for nothing. I just wanted to be up front about it."

Nikki scrambled to her feet, and her nails made clicking sounds on the tile as she followed Caitlin from the room.

Mick rubbed a hand across his jaw. Maybe having Caitlin stay wasn't as good an idea as it had seemed. He had tried getting to know her better, but just when he thought she was opening up, she blindsided him with something that pushed him away.

He noticed that she had left her medicine on the table. He started to call after her, but thought better of it. Tucking the pills in his shirt pocket, he listened to her running up the stairs. Was she running away from him?

Lord, what is it going to take to make that woman start trusting me? I really could use some help here.

Chapter 12

Caitlin pounded up the stairs and hurried into her room. "I can't believe I said that!" She dropped onto the bed and turned her head to stare at the dog that had followed her. "I can't even *believe* I said that."

She flopped backward on the bed and covered her face with her hands. "This is totally humiliating."

She'd ruined everything with her big mouth. He'd toss her out for sure now that she'd insulted him. And to think she had wondered if he might be interested in her. Interested, ha! Mick might be interested in a bright woman like Sandra, but not a dummy like Caitlin Williams.

Nikki laid her head on the bed and whined.

"Did you see his face? If I'd asked him to cook you for supper, I don't think he could have looked more stunned."

She pushed the dog's nose aside. "I had a right to say something, didn't I? Now we can both relax."

No, if Mick wasn't outright insulted, he was probably laughing about the very idea right now.

Caitlin sprang to her feet and paced the floor. She didn't have to wait for Mick to ask her to leave or to laugh at her. She'd leave now. There were plenty of places she could go. Only, if she left, she'd have to walk right past him downstairs and there was no way she wanted to do that.

It was either go down and face him or toss her bag out the window and escape. Right now, jumping from a second-story window held a certain appeal. She sat down on the edge of the bed and waited.

An hour later a knock at the door caused her heart to leap in her chest. Emotionally, she braced herself. She'd been thrown out on the street more than once. She'd survive. Taking a deep breath, she said, "Come in."

It wasn't Mick, but his mother who looked in. "Caitlin, Mick wanted me to give you these and to tell you that dinner is almost ready."

She held out the vial of pills Caitlin had left on the table. Caitlin took them from her outstretched hand.

"Did he say anything else?"

"Not really, why?"

"I thought maybe he'd want me to leave now."

"Why would you think that?"

"I said something to him that I shouldn't have."

"I see. Do you want to tell me about it?"

"No. I think it's best that I find somewhere else to stay."

Elizabeth stepped inside the room. "Are you unhappy here? Have we done something to offend you?"

"No. You've been super to me." Caitlin pulled the purple cat into a close embrace.

"Then why do you want to leave?"

Caitlin shrugged, but couldn't meet her gaze. "I like living on my own, that's all."

"Do you like it? I mean, do you really?"

"Sure."

Elizabeth sat down beside her. "Caitlin, dear, you are a poor liar. I don't think you like being alone, but for some reason you believe you don't deserve anything better."

Caitlin bit the corner of her lip. "That's not true."

"How right you are. You deserve *much better.* And your daughter deserves better. I want you to stay. Mick wants you to stay. Right now, the thing he wants most in the world is to see that your little girl doesn't end up living a hand-to-mouth existence in some slum. He believes the only way to guarantee that is by helping you."

"I can take care of myself."

"In time, I firmly believe you can, but do you want your daughter living the way you've had to live until that day comes along?"

Caitlin swallowed hard at the prospect. "No."

"I didn't think so. Whatever your feelings are for Mick or for myself, Beth is really the important one, isn't she?"

Why did she have to make so much sense? Caitlin searched Elizabeth's face and felt her affection and respect for the woman deepen.

"Please say you'll stay," Elizabeth coaxed.

"Okay. But only until I can get a place of my own."

"Good. That's all we're asking. Once you find a job you can pay Mick back if you feel you must."

"I will."

"You can start by coming down and pretending to like the way he cooks."

"It's not that bad."

"You must be kidding?"

"It's better than eating out of a garbage can."

Elizabeth's smile slipped a little. "I shall simply have to take your word on that. Now, come on. The food is getting cold."

Once seated at the kitchen table, Caitlin cast a covert glance at Mick. He didn't look angry. Relief made her realize how hungry she was. She picked up a piece of bread and took a quick bite. Looking up, she saw that Mick and Elizabeth were watching her. He had one hand on his mother's injured shoulder. Both he and Elizabeth extended a hand toward Caitlin.

"What?" she mumbled.

"We'd like to give thanks," Mick said.

"That's fine." She took another bite.

Mick seemed to choke back a laugh, but quickly composed his face. "Please join us. We all have things to be thankful for."

Caitlin wiped her fingers on her jeans and joined hands with them. Mick's hand was large and warm. His mother's hand was soft and dainty.

Mick bowed his head. "Dear Lord, bless this food before us. As we gather here, make us ever mindful of Your presence in our lives and grateful for the gifts You have bestowed upon us."

Caitlin listened to his words and heard the deep sincerity in his voice. She never realized that people who got three squares a day might be as thankful for their food as people who had to hustle for it. Mick had a way of mixing up her ideas of how the world worked. He was unlike anyone she'd ever met. It was no wonder she found him so attractive.

He had come into her life at a time when she and Beth needed help the most. His kindness and concern were as foreign to her as bubble baths. In the depths of her heart she realized that his quiet strength came from his deep belief in God. For once in her life she was on the receiving end of goodness from people who asked for nothing in return. Maybe Mick was right, maybe God did care what happened to Caitlin Williams.

When Mick finished saying grace, Caitlin added a hearty "Amen."

During the meal that followed, she didn't find a thing wrong with Mick's cooking. His mother kept up a running conversation that covered the lulls in both Mick's and Caitlin's contributions.

"Do you cook, Caitlin?" Elizabeth asked as she pushed a chunk of fatty meat to the side of her plate.

"Enough to get by. Burgers and stuff like that."

His mother cast a cheeky grin at Mick, then leaned toward Caitlin. "I have a great Italian cookbook that you can borrow. Spaghetti is an easy dish to fix and Mick goes on and on about the kind he gets at work."

Caitlin stirred her stew. Following a simple recipe was one more thing she couldn't do without knowing how to read. How stupid had she been to think Mick might be interested in someone like her?

In the past she might have made some rude comment to change the subject, but she found she didn't want to hurt Elizabeth's feelings. Mick seemed to sense her discomfort.

"I've had all the spaghetti I can stand at the firehouse this week. At home, burgers would be fine if you'd like to cook. Please don't think we mean to have you slaving in the kitchen."

Grateful for his intervention, she met his gaze. "How do you like your hamburgers?"

"Cooked, but not burnt."

Seeing his grin as he tossed her own words back at her erased the last of her doubt. He wasn't angry with her. Her heart lightened. She liked him, she liked him more than was good for her, but she couldn't seem to help it. She would be the perfect houseguest from now on. Anything to make him happy.

Over the next week, Caitlin was drawn into the lives of Mick and Elizabeth. She discovered that Elizabeth had founded Mercy House and still worked to keep it running by raising money and finding volunteers. Mick worked his days at the firehouse and on his days off he helped out at Mercy House and drove Caitlin to spend time with Beth.

Slowly, the strangeness of living in a real house with a real family faded and Caitlin began to feel that she belonged. Her affection for both Mick and his mother deepened daily.

One evening, Caitlin sat curled up on the sofa with Nikki while his mother shared the other end. Mick lounged in his favorite chair. They all laughed at the latest sitcom on TV.

Was this truly how people lived? Caitlin wondered. Did families laugh together in the evening? Did they bow their heads and say grace before meals? Looking around, Caitlin knew this was the kind of life she wanted for Beth. Only, how could she ever provide it?

When the nightly news came on, Elizabeth excused herself and headed up to bed. After the sports report, Mick clicked off the TV. "I think it's time we got some sleep."

"Mick, I haven't thanked you for everything you've done for me, and especially for what you've done for Beth."

"There's no need to thank me."

"But there is. Without you, neither one of us would have had a chance. I've never met anyone like you."

He shrugged. "You don't hang out at enough fire stations. Guys like me are a dime a dozen there."

"No, I don't think so."

"Okay, I'm one in a million, but it's still past your bedtime." He tipped his head toward the stairs.

Caitlin stared at her hands. "Do you believe God grants us special gifts?"

"Every time I see Beth, I know I'm face-to-face with one."

She nodded. "Whatever God wants from me He can have as long as she is okay."

"Caitlin, God doesn't make deals."

"Then what does He want?"

"He wants us to love Him above all else and for us to love each other. We have to open our hearts and trust in His will. We do it by letting go. By giving up thinking that we're in charge of our lives and realizing that He's in charge."

"How do *you* do it?"

Mick chuckled. "Not very well at times. I'm no saint. I struggle with my temper. I get impatient with people."

Mick might not be a saint, but Caitlin knew he was

a good, decent man. The fact that Mick O'Callaghan had come into her life was the closest thing to a miracle that she had ever seen.

He might be able to shrug off her thanks, but it didn't lessen her gratitude.

"Go on," he said. "Hit the sack."

She nodded and did as he asked.

Once in bed, sleep eluded Caitlin. Turning over, she flipped her pillow searching for a cool place and kicked aside the sheets. Mick O'Callaghan was a good man—a genuinely good man. Everything she learned about him only made him that much more special. He was an easy man to love.

She sat bolt upright in bed.

She was in love with him. She hadn't wanted to, hadn't planned to, but here in the darkness she saw the truth. She was in love with Mick O'Callaghan.

"Are we ready for the big moment?" Dr. Wright asked, standing beside Caitlin's chair.

"I am *so* ready," Caitlin replied. She waited with Mick beside Beth's bed in the NICU. Beth was being taken off her ventilator for the first time in her young life.

"Okay, let's do it," the doctor said with a happy smile.

With the help of a nurse and a respiratory therapist, she removed Beth's breathing tube, and Caitlin heard her baby cry for the very first time. Tears sprang to her eyes at the sound of that weak, hoarse, pitifully tiny wail. It was the most beautiful sound she'd ever heard.

A hand closed over hers, and she looked over to see Mick smiling at her in understanding.

"That a girl," Dr. Wright coaxed the baby, "tell us

all about it. What do you think, Mommy? Isn't she cute without all that tape on her face?"

"I think she's gorgeous," Caitlin managed to say through the emotion that threatened to choke her.

The doctor quickly adjusted a thick, stiff tubing with small prongs that fit into Beth's nose. Velcro straps attached to a colorful stocking cap held the tubing in place.

"This awkward-looking thing is called C-PAP," Dr. Wright explained. "It blows oxygen in under low pressure and that makes it easier for her to breathe, but from now on, every breath she takes is on her own."

When the doctor left the bedside, Caitlin glanced at Mick. He was grinning like an idiot. He touched the tubing in Beth's nose and said, "It looks like she's wearing the face guard of a football helmet."

"If you're thinking she'll be the next linebacker for the Bears, you can forget it."

He chuckled. "I can't believe how big she's getting. Even her cheeks are getting chubby."

"Well, she weighs a pound more than when she was born. She's three pounds and two ounces now."

Mick leaned closer. "You know, I think she has your mouth."

"Do you?"

His gaze rested on Caitlin's lips until she grew uncomfortable with his scrutiny. The atmosphere between the two of them had been strained in the last week. Oh, he had been as kind and as considerate as ever, but often she'd seen him staring at her intently. She was desperately afraid that he would discover just how much she had come to care for him.

She reached to hold Beth's foot. "She has her dad's knobby knees," she said to change the subject.

"Hey. My knees aren't—"

Caitlin's glance flew to his face. He looked stunned. Slowly, the joy faded from his face. He sent Caitlin a rueful smile. "I forgot for a second that she isn't really mine."

"Mick, I…" She what? Caitlin had no idea what to say.

He stood suddenly. "Well, I've got to run."

"I thought you were going to stay?"

"I can't. I have something I have to take care of. I'll pick you up out front at four o'clock."

"Okay." She managed a smile.

He leaned down and dropped a kiss on Beth's head and quickly left the unit. Watching him, Caitlin bit the inside corner of her lip. A man like Mick would make a wonderful father. A jerk like Vinnie didn't deserve to have a dog, let alone a daughter as beautiful as Beth. There had been a time in Caitlin's life when she would have given anything to know who her father was, to be able to see him just once. Vinnie wasn't much, but Beth should know who he was; not knowing, always wondering and dreaming, it was no good.

Someday Beth would want to know what her father had been like—if she looked like him, if she had his eyes or his smile.

Caitlin picked up her sketch pad and began to draw Vinnie as she remembered him, concentrating on the good times they had had together. She could see that Beth would have this much.

When she finished her second sketch of Vinnie, she flipped the page and began a drawing of Beth without her ventilator tube to add to the growing number of pictures she had compiled of the baby's days in the hospital. A nurse came to the bedside and began to take Beth's temperature. Finishing that, she picked up the stethoscope and placed it on the baby's chest. Quickly, Caitlin added the nurse's hand holding the stethoscope to her picture. After all, Beth had needed lots of helping hands to get her this far.

"What do you have there?"

Caitlin looked up to see Dr. Wright peering over her shoulder. "It's okay if I draw, isn't it? I can put it away."

"Of course it's okay. I'm simply admiring your work. Why, it's wonderful. Ladies, come look at this."

A group of nurses gathered beside Caitlin's chair. She heard compliments and exclamations of delight exchanged all around her, and she grew embarrassed at being the center of attention.

"Do you ever sell any?" someone asked.

"Sometimes I sell portraits over at the Navy Pier," Caitlin admitted.

"Really? How much do you charge?"

"Do you have a studio?"

The questions came faster than she could answer them.

"I'd love to have a portrait of Beth," Dr. Wright said. "She's been such a special little girl."

"I can do that." Caitlin flipped back through the pages until she came to one with Dr. Wright leaning over Beth to examine her. Carefully, she pulled the sketch from the book and handed it to the doctor.

"My goodness, you certainly flatter me," the woman said beaming. "I don't usually look this good after a night on call. Why is it that I've never noticed you sketching before?"

"Mostly, I draw when I'm at home."

"From memory? You can draw a detailed picture like this solely from memory?"

"Things I see just sort of stick in my head."

"What an extraordinary talent." Dr. Wright stared at the picture she held, then looked at Caitlin as if she had never truly seen her before. "How much do I owe you for this?"

"Nothing."

"Nonsense. You can't give it away for free."

"Sure I can. You've done more than enough for Beth and me. I'm not going to charge you for a little picture."

"Very well, I'll accept this one, but the rest I insist on paying for."

"The rest?"

"I've been wanting to get some new pictures for my office walls." She held up the sketch. "This would be perfect in a light blue mat with a silver frame."

"A grouping of three would be nice," one nurse suggested.

"I know—three of Beth, one on the vent, one when she's bigger and one when she's ready to go home."

"What a neat idea."

Like traffic on a busy street, their chatter flowed around Caitlin. She couldn't believe all the enthusiasm for her work.

"How soon could you have six more done?" Dr. Wright asked.

It took a minute for Caitlin to find her voice. "Six?"

"I have two walls that I'd like to put groups on. How much do you charge?"

Dr. Wright wanted to display her pictures on the walls of her office. Her pictures!

A doctor wouldn't want the kind of quick portraits that Caitlin did down on the pier. She would want ones with a lot of detail. The other women seemed interested, too. Maybe some of them would buy her work. But how much should she charge? If she named a price too high, they wouldn't want them.

She settled on a price that was twice as high as she usually charged down on Dock Street.

"Oh, no," Dr. Wright said quickly, and Caitlin's hopes fell. "I've purchased original works in galleries, and I'm not going to allow you to give these away." She then named a price that made Caitlin's jaw drop. It was five times what she had suggested.

"Which babies would you like me to sketch?" Caitlin managed to ask.

"That's a good question. Beth, of course, but who else?"

"You'll need to get permission from the parents," a nurse reminded her.

"I don't imagine that will be hard, not once they see what a wonderful job Ms. Williams does."

Caitlin cleared her throat. "Little Jacob, down on the end, his mother asked me to do a sketch of him."

"Excellent. See, what did I tell you?"

Dr. Wright's brows drew together in a slight frown. "I don't want to monopolize your time. I know you come here to be with your daughter, and I don't want to detract from that."

For that much money, Caitlin would draw standing on her head in a corner while she visited Beth. "No problem, Doc. I'm here every day, anyway. I can't always hold her, so I can draw while she's asleep."

"If you're sure you don't mind?"

"I don't. It'll be good to have something to keep me busy." And something to put money in her pocket—more money than she would have made in a month washing dishes at Harley's—and simply for doing something she loved. God was surely smiling on her today.

Dr. Wright stood. "Great. Let me show this sketch to some of the other parents and see if they'll give their permission to have you draw their children. And let me get you an advance for the ones I've ordered in case you need to get more supplies. Would fifty dollars cover your expenses?"

Caitlin stared at her in astonishment. "Sure."

"Okay, good. I'll be right back with it."

"Ms. Williams, do you think you could do a portrait of my two children?" a short, dark-haired nurse asked. "They aren't babies, they're two and five. It would make a perfect birthday gift for their grandmother."

Bemused, Caitlin smiled and nodded. "I'm sure we can work something out."

She would be earning her own money. Mick was going to be so proud of her.

Chapter 13

As promised, Mick pulled up to the front of the hospital at four o'clock and spied Caitlin waiting on a bench out front. She waved and hurried toward him. His spirits soared at the sight of her. Her smile was like sunshine. It warmed him all the way to his toes. Since she had moved into his home, he couldn't ever remember being happier.

She was grinning from ear to ear as she threw her duffel bag on the floor and climbed in beside him.

"You'll never guess what happened." Excitement electrified her voice and sparkled in her eyes.

"Okay, I won't try. What?"

"They want to buy my artwork!" With a squeal of delight, she threw her arms around his neck. "I can't believe it."

"Whoa!" He returned her enthusiastic hug. "Slow down and tell me what you're talking about."

She pulled back a fraction, still grinning. "Dr. Wright saw me sketching Beth, and she wants to buy some of my prints to hang in her office. She's going to pay me for them. She even gave me an advance."

Her announcement stunned him. She was earning her own money. But not enough to live on, of course. No, she still needed his help. "That's terrific. I told you someone would recognize your talent."

Suddenly, he realized how close her face was—how close her lips were. He shifted his gaze to her eyes— her wonderful, beautiful eyes. The pace of his heart accelerated and the excitement changed, deepening into something different. She sensed it, too. With a sheepish grin, she moved away and settled herself on her side of the car, taking her time about buckling her seat belt.

"How's Beth?" he asked.

"Dr. Wright said she might be able to do without the C-PAP in a few days. Course, she'll still be on oxygen for a while. Where are we going?" she asked as he pulled out into the street.

"I have one more stop to make."

"Where?"

"Mercy House."

"Oh."

The flat tone of her voice caused him to look at her sharply. "Is something wrong?"

"No," she said at last.

Mick glanced at her frequently as he drove into a section of town where abandoned buildings grew more frequent between run-down homes and boarded-up businesses. She didn't speak, and he wondered what he had done or said to upset her.

He pulled to a stop in front of a renovated three-story clapboard house with a wide porch across its front. A tall sign in the sparse grass beside the broad steps read Mercy House Shelter for Women and Children. The sign was somewhat misleading as the soup kitchen that occupied the spacious basement served anyone who came to the door, but the bedrooms in the house were given over to housing women who found themselves and their children without a place to live.

Stepping out of his SUV, Mick went to the back and opened the hatch. Caitlin stood on the sidewalk staring at the house. "Give me a hand, will you?" he asked. She joined him, and he handed her a small cardboard box, then he grabbed a bigger one for himself.

The front door of the shelter opened and an elderly man came down the steps toward them. He wore a beige polo shirt that was tucked into brown polyester pants belted high on his waist letting a good three inches of his pale blue socks show above scuffed black loafers.

"Hi ya, Mick," he called. Stopping beside Caitlin, the fellow took the box from her unresisting grip with hands that trembled faintly. "You shouldn't be liftin' stuff," he scolded.

Caitlin's eyebrows flew up. "Eddy?"

A wide, tooth-gapped grin appeared on his face. "Yup. Told ya I cleaned up pretty good, didn't I, Mick?"

"Yes, you did," Mick agreed. He never would have recognized the man without his tattered overcoat, thick gray beard and long hair if he hadn't spoken.

"How's that baby?" Eddy asked.

"She's doing better," Caitlin answered. "Eddy, you look great."

"Nah, I don't, but thanks, anyway. I'm gettin' some

help with my drinkin' and Pastor Frank, he gave me a job here." His skinny chest puffed out. "I'm his right-hand man, now."

Pastor Frank appeared in the doorway. "You certainly are, Eddy. I don't know how I managed without you."

Mick nodded toward the box he held. "The guys at the station donated some clothing. Where do you want these?"

"Bring them into the living room, and I'll let the ladies know that they're here. It's good of you to help us like this, my boy."

Smiling, the pastor came down the steps and extended his hand toward Caitlin. "And you must be the young woman I've heard so much about."

"Caitlin Williams," she replied as she took his hand.

"I'm glad to hear your daughter is doing better. Mick's been keeping me informed. He thinks the world of your little girl, but then, he thinks the world of all children. I've never known anyone with quite the gift he has for making them happy."

The man took Caitlin by the elbow and walked up the steps beside her. "Welcome to Mercy House. I'm sorry I couldn't offer you a place here when Mick first called, but we've been full to the rafters. It's sad how many women and children have no place to go." He held open the door and waited for Caitlin to proceed.

Caitlin didn't answer him. She glanced back at Mick, but he was talking to Eddy. She bit the corner of her lip and walked inside with a sinking feeling.

"Caitlin, would you excuse us?" Pastor Frank asked. At her nod, he turned to Mick. "Could I see you in my office for a moment?"

Mick followed the pastor into his office. Frank moved to his chair at the small, scarred oak desk that along with a large gray filing cabinet was the only furnishing in the Spartan room. "I've known you since you were five, Mick. Your mother is a dear friend. Obviously, your intentions are good, but are you going about this in the right way?"

"I don't know what you mean."

"I have room for Caitlin now. Don't you think it would be better if she were living here?"

"She's fine at my place. There isn't any need for her to move in here."

"How much longer will your mother be staying with you? Now that she's better, I know she's anxious to get back to her own home and to her friends."

"I thought she'd stay until Beth was out of the hospital. Has she told you she wants to leave?"

"Not in so many words, but surely you must see that having Caitlin living with you is putting your mother in a difficult spot? She can't leave the two of you there alone."

"I didn't intend to offer Caitlin a place to live, but now that I have, I won't go back on my word. I want to protect this woman—to see that she and her baby don't slip through the cracks and end up as two more lost souls in a city that already has far too many."

Mick moved to stare out the window at the children playing in the backyard. "Caitlin's mother was an addict and she never knew her father. She's a throwaway kid. You see them every day—you know what they're like. They don't trust anyone. She'd rather starve in a back alley than ask for help because she doesn't believe she needs it or deserves it. She's learning to trust, maybe for the first time in her life. I won't do anything to destroy that. She needs someone to take care of her."

"She isn't a child. What she needs isn't someone to take care of her. She needs to be able to take care of herself. Give her the tools to do that, show her that you believe she can, and you will have helped her more than any amount of free room and board ever will."

Mick pondered the pastor's words. If Caitlin could manage on her own what would it mean for him? He hated considering the idea. He wanted both of them in his life.

Frank picked up his pen and began to scribble notes on a pad. "I'll do what I can to find her a job. Does she have any technical training? Has she expressed an interest in going to school to learn a trade?"

"No, but you should see her artwork. She has a rare gift."

"That's something. Talk to her—find out if there's anything she'd like to do. I'll work on locating a place for her and the baby to live. This may take some time. Is she going to be okay with that?"

"I'll see that she is."

Caitlin leaned against the living room wall and watched the office door as she worried her lower lip between her teeth. They were talking about her in there, she was sure of it. Did Mick intend to leave her here? He wouldn't do that without telling her first, would he?

She bit down on the nail of her index finger and tore the corner of it. Who was she kidding? Her own mother had put her in a Dumpster and forgotten about her. Why should anyone else care what happened to her?

Maybe this was what God wanted from her? Mick had talked about trusting God's will. Maybe God wanted her to give up her nice place in exchange for Beth getting better? If that were the case, she'd do it and not complain.

She had money in her pocket and a chance to earn more. She was better off than she had been in a long time. She looked around the room. This wouldn't be a bad place to stay.

The office door opened and Mick came out. He smiled at her and her heart tripped into double time. Man, she had it bad for him. All he had to do was smile at her and she was willing to forgive him anything. Even if he left her here she wouldn't hold it against him.

He stopped in front of her. "Ready to go? I don't know about you, but I'm starving. Let's get something to eat on the way home."

A ton of tension drained out of her. She realized she was biting her fingernail and quickly tucked that hand under her arm. "That would be great."

Later, with a burger in one hand and a box of hot, crispy fries balancing on her lap, Caitlin asked the question that had been turning itself over and over in her mind. "Did you ask Pastor Frank if I could stay at Mercy House?"

"Is that what you want to do?"

She shrugged. "Not really." She wanted to stay with Mick forever, but that wasn't going to happen. She was lucky to have stayed this long.

Mick gave her a sidelong glance. "We've never talked about what you would like to do—for a job, I mean."

"I'll take whatever I can get."

"Still, you must have something that you're interested in. You're such a talented artist. Have you thought about going back to school to study art?"

She paused with her burger halfway to her mouth. Back to school? There was a joke.

"No. Drawing is a hobby. I can make a few extra bucks on the side with it, but I need something full-time to pay the bills."

"Pastor Frank is willing to try to find you a place of your own. When you're ready, that is. There isn't any rush, and I mean that. He can help find you work, too. He does it all the time for the women who come to the shelter."

Pastor Frank would send her to job interviews where she would have to fill out applications.

"I can get my own job, thank you. I haven't started looking because Beth has been so sick."

"I understand. Like I said, there isn't any hurry."

"No, she's better, and it's time I got busy."

"You can start with the paper when we get home. Something might jump out at you."

Sure, she thought, like the one or two words that she recognized in print. "I'll start tomorrow."

"But I'm on duty tomorrow."

"So?"

"Nothing, I guess, but I thought maybe I could drive you to some job interviews."

"I can take the bus."

"It would be easier if you'd wait until I could take you."

"Mick, I can manage."

"I'd like to help."

"And I'd like to be able to eat a burger without you thinking you need to wipe my face between bites," she snapped, and turned to stare out the window.

He was dense as pavement. She hated acting like this, but she would have to find her own job. She couldn't let Mick or anyone else discover that she couldn't read.

"I'm sorry," he said after a long silence.

"Forget it."

"No, you're right. I tend to forget that you aren't helpless."

She twisted around in the seat to face him. "I can't forget it. Not ever! I'm the one who has to hold down a job and take care of Beth."

"Caitlin, I'll always be here if you need something."

"You don't get it, do you? You've got your own life. Beth and I, we can't be waiting for you to find time for us. I've seen it happen more than I care to tell. A guy gets involved with a girl, he likes her, likes her kid, but it isn't his kid and sooner or later, he stops coming around."

"I won't be that way."

"Maybe not," she conceded. "But I can't take that chance. It's hard for me to say thanks and the truth is, I'll never be able to repay you for the help you've given me, but I have to be able to survive on my own."

"Life is about more than surviving."

She looked away. "Not for some of us. Not for me."

"Caitlin, I can't let Beth lead that kind of life."

"You don't have a choice."

"You forget, I'm her legal father."

She hadn't forgotten, but until now, she had assumed that he wouldn't press the issue. Did he still think that he could take Beth away from her? Cold fear gripped her heart. "Is that a threat?"

Mick turned the car into his driveway and stopped.

He shut off the engine, then looked at her. "Of course not. It's only that I want life to be about more than surviving for you and Beth. You deserve more, Caitlin. You deserve a life of comfort and security with someone who cares about you."

"Until that comes along, I'll manage by myself."

He stared at her, and she could see the struggle going on inside of him. "If things were different for us—"

"But they're not. I don't need you feeling sorry for me."

"You're wrong. I don't feel sorry for you. I admire you, very much. I care about you."

"I care for you, too, Mick, and for your mother. You've both been very kind to me. But now that I'm well, I need to stop depending on you and start taking care of myself."

"But I want to take care of you. I'm saying this all wrong."

He covered her hands with his and her heart raced. She tried to read his eyes, but she didn't trust what she saw there.

"Caitlin, I care about you deeply. You know that I love Beth like she was my own flesh and blood. I'll be a good father to her. I guess what I'm trying to say is that I want to marry you."

She didn't know how to respond. She longed to tell him of her love, but she knew she wasn't worthy of him. Once he discovered her secret he would be as ashamed of her as Vinnie had been. She'd never be able to go out to eat with him and his friends because she couldn't read a menu. She wouldn't be able to read bedtime stories to Beth, or write a birthday card to his mother. Mick deserved better.

He loved Beth. He was willing to marry Beth's

mother to keep her safe. He was so noble. It was almost more than Caitlin could bear.

"Thank you, but no. Taking care of people is what you do. I understand that. But this isn't the way. I won't pretend that your offer isn't tempting. It is. Only, not for the right reasons."

"You'd never have to worry about food or a place to sleep ever again. Beth would have a mother and a father to look after her. What better reason is there?"

"Love for a child isn't enough. I wish it were."

He looked so bewildered. She opened her car door and turned away to keep her face hidden from him. She knew there was little hope that she didn't look like a woman whose heart had just been broken.

Chapter 14

Early the next morning, Caitlin stood at the curb and waited for the bus with her duffel bag slung over one shoulder. After tossing and turning for much of the night, she didn't see that she had any choice. She had to get out of Mick's life. She couldn't face him day after day loving him the way she did.

Both Mick and Elizabeth had still been asleep when Caitlin let herself out of the house. She hated sneaking away, but she knew she couldn't face them and not break down. She'd call as soon as she got settled. She could handle a phone conversation, but looking Mick in the face when she said goodbye was more than she could take.

At last, the bus pulled up in front of her. When the tall door slid open, she hesitated. No one got off and there wasn't anyone else waiting to get on.

The stout woman driving asked, "Well? Are you coming?"

Caitlin chewed the corner of her lip for a second. "Is this the bus to Grand?"

"If that's what it says on the front, honey, then it must be. Are you getting on, or not?"

Struggling to hide the shame that burned like acid in the pit of her stomach, Caitlin climbed the steps and dropped her fare in the slot. She found a seat and gazed out the window, taking note of the houses and landscape along the route. Once she got to Grand Avenue, she'd be able to find her way around. She knew that area. Finding her way back would be the tricky part. Street names didn't mean anything unless they were numbers. Numbers she knew.

When the bus reached an area she was familiar with, Caitlin got off and walked the remaining blocks to Mercy House. Relief flooded her when she spied Eddy working in the front yard. She walked over to where he was weeding a small flower bed.

"Hi, Eddy."

The old man looked up, peering over the rim of a pair of glasses missing an earpiece. "Caitlin, is that you? How's that baby doin'?"

"She's getting better."

"I'm glad to hear it. I pray for her every day. What are you doin' here?"

"I'm here to stay for a while."

"I'm sorry, Caitlin. We don't have a room for you."

"What? Are you sure?"

"I'm real sure. Pastor Frank thought you was gonna be stayin' with Mick for a while. Last night a lady with four little kids came and Pastor Frank gave them the last room. I'm sure sorry about that. You want to check with Pastor Frank?"

"No." Her hopes fell. So much for her great plan. "I guess I can stay with Mick a while longer. I was just hoping to get out from under his feet, that's all. Maybe you can help me with something else."

"What kinda help can an old, crazy fella like me give you?"

"I need a job."

His brow wrinkled even more. "I don't know of any work."

"I do. I've got the want ads with me." Caitlin handed him the paper.

Looking puzzled, he said, "I still don't understand."

Caitlin glanced around to make sure no one could overhear her, then leaned closer. "I need your help because…because I can't read."

"That ain't a crime."

"I never said it was."

"You're actin' like it is what with this whisperin' an' all."

Straightening, Caitlin regretted sharing her secret. "I don't like other people knowing how stupid I am."

"You ain't stupid."

"It'll look that way when I can't fill out a job application. I need to find work before Beth comes home. I have to be able to support us."

"Pastor Frank can help. You're not the only woman who has trouble reading."

"Pastor Frank might tell Mick. I don't want him to know. He'll think I can't take care of Beth. But I can. I just need to get a job."

"Okay, calm down. What can I do?"

Caitlin led Eddy to a small bench in the yard. She sat down and handed him the paper. "Read these ads and help me find a job that I can do. I'll do anything if it means being able to keep Beth."

"Okay, sure, but what are you gonna do when you have to fill out their forms and such?"

"That's why I need you to come with me. If they want me to fill out an application, I'll ask if I can take it home. If they say yes, I'll bring it outside, and you can fill it out for me. If they say no, I'll find some way to sneak one out to you. I've got to have a job. Will you help me?"

He patted her arm. "Sure, I'll help. You was always nice to me."

"Thanks, Eddy. You don't know what this means to me."

Two weeks later, Caitlin looked up from her sketching to smile at Beth sleeping soundly inside her incubator. It was wonderful to see her making progress after all that had happened. Each day, Caitlin discovered something new about her daughter. Beth liked to sleep on her left side. She woke up hollering, but she calmed down as soon as someone spoke to her. She even seemed to like her mother's off-key singing.

Studying her baby's sweet face, Caitlin wondered if her own mother had ever watched her sleep this way. Had Dotty seen anything beautiful in her, or had she only seen a burden?

Pity for the woman who would never know her granddaughter welled up in Caitlin, and some of the anger she harbored toward her mother crumbled away.

Maybe this is what Mick means when he talks about forgiving those that have sinned against us.

Shaking off her somber thoughts, Caitlin concentrated on Beth once more. She needed only a small amount of oxygen and she was tolerating tube feedings of milk and sucking on a pacifier. Twice a day, Caitlin gave her small amounts of milk from a bottle. Beth slurped it down. If nothing else went wrong, she would be big enough to be discharged in a few weeks. But to where?

Caitlin was still staying at Mick's, but things were tense between them. She'd been avoiding him because, sooner or later, her guard was bound to slip, and he'd see that she was in love with him.

In spite of Eddy's help, Caitlin hadn't been able to find work. The money from the sales of her sketches was adding up, but it wouldn't be enough to last more than a few weeks even if she found a cheap place to live.

Beth's monitor beeped loudly. Caitlin looked up expecting the usual false alarm. Beth had become a whiz at getting her toes or fingers tangled in her lead wires and pulling them loose. This time it wasn't a false alarm; Beth's heart rate had slowed to less than eighty.

Caitlin sprang to her feet. "Sandra, something's wrong!"

The nurse came quickly. She opened one of the round portholes, stuck her hand in and began to rub the baby's back, but her gaze stayed focused on the monitor. When Beth's heart rate began climbing, Sandra looked in at Beth and asked, "Are you trying to scare your mother?"

"If she is, she's doing a fine job. What's wrong?"

"It looks like she had an apnea spell. It means she

forgot to breathe. It's common in premature babies, but it can also be a sign of a seizure. Did you notice her yawning or twitching or doing anything unusual?"

"No."

"Then it may have been simple apnea. Preemies have nervous systems that are immature and sometimes, especially when they're sleeping, they simply stop breathing. If it lasts long enough, their heart rate slows down, too."

"Babies die from that, don't they?"

"You're thinking about SIDS—sudden infant death syndrome. It isn't the same thing, but premature babies are more at risk for developing SIDS. I'll let the doctors know about this. They may want to do a few more tests."

"Like what?"

"Like checking her blood to see if the level of her seizure medication is right. It has to be adjusted as she gets bigger otherwise she'll outgrow her dose."

"If it's this apnea stuff, what will they do?"

"We usually start them on a drug called caffeine. It's the same thing you get in coffee or soda. Coffee keeps you awake and gives you a lift. This does the same thing for Beth. It will help keep her breathing when she does fall asleep. Most babies grow out of these spells before they go home."

"What if they don't?"

"In that case, they stay on the caffeine and they go home on a monitor that will alarm if their heart rate or their breathing gets too slow."

"I'd feel better having a monitor. How do I get one?"

Sandra patted Caitlin's arm. "You're getting ahead of yourself. If Beth needs one, the doctors will arrange for it. If she doesn't, you'll have to treat her like a regular baby."

"I'm not sure I can."

"I know, but it'll get easier. How would you like to try nursing her this time?"

"Really? That would be fantastic! Only, I don't know what to do. I mean… I've never actually…well… she's never…you know, nursed from me."

Sandra smiled. "I think together we can find a way to manage. But I don't want you to expect too much this first time. It will be new for Beth, too. Lots of premature babies don't know what to do right off the bat. They can learn, we have ways to help, but don't be too disappointed if she doesn't latch on right away. I'll get a pillow for you, and I'll show you how to get ready for her."

Sandra pulled the curtain around the cubicle to give them some privacy.

A few minutes later, Mick entered the nursery and made his way toward Beth's spot hoping that he wasn't too late for the afternoon feeding. Beth was still being limited to only short times out of her incubator, and he didn't want to miss a chance to hold her. He saw that the curtain was drawn around her bed and wondered why. The sound of a giggle reached him and he listened intently.

"She's getting it all over her face." It was Caitlin's voice, and she was clearly amused.

"Just stroke down on her lips until she opens her mouth wide, then shove it in." Sandra's voice followed. She, too, sounded as if she were struggling not to laugh.

"I think she's got it."

"I don't think so, but she's trying," Sandra answered.

"Wow! I feel that."

Sandra laughed. "Okay, that is a positive sign."

"She's doing it." Caitlin's voice was full of joy.

Mick knew he should leave, but his feet were rooted to the spot. Bands of love, pride and happiness tangled around his heart and squeezed. Caitlin had worked so hard to be a successful nursing mother. The two of them deserved this special time together.

Sandra said, "I'll be back in a few minutes to check on you. Call if you need anything."

Mick took his cue and left the room before they knew he was listening in. Fifteen minutes later, he came in again and saw the curtain was open. Caitlin held Beth in the crook of her arm. A soft light shone in her eyes and a happy smile curved her lips. "Mick, I'm glad you're here."

He smiled back feeling foolishly proud as he settled into a chair beside her.

During the past weeks, Caitlin had been avoiding him. Using the excuse of job hunting, she had been gone from the house for long hours if he was home. Whenever he tried to bring up how he felt about her, she practically ran out of the room. He tried to remember not to push, but it got harder every day.

Sandra came back to the bedside. "There are some people in the waiting room who would like to see both of you."

Caitlin looked curious. "Who is it?"

"They said they were friends of yours. One of them is a pastor."

"It must be Pastor Frank," Caitlin said. "It's fine if he comes in."

A few minutes later, Caitlin looked up and smiled. "Eddy! What a surprise. Come in."

"Are you sure it's okay?"

"Of course it is. Come and meet Beth." She raised the baby higher in the crook of her elbow. "Eddy, meet Elizabeth Anne Williams. Beth, this is the fellow who saved us both by getting the ambulance the day you were born."

Eddy propped his trembling hands on his thighs as he leaned forward. "Sheesh! I ain't never seen a baby so small."

"She's a lot bigger now than when she was born," Mick said, hiding his hurt and disappointment. Caitlin had called her Elizabeth Anne Williams, not O'Callaghan. He shouldn't have expected Caitlin to think of Beth as bearing his name. Legally she did, but not in her mother's eyes.

"Sheesh," Eddy said again, clearly in awe.

"Sit down," Caitlin patted the chair beside her. "Would you like to hold her?"

Eddy straightened and waved his hands. "Oh, no. She's too little. I might drop her or something. Maybe when she's bigger—and walkin'. I got a present for her down at Mercy House."

"You didn't have to get us anything."

"I know. It ain't much, but you'll be needin' it."

"What is it?"

"I ain't gonna tell ya, but when you take this cutie to yer new home, it'll be waitin."

Caitlin sent Mick a questioning look. He shook his head. He had no idea what Eddy was talking about.

"What do you mean, my new home?" she asked.

"Oh, I wasn't supposed to say nothin'. Pastor Frank

was gonna tell ya himself. I guess I'd better go and let him come in. She's real cute, honey. Thanks for lettin' me see her." He gave a short nod, sniffed once, wiped at his eye then fled from the room.

A few minutes later, the pastor joined them. He grinned at Caitlin and the baby. "My, she is a tiny one. Babies never cease to amaze me. What a wonderful way God chose to start people."

He took the seat beside Caitlin. "I have some good news, but I think Eddy spoiled my surprise. I've found an apartment for you. It's not much, only two rooms over a garage, but it's sound, and it's close to the hospital. And the first three months rent will be free."

"A place of our own, for real? How?" She looked at Mick.

"It wasn't me." He listened to Pastor Frank's news with a sinking heart. It often took the man months to find homes for the women at his shelter. Mick had expected Caitlin would be with him for weeks yet. Certainly until after the baby came home. He didn't want her leaving. Not now—not ever. He wanted to see her bright and beautiful face every day.

"The Lord moves in mysterious ways," Pastor Frank continued. "Out of the blue I received a call from one of my parishioners about having a place for someone. It was too small for the women at the shelter who all have several children and the two elderly women with us couldn't manage the stairs. But it seemed perfect for you. The place is empty now. You can move in right away. It even has some furniture."

"A place of our own," Caitlin tried to infuse some joy into her voice. It was what she wanted only she wasn't ready to leave Mick.

Sandra came to stand beside Caitlin's chair. "It's time for Beth to go back in her bed. We don't want her wasting her calories keeping warm. We want her to use them to grow."

"But Mick hasn't gotten to hold her," Caitlin protested.

"I'll hold her tomorrow," he said. "Let her sleep now."

She tried to read his face, but she couldn't tell what he was thinking. Was he sad to know she would be leaving, or relieved to get rid of her?

Pastor Frank excused himself and left. Mick walked with him out of the unit. Caitlin let Sandra put Beth back to bed, then she left as well.

Mick was waiting by his SUV in the hospital parking lot. He held open the door for her. Climbing in, she tried again to find out what he was thinking. "Pastor Frank didn't waste any time getting me a place."

"No, he didn't." Mick shut her door and walked around. He seemed angry. She waited until he got in and started the engine.

"It sounds like a nice place," she ventured.

"It sounds small."

"Compared to your place, maybe. But for just Beth and me, it sounds okay."

"We'll see."

"What does that mean?"

"I'm not going to let you and Beth move into some dump."

"Did I hear you right? You aren't going to *let* me? What makes you think that *you* can tell me what to do?"

"Don't get your hackles up. I didn't mean it like that."

"And just how did you mean it?"

"All I meant was that I want to check the place out."

"You want to check out the place *I'm* going to live? Why?"

"You know why."

"I want to hear you say it." Angry now, she didn't try to hide the fact.

"All right! Because it might not be the kind of place you should take a baby who has spent the last two months in a hospital."

"I can't believe you think I'd let her stay in a place that wasn't okay."

"Let me see," he said, sarcasm cutting deep through his voice. "Oh, like the place I found you in! Now that was okay, wasn't it?"

"I didn't have a choice then. I was working on getting a decent place, only Beth came too soon."

"There will always be problems that come up. I just don't see how you can take care of her by yourself."

She turned away from him and stared out the window. She had to be strong. Now more than ever. She couldn't let her feelings for Mick blind her to what he could do. She drew in a deep, steadying breath. "Beth and I will be fine without your help."

He gave an exasperated sigh. "I know you love her, but love won't put food on the table, it won't pay the rent. Beth needs a father. I intend to be there for her. I grew up without a father, and so did you. You know what it's like. Why won't you let me take care of both of you?"

She jerked around to face him. "Yes, I grew up without a father, but I barely missed him because I never knew who he was. You know who I did miss? I missed my mother! I missed her every time she was too strung out to get out of bed while I went hungry because there wasn't any food. I missed her every time she left me alone and didn't come home for days. All I ever wanted was for her to love me. Me! Not the stuff she shot up her arm." Her voice broke, but she struggled to keep control.

"All I ever wanted was for my mother to love me the way that I love Beth. She's all I need, and I'm all she needs. Beth was never yours. I'm sorry you can't accept that."

"She isn't my blood, but she's mine in my heart. I don't want to fight, Caitlin."

She didn't, either, but she couldn't let him think that he could run her life. He had the power to take her child away if she failed to live up to the standards he set. She hardened her heart. Keeping Beth was all that mattered. She stared straight ahead and kept her voice level when she said, "Beth isn't some fantasy replacement for the children you can't have."

"That's not fair!"

She cringed at the pain she had inflicted, but there was no way to call the words back. Instead, she said, "Life ain't fair, Mick'O. I'm surprised you hadn't noticed. I'm going back inside and stay with Beth a while longer."

She reached for the handle and pushed open the door. He didn't try to stop her.

"Go home, Mick. I can find my own way from now on. You know, I'm looking forward to being out on my own again." It was, without a doubt, the biggest lie she had ever uttered.

Mick didn't answer. He simply stared at her. She couldn't bear the pain in his face. She closed the door and walked away.

* * *

It was barely a week later when a timid knock came from the front door of Caitlin's new home. She dropped the curtain rod she was hanging and hurried to open it. Maybe it was Mick.

It wasn't. His mother stood on the stoop. She held a large shopping bag in her hand. Her other arm remained in a sling, but the cast was gone. Caitlin stared in surprise at her unexpected guest.

Elizabeth smiled and wiggled two fingers in an awkward wave. "Hi. I hope you don't mind my dropping by. I was out shopping, and I saw the cutest baby clothes. I couldn't resist. I hope you don't mind."

"Ah—no, I don't mind at all. Come in."

"Thanks, but I have a few more bags in the cab." She pushed the one she held into Caitlin's hands and hurried down the steps. She returned with bag after bag until Caitlin wondered if the woman had been knocking over infant stores across the city and was trying to get rid of the stolen goods. As she set the last bag on the counter, Caitlin wondered if the gesture had been Mick's idea. She couldn't bring herself to ask.

Elizabeth looked around, and said, "My gracious sakes! What is that monstrosity?"

"I think it's called a pram. It's a present from a friend."

"It's a gigantic, black leather baby buggy with crooked wheels." She moved closer to examine it. "This thing must be a hundred years old. I don't think I've ever seen one except in movies. What are you going to do with it?"

"I'm going to use it as a baby bed."

"You're joking."

"I know a girl whose baby slept in the bottom drawer of her dresser. Why couldn't a baby buggy work as well?"

"I guess it could." Elizabeth bent to examine the pram then wrinkled her nose. "Thank goodness the baby isn't coming home yet. This is going to take some work to get it clean."

Looking instantly contrite, she straightened and said, "I'm sorry. That sounded heartless. I'm sure you wish your little girl were home no matter what. How is she doing?"

"Great, except that she still forgets to breathe sometimes. She's on a drug to help that, and she's still on one to control her seizures, but she's gaining weight. I nurse her three times a day now. If she keeps gaining, she'll get to move out of her incubator in a few more days."

"I'm glad. You've been very brave in the face of all that has happened."

Caitlin shook her head. "No, I'm not. I worry every minute that something else will go wrong."

"That's only natural. It's a mother thing." Moving around the apartment, Elizabeth picked up Caitlin's sketchbook from the stained-and-scarred coffee table. "May I?" At Caitlin's nod, she leafed through the book.

"These are wonderful. Mick told me you're an artist and that you are selling some of your work."

"Lately, every grandparent with a baby in the nursery wants to buy a portrait. Dr. Wright has even talked to a guy who owns a gallery. He's gonna take a look at my stuff."

"That's great."

"Maybe, maybe not. I don't want to get my hopes

up. How is Mick?" she asked, hoping she didn't sound too eager for information.

"Actually, I haven't seen much of him. I got my cast off two days ago, and I'm moving back into my own apartment. I've been busy setting things to rights there. I'm sure he's been busy with work."

Too busy to come to the hospital. Caitlin knew because she spent every day there, herself. He'd promised that he would always be there for Beth, but this was how Caitlin knew it would turn out. He was getting on with his life. Only, she hadn't expected it to hurt this much.

Elizabeth moved a step closer and laid a hand on Caitlin's shoulder. "I'd really like to keep in touch with you."

"I'd like that, too."

"Well, since I'm here, why don't I take you out to lunch?"

"You don't have to do that."

"Nonsense. You have to eat, don't you? I tell you what. In exchange for a meal, you can bring your young knees over to my apartment and take a broom to the dust buffalo under my bed and sofa. You'd be doing me a big favor."

"I thought they were dust bunnies."

"They've been growing since I've been at Mick's. Please say you'll come and tackle them for a crippled, old woman."

"Since you put it that way, sure."

"Excellent. I told the cabby to wait in case you said yes. I can't wait to show you my little place. I have quite a teapot collection that I think you'll like. That reminds me. Do you have a teapot? If not, I shall make you a present of one of mine. Good tea requires a good pot to brew in."

Caitlin smiled as she followed Elizabeth down the steps. Besides the fact that she truly liked Mick's mother, it would be easy now to find out how he was doing. She missed him more than she had ever thought possible.

It was after two in the morning when Mick entered the NICU and made his way to the incubator where Beth lay sleeping. Propped on her side, she held both fists close to her face like a tiny boxer getting ready to take on all comers. She was a fighter like her mother, and he thanked God for that. Life wasn't going to be easy for her.

He draped one arm on the top of her box and leaned in close, but he didn't speak, didn't open the porthole to caress her tiny head as he longed to do. She needed her sleep. She was doing so well now that the past months seemed like a fading nightmare. How many times had she cheated death while he paced in the waiting room? He had come to hate the sight of those blue tweed chairs. He'd never buy anything that color.

An alarm sounded a few beds down the aisle, and a nurse walked by to silence it. There was still a hustle in the nursery, but it was more muted at night. Perhaps it was the dimmed lights that kept everyone talking more quietly and slowed the frantic pace. He'd taken to visiting Beth in the small hours of the morning since Caitlin had moved out of his house.

Without her presence, he found it hard to sleep. Instead of tossing and turning in his lonely bed he came here. Here he didn't miss her scent—her vibrancy—the sound of her voice. Here he came to watch over Beth while she slept.

Each day, Beth grew stronger. And each day the child he thought of as his own slipped further away from him. He had to let her go. Just as he had let her mother go.

Knowing that Caitlin didn't want him in her life was tearing him apart. She wanted to live her own life. He understood that, even respected it, but the love he felt wasn't fading now that they were apart. Would it ever? How could he face a lifetime without Caitlin and Beth?

Lord, grant me Your wisdom and guidance. Please. Because I don't know what to do.

Chapter 15

"These are your going-home instructions. Do you have any questions?" A nurse Caitlin hadn't met before handed her a sheet of paper. Caitlin took it and stared at it trying to calm her fears. How could she possibly do this? How could she care for Beth without doctors and nurses there around the clock? What if there was something important in this paper?

Tell her. Tell her you can't read.

She opened her mouth to confess, but the words stuck in her throat. Would they let her take Beth home if they knew how stupid she was? The fear of losing her baby always lurked in the back of her mind. If they thought she couldn't take care of Beth, would they give her to Mick, instead?

She glanced at the car seat by her feet. Beth slept quietly, looking utterly adorable in a pink, frilly dress with a matching band around her head. No, Caitlin decided, she couldn't risk it. As soon as she had a chance, she'd take the paper and have Eddy look at it.

Caitlin forced a smile. "It all seems pretty clear."

"Good. Here are the prescriptions for Beth's medications. Take them to the pharmacy of your choice."

"But I'll still give her the same amounts, right?"

"That's right. Her caffeine is ten milligrams, that's one cc in the morning, and her phenobarbital is eight milligrams, two cc's at night. I've put several small oral medication syringes in this bag."

Caitlin nodded. She knew how to give the medications. She'd watched closely as Sandra had shown her how to draw two cc's of liquid from the round bottle and one cc from the oval bottle. Both medicines were red liquids, but she knew the round bottle was the drug that would control Beth's seizures and the oval bottle was the drug that would keep Beth from having apnea. "The pharmacy will give me the same medicines, right?"

"Yes, they'll be the same as what Beth was taking here. Do you have any questions about the home monitor?"

"No, the guy who set it up explained everything. I've had my CPR training. I know all the emergency numbers."

Dr. Wright came into the nursery just then followed by a small man in a sharply tailored, dark blue suit. Caitlin shook the hand that Dr. Wright held out.

"I wish you the best of luck, Ms. Williams. Before you go, let me introduce you to someone. This is Karl Wiltshire. Karl, this is the young woman I've been telling you about, Caitlin Williams."

"Ms. Williams, I've been looking forward to meeting you. I've been admiring some of your work in Dr. Wright's office. You have a remarkable talent."

"Thanks." Caitlin still felt embarrassed by the attention her work seemed to be getting.

The man held out a business card. "I own a gallery downtown. I'd be interested in displaying some of your work."

He smiled at Beth. "I can see that you're going to be busy for a while, but I'd like to get together with you. Would next Friday be too soon?"

Stunned, Caitlin took his card. Her work in a gallery? The idea blew her away. "Um, no. Next Friday will be fine."

"Excellent. Let's say ten o'clock?"

"Great. Would it be okay if I brought the baby?"

"Of course. Bring what you think is your best work and we'll discuss it." With that, he shook Caitlin's hand and followed Dr. Wright out of the unit.

"Well," the nurse said, "I guess that's everything."

Caitlin tucked Mr. Wiltshire's business card in the bag with Beth's things. Looking through the bag, she realized something was missing. "I don't see Beth's card. It has green shamrocks on it."

"You mean her Irish blessing. I think it's still on her crib. I'll get it for you."

A few moments later, she returned with the card in her hand. She read it aloud. "'May God grant you many years to live, for sure He must be knowing, the Earth has angels all too few, and heaven's overflowing.' Isn't that beautiful?"

"It's perfect." Tears pricked the back of Caitlin's eyes. Reaching out, she took the card from the woman's hand. Mick had chosen these words for Beth on the day she was born, and Caitlin would cherish them forever.

The nurse said, "I'm surprised Mick isn't here."

"He's been working a lot, I guess. He hasn't been able to come and see her lately."

"Except at night."

Caitlin frowned. "What do you mean?"

"I usually work the night shift. I'm covering for a nurse who is sick this morning. I've gotten used to seeing Mick here in the wee hours."

Caitlin blinked hard. Mick had been to see Beth, but he hadn't come to see Beth's mother. That hurt, although she knew it shouldn't. Did he still worry that she wouldn't be able to take care of Beth by herself?

Beth was going to be the only priority in Caitlin's life from now on. She would stop mooning over Mick O'Callaghan. She would stop missing him. Maybe someday, she'd even stop dreaming about him.

Slipping the strap of Beth's monitor over her shoulder, Caitlin picked up the car seat. "Please tell everyone I said thank you."

"Good luck, and don't be afraid to call us with questions."

Glancing around the unit once more, a sense of loss settled over Caitlin. Strangely enough, she was going to miss this place. She looked down at her baby and smiled. "Let's go home, jelly bean."

The cabdriver waited for them while Caitlin took Beth's prescriptions into a nearby pharmacy. She hurried, knowing the meter was still running. She had some money, but none to waste.

In the pharmacy, the woman behind the counter handed Caitlin the drugs in a small white paper sack.

It wasn't until she and Beth were back in the cab that Caitlin opened it and looked in. There were two identical oval, amber plastic bottles.

Caitlin stared at them in dismay. At the hospital, the seizure medication had been in a round bottle. Her heart hammered with panic. How was she going to tell them apart? She took a deep breath and tried to remain calm. She'd find a way to manage. She always found a way.

A few minutes later, the cab pulled up to the small apartment that she and Beth were going to call home. Caitlin leaned forward to pay the driver. "Could you help me carry some things in?"

"Sure. No problem," he replied.

Caitlin took one bottle of medication from the package and let it slip to the floor. Then she unbuckled Beth's car seat and lifted the baby out of the cab. "I'll take her if you can get her monitor and the diaper bag."

Caitlin was halfway up the outside stairs that led to her new home when the driver called out, "Hey, you forgot some medicine here."

She turned back frowning. "I don't think so. What is it?"

He peered at the bottle. "It says Caffeine Ci—something."

She sagged with relief. "Oh, yes, it's mine. It must have fallen out of my bag."

"Good thing I saw it." He tucked it in his shirt pocket, then lifted the diaper bag and the monitor from the cab.

Once inside the apartment, Caitlin set the bottle with Beth's seizure medication on the kitchen counter. She'd mark it with something that would let her tell the medicines apart right away. She set Beth's car seat on the floor beside the couch.

The driver carried in the diaper bag and Beth's VCR-sized monitor. "Where do you want these?"

"Anywhere is fine."

"Oops, she's spitting up," he said, pointing to Beth. "My youngest one was always doing that."

Caitlin took the diaper bag from him, and he moved aside as she found a cloth to wipe Beth's face. When she looked up, he was standing by the kitchen counter reading the bottle he held.

"I'll take that," she said.

"Oh, sure." He handed it to her. "What's it for, if you don't mind my asking?"

"She has apnea. The caffeine helps her to keep breathing."

"Wow. And the Pheno stuff?"

"It controls her seizures."

"Seizures? The poor kid." His voice held an edge of pity that annoyed Caitlin.

"The doctors think she'll outgrow them."

"That's good. Well, I'd better get going. Good luck to you both," he said.

Caitlin showed him to the door and closed it behind him, then she stared at the bottle in her hand. She had found a way this time, but it might not be so easy the next time. Not being able to read hadn't meant much when she only had herself to worry about. Street smarts had mattered more than the things she'd learned in school, but now she had Beth to think of.

Someday Beth would go to school, and she'd want her mother to help with homework and stuff. Caitlin bit down on her fingernail as she stared at her sleeping daughter.

Could she lie and fool her own daughter the way she had fooled others? She didn't want to, but she didn't want Beth to be ashamed of her, either.

Carrying the bottle in her hand to the kitchen, she set it on top of the refrigerator. She found a small rubber band in a drawer and put it over the neck of the bottle on the counter. It would be easy to tell them apart now. Next time she had them filled, she'd ask the pharmacy for two different kinds of bottles.

She crossed the room and sat down on the brown floral sofa that had come with the apartment and stared at her baby, still sleeping peacefully. The quiet of the small place surrounded them. They were home. She had her baby with her now and forever.

Beth stirred and began to fuss. Happily, Caitlin picked her up and began to nurse her. This was how she had always known it would be. Silently, Caitlin thanked God for the beautiful child He had given her.

Mick helped loop the long fire hose back onto the sides of the truck. He pushed back his helmet and wiped the sweat and soot from his forehead with the back of his coat sleeve. Woody secured his end, then turned to Mick. "Our shift ended forty minutes ago."

The small kitchen fire had produced a lot of smoke, but most of the home was still intact. The family stood huddled together on the sidewalk, thankful it hadn't been worse.

Mick looked over his shoulder at his friend. "Don't tell me you're complaining about overtime."

"Not me. I can always find ways to spend it. Now

that we're off, what are your plans for the next few days?"

"A hot shower, some breakfast and then I'm going to see Caitlin and Beth."

"You've waited—what? A whole week?"

"I wanted to give them time to get used to being in a new place, but I need to see how they're doing."

"Mick, they're doing fine."

"I know they're fine. I'm the basketcase. How am I going to convince Caitlin that I'm in love with her? She thinks I'm only interested in Beth."

The "fantasy replacement" for the child he couldn't have. Her comment had hurt, but in a way, it had been true—to start with. Only so much had changed since the day Beth was born. He had changed. He needed both of them in his life.

Woody slapped Mick's shoulder and pushed him toward the cab of the truck. "First, let's get back to the station and out of this gear, and then we can discuss your love life. The main thing is, don't rush her. Take it slow and easy. Be a friend."

On the ride back to the firehouse, Mick pondered Woody's advice. It made sense. Slow and easy, that would be the plan.

Please, Lord, let me prove to Caitlin that I love her. That I want us to be a family.

He'd show her he could be a dependable friend before anything else. She would be hard to convince. She was stubbornly independent. She had a little money now from her drawings, but that wouldn't last long. Soon she'd see that she needed him and he'd be there for her.

After showering and getting dressed in Levi's and

a blue plaid cotton shirt, Mick pulled a small bag from the top shelf of his locker. Inside was a plush pink bunny that played a child's prayer when its paws were squeezed. Today he would simply say that he had stopped by to see Beth and give her a welcome-home present. Caitlin would believe that.

Beth wouldn't quit crying. Caitlin paced the floor of her small apartment, switching the baby from one weary arm to the other. It was almost eight in the morning, and Beth had been crying since before midnight. Caitlin's feelings of frustration and inadequacy had long since given way to pure exhaustion.

"What's wrong? Tell me what you want," she pleaded, knowing she had already tried everything. "I've fed you and changed you and rocked you. What else do you need?"

Even the warm bath and wrapping Beth tightly had failed to calm her for more than a few minutes. Nothing worked.

Caitlin was due at the Wiltshire Gallery at ten o'clock. She had less than two hours to get presentable and get downtown. Having the gallery accept her work was so important. Why did Beth have to choose this night to have a case of colic? "Hush, baby, please."

Beth arched her back and flailed her arms as her cries continued. The last bit of Caitlin's patience vaporized. Crossing to the bedroom, she laid the baby abruptly in her oversize buggy. "Well, just cry then! I don't care!"

Shutting the door with a bang, Caitlin dropped onto the sagging sofa, pressed her hands over her ears and battled the need to burst into tears herself.

She waited, watching the hands of the clock tick slowly around. Five minutes. After ten minutes, she gave up. Dragging herself off the sofa, she returned to the bedroom. Beth's cries had subsided to ragged sobs and pitiful whimpering. She turned her tiny face toward Caitlin, her wide-eyed expression a picture of panic and fear.

Consumed with guilt, Caitlin scooped her up and held her close. "I'm sorry, I'm sorry. I'm a terrible mother, only I just don't know what else to do."

A knock sounded at the front door and Beth began crying loudly once more.

Now what? Carrying her screaming child, Caitlin yanked open the door, then sagged with relief. "Mick. Oh, I'm so glad to see you."

"What's wrong?" His concern was her undoing.

A sob escaped her. "I don't know." She thrust the baby toward him. "She just keeps crying and crying. I've done everything I can think of."

Taking the baby from her, he balanced Beth in one arm and draped his free arm over Caitlin's shoulders. "Okay. It's going to be all right. Babies get fussy sometimes."

"Not like this."

He led her to the sofa and sat beside her. "When did this start?"

"I don't know. The day before yesterday, I think. She started having high heart-rate alarms on her monitor."

"But no apnea?"

"No, and she won't eat. Maybe there's something wrong with my milk again."

Caitlin watched anxiously as Mick laid the baby in his lap and checked her over. Laying two fingers on the inside of Beth's elbow, he checked her pulse as Caitlin had learned to do.

"Did you give her any caffeine this morning?"

"No, not for the past two days. Her pulse was too high. I count it every time just like they showed me at the hospital."

"She doesn't feel warm, I don't think she has a fever, but her pulse is way too fast."

"What should I do?"

"I think we had better get her in to see a doctor."

"You think she's sick? I thought she was just having colic." Guilt and remorse rose like bile in her throat. She should have taken her to the doctor last night. Instead, she had let her baby suffer for hours.

"I'll take you to the E.R. Bring her medicine, they'll want to know what she's on."

Trying desperately to stave off a wave of panic, Caitlin gathered Beth's things and followed Mick down to his car. He fastened the baby's car seat into the center of the rear seat, and Caitlin got in beside her daughter. Beth continued to cry as Mick drove. It broke Caitlin's heart not to be able to pick her up. Suddenly, the baby's crying became a choking gurgle. She stiffened and arched as her face twisted into a grimace.

"Mick, she's having a seizure."

"Is she breathing?"

"Yes. What do I do?" *Please God, help her.*

"Just make sure she's breathing," Mick said.

After nearly a minute, Beth stopped arching and went limp. The color of her face paled and slowly took on a blue tinge. Leaning her cheek close to the baby's nose confirmed Caitlin's worst fears. She fumbled with the straps of the car seat. "She's not breathing now."

"We're almost there."

"I'm starting CPR. God, please help me do this!" Pulling Beth to her lap, Caitlin bent and covered her daughter's mouth and nose with her own mouth and delivered two small puffs of air. Beth's chest rose and fell and Caitlin knew she had done it right. She continued to deliver puffs of air until Beth suddenly drew in a breath of her own and let out a cry.

"Thank You, Lord." Mick's voice wavered with emotion.

Seconds later, the car skidded to a stop in front of the hospital's E.R. He jumped out and jerked open Caitlin's door. "I'll take her."

Caitlin handed Beth to him and followed close behind as he hurried through the hospital doors. His tense explanation to the clerk on duty got them ushered quickly into a room. A nurse took Beth and laid her in the center of a large cot.

Caitlin pressed a hand to her trembling lips. Beth looked so small and helpless. A doctor entered the room and began to examine Beth. He asked question after question. Mick stood silently behind Caitlin with his hands on her shoulders. She was so thankful that he was there.

When the doctor was done with his examination, he gave the nurse instructions for lab work and then suggested to Caitlin that she might like to step out while they drew blood.

"No, I've seen her stuck before. I want to stay."

"I'll stay as well," Mick said.

Together they helped to hold Beth still while a man from the lab stuck her arm. When it was all over, Caitlin picked up her sobbing baby and held her close.

The nurse indicated a chair. "You might as well be seated. It'll be a while before the test results come back."

Nodding, Caitlin sat down and Mick took a seat beside her. The nurse held out a clipboard. "We'll need some paperwork filled out."

Mick reached for Beth. "I'll hold her while you do it."

"No, she needs me right now." Caitlin glared at the nurse. "Can't that wait? Can't you see how upset she is?"

With an apologetic look to the nurse, Mick took the clipboard from her. "I'll fill it out."

"All right, just be sure and have Mom sign it."

The nurse left the room and Caitlin avoided Mick's gaze as she concentrated on calming Beth. After a few minutes of silence, she said, "Good ol' Mick to the rescue, again. Do you have some kind of radar that lets you know when I'm in trouble?"

"I only stopped by to give Beth a homecoming present and to see how you were doing."

"We were doing fine until last night." She knew she sounded defensive, but once again he had proven that he knew Beth better than she did. It irked her that she had needed his help, even as she admitted to herself that she had never been happier to see anyone when she had opened her door.

"Thanks for bringing us to the hospital. You don't have to stay if you're busy."

"I'm not busy." He finished filling out the form, then leaning forward, he clasped his hands together and waited in silence.

Thirty minutes later, the doctor walked in. He was frowning as he stared at the papers in his hand. "I understand that Beth was sent home on phenobarbital and also on caffeine, is that right?"

"That's right," Caitlin answered. Something was wrong, she knew it by the way he wouldn't meet her gaze.

He looked at Mick. "You're listed as the father, but I see you have a different address."

"Caitlin and I don't live together."

The doctor stared hard at Caitlin. "Do you have Beth's medication with you?"

Caitlin fought down the need to take Beth and run. She had done everything just as the nurses in the NICU had told her to. She hadn't done anything wrong. She pulled them from her bag and held them out.

"I've been giving them just like I was taught." Caitlin drew a quick, deep breath. She was suffocating in the small room. The walls pressed in closer and closer. Mick and the doctor were staring at her intently.

The doctor walked to the cart in the corner of the room. After a moment, he turned around and held out both bottles and two syringes. "Show me how you've been giving them. Let's let Dad hold Beth for a minute."

Caitlin licked her dry lips. "I can hold her."

Mick rose and took Beth from her arms. "Show the doctor how you've been giving Beth her medicine."

The doctor knew. Caitlin didn't know how, but she was sure of it. Was it possible she had mixed up the medicines? She had been so careful to keep them apart. She took the bottles from him with hands that trembled. Looking down, she saw neither one had a rubber band on it.

"Draw up the phenobarbital first," the doctor suggested.

Which was which? What should she do? She looked from the doctor to Mick. Now he would see how stupid she was.

"I can't," she admitted in anguish.

"Why not?" the doctor asked gently.

"I had it marked. You took the rubber band off. I know it was the right one. It was, wasn't it? The rubber band was on her seizure medicine. It was two cc's every night in a little bit of milk so she'd take it all before I fed her, and the apnea medicine was one cc in the morning. I had it right. I know I did. Only, maybe—maybe the cabdriver mixed them up." Panic choked her. What had she done?

"Let me see." Mick took the bottles from her limp hand. "This one is phenobarbital and this one is caffeine. What do you mean the cabdriver mixed them up?"

A strange calm settled over Caitlin. The life she had dreamed of with her daughter disappeared before her the way the winds scattered the morning mist that rose from the lake. She had nothing left to lose.

"I pretended to leave one in his cab and when he asked if it was mine, I had him read the label. He had the caffeine in his hand so I knew I had her seizure medicine. I put it down on the counter. He must have switched them. I thought it was such a good plan."

"I don't understand," Mick looked more confused than ever.

"I—I can't read. But I would never hurt, Beth. Never."

"You wouldn't hurt her? You've been giving her the wrong doses of medicine. This is phenobarbital! You could have killed her!"

The anger and loathing in his eyes was painful to

see. Beth whimpered and Caitlin reached for her, but Mick turned away and hushed the baby, murmuring words of comfort as he held her close. Caitlin stared at his back. She didn't blame him. Mick would never let anything hurt Beth.

She'd been crazy to think that she could raise Beth. She was no better than her own mother. Dotty had her drugs to blame. Caitlin couldn't blame anyone or anything but herself. Beth would be better off with Mick. He would never hurt her.

The door opened beside Caitlin as the nurse came in, and in a moment of agony unlike anything she had ever faced, Caitlin knew what she had to do. She had to give up her baby. She had to go where she could never, ever hurt Beth or Mick again.

One last glimpse of Beth's face was all she wanted. Only Mick held her close and Caitlin couldn't see her. Tears blurred her vision and tightened her throat.

God, please forgive me.

Quietly, she turned away and slipped out of the room.

Chapter 16

The doctor scrawled on Beth's chart, then handed it to the nurse. "I'm going to admit the child for observation overnight. It's a simple matter to get her phenobarbital level back up, but the caffeine will have to wear off on its own. She'll need to be on a monitor until her heart rate is more normal."

The nurse left the room and the doctor spoke to Mick. "You'll be able to stay with her tonight."

Mick nodded, too angry and upset to speak. How could Caitlin have taken such a chance with Beth's health? He glanced around, but Caitlin had left the room.

The doctor laid a hand on Mick's arm. "I take it you didn't know she couldn't read?"

He shook his head. "I had no idea. How did you know?"

"I didn't. The nurse suspected something when the baby's mother became belligerent about filling out the paperwork. We see it more than you'd think. When your daughter's lab reports came back, I knew either the pharmacy had filled the prescriptions incorrectly, or it had been given incorrectly. That's why I asked to see the bottles. She had a rubber band around one. I was pretty sure then. When I took that off, she couldn't tell the bottles apart. Somehow, she must have marked the wrong one."

Beth whimpered and Mick gently bounced her until she quieted. "Caitlin loves Beth. She'd never knowingly hurt her. I don't understand why she didn't tell me."

"Fear, I imagine."

"Of what?"

"Fear of ridicule, shame, the reasons are often deep-seated and difficult for the illiterate person to define. Many of them become incredibly skillful at hiding the truth even from family members."

The door opened and the nurse looked in. "The peds floor has a bed ready now. I'll take you upstairs."

"Did you tell her mother that Beth is being admitted?" Mick asked.

"I looked for her, but I couldn't find her."

He shouldn't have yelled at her. Of course, she hadn't meant to hurt Beth. "Did anyone see where she went?"

"No, but I've sent someone to look for her. Beth needs to be on a monitor. We shouldn't delay."

Reluctantly, Mick agreed. In the room where Beth would spend the night, he impatiently answered the staff's questions and glanced frequently toward the door, but Caitlin never appeared. Where was she?

When Beth fell asleep at last, he went searching for Caitlin himself. What did she think she was going to accomplish by ducking out like this? Maybe he had reacted badly, but surely she knew he didn't believe she would intentionally hurt Beth.

It didn't matter how independent Caitlin wanted to be, she would have to accept the fact that he was going to be a part of their lives from now on—a big part of it.

Why on earth hadn't she told him the truth? Why hadn't she asked for his help? He would have given it gladly. She had no right to jeopardize Beth's health for nothing more than her pride. When she did show up, he intended to give her a piece of his mind. Making a mistake was one thing, but this juvenile behavior of running away from her problems had to stop.

So she couldn't read—big deal. All she had to do was to say so. But no, she was too pigheaded for that. Now that he knew, he could remember a dozen times in the past when he should have suspected something. Maybe he could understand that her pride had prevented her from telling others, but why hadn't she trusted him? He loved her.

He dropped his gaze to stare at the floor. He loved her, but he had never told her that—he had kept his secrets, too.

As the hours dragged by and she didn't come in, he began to worry. A cold fear started to uncoil inside him.

She had looked so scared in the E.R. Like a jerk, he had yelled at her, and her face had gone white. Something in her beautiful eyes changed, and she had looked so remote. Wrapped up in his own concerns for Beth, he hadn't recognized what he saw until now. It had been hopelessness.

Tears blurred Caitlin's vision as she ran down the sidewalk. It didn't matter where she went. She only wanted to get away—away from the look on Mick's face—away from the knowledge that she had almost killed Beth. She ran until pain clenched her side in a tight grip and her breath came in short ragged gasps.

Anguish, guilt and regret choked her. She had abandoned her baby. Love for her daughter almost made her turn around, but then she remembered Beth's face twisted in pain as spasms jerked her little body. She had done that to her baby. Her ignorance had done that.

Desperately, she wished that she had trusted Mick enough to tell him the truth. Instead, she saw his angry face and heard his voice as he shouted, "You could have killed her."

The pain in her side made her slow down, but she kept moving. If she stopped putting one foot in front of the other, she would sink into a heap of despair.

This is for the best. I can't take care of her.

She would only end up hurting Beth again. She saw that now. Leaving Beth with Mick was the right thing to do. Beth would be safe with him.

The gray world around her gradually turned into darkness as night fell and still Caitlin walked, turning this way and that, down streets whose names she couldn't read, past stores whose signs she didn't understand.

Beth would be okay. Mick would look after her. He could give her a life of security and love.

Cars streaked past Caitlin as she plodded on, but she barely noticed. Slowly, towering buildings replaced the houses along the streets. There were people around her now, laughing, calling out for cabs, hurrying past with cell phones pressed to their ears or shopping bags clutched tightly in their hands. No one noticed her. Funny how easily she had slipped back into being another invisible street person.

That thought made her pause. She had spent years rarely making eye contact with anyone, surviving on the fringes of society and sometimes wondering if she really existed at all. Going back to that kind of life would be unbearable after Mick and after Beth. Never seeing Beth again, never holding her close, that would be unbearable, too.

Ahead of Caitlin rose the white, ornate pylons of the Michigan Avenue Bridge. Across the bridge, the lights of Chicago's Magnificent Mile stretched like a glittering chasm of glass and steel, a world in which she had no part. Below her, curving along the edge of the river lay Wacker Drive and farther on, Lower Wacker Drive. In her early days on the streets, she had lived by staying warm, huddled in a cardboard box on the grates on Lower Wacker with dozens of other street people. They had taught her how to survive. Only now, surviving wasn't enough. Mick had made her believe that.

Fog drifted in ghostly curtains across the bridge as if drawn along by the flow of the water beneath it. Caitlin kept to the walkway until she reached the center of the bridge. There she leaned on the rail and stared at the dark, churning water below her. A lifetime without her baby—without Mick—what was it worth?

Down there was an end to her pain and grief. She

wouldn't have to face a lifetime of missing Beth and missing Mick, of knowing how badly she had failed both of them. Her hands tightened on the rail. It would be so easy to close her eyes and take a simple step over the side into nothingness.

Caitlin raised her face to the night sky. Suddenly filled with anger, she shouted, "Is this Your great plan, God? Well, it stinks! Do You hear me? It stinks!"

She sank to her knees by the rail. Tears streamed unheeded down her cheeks. Everything she loved was lost.

With her face pressed against the cold railing, Caitlin watched the inky water swirl below the bridge. One easy step and it would all be over. She closed her eyes and pictured her baby cradled in Mick's gentle arms.

"Beth, I never meant to hurt you," she whispered. "Mick will keep you safe. He's so strong. Only—I don't want you to grow up thinking that I never loved you, because I love you with all my heart."

Who will tell her that if you kill yourself?

The thought came from deep within her heart. From the place Mick had once told her she could find God. Caitlin rubbed the tears from her eyes to clear her vision. Slumped against the railing, she drew her knees up and wrapped her arms around them to ward off the chill of the night.

Is this what You wanted, God? For me to give up Beth so she'd be safe and loved? If that's so, then I guess this is okay because that's all I want, too. Honest. Only how can I live without her? I give up, Lord. Please, help me. I can't do this alone.

Slowly, a sense of calm and peace grew inside her,

pushing away the chill with a feeling of warmth. Whatever He wanted, it wasn't for her to end her life here.

Pulling herself to her feet, Caitlin walked off the
bridge with unsteady steps, but she kept walking.

Hours later, on the verge of exhaustion, she sank
into a corner of an alley a few streets back from West
Madison. Wrapping her arms around her drawn-up
knees, she rested her head on them and tried to sleep,
but she couldn't. Her grief and pain were impossible
to ignore.

Please, Lord. Give me the strength to go on.

Beth would grow up happy and loved with Mick as
her father, but wouldn't she always wonder why her
mother had abandoned her? Caitlin couldn't add that
burden to her child's life. Someday, when Beth was
old enough, someone needed to explain it to her. Besides Mick, there was only one person Caitlin thought
might understand.

What Beth might someday think about her was more
important than what anyone had ever thought of her
in the past. She wanted to be someone Beth would be
proud of. To do that, she had to become something better than what she was. And she couldn't do it alone.
Help me, God. Show me the way.

When the sun rose at last, Caitlin tilted her head
back to stare at the strip of blue sky overhead and a new
sense of determination filled her. She had lost everything that was important, but she wouldn't be ashamed
anymore. God had shown her that.

She rose stiffly to her feet. Although she had been to
the area only once before, she knew she could find the
way. When she judged it to be late enough, she made
her way to the apartment building on the corner. She

passed a group of boys playing stickball in the street and wondered if Mick had ever played ball like that. Maybe he would teach Beth how, someday.

Caitlin realized she would never watch her daughter at play, never see her take her first steps, never hear her first words. Sadness, sharp as a knife, cut through her, but she walked on. She couldn't go another hour without knowing how Beth was.

Inside the lobby, tastefully decorated in shades of gray and muted blues, she gathered her newfound courage close and pressed the elevator button.

On the fifth floor, she made her way to apartment 516. Overwhelmed by the temptation to turn and run away, she knocked quickly before she could change her mind. The door opened before she was ready. Elizabeth O'Callaghan's face took on a look of absolute shock.

"Caitlin, what on earth are you doing here? My dear, everyone was so worried about you. Mick is simply frantic. Are you all right?"

"How's Beth?" Her words came out in a husky whisper because she couldn't talk around the lump in her throat.

"She's fine. She went home from the hospital this morning."

It was the news she needed to hear. Nothing else mattered. Relief left her weak and shaking.

Elizabeth grasped Caitlin's elbow. "Come inside and sit down. You look as pale as a sheet."

Caitlin shook her head. "I won't impose on you. I just had to know she was all right. I came here because I want you to tell Beth when she's old enough to understand that..."

Words failed her as she struggled to hold back her

tears. "Tell her that I loved her with all my heart, but I couldn't take care of her. Tell her I left *because* I loved her. And tell Mick…tell him…"

"Tell him yourself." His voice came from behind her, and she froze.

Chapter 17

Caitlin couldn't move, couldn't speak, as pain crashed like a tidal wave through her. She didn't dare turn around. *Please, Lord, I'm not strong enough for this.*

She kept her eyes down. If Mick had Beth—if she saw her baby girl just once—she'd never be able to leave her again.

She forced her wooden legs to start walking toward the stairs at the end of the hall.

"Running again, Caitlin?" he called after her. "I thought you said you loved her?"

Her feet stopped even as her mind screamed for her to keep going. She tilted her head back to stare at the ceiling. "What do you want from me, Mick?"

"I want answers."

"I don't have any."

"I need to know why you abandoned your child. Why?"

Abruptly, anger at Mick replaced her desire to flee. If he wanted answers, then she'd give him what he wanted to hear.

"Because I couldn't do it, okay?" she shouted. "You were right all along. I couldn't take care of her. I couldn't be a mother. I couldn't manage because I'm too stupid to learn how to read."

"You aren't stupid." His voice was right behind her.

"I am. You said it yourself. I could have killed her." Tears slipped unheeded down her cheeks.

She took a deep breath and steadied her voice. "Anyway, she's better off with you. You'll give her a good life. A life with a real home and clothes that don't come from a thrift store. She'll have all the things I'd never be able to afford."

"That's a lie, and you know it. This isn't about things. I deserve to hear the truth."

Stunned by the pain in his voice, she spun around. Just as she feared, Beth lay snuggled in the crook of his arm. Caitlin pressed a hand to her lips to hold back a sob.

Her baby. She was so beautiful—more beautiful even than Caitlin remembered, and her heart swelled with painful happiness and pride.

"How could you walk out on her?" he demanded. "How could a mother do that?"

Caitlin closed her eyes. Suddenly, weary beyond words, she knew he wouldn't go until she admitted the bitter truth.

"I did it for her—to keep her safe. May God forgive me."

"I don't understand."

He didn't. She had to make him understand. She struggled to find the words. "I hurt her, Mick."

"I know you didn't mean to."

"My mother never meant to hurt me, but she did. So many times! And I forgave her every time. I believed her each time she said she'd change—but she never did. Listening to her say how sorry she was didn't erase any of the pain. It didn't ease my hunger when she spent money on dope instead of food. It didn't make the slaps and punches less painful when I wouldn't sell drugs for her pimp of a boyfriend. Then one day, I just ran out of forgiveness, and I started to hate her."

Caitlin raised her face, her gaze drawn to her sweet baby. "I didn't want that for Beth."

With her heart in broken pieces, she looked away. "I couldn't take care of her any more than my mom could take care of me. Maybe the reasons are different, but that doesn't matter. Yesterday in the E.R., when I heard myself stammering the same excuses—I was sorry—I didn't mean it   I'll do better—I realized I was just like her. That's why I left. So I'd never hurt Beth again. I know you love her. I know she'll always be safe with you."

Looking up at Mick, a ghost of a smile crossed her face. "God must truly love you, Mick O'Callaghan. He's given you the greatest gift."

Mick studied Caitlin's pain-filled, tear-streaked face. Slowly his anger and confusion faded. Whatever he had expected, it hadn't been this. Compassion welled up in him. As a child, she had suffered what no child ever should. Now she was willing to suffer even more to spare her daughter the same fate.

Like the two women who came before King Solomon, the true mother had been willing to give up her child rather than see him harmed. Mick felt humbled in the face of Caitlin's sacrifice.

Lord, make me worthy of this woman.

He loved her. He understood what she had done and what it had cost her. Even if she didn't love him, he couldn't separate her from Beth. He needed both of them in his life. But how could he convince Caitlin of that when she believed he only wanted her child?

He glanced from Caitlin to Beth—his daughter in every sense of the word except one—and his heart ached for what he knew he must do. There was only one way he could prove to Caitlin that he believed in her, that he forgave her.

Forgive my arrogance and my pride, Lord. Grant me Your wisdom. I've never needed it as much as I need it now.

"Caitlin, you are not your mother," he said gently. "Everything you did—even leaving—was because you wanted what was best for Beth. No one can love Beth more than that. She doesn't need things. She needs her mother's love—your love."

Startled, Caitlin's gaze flew to his face. Had she heard right? Was he offering her a chance to gain back everything she had thrown away? "What are you saying?"

"I'm saying that Beth needs her mother, and I think her mother needs Beth even more."

A powerful joy unfolded in Caitlin. With trembling hands, she took Beth from him and drew her close. The sweet fragrance of her baby was her undoing. She broke into gut-wrenching sobs. "I'm so sorry, Beth. I'll never leave you again. Never! Never! Thank You, God. Thank You."

Elizabeth held her door open wide and Mick helped Caitlin to the sofa. It was several long minutes until she regained a measure of control. When she was able to stop crying, she kissed Beth's face, then looked at him. "I don't know what to say. I don't have words to tell you how much this means to me. How can you forgive me for what I did?"

Choking back the lump that filled his throat, he said, "I know you love Beth, and I knew you would come back."

"I came back to make sure she was okay, not to take her away from you. Only to tell her why I had to leave, and to tell her that I always loved her. I just need to get my head on straight, first."

He tilted his. "It doesn't look crooked to me."

She smiled, but quickly looked down. He lifted her chin with one finger. Fear and indecision gathered in her bright eyes. "What if I can't do it? What if I *am* like my mother?"

"You're not."

"I think I'm scared."

"I know. So am I."

"You? Of what?"

"The same things you are. That I'll make a lousy parent, that I'll be too strict, or too lenient. That she'll run into the street when I'm not looking, or that she'll break my heart when some guy wants to marry her. It scares me to death, but I know that God loves her and she is always in His tender care."

"Yes." Caitlin gripped his hand and squeezed. "I believe that, now. He was never far away. I just wasn't looking with my heart."

* * *

Early on a Sunday morning two weeks later, Mick stood in his own kitchen trying to find a pot holder. "It's coming, it's coming. Take it easy," he said in a harried voice.

Beth was screaming in her bouncy chair on the kitchen table. Nikki whined in sympathy and got in Mick's way as he hurried to fix her formula. He pulled the bottle from the pan and checked the temperature by shaking a few drops onto his wrist. It was almost warm enough. He put the bottle back in the water and turned off the heat. Grasping the handle of the pan on the stove with his shirttail, he turned and headed for the sink but stumbled over the dog. He lost his grip on the pan of hot water and it crashed to the floor. The bottle of milk went rolling under the table.

Nikki dashed after it. Proudly, she came back to sit in front of him. The bottle swayed from the nipple clenched in her mouth.

Two nights of getting up every three hours to feed Beth had worn him to a nub. *Please, let Caitlin get here soon.*

"Give me that!" Exasperated, he yanked the bottle away from the dog, but the nipple stayed firmly in her teeth, and milk sprayed from the topless container in a wide arch that hit Beth, the table and the kitchen wall.

After a moment of stunned silence, Beth's wailing skyrocketed, Nikki dropped her prize to lap up the spilled milk, and the doorbell rang.

In a daze, Mick stared at the disaster. The doorbell chimed again. He lifted Beth from her chair, wiped her dripping face on his sleeve and carried the still-screaming baby with him to the front door. His hope that it might not be Caitlin died swiftly when he pulled open the door and saw her.

His heart jumped into double time. The words *I love you madly* hovered on his lips, but he held them back. This wasn't the right moment.

"Perfect timing!" he growled. "Now you get to see my inept attempt at being a parent."

"Hello, to you, too, Mick. And how's my little precious girl? Did you miss me?" Caitlin plucked the wet baby from his arms, relieved him of the empty bottle and marched toward the kitchen. At the doorway, she halted. "Oh, my!"

She looked back at Mick and burst into laughter.

With the sound of her adorable mirth still ringing in his ears, Mick retreated to the living room and sank into his chair. It was there that she joined him ten minutes later. Beth, clean and dressed in fresh clothes, sucked contentedly on a pacifier.

He gave Caitlin a rueful grin. "I'm *so* glad you're home. I had no idea what I was getting myself into when I said I'd watch her for two days. How did your show go?"

Her smile was beautiful to see. It warmed him all the way to the bottom of his heart.

"It went well. I sold enough prints to keep Beth in disposable diapers for—oh—at least a month."

"We missed you."

"I missed you, too. Was it really bad?"

"I don't know how you find time to do portraits and take care of her. You amaze me."

"Thanks, Mick. That means a lot." She paused as if she wanted to say more, but rose instead. "I'd better get going."

"There isn't any rush." He racked his mind for something else to say, for some way to keep her close a little longer.

"Beth and I'll be late for church if I don't get going. Your mother's expecting me to help with the nursery today."

"Send the cab away. I can give you a ride to church."

Her face brightened. "I'd like that. If you don't mind?"

"Not at all. I'll be ready in two minutes. What do you think of Pastor Frank's little church?"

"Everyone at the Westside Christian Church has been wonderful. You can really feel God's grace in the way people care about each other there. I've been so blessed, and a lot of it is due to you, Mick."

"You found the Lord in your own heart, Caitlin."

"I know He was there all along, but you're the one who helped me to understand that. I don't know how I'll ever be able to repay that gift. You're a very special person."

Mick felt the heat rise to his face and knew he was blushing. "Have lunch with me after church, and I'll consider us even."

Was it too soon to let her know he had grown more than fond of her? He didn't want to press her or scare her off. He waited with his heart pounding in his throat for her answer.

"I have a better idea. I've invited your mother over for lunch. Why don't you join us? I've been learning to cook some new things. I'm making spaghetti today."

Mick blinked twice. His smile slipped a little.

Caitlin gave him a puzzled look. "You don't have to come if you don't want to."

"I want to," he answered quickly. Gazing at her,

his heart grew light at the sight of the soft smile on her face.

Thank You, Lord, for bringing this woman into my life. This time, I'm not going to lose her so please forgive this little white lie.

"The fact is," he said, "I love spaghetti."

Epilogue

Caitlin lifted Beth in her car seat from the back of a cab. Now seven months old, her tiny premature daughter had grown into a happy baby with a sweet smile and chubby arms and legs. The pediatrician's scale showed she was definitely making up for her slow start. Caitlin asked the driver to wait, then turned to see Mick sprinting down the steps of his house toward her. Her heart did this crazy flip-flop whenever she saw him. How much longer could she hide the fact?

She was head over heels in love with the guy, and he continued to act like a perfect gentleman. But sometimes she was sure he saw her as more than a friend, and Beth's mother. But if she were wrong, she might jeopardize the easy relationship they shared. For Beth's sake, she didn't want that to happen. Then yesterday something occurred that gave her renewed hope.

Mick reached her side in a few long strides. "Let me give you a hand." His voice seemed more breathless than the short trip to the curb warranted.

"Thanks." She handed him the baby's carrier and tried to stay calm as she walked ahead of him up to the house.

"What time will you be back?" he asked, holding the door.

"I meet with my reading tutor until noon, then I'm working at the gallery until four-thirty, so let's say five. Will that be a problem?"

"Not at all. You know I'll keep Beth any chance I get. How's the new job going?" He set Beth's carrier on the floor.

"It's great. I put my nose in the air and pretend I know more about art than the people who come in to buy it. Most of them can't resist a piece if a snob tells them it's a steal."

"I can just see it. By the way, have I told you how proud I am that you are learning to read?" he asked quietly.

She looked up to find him staring at her intently. A flush heated her cheeks. "You are?"

"Yes, I am. That took a lot of courage."

Looking to her child asleep at her feet, Caitlin said, "No, it didn't. Not after what happened to Beth."

From outside, the cab honked once. "I guess you'd better get going," Mick said.

"In a minute. Woody came into the gallery yesterday. He told me something interesting."

"Oh, yeah?"

"I mentioned you were coming over for dinner Friday, and he said as long as I didn't feed you spaghetti I'd be safe."

"Woody has a big mouth."

"I've fixed you spaghetti a dozen times in the past few months. You've never complained once."

"Well—I—I like it the way you fix it."

"You do?" She smiled to herself. Yes, there was definitely hope for her. "Guess I'd better run."

He caught her arm as she turned away. "Aren't you forgetting something?"

His touch sent a tingling spiral of warmth through her. Her gaze moved from his hand to his face. "What?" she managed to ask in a husky whisper.

"A goodbye kiss—for Beth."

"She's asleep. I don't want to wake her." The tingling grew stronger. He pulled her closer.

"I could save one for her. For later," he suggested.

"Yeah…that's…a good idea." Caitlin didn't care that they weren't making any sense because as soon as his lips touched hers, she only wanted to keep on kissing him. Her arms circled his neck. All the joy she had kept hidden in her heart bubbled to the surface leaving her giddy with happiness.

The cab honked again, and Mick broke the kiss. Caitlin pressed her cheek against his chest and was thrilled with the feel of his strong arms around her.

"Whoa!" he said between deep breaths.

"If you say you're sorry, I'll hit you," she threatened.

He chuckled and kissed the top of her head. "Sorry? No, sorry wasn't what came to mind."

"Well, it should be!"

"Why should I be sorry?" Concern filled his voice.

"Because you took so long to do this!"

"Honey, I wasn't sure how you felt. I didn't want to rush you into anything that you weren't ready for. You've had so many big changes in your life."

She pulled back and gazed into his eyes. "I love you, Mick O'Callaghan. I love you. I've been waiting months to tell you that."

"I love you, too. More than you'll ever know. I love you the way the night sky loves the stars. The way the sun—"

"Shut up and kiss me again."

He did, and quite thoroughly.

When they broke apart, he stroked her cheek with his knuckles, then slipped his hand behind the nape of her neck and pulled her close until his forehead touched hers. "Will you marry me?"

"Yes."

"No hesitation?"

"God brought you into my life so that we could be together as a family. Who am I to argue with a plan that good?"

"I don't deserve you, but I'm going to spend the rest of my life trying to make you happy."

"You do that without even trying."

Vaguely, she heard the cab honking. Mick held her out at arm's length. "Your driver is getting impatient."

She nodded in resignation. "I'm going to be late for class." In her carrier, Beth began to fuss.

"You could skip today," he offered.

Oh, how she wanted to. At one time, she would have, but Caitlin shook her head. "And set a bad example for our daughter? I don't think so."

"Say that again."

She wrinkled her brow. "I don't think so?"

"No, the part where you said 'our daughter.'"

Caitlin grinned, happier than she ever remembered being. "*Our daughter* is awake and if you don't have her bottle ready in two minutes or less, she'll scream the house down." As if on cue, Beth's crying rose in volume.

He let go of Caitlin and lifted the baby from her carrier. "She's a lot like her mother in that respect," he said with a knowing smile. Taking Caitlin by the elbow, he walked her to the door. "Tonight, you and I are going to have a long talk."

"Talk? I had more kissing in mind."

"Okay, a little of that, too." He gave her a quick peck, then a gentle push toward the street.

Reluctantly, Caitlin climbed into the cab. As it pulled away, she rolled down the window and blew a kiss toward the two people she loved more than anything in the world and gave thanks to God for the blessing He had showered upon her.

Mick's shout reached her as the cab turned the corner and she sank back onto the seat with a contented smile. She met the driver's eyes in the rearview mirror and sighed. "Wasn't that the most beautiful thing you ever heard?"

"I missed it, lady. What did he say?"

"He said 'Hurry home. We'll be waiting for you.'"

* * * * *

We hope you enjoyed reading
NEVER TOO LATE
by *New York Times* bestselling author
RAEANNE THAYNE
&
HIS BUNDLE OF LOVE
by *USA TODAY* bestselling author
PATRICIA DAVIDS

Both were originally **Harlequin®** SERIES stories!

Uplifting romances of faith, forgiveness and hope.

From passionate, suspenseful and dramatic
love stories to inspirational or historical,
Harlequin offers different lines to
satisfy every romance reader.
New books available every month.

⬡ HARLEQUIN®

www.Harlequin.com
www.LoveInspired.com

NYTHRS0618

SPECIAL EXCERPT FROM

Love Inspired®

Her family's future in the balance, can Clara Fisher find a way to save her home?

Read on for a sneak preview of
*HIS NEW AMISH FAMILY by **Patricia Davids**,*
*the next book in **THE AMISH BACHELORS** miniseries,*
available in July 2018 from Love Inspired.

Paul Bowman leaned forward in his seat to get a good look at the farm as they drove up. Both the barn and the house were painted white and appeared in good condition. He made a quick mental appraisal of the equipment he saw, then jotted down numbers in a small notebook he kept in his pocket.

"What is she doing here?" The anger in his client Ralph's voice shocked Paul.

He followed Ralph's line of sight and spied an Amish woman sitting on a suitcase on the front porch of the house. She wore a simple pale blue dress with an apron of matching material and a black cape thrown back over her shoulders. Her wide-brimmed black traveling bonnet hid her hair. She looked hot, dusty and tired. She held a girl of about three or four on her lap. The child clung tightly to her mother. A boy a few years older leaned against the door behind her holding a large calico cat.

"Who is she?" Paul asked.

"That is my annoying cousin, Clara Fisher." Ralph opened his car door and got out. Paul did the same.

LIEXP0618

The woman glared at both men. "Why are there padlocks on the doors, Ralph? Eli never locked his home."

"They are there to keep unwanted visitors out. What are you doing here?" Ralph demanded.

"I live here. May I have the keys, please? My children and I are weary."

Ralph's eyebrows snapped together in a fierce frown. "What do you mean you live here?"

"What part did you fail to understand, Ralph? I… live…here," she said slowly.

Ralph's face darkened with anger. Paul had to turn away to keep from laughing.

She might look small, but she was clearly a woman to be reckoned with. She reminded him of an angry mama cat all fluffed up and spitting-mad. He rubbed a hand across his mouth to hide a grin. His movement caught her attention, and she pinned her deep blue gaze on him. "Who are you?"

He stopped smiling. "My name is Paul Bowman. I'm an auctioneer. Mr. Hobson has hired me to get this property ready for sale."

Don't miss
HIS NEW AMISH FAMILY by Patricia Davids,
available July 2018 wherever
Love Inspired® books and ebooks are sold.

www.LoveInspired.com

Copyright © 2018 by Patricia MacDonald

LIEXP0618

Love Inspired®

Uplifting romances of faith, forgiveness and hope.

Save $1.00

on the purchase of ANY
Love Inspired® book.

Available wherever books are sold, including most bookstores, supermarkets, drugstores and discount stores.

✂

Save $1.00

on the purchase of any Love Inspired® book.

Coupon valid until September 30, 2018.
Redeemable at participating outlets in the U.S. and Canada only.
Not redeemable at Barnes & Noble stores. Limit one coupon per customer.

52615809

Canadian Retailers: Harlequin Enterprises Limited will pay the face value of this coupon plus 10.25¢ if submitted by customer for this product only. Any other use constitutes fraud. Coupon is nonassignable. Void if taxed, prohibited or restricted by law. Consumer must pay any government taxes. Void if copied. Inmar Promotional Services ("IPS") customers submit coupons and proof of sales to Harlequin Enterprises Limited, P.O. Box 31000, Scarborough, ON M1R 0E7, Canada. Non-IPS retailer—for reimbursement submit coupons and proof of sales directly to Harlequin Enterprises Limited, Retail Marketing Department, 22 Adelaide St. West, 40th Floor, Toronto, Ontario M5H 4E3, Canada.

U.S. Retailers: Harlequin Enterprises Limited will pay the face value of this coupon plus 8¢ if submitted by customer for this product only. Any other use constitutes fraud. Coupon is nonassignable. Void if taxed, prohibited or restricted by law. Consumer must pay any government taxes. Void if copied. For reimbursement submit coupons and proof of sales directly to Harlequin Enterprises, Ltd 482, NCH Marketing Services, P.O. Box 880001, El Paso, TX 88588-0001, U.S.A. Cash value 1/100 cents.

5 65373 00076 2   (8100)0 12370

® and ™ are trademarks owned and used by the trademark owner and/or its licensee.

© 2018 Harlequin Enterprises Limited

NYTCOUP0618